KU-201-439

He held a number of jobs in Nairobi, Rhodesia and South Africa, and then became a journalist there. In 1962 he began to write a novel, *The Golden Keel*; after its successful publication in 1963 he and his wife returned to England, and he has been a full-time novelist ever since. He now lives in Guernsey.

Desmond Bagley has now written twelve highly-praised novels, each more successful than the last: all have been bestsellers in England and America, and they have now been translated into nineteen foreign languages. His most recent book, *Flyaway*, was published in 1978.

DESMOND BAGLEY

Wyatt's Hurricane

FONTANA / Collins

First published in 1966 by William Collins Sons & Co Ltd
First issued in Fontana Books 1968
Twenty-third Impression June 1983

© 1966 by Desmond Bagley   ·

Made and printed in Great Britain by
William Collins Sons & Co Ltd, Glasgow

With the blast of thy nostrils the waters were gathered together, the floods stood upright as a heap, and the depths were congealed in the heart of the sea.

The enemy said, I will pursue, I will overtake, I will divide the spoil; my lust shall be satisfied upon them; I will draw my sword, my hand shall destroy them.

Thou didst blow with thy wind, the sea covered them; they sank as lead in the mighty waters.

EXODUS: ch. 15, vv. 8-10

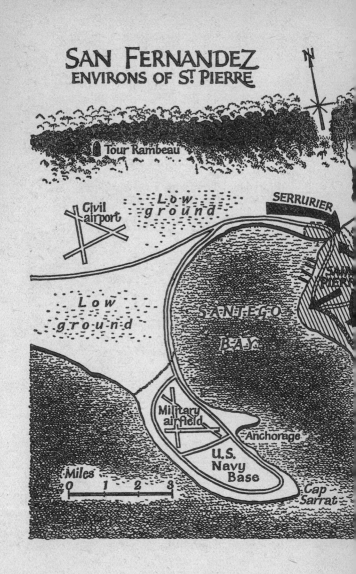

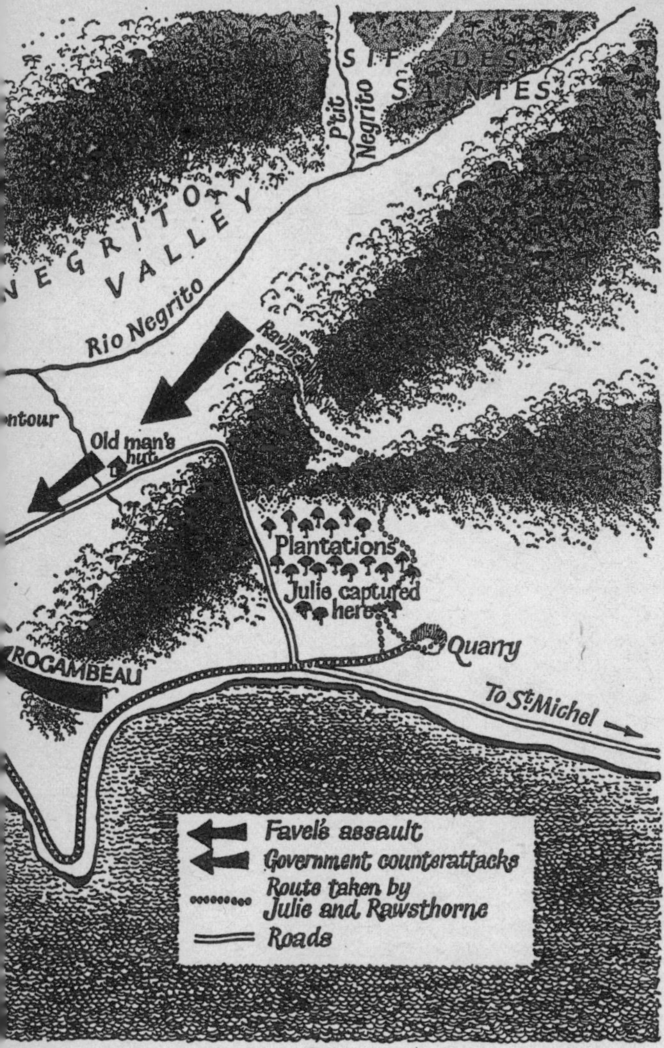

SIF DES SAINTES
P'tit Negrito
NEGRITO VALLEY
Rio Negrito
Ravine
ntour
Old man's hut
Plantations
Julie captured here
Quarry
ROGAMBEAU
To St. Michel
Favel's assault
Government counterattacks
Route taken by Julie and Rawsthorne
Roads

This one is for Jimmy Brown

One

The Super-Constellation flew south-east in fair weather, leaving behind the arc of green islands scattered across the crinkled sea, the island chain known as the Lesser Antilles. Ahead, somewhere over the hard line of the Atlantic horizon, was her destination—a rendezvous with trouble somewhere north of the Equator and in that part of the Atlantic which is squeezed between North Africa and South America.

The pilot, Lieutenant-Commander Hansen, did not really know the exact position of contact nor when he would get there—he merely flew on orders from a civilian seated behind him—but he had flown on many similar missions and knew what was expected of him, so he relaxed in his seat and left the flying to Morgan, his co-pilot. The Lieutenant-Commander had over twelve years' service in the United States Navy and so was paid $660 a month. He was grossly underpaid for the job he was doing.

The aircraft, one of the most graceful ever designed, had once proudly flown the North Atlantic commercial route until edged out by the faster jets. So she had been put in mothballs until the Navy had need of her and now she wore United States Navy insignia. She looked more battered than seemed proper in a Navy plane—the leading edge of her wings was pitted and dented and the mascot of a winged cloud painted on her nose was worn and abraded—but she had flown more of these missions than her pilot and so the wear and tear was understandable.

Hansen looked at the sky over the horizon and saw the first faint traces of cirrus flecking the pale blue. He flicked a switch and said, " I think she's coming up now, Dave. Any change of orders?"

A voice crackled in his earphones. "I'll check on the display."

Hansen folded his hands across his stomach and stared ahead at the gathering high clouds. Some Navy men might have resented taking instructions from a civilian, especially from one who was not even an American, but Hansen knew

9

better than that; in this particular job status and nationality did not matter a damn and all one needed to know was that the men you flew with were competent and would not get you killed—if they could help it.

Behind the flight deck was the large compartment where once the first-class passengers sipped their bourbon and joshed the hostesses. Now it was crammed with instruments and men; consoles of telemetering devices were banked fore and aft, jutting into promontories and forming islands so that there was very little room for the three men cramped into the maze of electronic equipment.

David Wyatt turned on his swivel stool and cracked his knee sharply against the edge of the big radar console. He grimaced, reflecting that he would never learn, and rubbed his knee with one hand while he switched on the set. The big screen came to life and shed an eerie green glow around him, and he observed it with professional interest. After making a few notes, he rummaged in a satchel for some papers and then got up and made his way to the flight deck.

He tapped Hansen on the shoulder and gave the thumbs-up sign, and then looked ahead. The silky tendrils of the high-flying cirrus were now well overhead, giving place to the lower flat sheets of cirrostratus on the horizon, and he knew that just over the edge of the swelling earth there would be the heavy and menacing nimbostratus—the rain-bearers. He looked at Hansen. "This is it," he said, and smiled.

Hansen grunted in his throat. "No need to look so goddam happy."

Wyatt pushed a thin sheaf of photographs at him. "This is what it looks like from upstairs."

Hansen scanned the grained and streaky photographs which had been telemetered to earth from a weather satellite. "These from Tiros IX?"

"That's right."

"They're improving—these are okay," said Hansen. He checked the size of the swirl of white against the scale on the edge of the photograph. "This one's not so big; thank God for that."

"It's not the size that counts," said Wyatt. "It's the pressure gradient—you know that. That's what we're here for."

"Any change in operating procedure?"

Wyatt shook his head. "The usual thing—we go in counterclockwise with the wind, edging in all the time. Then, when we get to the south-west quadrant, we turn for the centre."

Hansen scratched his cheek. "Better make sure you get all your measurements first time round. I don't want to do this again." He cocked his head aft. "I hope your instrumentation works better than last time."

Wyatt grimaced. "So do I." He waved cheerily and went back aft to check on the big radar display. Everything was normal with no anomalies—just the usual dangerous situation ahead. He glanced at the two men under his command. Both were Navy men, skilled specialists who knew everything there was to know about the equipment in their charge, and both had flown on these missions before and knew what to expect. Already they were checking their webbing straps to see there would be no chafe when unexpected strain was thrown on them.

Wyatt went to his own place and strapped himself into the seat. As he snapped down the lever which prevented the seat turning he at last admitted to himself that he was frightened. He always felt scared at this stage of the operation—more scared, he was sure, than any other man aboard. Because he knew more about hurricanes than even Hansen ; hurricanes were his job, his life study, and he knew the ravening strength of the winds which were soon to attack the plane in an effort to destroy it. And there was something else, something newly added. From the moment he had seen the white smear on the satellite photographs back at Cap Sarrat he had sensed that this was going to be a bad one. It was not something he could analyse, something he could lay on paper in the cold symbols and formulae of meteorological science, but something he felt deep in his being.

So this time he was even more frightened than usual.

He shrugged and applied himself to his work as the first small buffet of wind hit the plane. The green trace on the radar screen matched well with the satellite photographs and he switched on the recorder which would put all that data on to a coiled strip of plastic magnetic tape to be correlated in the master computer with all the other information that was soon to come pouring in.

Hansen stared ahead at the blackness confronting the plane. The oily black nimbostratus clouds heaved tumultuously, driven by the wind, the formations continually building up and shredding. He grinned tightly at Morgan. "Let's get on with it," he said, and gently turned to starboard. Flying in still air at this particular throttle-setting the Super-Constellation should have cruised at 220 knots, and so his air-speed indicator showed, but he was willing to bet that their ground speed was nearer 270 knots with this wind behind them.

That was the devil in this job; instruments did not read true and there was no hope of getting a valid ground-sighting because even if the clouds broke—which they never did—merely to see a featureless stretch of ocean would be useless.

Suddenly the plane dropped like a stone—caught in a down-draught—and he fought with the controls while watching the altimeter needle spin like a top. He got her on to an even keel once more and set her into a climb to regain his altitude and, almost before he knew what was happening, the plane was caught in an updraught just as fierce and he had to push the control column forward to avoid being spewed from the top of the wind system.

Through the toughened glass he saw rain and hail being driven upwards, illuminated by the blue glare of lightning. Looking back, he saw a coruscating flash spreading tree-wise from the wingtip and knew they had been struck. He also knew that it did not matter; there would be a mere pin-hole in the metal to be filled in by the ground staff and that was all—except for the fact that the plane and everything in it was charged up with several thousand volts of electricity which would have to be dissipated when landing.

Carefully he edged the Constellation deeper into the storm, flying a spiral course and finding the stronger winds. The lightning was now almost continuous, the whipcrack of the close discharges drowning out the noise of the engines. He switched on his throat mike and shouted to the flight engineer, "Meeker, everything okay?"

There was a long pause before Meeker replied. "Ever . . . . . . ng fine." The words were half drowned in static.

Hansen shouted, "Keep things that way," and started to do some mental arithmetic. From the satellite photograph he had judged the diameter of the hurricane at 300 miles, which would give a circumference of about 950 miles. To get to the south-west quadrant where the winds were least strong and where it was safest to turn inwards to the centre he would have to fly a third of the way round—say, 230 miles. His air-speed indicator was now fluctuating too much to be of any use, but from past experience he judged his ground-speed to be a little in excess of 300 knots—say, 350 miles an hour. They had been in the storm nearly half an hour, so that left another half-hour before the turning-point.

Sweat beaded his forehead.

In the instrument compartment Wyatt felt that he was being beaten black and blue and he knew that when he got back to Cap Sarrat and stripped he would find weals where his harness had bitten into him. The stark functional lighting dimmed and flared as lightning flashes hit the plane and momentarily overloaded the circuits, and he hoped that the instrumentation held up under the beating.

He cast a glance at the other two men. Smith was hunched in his seat, expertly rolling as the plane lurched and occasionally resetting a knob. He was all right. Jablonsky's face had a greenish tinge and, as Wyatt looked, he turned and was violently sick. But he recovered quickly and applied himself to his job, and Wyatt smiled briefly.

He looked at the clock set into the panel before him and began to calculate. When they turned in towards the centre of the hurricane they would have to fly a little over a hundred miles to get to the " eye ", that mysterious region of calm in the midst of a wilderness of raging air. There would be fierce crosswinds and the ride would be rough and Wyatt estimated it would take nearly three-quarters of an hour. But then they would be able to idle and catch their breaths before plunging into the fray again. Hansen would circle for fifteen minutes in that wondrous stillness while Wyatt did his work, and they would all rub the soreness from their battered bodies and gird themselves for the flight out.

From the moment they turned in to the centre all instruments would be working, recording air pressure, humidity, temperature and all the other variables that go to make up the biggest wind on earth. And on the way through the hurricane they would drop what Wyatt called to himself their " bomb load "—marvellously complex packages of instruments jettisoned into the storm, some to be tossed for an hour or so in the wind before touching down, some to plunge down to float on the raging sea, others that would sink to a predetermined depth beneath the waves. But all would be sending radio signals to be caught by the complex of receiving instrumentation in the plane and recorded on tape.

He steadied himself in the seat and began to dictate into his throat mike which was hooked up to a small recording machine. He hoped he would be able to disentangle his own voice from the storm noises when he replayed the tape back at base.

Half an hour later Hansen turned in towards the centre, buzzing Wyatt as he did so. Immediately he felt a difference in the quality of the wind's attack on the plane; there was a new set of noises added to the cacophony and the controls reacted differently under his hands. The Constellation became more difficult to control in the crosswinds which he knew were gusting at perhaps 130 miles an hour; she plunged and bucked and his arms began to ache with the constant corrective movements he was forced to apply. The gyro-compass had long since toppled out of action and the card of the magnetic compass was swinging violently in the bowl.

Wyatt and his crew were very busy. Deafened by the murderous sound and shaken like dice in a cup, they still managed to get on with their work. The instrument capsules were dropped with precision at regular intervals and the information which they immediately began to radio back was stored on the inch-wide, thirty-two track tapes which Smith and Jablonsky hovered over solicitously. In the intervals between dropping the capsules Wyatt continued his running commentary on to his private tape; he knew this data was subjective and not to be used for serious analysis, but he liked to have it for his private information and to compare later with the numerical findings.

It was with relief that he heard the racket end with almost shattering abruptness and knew they had penetrated to the eye of the hurricane. The plane stopped bucking and seemed to float through the air and, after the noise of the storm, the roar of the engines seemed to be the most peaceful sound he had ever heard. Stiffly he unbuckled his straps and said, "How are things going?"

Smith waggled his hand. "Average score. No humidity readings from number four; no air temperature from number six; no sea temperature from number seven." He grimaced.

"Not a cheep of anything from number three, and none of the sinkers worked at all."

"Damn those sinkers!" said Wyatt feelingly. "I always said that system was too bloody complicated. How about you, Jablonsky? What about direct readings?"

"Everything's okay with me," said Jablonsky.

"Keep at it," said Wyatt. "I'm going to see the skipper." He made his way forward to the flight deck to find Hansen massaging his arms while Morgan flew the plane in a tight circle. He smiled faintly.

"This one's a bastard," said Hansen. "Too rough for this mother's son. How about you?"

"The usual crop of malfunctions—only to be expected. But none of the sinkers worked at all."

"Have they ever?"

Wyatt smiled ruefully. "It's asking a bit much, isn't it?" he said. "We drop a very complicated package into the sea in the middle of a hurricane so that it will settle to a pre-determined depth. It broadcasts by sonar a signal which is supposed to be picked up by an equally complicated floating package, turned into a radio wave and picked up by us. There's one too many links in that chain. I'll write a report when I get back—we're tossing too much money into the sea for too little return."

"*If* we get back," said Hansen. "The worst is yet to come. I've never known winds so strong in the south-west quadrant, and it'll be a damn' sight worse heading north."

"We can scrub the rest of it, if you like," offered Wyatt. "We can go out the way we came in."

"If I could do it I would," said Hansen bluntly. "But we haven't the gas to go all the way round again. So we'll bull our way out by the shortest route and you can drop the other half of the cargo as planned—but it'll be a hell of a rough ride." He looked up. "This one is really bad, Dave."

"I know," said Wyatt soberly. "Give me a buzz when you're ready to move on." He returned to the instrument section.

It was only five minutes before the buzzer went and Wyatt knew that Hansen was really nervous because he usually idled for much longer in the eye. He hastily fastened his straps and tensed his muscles for the wrath to come. Hansen had been right—this was a really bad one, it was small, tight and vicious. He would be interested to know what the pressure gradient was that could whip up such high winds.

If what had gone before was purgatory, then this was pure unadulterated hell. The whole fabric of the Constellation creaked and groaned in anguish at the battering it was receiving; the skin sprang leaks in a dozen places and for a time Wyatt was fearful that it was all too much, that the wings would be torn off in spite of the special strengthening and the fuselage would smash into the boiling sea. He was plagued by a stream of water that cascaded down his neck, but managed to get rid of the rest of the capsules with the same well-timed precision.

For nearly an hour Hansen battled with the big wind and, just when he thought he could bear it no longer, the plane was thrown out of the clouds, spat forth as a man spits out an orange pip. He signalled for Morgan to take over and sagged back in his seat completely exhausted.

As the buffeting lessened Wyatt took stock. Half of Jablonsky's equipment had packed up, the tell-tale dials recording zero. Fortunately the tapes had kept working so all was not lost. Smith's tale was even sorrier—only three of a round dozen capsules had returned signals, and those had suddenly ceased half-way through the flight when the recorder had been torn bodily from its mounting with a sputter of sparks and the tapes had stopped.

"Never mind," said Wyatt philosophically. "*We* got through."

Jablonsky mopped water from the top of his console. "That was too goddam rough. Another one like that and I'll take a ground job."

Smith grunted. "You and me both."

Wyatt grinned at them. "You're not likely to get another like that in a hurry," he said. "It was my worst in twenty-three missions."

He went up to the flight deck and Jablonsky looked after him. "Twenty-three missions! The guy must be nuts. Ten is my limit—only two more to go."

Smith rubbed his chin reflectively. "Maybe he's got the death wish—you know, psychology and all that. Or maybe he's a hurricane lover. But he's got guts, that's for sure—I've never seen a guy look so unconcerned."

On the flight deck Hansen said heavily, " I hope you got everything you wanted. I'd hate to go through that again."

" We'll have enough," said Wyatt. " But I'll be able to tell for certain when we get home. When will that be?"

" Three hours," said Hansen.

There was a sudden change in the even roar and a spurt of black smoke streaked from the port outer engine. Hansen's hand went like a flash to the throttles and then he feathered the airscrew. " Meeker," he roared. " What's wrong?"

" Dunno," said Meeker. " But I reckon she's packed in for the rest of the trip. Oil pressure's right down." He paused. " I had some bother with her a little while back but I reckoned you didn't feel like hearing about it just then."

Hansen blew out his cheeks and let forth a long sigh. " Jesus!" he said reverently and with no intention to swear. He looked up at Wyatt. " Make it nearly four hours."

Wyatt nodded weakly and leaned against the bulkhead. He could feel the knots in his stomach relaxing and was aware of the involuntary trembling of his whole body now that it was over.

II

Wyatt sat at his desk, at ease in body if not in mind. It was still early morning and the sun had not developed the power it would later in the day, so all was still fresh and new. Wyatt felt good. On his return the previous afternoon he had seen his precious tapes delivered to the computer boys and then had indulged in the blessed relief of a hot bath which had soaked away all the soreness from his battered body. And that evening he had had a couple of beers with Hansen.

Now, in the fresh light of morning, he felt rested and eager to begin his work, although, as he drew the closely packed tables of figures towards him, he did not relish the facts he knew he would find. He worked steadily all morning, converting the cold figures into stark lines on a chart—a skeleton of reality, an abstraction of a hurricane. When he had finished he looked at the chart with blank eyes, then carefully pinned it on to a large board on the wall of his office.

He had just started to fill in a form when the phone rang, and his heart seemed to turn over as he heard the well-remembered voice. " Julie!" he exclaimed. " What the devil are you doing here?"

The warmth of her voice triumphed over electronics. "A week's vacation," she said. "I was in Puerto Rico and a friend gave me a lift over in his plane."

"Where are you now?"

"I've just checked into the Imperiale—I'm staying here and, boy, what a dump!"

"It's the best we've got until Conrad Hilton moves in—and if he has any sense, he won't," said Wyatt. "I'm sorry about that ; you can't very well come to the Base."

"It's okay," said Julie. "When do I see you?"

"Oh, hell!" said Wyatt in exasperation. "I'll be tied up all day, I'm afraid. It'll have to be to-night. What about dinner?"

"That's fine," she said, and Wyatt thought he detected a shade of disappointment. "Maybe we can go on to the Maraca Club—if it's still running."

"It's still on its feet, although how Eumenides does it is a mystery." Wyatt had his eye on the clock. "Look, Julie, I've got a hell of a lot to do if I'm to take the evening off ; things are pretty busy in my line just now."

Julie laughed. "All right ; no telephonic gossip. It'll be better face to face. See you to-night."

She rang off and Wyatt replaced the handset slowly, then swivelled his chair towards the window where he could look over Santego Bay towards St. Pierre. Julie Marlowe, he thought in astonishment, well, well! He could just distinguish the Imperiale in the clutter of buildings that made St. Pierre, and a smile touched his lips.

He had not known her long, not really. She was an air hostess on a line covering the Caribbean from Florida and he had been introduced to her by a civilian pilot, a friend of Hansen's. It had been good while it lasted—San Fernandez had been on her regular route and he had seen her twice a week. They had had three months of fun which had come to a sudden end when the airline had decided that the government of San Fernandez, President Serrurier in particular, was making life too difficult, so they dropped St. Pierre from their schedule.

Wyatt pondered. That had been two years ago—no, nearer three years. He and Julie had corresponded regularly at first, but with the passage of time their letters had become sparser and more widely spaced. Friendship by letter is difficult, especially between a man and a woman, and he had expected at any moment to hear that she was engaged—or married—and that would be the end of it, for all practical purposes.

He jerked his head and looked at the clock, then swung round to the desk and pulled the form towards him. He had nearly finished when Schelling, the senior Navy meteorologist on Cap Sarrat Base, came in. "This is the latest from Tiros on your baby," he said, and tossed a sheaf of photographs on to the desk.

Wyatt reached for them and Schelling said, "Hansen tells me you took quite a beating."

"He wasn't exaggerating. Look at that lot." Wyatt waved at the chart on the wall.

Schelling walked over to the board and pursed his lips in a whistle. "Are you sure your instrumentation was working properly?"

Wyatt joined him. "There's no reason to doubt it." He stretched out a finger. "Eight hundred and seventy millibars in the eye—that's the lowest pressure I've encountered anywhere."

Schelling ran a practised eye over the chart. "High pressure on the outside—1040 millibars."

"A pressure gradient of 170 millibars over a little less than 150 miles—that makes for big winds." Wyatt indicated the northern area of the hurricane. "Theory says that the wind-speeds here should be up to 170 miles an hour. After flying through it I have no reason to doubt it—and neither has Hansen."

Schelling said, "This is a bad one."

"It is," said Wyatt briefly, and sat down to examine the Tiros photographs with Schelling looking over his shoulder. "She seems to have tightened up a bit," he said. "That's strange."

"Makes it even worse," said Schelling gloomily. He put down two photographs side by side. "She isn't moving along very fast, though."

"I made the velocity of translation eight miles an hour—about 200 miles a day. We'd better check that, it's important." Wyatt drew a desk calculator and, after checking figures marked on the photographs, began to hammer the keys. "That's about right; a shade under 200 miles in the last twenty-four hours."

Schelling blew out his cheeks with a soft explosion of relief. "Well, that's not too bad. At that rate it'll take her another ten days to reach the eastern seaboard of the States, and they usually don't last longer than a week. That's if she moves in a straight line—which she won't. The Coriolis force will move her eastward in the usual parabola and my guess is that she'll peter out somewhere in the North Atlantic like most of the others."

"There are two things wrong with that," said Wyatt flatly. "There's nothing to say she won't speed up. Eight miles an hour is damned slow for a cyclone in this part of the world— the average is fifteen miles an hour—so it's very probable she'll last long enough to reach the States. As for the Coriolis effect, there are forces acting on a hurricane which cancel that out very effectively. My guess is that a high-altitude jet stream can do a lot to push a hurricane around, and we know damn' little about those and when they'll turn up."

Schelling began to look unhappy again. "The Weather Bureau isn't going to like this. But we'd better let them know."

"That's another thing," said Wyatt, lifting the form from his desk-top. "I'm not going to put my name to this latest piece of bureaucratic bumff. Look at that last request—'State duration and future direction of hurricane.' I'm not a fortune-teller and I don't work with a crystal ball."

Schelling made an impatient noise with his lips. "All they want is a prediction according to standard theory—that will satisfy them."

"We don't have enough theory to fill an eggcup," said Wyatt. "Not that sort of theory. If we put a prediction on that form then some Weather Bureau clerk will take it as gospel truth—the scientists have said it and therefore it *is* so —and a lot of people could get killed if the reality doesn't match with theory. Look at Ione in 1955—she changed direction seven times in ten days and ended up smack in the mouth of the St. Lawrence way up in Canada. She had all the weather boys coming and going and she didn't do a damn' thing that accorded with theory. I'm not going to put my name to that form."

"All right, I'll do it," said Schelling petulantly. "What's the name of this one?"

Wyatt consulted a list. "We've been running through them

pretty fast this year. The last one was Laura—so this one will be Mabel." He looked up. "Oh, one more thing. What about the Islands?"

"The Islands? Oh, we'll give them the usual warning."

As Schelling turned and walked out of the office Wyatt looked after him with something approaching disgust in his eyes.

III

That evening Wyatt drove the fifteen miles round Santego Bay to St. Pierre, the capital city of San Fernandez. It was not much of a capital, but then, it was not much of an island. As he drove in the fading light he passed the familiar banana and pineapple plantations and the equally familiar natives by the roadside, the men dingy in dirty cotton shirts and blue jeans, the women bright in flowered dresses and flaming headscarves, and all laughing and chattering as usual, white teeth and gleaming black faces shining in the light of the setting sun. As usual, he wondered why they always seemed to be so happy.

They had little to be happy about. Most were ground down by a cruel poverty made endemic by over-population and the misuse of the soil. At one time, in the eighteenth century, San Fernandez had been rich with sugar and coffee, a prize to be fought over by the embattled colonizing powers of Europe. But at an opportune moment, when their masters were otherwise occupied, the slaves had risen and had taken command of their own destinies.

That may have been a good thing—and it may not. True, the slaves were free, but a series of bloody civil wars engendered by ruthless men battling for power drained the economic strength of San Fernandez and population pressure did the rest, leaving an ignorant peasantry eking out a miserable living by farming on postage-stamp plots and doing most of their trade by barter. Wyatt had heard that some of the people in the central hills had never seen a piece of money in their lives.

Things had seemed to improve in the early part of the twentieth century. A stable government had encouraged foreign investment and bananas and pineapples replaced coffee, while the sugar acreage increased enormously. Those were the good days. True, the pay on the American-owned plantations was small, but it was regular and the flow of money to the island was enlivening. It was then that the Hotel Imperiale was built and St. Pierre expanded beyond the confines of the Old City.

But San Fernandez seemed to be trapped in the cycle of its own history. After the Second World War came Serrurier, self-styled Black Star of the Antilles, who took power in bloody revolution and kept it by equally bloody government, ruling by his one-way courts, by assassination and by the power of the army. He had no opponents—he had killed them all—and there was but one power on the island—the black fist of Serrurier.

And still the people could laugh.

St. Pierre was a shabby town of jerry-built brick, corrugated iron and peeling walls, with an overriding smell that pervaded the whole place compounded of rotting fruit, decaying fish, human and animal ordure, and worse. The stench was everywhere, sometimes eddying strongly in the grimmer parts of town and even evident in the lounge of the Imperiale, that dilapidated evidence of better times.

As Wyatt peered across the badly lit room he knew by the dimness that the town electricity plant was giving trouble again and it was only when Julie waved that he distinguished her in the gloom. He walked across to find her sitting at a table with a man, and he felt a sudden unreasonable depression which lightened when he heard the warmth in her voice.

"Hello, Dave. I *am* glad to see you again. This is John Causton—he's staying here too. He was on my flight from Miami to San Juan and we bumped into each other here as well."

Wyatt stood uncertainly, waiting for Julie to make her excuses to Causton, but she said nothing, so he drew up another chair and sat down.

Causton said, "Miss Marlowe has been telling me all about you—and there's one thing that puzzles me. What's an Englishman doing working for the United States Navy?"

Wyatt glanced at Julie, then sized up Causton before answering. He was a short, stocky man with a square face, hair greying at the temples and shrewd brown eyes. He was English himself by his accent, but one could have been fooled by his Palm Beach suit.

"To begin with, I'm not English," said Wyatt deliberately. "I'm a West Indian—we're not all black, you know. I was born on St. Kitts, spent my early years on Grenada and was educated in England. As for the United States Navy, I don't work *for* them, I work *with* them—there's a bit of a difference there. I'm on loan from the Meteorological Office."

Causton smiled pleasantly. "That explains it."

Wyatt looked at Julie. "What about a drink before dinner?"

"That *is* a good idea. What goes down well in San Fernandez?"

"Perhaps Mr. Wyatt will show us how to make the wine of the country—Planter's Punch," said Causton. His eyes twinkled.

"Oh, yes—do," exclaimed Julie. "I've always wanted to drink Planter's Punch in the proper surroundings."

"I think it's an overrated drink, myself," said Wyatt. "I prefer Scotch. But if you want Planter's Punch, you shall have it." He called a waiter and gave the order in the bastard French that was the island *patois*, and soon the ingredients were on the table.

Causton produced a notebook from his breast pocket. "I'll take notes, if I may. It may come in useful."

"No need," said Wyatt. "There's a little rhyme for it which, once learned, is never forgotten. It goes like this:

> One of sour,
> Two of sweet,
> Three of strong
> And four of weak.

"It doesn't quite scan, but it's near enough. The sour is the juice of fresh limes, the sweet is sugar syrup, the strong is rum—Martinique rum is best—and the weak is iced water. The rhyme gives the proportions."

As he spoke he was busy measuring the ingredients and mixing them in the big silver bowl in the middle of the table. His hands worked mechanically and he was watching Julie. She had not changed apart from becoming more attractive, but perhaps that was merely because absence had made the heart fonder. He glanced at Causton and wondered where he came in.

"If you go down to Martinique," he said, "you can mix your own Planter's Punch in any bar. There's so much rum in Martinique that they don't charge you for it—only for the limes and the syrup."

Causton sniffed. "Smells interesting."

Wyatt smiled. "Rum does pong a bit."

"Why have we never done this before, Dave?" asked Julie. She looked interestedly at the bowl.

"I've never been asked before." Wyatt gave one final stir. "That's it. Some people put a lot of salad in it like a fruit cup, but I don't like drinks I have to eat." He lifted out a dipperful. "Julie?"

She held out her glass and he filled it. He filled the other glasses then said, "Welcome to the Caribbean, Mr. Causton."

"It's wonderful," said Julie. "So smooth."

"Smooth and powerful," said Wyatt. "You wouldn't need many of these to be biting the leg of the table."

"This should get the evening off to a good start," said Julie. "Even the Maraca Club should look good." She turned to Causton. "Now there's an idea—why don't you come with us?"

"Thank you very much," said Causton. "I *was* wondering what to do with myself to-night. I was hoping that Mr. Wyatt, as an old island hand, could give me a few pointers on sight-seeing on San Fernandez."

Wyatt looked blankly at Julie, then said politely, "I'd be happy to." He felt depressed. He had hoped that he had been the attraction on San Fernandez, but apparently Julie was playing the field. But why the hell had she to come to San Fernandez to do it?

It turned out that Causton was foreign correspondent for a big London daily and over dinner he entertained them with a hilarious account of some of his experiences. Then they went on to the Maraca, which was the best in the way of a night club that St. Pierre had to offer. It was run by a Greek, Eumenides Papegaikos, who provided an exiguous South American atmosphere with the minimum of service at the highest price he could charge; but apart from the Officers' Club at Cap Sarrat Base it was the only substitute for a civilized evening, and one did get bored with the Base.

As they entered the smoke-filled, dimly-lit room someone waved, and Wyatt waved back as he recognized Hansen, who was whooping it up with his crew. At the far end of the room a loud-voiced American was bellowing, and even at that distance it was easy to hear that he was retailing, blow by blow, his current exploits as a game fisherman. They found a table, and as Causton ordered drinks in perfect and fluent French which the waiter could not understand, Wyatt claimed Julie for a dance.

They had always danced well together but this time there seemed to be a stiffness and a tension between them. It was not the fault of the orchestra, poor though it was, for while the tune was weird, the rhythm was perfect. They danced in silence for a while, then Julie looked up and said softly, "Hello, Dave. Seen any good hurricanes lately?"

"See one, you've seen them all," he said lightly. "And you?"

"About the same. One flight is very like another. Same places, same air, same passengers. I sometimes swear that the air traveller is a different breed from the rest of us common humanity; like Dawson—that man over there."

Wyatt listened to the raucous voice spinning its interminable fishing yarn. "You know him?"

"Don't you?" she said in surprise. "That's Dawson, the writer—Big Jim Dawson. Everyone's heard of him. He's one of the regulars on my flight, and a damn' nuisance he is, too."

"I've heard of him," said Wyatt. Julie was right—there could not have been a corner of the world where the name of Big Jim Dawson was not known. He was supposed to be a pretty good writer, although Wyatt did not feel himself equipped to judge; at any rate, the critics appeared to think so.

He looked down at Julie and said, "You don't appear to find Causton a nuisance."

"I like him. He's one of these polite, imperturbable Englishmen we're always reading about—you know, the quiet kind with hidden depths."

"Is he one of your regulars?"

"I met him for the first time on my last flight. I certainly didn't expect to find him here in San Fernandez."

"You certainly went out of your way to make him feel at home."

"That was just hospitality—looking after a stranger in a strange land." Julie looked up with a mischievous glint in her eye. "Why, Mr. Wyatt, I do believe you're jealous."

"I might be," said Wyatt bluntly. "If I had anything to be jealous about."

Julie dropped her eyes and went a little pale. They danced in stiff silence until the melody was finished, then turned to go back to their table, but Julie was whirled away by the exuberant Hansen. "Julie Marlowe! What are you doing in this dump? I'm stealing her, Davy Boy, but I'll return her intact." He swept her on to the floor in a caricatured rumba, and Wyatt returned glumly to Causton.

"Powerful stuff." said Causton, holding a bottle to the light. He waved it. "Have one?"

Wyatt nodded. He watched Causton fill his glass, and said abruptly, "Here on business?"

"Good lord, no!" said Causton. "I was due for a week's holiday, and since I was in New York, I decided to come down here."

Wyatt glanced at Causton's shrewd eyes and wondered how far that was true. He said, "There's not much here for a holiday; you'd have been better off in the Bermudas."

"Maybe," said Causton noncommittally. "Tell me something about San Fernandez. Does it have a history?"

Wyatt smiled sourly. "The same as any other Caribbean island—but a bit more so. First it was Spanish, then English, and finally French. The French made the deepest impression —you can see that in the language—although you do find the natives referring to St. Pierre and San Pedro and Peter's Port, and the language is the most mixed-up you've heard."

Causton nodded ruefully, thinking of his recent difficulties with the waiter.

Wyatt said, "When Toussaint and Cristophe threw the French out of Haïti at the beginning of the 1800's, the locals here did the same, though it hasn't had the same publicity."

"Um," said Causton. "How did an American base get here?"

"That happened at the turn of this century," said Wyatt. "Round about the time the Americans were flexing their muscles. They found they were strong enough to make the Monroe Doctrine stick, and they'd just got over a couple of wars which proved it. There was a lot of talk about 'Manifest Destiny' and the Yanks thought they had a big brotherly right to supervise other people's business in this part of the world. San Fernandez was in pretty much of a mess in 1905 with riots and bloody revolution, so the Marines were sent ashore. The island was American administered until 1917 and then the Americans pulled out—but they hung on to Cap Sarrat."

"Didn't something of the sort happen in Haïti as well?"

"It's happened in most of the islands—Cuba, Haïti, the Dominican Republic."

Causton grinned. "It's happened more than once in the Dominican Republic." He sipped his drink. "I suppose Cap Sarrat is held under some kind of treaty?"

"I suppose you could call it that," agreed Wyatt. "The Americans leased the Cap in 1906 for one thousand gold dollars a year—not a bad sum for those days—but depreciation doesn't work in favour of San Fernandez. President Serrurier now gets $1693." Wyatt paused. "And twelve cents," he added as an afterthought.

Causton chuckled. "Not a bad bit of trading on the part of the Americans—a bit sharp, though."

"They did the same in Cuba with Guantanamo Base," said Wyatt. "Castro gets twice as much—but I think he'd rather have Guantanamo and no Americans."

"I'll bet he would."

"The Navy is trying to build up Cap Sarrat as a substitute for Guantanamo in case Castro gets uppity and takes it from them. I suppose there is a possibility that it might happen."

"There is," said Causton. "I don't think he could just take it by force, but a bit of moral blackmail might do it, given the right political circumstances."

"Anyway, here is Cap Sarrat," said Wyatt. "But it's not nearly as good as Guantanamo. The anchorage in Santego Bay is shallow—all it will take is a light cruiser—and the base facilities will take twenty years and a couple of hundred million dollars to even approach Guantanamo. It's very well equipped as an air base, though; that's why we use it as a hurricane research centre."

"Miss Marlowe was telling me about that——" began Causton, but he was interrupted by the return of Hansen and Julie and he took the opportunity of asking Julie to dance.

"Aren't you going to ask me to have a drink?" demanded Hansen.

"Help yourself," said Wyatt. He saw Schelling come into the room with another officer. "Tell me, Harry; how did Schelling come to make Commander in your Navy?"

"Dunno," said Hansen, sitting down. "Must be because he's a good meteorologist, because he's an officer like a bull's got tits."

"Not so good, eh?"

"Hell, one thing an officer's got to do is to lead men, and Schelling couldn't be a Den Mother for a troop of Girl Scouts. He must have got through on the specialist side."

"Let me tell you something," said Wyatt, and told Hansen about his conversation that morning with Schelling. He ended up by saying, "He thinks that meteorology is an exact science and that what the textbooks say is so. People like that frighten me."

Hansen laughed. "Dave, you've come across a type of officer that's not uncommon in the good old U.S.N. The Pentagon is swarming with them. He goes by the book for one reason and one reason only—because if he goes by the book he can never be proved wrong, and an officer who is never wrong is regarded as a good, safe man to have around."

"Safe!" Wyatt almost lost his voice. "In his job he's about as safe as a rattlesnake. The man has lives in his hands."

"Most Navy officers have men's lives in their hands at one time or another," said Hansen. "Look, Dave, let me tell you the way to handle guys like Schelling. He's got a closed mind, and you can't go through him—he's too solid. So you go round him."

"It's a bit difficult for me," said Wyatt. "I have no status. I'm not a Navy man—I'm not even an American. He's the chap who reports to the Weather Bureau, and he's the chap they'll believe."

"You're getting pretty steamed up about this, aren't you? What's on your mind?"

"I'm damned if I know," admitted Wyatt. "It's just that I've got a funny feeling that things are going to go wrong."

"You're worried about Mabel?"

"I think it's Mabel—I'm not too sure."

"I was worried about Mabel when I was rumbling about in her guts," said Hansen. "But I'm pretty relaxed about her now."

Wyatt said, " Harry, I was born out here and I've seen some pretty funny things. I remember once, when I was a kid, we. had news that a hurricane was coming but that we'd be all right, it would miss Grenada by two hundred miles. So nobody worried except the people up in the hills, who never got the warning anyway. There's a lot of Carib Indian in those people and they've had their roots down in the Caribbean for thousands of years. They battened down the hatches and dug themselves in. When that hurricane came up to Grenada it made a right-angle swerve and pretty near sank the island. Now how did those hill people know the hurricane was going to swerve like that?"

" They had a funny feeling," said Hansen. " And they had the sense to act on it. It's happened to me. I was once flying in a cloud when I got that feeling, so I pushed the stick forward a bit and lost some height. Damned if a civilian ship —one of those corporation planes—didn't occupy the air space I'd been in. He missed me by a gnat's whisker."

Wyatt shrugged. " As a scientist I'm supposed to go by the things I can measure, not by feelings. I can't show my feelings to Schelling."

" To hell with Schelling," said Hansen. " Dave, I don't think there's a competent research scientist alive who hasn't gone ahead on a hunch. I still say you should bypass Schelling. What about seeing the Commodore?"

" I'll see how Mabel behaves to-morrow," said Wyatt. " I want to see if she's a really bad girl."

" Don't forget your feelings about her," said Hansen.

Julie's cool voice spoke from behind Wyatt. " Do you really have feelings for this bad girl, Mabel?"

Hansen laughed and began to get up, but Julie waved him down. " I'm having my feet danced off, and I haven't had a drink yet. Let's sit this one out." She looked at Wyatt. " Who's Mabel?"

Hansen chuckled. " One of Dave's girls. He's got a string of them. Dave, remember Isobel last year? You certainly had fun and games with her."

Wyatt said, " She roughed you up a bit, if I remember rightly."

" Ah, but I escaped from her clutches."

Causton snapped his fingers and said with sudden perception, " You're talking about hurricanes, aren't you?"

Julie said with asperity, "Why must they give girls' names to hurricanes?"

"They're easy to remember," said Wyatt with a straight face. "And so hard to forget. I believe the Association of Womens' Clubs of America put in an objection to the Weather Bureau, but they were overruled. One round won in the battle of the sexes."

"I'd be interested to see your work," said Causton. "From a professional point of view, that is."

"I thought you were on holiday."

"Newspapermen are never really on holiday—and news is where you find it."

Wyatt discovered that he rather liked Causton. He said, "I don't see why you shouldn't come up to the Base."

Hansen grinned. "Schelling won't object; he's a sucker for publicity—of the right kind."

"I'd try not to write any unkind words," said Causton. "When could I come?"

"What about to-morrow at eleven?" said Wyatt. He turned to Julie. "Are you interested in my hurricanes? Why don't you come too?" He spoke impersonally.

"Thank you very much," she said, equally impersonally.

"That's fixed, then," said Causton. "I'll bring Miss Marlowe with me—I'm hiring a car." He turned to Hansen. "Do you have any trouble with the island government at the Base?"

Hansen's eyes sharpened momentarily, then he said lazily, "In what way?"

"I gather that Americans aren't entirely popular here. I also understand that Serrurier is a rough lad who plays rough games and he's not too particular about the methods he uses. In fact, some of the stories I've heard give me the creeps—and I'm not a particularly shivery man."

Hansen said shortly, "We don't interfere with them and they don't interfere with us—it's a sort of unspoken agreement. The boys on the Base are pretty firmly disciplined about it. There *have* been a few incidents and the Commodore cracked down hard."

"What kind of——" Causton began, but a booming voice drowned his question. "Say, weren't you the hostess on my plane to Puerto Rico?"

Wyatt looked up, shadowed by the bull-like figure of Dawson. He glanced at Julie, whose face was transformed by a bright, professional smile. "That's right, Mr. Dawson."

"I didn't expect to find you here," roared Dawson. He seemed incapable of speaking in a normal, quiet tone, but that could have been because he was a little drunk. "What say you an' me have a drink?" He gestured largely. "Let's all have a drink."

Causton said quietly, "I'm in the chair, Mr. Dawson. Will you have a drink with me?"

Dawson bent and looked at Causton, squinting slightly. "Don't I know you from somewhere?"

"I believe we met—in London."

Dawson straightened and moved around so he could get a good view of Causton. He pondered rather stupidly for a moment, then snapped his fingers. "That's right," he said. "I know you. You are one of those smart-aleck reporters who roasted me when *The Fire Game* was published in England. I never forget a face, you know. You were one of the guys who came an' drank my liquor, then stuck a knife in my back."

"I don't believe I had a drink that morning," observed Causton equably.

Dawson exhaled noisily. "I don't think I will have a drink with you, Mr. Whatever-your-name-is. I'm particular of the company I keep." He swayed on his feet and his eyes flickered towards Julie. "Not like some people."

Both Wyatt and Hansen came to their feet, but Causton said sharply, "Sit down, you two ; don't be damn' fools."

"Aw, to hell with it," mumbled Dawson, passing a big hand over his face. He blundered away, knocking over a chair and heading for the lavatories.

"Not a nice man," said Causton wryly. "I'm sorry about that."

Wyatt picked up the fallen chair. "I thought you were a foreign correspondent?"

"I am," said Causton. "But I was in London a couple of years ago when half the staff was down with influenza, and I helped out on local stuff for a while." He smiled. "I'm not a literary critic, so I wrote a story on the man, not the writer. Dawson didn't like it one little bit."

"I don't like Dawson one little bit," said Hansen. "He sure is the Ugly American."

" The funny thing about him is that he's a good writer," said Causton. " I like his stuff, anyway ; and I'm told that his critical reputation is very high. The trouble is that he thinks that the mantle of Papa Hemingway has fallen on his shoulders —but I don't think it's a very good fit."

Wyatt looked at Julie. " How much of a nuisance was he?" he asked softly.

" Air hostesses are taught to look after themselves," she said lightly, but he noticed she did not smile.

The incident seemed to cast a pall over the evening. Julie did not want to dance any more so they left quite early. After taking Julie and Causton back to the Imperiale, Wyatt gave Hansen a lift back to the Base.

They were held up almost immediately in the Place de la Libération Noire. A convoy of military trucks rumbled across their path followed by a battalion of marching infantry. The troops were sweating under their heavy packs and their black faces shone like shoe-leather in the street lighting.

Hansen said, " The natives are restless to-night ; those boys are in war trim. Something must be happening."

Wyatt looked around. The big square, usually crowded even at this time of night, was bare except for groups of police and the unmistakable plainclothes men of Serrurier's security force. The cheerful babble of sound that pervaded this quarter was replaced by the tramp of marching men. All the cafés were closed and shuttered and the square looked dark and grim.

" Something's up," he agreed. " We had this before—six months ago. I never did find out why."

" Serrurier always was a nervous type," said Hansen. " Frightened of shadows. They say he hasn't been out of the Presidential Palace for over a year."

" He's probably having another nightmare," said Wyatt.

The column of marching men came to an end and he let in the clutch and drove round the square, past the impossibly heroic bronze statue of Serrurier and on to the road that led to the Base. All the way to Cap Sarrat he thought of Julie and the way she had behaved.

He also thought a little of Mabel.

Two

Causton was up early next morning, and after a token breakfast he checked a couple of addresses in his notebook, then went into the town. When he arrived back at the Imperiale to pick up Julie he was very thoughtful and inclined to be absent-minded, so there was little conversation as they drove to Cap Sarrat in the car he had hired. They were halted briefly at the gates of the Base, but a telephone call from the guardroom soon released them, and a marine led them to Wyatt's office.

Julie looked curiously at the charts on the walls and at the battered desk and the scuffed chairs. "You don't go in for frills."

"This is a working office," said Wyatt. "Please sit down."

Causton examined a wall chart with some misgivings. "I'm always baffled by boffins," he complained. "They usually make the simplest things sound hellishly complicated. Have mercy on us poor laymen."

Wyatt laughed, but spoke seriously. "It's the other way round, you know. Our job is to try to define simply what are really very complex phenomena."

"Try to stick to words of one syllable," pleaded Causton. "I hear you went to look at a hurricane at first hand the other day. It was more than a thousand miles from here—how did you know it was there?"

"That's simple to explain. In the old days we didn't know a hurricane had formed until it was reported by a ship or from an island—but these days we're catching them earlier." Wyatt spread some photographs on the desk. "We get photographs from satellites—either from the latest of the Tiros series or from the newer Nimbus polar orbit satellites."

Julie looked at the photographs uncomprehendingly and Wyatt interpreted. "This tells us all we need to know. It gives us the time the photograph was taken—here, in this corner. This scale down the edge gives the size of what we're looking at—this particular hurricane is about three hundred miles across. And these marks indicate latitude and longitude—so we know exactly where it is. It's simple, really."

Causton flicked the photograph. "Is this the hurricane you're concerned with now?"

"That's right," said Wyatt. "That's Mabel. I've just finished working out her present position and her course. She's a little less than six hundred miles south-east of here, moving north-west on a course that agrees with theory at a little more than ten miles an hour."

"I thought hurricanes were faster than that," said Julie in surprise.

"Oh, that's not the wind speed; that's the speed at which the hurricane as a whole is moving over the earth's surface. The wind speeds inside this hurricane are particularly high—in excess of 170 miles an hour."

Causton had been thinking deeply. "I don't think I like the sound of this. You say this hurricane is south-east of here, and it's moving north-west. That sounds as though it's heading directly for us."

"It is," said Wyatt. "But fortunately hurricanes don't move in straight lines; they move in curves." He paused, then took a large, flat book from a near-by table. "We plot the paths of all hurricanes, of course, and try to make sense of them. Sometimes we succeed. Let me see—1955 gives an interesting variety."

He opened the book, turned the leaves, then stopped at a chart of the Western Atlantic. "Here's 1955. Flora and Edith are textbook examples—they come in from the south-east then curve to the north-east in a parabola. This path is dictated by several things. In the early stages the hurricane is really trying to go due north but is forced west because of the earth's rotation. In the latter stages it is forced back east again because it comes under the influence of the North Atlantic wind system."

Causton looked closely at the chart. "What about this one?"

Wyatt grinned. "I thought you'd spot Alice. She went south and ended up in North Brazil—we still don't know why. Then there's Janet and Hilda—they didn't curve back according to theory and went clear across Yucatan and into North Mexico and Texas. They killed a lot of people."

Causton grunted. " It seems to me there's something wrong with your theory. What about this wiggly one?"

" Ione? I was talking about her only yesterday. It's true she wriggled like a snake, but if you smooth her course you'll see that she fits the theoretical pattern. But we still don't know exactly what makes a hurricane change course sharply like that. I have an idea it may be because it's influenced in some way by a high-altitude jet stream, but that's difficult to tie in because a hurricane is very shallow—it doesn't extend more than a few thousand feet up. That's why contact with land destroys it—it will batter itself to death against a ridge, but it does a lot of damage in the process."

Julie looked at the lines crawling across the chart. " They're like big animals, aren't they? You'd swear that Ione wanted to destroy Cape Hatteras, then turned away because she didn't like the land."

" I wish they were intelligent," said Wyatt. " Then we might have a bit of luck in predicting what they're going to do next."

Causton had his notebook out. " Next thing—what causes hurricanes?"

Wyatt leaned back in his chair. " You need a warm sea and still air, and you will find those conditions in the doldrums in the late summer. The warm air rises, heavy and humid, full of water vapour. Its place is taken by air rushing in from the sides, and, because of the earth's rotation, this moving air is given a twist so that the whole system begins to revolve."

He sketched it on a scrap pad. " The warm air that is rising meets cooler air and releases its water vapour in the form of rain. Now, it has taken a lot of energy for the air to have lifted that water vapour in the first place, and this energy is now released as heat. This increases the rate of ascent of the air—the whole thing becomes a kind of vicious circle. More water is released and thus more heat, and the whole thing goes faster and faster and becomes much bigger. As much as a million tons of air may be rising each second."

He drew arrows on the scrap pad, spiralling inwards. " Because the wind system is revolving, centrifugal force tends to throw the air outwards, and so the pressure in the centre becomes very low, thus forming the eye of the hurricane. But the pressure on the outside is very high and something must give somewhere. So the wind moves faster and faster in an attempt to fill that low pressure area, but the faster it moves the more the centrifugal force throws it outwards. And so we have these very fast circular winds and a fully fledged hurricane is born."

He drew another arrow, this one moving in a straight line. " Once established, the hurricane begins to move forward, like a spinning top that moves along the ground. This brings it in contact with more warm sea and air and the process becomes self-sustaining. A hurricane is a vast heat engine, the biggest and most powerful dynamic system on earth." He nodded to the chart on the wall. " Mabel, there, has more power in her than a thousand hydrogen bombs."

" You sound as though you've fallen in love with hurricanes," said Julie softly.

" Nonsense!" Wyatt said sharply. " I hate them. All West Indians hate them."

" Have you had a hurricane here—in San Fernandez?" asked Causton.

" Not in my time," said Wyatt. " The last one to hit San Fernandez was in 1910. It flattened St. Pierre and killed 6,000 people."

" One hurricane in nearly sixty years," mused Causton. " Tell me—I ask out of personal interest—what is the likelihood of your friend Mabel coming this way?"

Wyatt smiled. " It *could* happen, but it's not very likely."

" Um," said Causton. He looked at the wall chart. " Still, I'd say that Serrurier is a much more destructive force than any of your hurricanes. At the last count he's caused the death of more than 20,000 people on this island. A hurricane might be pleasanter if it could get rid of him."

" Possibly," said Wyatt. " But that's out of my province. I'm strictly non-political." He began to talk again about his work until he saw their interest was flagging and they were becoming bored with his technicalities, and then he suggested they adjourn for lunch.

They lunched in the Officers' Mess, where Hansen, who was to join them, was late and apologetic. " Sorry, folks, but I've been busy." He sat down and said to Wyatt, " Someone's got a case of jitters—all unserviceable aircraft to be made ready for flight on the double. They fixed up my Connie pretty fast ;

I did the ground tests this morning and I'll be taking her up this afternoon to test that new engine." He groaned in mock pain. "And I was looking forward to a week's rest."

Causton was interested. "Is it anything serious?"

Hansen shrugged. "I wouldn't say so—Brooksie isn't the nervous type."

"Brooksie?"

"Commodore Brooks—Base Commander."

Wyatt turned to Julie and said in a low voice, "What are you doing for the rest of the day?"

"Nothing much—why?"

"I'm tired of office work," he said. "What about our going over to St. Michel? You used to like that little beach we found, and it's a good day for swimming."

"That sounds a good idea," she agreed. "I'd like that."

"We'll leave after lunch."

"How's Mabel?" asked Hansen across the table.

"Nothing to report," said Wyatt. "She's behaving herself. She just missed Grenada as predicted. She's speeded up a bit, though; Schelling wasn't too happy about that."

"Not with the prediction he made." Hansen nodded "Still, he'll have covered himself—you can trust him for that."

Causton dabbed at the corner of his mouth with his napkin. "To change the subject—have any of you heard of a man called Favel?"

"Julio Favel?" said Hansen blankly. "Sure—he's dead."

"Is he now!"

"Serrurier's men caught up with him in the hills last year. There was a running battle—Favel wasn't going to be taken alive—and he was killed. It was in the local papers at the time." He quirked an eyebrow at Causton. "What's the interest?"

"The rumour is going about that Favel is still alive," said Causton. "I heard it this morning."

Hansen looked at Wyatt, and Wyatt said, "That explains Serrurier's nightmare last night." Causton lifted his eyebrows, and Wyatt said, "There was a lot of troop movement in the town last night."

"So I saw," said Causton. "Who was Favel?"

"Come off it," said Wyatt. "You're a newspaperman—you know as well as I do."

Causton grinned. "I like to get other people's views," he said without a trace of apology. "The objective view, you know; as a scientist you should appreciate that."

Julie said in bewilderment, "Who was this Favel?"

Causton said, "A thorn in the side of Serrurier. Serrurier, being the head of government, calls him a bandit; Favel preferred to call himself a patriot. I think the balance is probably on Favel's side. He was hiding in the hills doing quite a bit of damage to Serrurier before he was reported killed. Since then there has been nothing—until now."

"I don't believe he's alive," said Hansen. "We'd have heard about it before now."

"He might have been intelligent enough to capitalize on the report of his death—to lie low and accumulate strength unworried by Serrurier."

"Or he might have been ill," said Wyatt.

"True," said Causton. "That might be it." He turned to Hansen. "What do you think?"

"All I know is what I read in the newspapers," said Hansen. "And my French isn't too good—not the kind of French these people write." He leaned forward. "Look, Mr. Causton; we're under military discipline here at Cap Sarrat, and the orders are not to interfere in local affairs—not even to appear interested. If we don't keep our noses clean we're in trouble. If we survive Serrurier's strong-arm boys, then Commodore Brooks takes our hides off. There have been a few cases, you know, mostly among the enlisted men, and they've got shipped back to the States with a big black demerit to spend a year or two in the stockade. I was going to tell you this last night when that guy Dawson busted in."

"I'm sorry," said Causton. "I apologize. I didn't realize the difficulties you people must have here."

"That's all right," said Hansen. "You weren't to know. But I might as well tell you that one thing that is specifically discouraged is talking too freely to visiting newsmen."

"Nobody likes us," said Causton plaintively.

"Sure," said Hansen. "Everyone has something to hide—but our reasons are different. We're trying to avoid stirring up any trouble. You know as well as I do—where you find a newsman you find trouble."

"I rather think it's the other way round," said Causton gently. "Where you find trouble you find a newsman—the trouble comes first." He changed the subject abruptly. "Speaking of Dawson, I find that he's staying at the Imperiale. When Miss Marlowe and I left this morning he was nursing a hangover and breakfasting lightly off one raw egg and the juice of a whisky bottle."

Wyatt said, "You're not really on holiday, are you, Causton?"

Causton sighed. "My boss thinks I am. Coming here was a bit of private enterprise on my part. I heard rumours and rumours of rumours. For instance, arms traffic to this part of the world has been running high lately. The stuff hasn't been going to Cuba or South America as far as I can find out, but it's being absorbed somewhere. I put it to my boss, but he didn't agree with my reasoning, or, as he put it, my non-reasoning. However, I have great faith in myself so I took a busman's holiday and here I am."

"And have you found what you're looking for?"

"You know, I really fear I have."

II

Wyatt drove slowly through the suburbs of St. Pierre, hampered by the throngs in the streets. The usual half-naked small boys diced with death before the wheels of his car, shrieking with laughter as he blew his horn; the bullock carts and sagging trucks created their usual traffic jams, and the chatter of the crowds was deafening—the situation was normal and Wyatt relaxed as he got out of the town and was able to increase speed.

The road to St. Michel wound up from St. Pierre through the lush Negrito Valley, bordered with banana, pineapple and sugar plantations and overlooked by the frowning heights of the Massif des Saints. "It seems that last night's disturbance was a false alarm," said Wyatt. "In spite of what Causton said this morning."

"I don't know if I really like Causton, after all," said Julie pensively. "Newspaper reporters remind me of vultures, somehow."

"I have a fellow feeling for him," said Wyatt. "He makes a living out of disaster—so do I."

She was shocked. "It's not the same at all. At least you are trying to minimize disaster."

" So is he, according to his lights. I've read some of his stuff and it's very good; full of compassion at the damn' silliness of the human race. I think he was truly sorry to find out he was right about the situation here—if he is right, of course. I hope to God he isn't."

She made an impatient movement with her shoulders. " Let's forget about him, shall we? Let's forget about him and Serrurier and—what's-his-name—Favel."

He slowed to avoid a wandering bullock cart loaded with rocks and jerked his head back at the armed soldier by the road. " It's not so easy to forget Serrurier with that sort of thing going on."

Julie looked back. " What is it?"

" The *corvé*—forced labour on the roads. All the peasants must do it. It's a hangover from pre-revolutionary France which Serrurier makes pay most handsomely. It has never stopped on San Fernandez." He nodded to the side of the road. " It's the same with these plantations; they were once owned by foreign companies—American and French mostly. Serrurier nationalized the lot by expropriation when he came to power. He runs them as his own private preserve with convict labour—and it doesn't take much to become a convict on this island, so he's never short of workers. They're becoming run down now."

She said in a low voice, " How can you bear to live here— in the middle of all this unhappiness?"

" My work is here, Julie. What I do here helps to save lives all over the Caribbean and in America, and this is the best place to do it. I can't do anything about Serrurier; if I tried I'd be killed, gaoled or deported and that would do no one any good. So, like Hansen and everyone else, I stick close to the Base and concentrate on my own job."

He paused to negotiate a bad bend. " Not that I like it, of course."

" So you wouldn't consider moving out—say, to a research job in the States?"

" I'm doing my best work here," said Wyatt. " Besides, I'm a West Indian—this is my home, poor as it is."

He drove for several miles and at last pulled off the road on to the verge. " Remember this?"

" I couldn't forget it," she said, and left the car to look at the panorama spread before her. In the distance was the sea, a gleaming plate of beaten silver. Immediately below were the winding loops of the dusty road they had just ascended and between the road and the sea was the magnificent Negrito Valley leading down to Santego Bay with Cap Sarrat on the far side and St. Pierre, a miniature city, nestling in the curve of the bay.

Wyatt did not look at the view—he found Julie a more satisfying sight as she stood on the edge of the precipitous drop with the trade wind blowing her skirt and moulding the dress to her body. She pointed across the valley to where the sun reflected from falling water. "What's that?"

"La Cascade de l'Argent—it's on the P'tit Negrito." He walked across and joined her. "The P'tit Negrito joins the Gran' Negrito down in the valley. You can't see the confluence from here."

She took a deep breath. "It's one of the most wonderful sights I've ever seen. I wondered if you'd show it to me again."

"Always willing to oblige," he said. "Is this why you came back to San Fernandez?"

She laughed uncertainly. "One of the reasons."

He nodded. "It's a good reason. I hope the others are as good."

Her voice was muffled because she had dropped her head. "I hope so, too."

"Aren't you sure?"

She lifted her head and looked him straight in the eye. "No, Dave, I'm not sure. I'm not sure at all."

He put his hands on her shoulders and drew her to him. "A pity," he said, and kissed her. She came, unresisting, into his arms and her lips parted under his. He felt her arms go about him, drawing him closer, until at last she broke away.

"I don't know about that," she said. "I'm still not sure —but I'm not sure about being not sure."

He said, "How would you like to live here—on San Fernandez?"

Julie looked at him warily. "Is that a proposition?"

"I suppose you could call it a proposal," Wyatt said, rubbing the side of his jaw. "I couldn't go on living at the Base, not with you giving up the exotic life of an air hostess, so we'd have to find a house. How would you like to live somewhere up here?"

"Oh, Dave, I'd like that very much," she cried, and they were both incoherent for a considerable time.

After a while Wyatt said, "I don't understand why you were so standoffish; you clung on to Causton like a blood brother last night."

"Damn you, Dave Wyatt," Julie retorted. "I was scared. I was chasing a man and women aren't supposed to do that. I got cold feet at the last minute and was frightened of making a fool of myself."

"So you did come here to see me?"

She ruffled his hair. "You don't see much in people, do you, Dave? You're so wrapped up in your hurricanes and formulas. Of course I came to see you." She picked up his hand and examined the fingers one by one. "I've been out with lots of guys and sometimes I've wondered if this time it was the *one*—women do think that way, you know. And every time you got in the way of my thinking, so I knew I had to come back to straighten it out. I had to have you in my heart altogether or I had to get you out of my system completely—if I could. And you kept writing those deadpan letters of yours which made me want to scream."

He grinned. "I was never very good at writing passion. But I see I've been properly caught by a designing woman, so let's celebrate." He walked over to the car. "I filled a Thermos with your favourite tipple—Planter's Punch. I departed from the strict formula in the interests of sobriety and the time of day—this has less rum and more lime. It's quite refreshing."

They sat overlooking the Negrito and sampled the punch. Julie said, "I don't know much about you, Dave. You said last night that you were born in St. Kitts—where's that?"

Wyatt waved. "An island over to the south-east. It's really St. Christopher, but it's been called St. Kitts for the last four hundred years. Christophe, the Black Emperor of Haïti, took his name from St. Kitts—he was a runaway slave. It's quite a place."

"Has your family always lived there?"

"We weren't aborigines, you know, but there have been Wyatts on St. Kitts since the early sixteen hundreds. They were planters, fishermen—sometimes pirates, so I'm told—a motley crowd." He sipped the punch. "I'm the last Wyatt of St. Kitts."

" That's a shame. What happened?"

" A hurricane in the middle of the last century nearly did for the island. Three-quarters of the Wyatts were killed; in fact, three-quarters of the population were wiped out. Then came the period of depression in the Caribbean—competition from Brazilian coffee, East African sugar and so on, and the few Wyatts that were left moved out. My parents hung on until just after I was born, then they moved down to Grenada where I grew up."

" Where's Grenada?"

" South along the chain of islands, north of Trinidad. Just north of Grenada are the Grenadines, a string of little islands which are as close to a tropical paradise as you'll find in the Caribbean. I'll take you down there some day. We lived on one of those until I was ten. Then I went to England."

" Your parents sent you to school there, then?"

He shook his head. " No, they were killed. There was another hurricane. I went to live with an aunt in England; she brought me up and saw to my schooling."

Julie said gently, " Is that why you hate hurricanes?"

" I suppose it is. We've got to get down to controlling the damn' things some time, and I thought I'd do my bit. We can't do much yet beyond organizing early warning systems and so on, but the time will come when we'll be able to stop a hurricane in its tracks, powerful though it is. There's quite a bit of work being done on that." He smiled at her. " Now you know all about David Wyatt."

" Not all, but there's plenty of time for the rest," she said contentedly.

" What about your life story?"

" That will have to wait, too," she said, pushing away his questing hand and jumping up. " What about that swim you promised?"

They got into the car and Julie stared up at the viridian-green hills of the Massif des Saints. Wyatt said, " That's bad country—infertile, pathless, disease-ridden. It's where Favel held out until he was killed. An army could get lost up there —in fact, several have."

" Oh! When was this?"

" The first time was when Bonaparte tried to crush the Slave Revolt. The main effort was in Haïti, of course, but as a side-issue Le Clerc sent a regiment to San Fernandez to stifle the slave rebellion here. The regiment landed without difficulty and marched inland with no great opposition. Then it marched up there—and never came out."

"What happened to it?"

Wyatt shrugged. "Ambushes—snipers—fever—exhaustion. White men couldn't live up there, but the blacks could. But it swallowed another army—a black one this time—not very long ago. Serrurier tried to bring Favel to open battle by sending in three battalions of the army. They never came out, either; they were on Favel's home ground."

Julie looked up at the sun-soaked hills and shivered. "The more I hear of the history of San Fernandez, the more it terrifies me."

Wyatt said, "We West Indians laugh when you Americans and the Europeans think the Antilles are a tropical paradise. Why do you suppose New York is flooded with Puerto Ricans and London with Jamaicans? They are the true centres of paradise to-day. The Caribbean is rotten with poverty and strife and not only San Fernandez, although it's just about as bad here as it can get." He broke off and laughed embarrassedly. "I was forgetting you said you would come here to live—I'm not giving the place much of a build-up, am I?" He was silent for a few minutes, then said thoughtfully, "What you said about doing research in the States makes sense, after all."

"No, Dave," said Julie quietly. "I wouldn't do that to you. I wouldn't begin our lives together by breaking up your job—it wouldn't be any good for either of us. We'll make our home here in San Fernandez and we'll be very happy." She smiled. "And how long do I have to wait before I have my swim?"

Wyatt started the car and drove off again. The country changed as they went higher to go over the shoulder of the mountains, plantations giving way to thick tangled green scrub broken only by an occasional clearing occupied by a ramshackle hut. Once a long snake slithered through the dust in front of the slowly moving car and Julie gave a sharp cry of disgust.

"This is a faint shadow of what it's like up in the mountains," observed Wyatt. "But there are no roads up there."

Suddenly he pulled the car to a halt and stared at a hut by

the side of the road. Julie also looked at it but could see nothing unusual—it was merely another of the windowless shacks made of rammed earth and with a roughly thatched roof. Near the hut a man was pounding a stake into the hard ground.

Wyatt said, "Excuse me, Julie—I'd like to talk to that man."

He got out of the car and walked over to the hut to look at the roof. It was covered by a network of cords made from the local sisal. From the net hung longer cords, three of which were attached to stakes driven into the ground. He went round the hut twice, then looked thoughtfully at the man who had not ceased his slow pounding with the big hammer. Formulating his phrases carefully in the barbarous French these people used, he said, "Man, what are you doing?"

The man looked up, his black face shiny with sweat. He was old, but how old Wyatt could not tell—it was difficult with these people. He looked to be about seventy years of age, but was probably about fifty. "*Blanc*, I make my house safe."

Wyatt produced a pack of cigarettes and flicked one out. "It is hard work making your house safe," he said carefully.

The man balanced the hammer on its head and took the cigarette which Wyatt offered. He bent his head to the match and, sucking the smoke into his lungs, said, "Very hard work, *blanc*, but it must be done." He examined the cigarette. "American—very good."

Wyatt lit his own cigarette and turned to survey the hut. "The roof must not come off," he agreed. "A house with no roof is like a man with no woman—incomplete. Do you have a woman?"

The man nodded and puffed on his cigarette.

"I do not see her," Wyatt persisted.

The man blew a cloud of smoke into the air, then looked at Wyatt with blood-flecked brown eyes. "She has gone visiting, *blanc*."

"With all the children?" said Wyatt quietly.

"Yes, *blanc*."

"And you fasten the roof of your house." Wyatt tapped his foot. "You must fear greatly."

The man's eyes slid away and he shuffled his feet. "It is a time to be afraid. No man can fight what is to come."

"The big wind?" asked Wyatt softly.

The man looked up in surprise. "Of course, *blanc*, what else?" He struck his hands together smartly and let them fly up into the air. "When the big wind comes—*li tomber boum*."

Wyatt nodded. "Of course. You do right to make sure of the roof of your house." He paused. "How do you know that the wind comes?"

The man's bare feet scuffled in the hot dust and he looked away. "I know," he mumbled. "I know."

Wyatt knew better than to persist in that line of questioning —he had tried before. He said, "When does the wind come?"

The man looked at the cloudless blue sky, then stooped and picked up a handful of dust which he dribbled from his fingers. "Two days," he said. "Maybe three days. Not longer."

Wyatt was startled by the accuracy of this prediction. If Mabel were to strike San Fernandez at all then those were the time limits, and yet how could this ignorant old man know? He said matter-of-factly, "You have sent your woman and children away."

"There is a cave in the hills," the man said. "When I finish this, I go too."

Wyatt looked at the hut. "When you go, leave the door open," he said. "The wind does not like closed doors."

"Of course," agreed the man. "A closed door is inhospit-able." He looked at Wyatt with a glint of humour in his eyes. "There may be another wind, *blanc*; perhaps worse than the hurricane. Favel is coming down from the mountains."

"But Favel is dead."

The man shrugged. "Favel is coming down from the mountains," he repeated, and swung the hammer again at the top of the stake.

Wyatt walked back to the car and got into the driving seat. "What was all that about?" asked Julie.

"He says there's a big wind coming so he's tying down the roof of his house. When the big wind comes—*li tomber boum*."

"What does that mean?"

"A very free translation is that everything is going to come down with a hell of a smash." Wyatt looked across at the hut and at the man toiling patiently in the hot sun. "He knows enough to leave his door open, too—but I doubt if I could tell you why." He turned to Julie. " I'm sorry, Julie, but I'd like to get back to the Base. There's something I must check."

" Of course," said Julie. " You must do what you must."

He turned the car round in the clearing and they went down the road. Julie said, " Harry Hansen told me you were worried about Mabel. Has this anything to do with it?"

He said, " It's against all reason, of course. It's against everything I've been taught, but I think we're going to get slammed. I think Mabel is going to hit San Fernandez." He laughed wryly. " Now I've got to convince Schelling."

" Don't you think he'll believe you?"

"What evidence can I give him? A sinking feeling in my guts? An ignorant old man tying on his roof? Schelling wants hard facts—pressure gradients, adiabatic rates—figures he can measure and check in the textbooks. I doubt if I'll be able to do it. But I've got to. St. Pierre is in no better condition to resist a hurricane than it was in 1910. You've seen the shanty town that's sprung up outside—how long do you suppose those shacks would resist a big wind? And the population has gone up—it's now 60,000. A hurricane hitting now would be a disaster too frightening to contemplate."

Unconsciously he had increased pressure on the accelerator and he slithered round a corner with tyres squealing in protest. Julie said, " You won't make things better by getting yourself killed going down this hill."

He slowed down. " Sorry, Julie ; I suppose I'm a bit worked up." He shook his head. " It's the fact that I'm helpless that worries me."

She said thoughtfully, " Couldn't you fake your figures or something so that Commodore Brooks would have to take notice? If the hurricane *didn't* come you'd be ruined professionally—but I think you'd be willing to take that chance."

" If I thought it would work I'd do it," said Wyatt grimly. "But Schelling would see through it; he may be stupid but he's not a damn' fool and he knows his job from that angle. It can't be done that way."

"Then what are you going to do?"

"I don't know," he said. "I don't know."

III

He dropped Julie at the Imperiale and headed back to the Base at top speed. He saw many soldiers in the streets of St. Pierre but the fact did not impinge on his consciousness because he was busy thinking out a way to handle Schelling. When he arrived at the main gate of the Base he had still not thought of a way.

He was stopped at the gateway by a marine in full battle kit who gestured with a sub-machine-gun. " Out, buddy! "

" What the devil's going on? "

The marine's lips tightened. " I said ' out '. "

Wyatt opened the door and got out of the car, noticing that the marine backed away from him. He looked up and saw that the towers by the gateway were fully manned and that the ugly snouts of machine-guns covered his car.

The marine said, " Who are you, buster? "

" I'm in the Meteorological Section, " said Wyatt. " What damned nonsense is all this? "

" Prove it, " said the marine flatly. He lifted the gun sharply as Wyatt made to put his hand to his breast pocket. " Whatever you're pulling out, do it real slow. "

Slowly Wyatt pulled out his wallet and offered it. " You'll find identification inside. "

The marine made no attempt to come closer. " Throw it down. "

Wyatt tossed the wallet to the ground, and the marine said, " Now back off. " Wyatt slowly backed away and the marine stepped forward and picked up the wallet, keeping a wary eye on him. He flicked it open and examined the contents, then waved to the men in the tower. He held out the wallet and said, " You seem to be in the clear, Mr. Wyatt. "

" What the hell's going on? " asked Wyatt angrily.

The marine cradled the sub-machine-gun in his arms and stepped closer. " The brass have decided to hold security exercises, Mr. Wyatt. I gotta go through the motions—the Lieutenant is watching me. "

Wyatt snorted and got into his car. The marine leaned against the door and said, " I wouldn't go too fast through the gate, Mr. Wyatt; those guns up there are loaded for real. " He shook his head sadly. " Someone's gonna get killed on this exercise for sure. "

"It won't be me," Wyatt promised.

The marine grinned and for the first time an expression of enthusiasm showed. "Maybe the Lieutenant will get shot in the butt." He drew back and waved Wyatt on.

As Wyatt drove through the Base to his office he saw that it was an armed camp. All the gun emplacements were manned and all the men in full battle kit. Trucks roared through the streets and, near the Met. Office, a rank of armoured cars were standing by with engines ticking over. For a moment he thought of what the old man had said— Favel is coming down from the mountains. He shook his head irritably.

The first thing he did in his office was to pick up the telephone and ring the clearing office. "What's the latest on Mabel?"

"Who? Oh—Mabel! We've got the latest shots from Tiros; they came in half an hour ago."

"Shoot them across to me."

"Sorry, we can't," said the tinny voice. "All the messengers are tied up in this exercise."

"I'll come across myself," said Wyatt, and slammed down the phone, fuming at the delay. He drove to the clearing office, picked up the photographs and drove back, then settled down at his desk to examine them.

After nearly an hour he had come to no firm conclusion. Mabel was moving along a little faster—eleven miles an hour —and was on her predicted course. She would approach San Fernandez no nearer than to give the island a flick of her tail— a few hours of strong breezes and heavy rain. That was what theory said.

He pondered what to do next. He had no great faith in the theory that Schelling swore by. He had seen too many hurricanes swerve on unpredictable courses, too many islands swept bare when theory said the hurricane should pass them by. And he was West Indian—just as much West Indian as the old black man up near St. Michel who was guarding his house against the big wind. They had a common feeling about this hurricane; a distrust which evidenced itself in deep uneasiness. Wyatt's people had been in the Islands a mere four hundred years, but the black man had Carib Indian in his ancestry who had worshipped at the shrine of Hunraken, the Storm God. He had enough faith in his feelings to take positive steps, and Wyatt felt he could do no less, despite the fact that he could not prove this thing in the way he had been trained.

He felt despondent as he went to see Schelling.

Schelling was apparently busy, but then, he always was apparently busy. He raised his head as Wyatt entered his office, and said, " I thought you had a free afternoon."

" I came back to check on Mabel," said Wyatt. " She's speeded up."

" Oh!" said Schelling. He put down his pen and pushed the form-pad away. " What's her speed now?"

" She's covered a hundred miles in the last nine hours— about eleven miles an hour. She started at eight—remember?" Wyatt thought this was the way to get at Schelling—to communicate some unease to him, to make him remember that his prediction sent to the Weather Bureau was now at variance with the facts. He said deliberately, " At her present speed she'll hit the Atlantic Coast in about six days; but I think she'll speed up even more. Her present speed is still under the average."

Schelling looked down at the desk-top thoughtfully. " And how's her course?"

This was the tricky one. " As predicted," said Wyatt carefully. " She could change, of course—many have."

" We'd better cover ourselves," said Schelling. " I'll send a signal to the Weather Bureau; they'll sit on it for a couple of days and then announce the Hurricane Watch in the South-Eastern States. Of course, a lot will depend on what she does in the next two days, but they'll know we're on the ball down here."

Wyatt sat down uninvited. He said, " What about the Islands?"

" They'll get the warning," said Schelling. " Just as usual. Where exactly is Mabel now?"

" She slipped in between Grenada and Tobago," said Wyatt. " She gave them a bad time according to the reports I've just been reading, but nothing too serious. She's just north of Los Testigos right now." He paused. " If she keeps on her present course she'll go across Yucatan and into Mexico and Texas just like Janet and Hilda did in 1955."

" She won't do that," said Schelling irritably. " She'll curve to the north."

" Janet and Hilda didn't," pointed out Wyatt. " And supposing she *does* curve to the north as she's supposed to do. She only has to swing a little more than theory predicts and we'll have her right on our doorstep."

Schelling looked up. "Are you seriously trying to tell me that Mabel might hit San Fernandez?"

"That's right," said Wyatt. "Have you issued a local warning?"

Schelling's eyes flickered. "No, I haven't. I don't think it necessary."

"You don't think it necessary? I would have thought the example of 1910 would have made it very necessary."

Schelling snorted. "You know what the government of this comic opera island is like. We tell them—they do precisely nothing. They've never found it necessary to establish a hurricane warning system—that would be money right out of Serrurier's own pocket. Can you see him doing it? If I warn them, what difference would it make?"

"You'd get it on record," said Wyatt, playing on Schelling's weakness.

"There is that," said Schelling thoughtfully. Then he shrugged. "It's always been difficult to know whom to report to. We have told Descaix, the Minister for Island Affairs, in the past, but Serrurier has now taken that job on himself—and telling Serrurier anything is never easy, you know that."

"When did this happen?"

"He fired Descaix yesterday—you know what that means. Descaix is either dead or in Rambeau Castle wishing he were dead."

Wyatt frowned. So Descaix, the chief of the Security Force, was gone—swept away in one of Serrurier's sudden passions of house-cleaning. But Descaix had been his right arm; something very serious must have happened for him to have fallen from power. *Favel is coming down from the mountains.* Wyatt shook the thought from him—what had this to do with the violence of hurricanes?

"You'd better tell Serrurier, then," he said.

Schelling smiled thinly. "I doubt if Serrurier is in any mood to listen to anything he doesn't want to hear right now." He tapped on the desk. "But I'll tell someone in the Palace —just for the record."

"You've told Commodore Brooks, of course," said Wyatt idly.

"Er . . . he knows about Mabel . . . yes."

"He knows *all* about Mabel?" asked Wyatt sharply. "The type of hurricane she is?"

"I've given him the usual routine reports," said Schelling stiffly. He leaned forward. "Look here, Wyatt, you seem to have an obsession about this particular hurricane. Now, if you have anything to say about it—and I want facts—lay it on the line right now. If you haven't any concrete evidence, then for God's sake shut up and get on with your job."

"You've given Brooks 'routine' reports," repeated Wyatt softly. "Schelling, I want to see the Commodore."

"Commodore Brooks—like Serrurier—has no time at the present to listen to weather forecasts."

Wyatt stood up. "I'm going to see Commodore Brooks," he said obstinately.

Schelling was shocked. "You mean you'd go over my head?"

"I'm going to see Brooks," repeated Wyatt grimly. "With you or without you."

He waited for the affronted outburst and for a moment he thought Schelling was going to explode, but he merely said abruptly, "Very well, I'll arrange an appointment with the Commodore. You'd better wait in your office until you're called—it may take some time." He smiled grimly. "You're not going to make yourself popular, you know."

"I haven't entered a popularity contest," said Wyatt evenly. He turned and walked out of Schelling's office, puzzled as to why Schelling should have given in so easily. Then he chuckled bleakly. The reports that Schelling had given Brooks must have been very skimpy, and Schelling couldn't afford to let him see Brooks without getting in his version first. He was probably with Brooks now, spinning him the yarn.

The call did not come for over an hour and a half and he spent the time compiling some interesting statistics for Commodore Brooks—a weak staff to lean on but all he had, apart from the powerful feeling in his gut that disaster was impending. Brooks would not be interested in his emotions and intuitions.

Brooks's office was the calm centre of a storm. Wyatt had to wait for a few minutes in one of the outer offices and saw the organized chaos that afflicts even the most efficient organization in a crisis, and he wondered if this was just another exercise. But Brooks's office, when he finally got there, was calm and peaceful; Brooks's desk was clean, a vast expanse of polished teak unmarred by a single paper, and the Commodore sat behind it, trim and neat, regarding Wyatt with a stony, but neutral, stare. Schelling stood to one side, his hands behind his back as though he had just been ordered to the stand-easy position.

Brooks said in a level voice, " I have just heard that there is a technical disputation going on among the Meteorological Staff. Perhaps you will give me your views, Mr. Wyatt."

" We've got a hurricane, sir," said Wyatt. " A really bad one. I think there's a strong possibility she may hit San Fernandez. Commander Schelling, I think, disagrees."

" I have just heard Commander Schelling's views," said Brooks, confirming the suspicions Wyatt had been entertaining. " What I would like to hear are your findings. I would point out, however, that pending the facts you are about to give me, I consider the possibility of a hurricane hitting this island to be very remote. The last one, I believe, was in 1910."

It was evident that he had been given a quick briefing by Schelling.

Wyatt said, " That's right, sir. The death roll on that occasion was 6,000."

Brooks's eyebrows rose. " As many as that?"

" Yes, sir."

" Continue, Mr. Wyatt."

Wyatt gave a quick résumé of events since Mabel had been discovered and probed. He said, " All the evidence shows that Mabel is a particularly bad piece of weather; the pressure gradient is exceptional and the winds generated are remarkably strong. Lieutenant-Commander Hansen said it was the worst weather he had ever flown in."

Brooks inclined his head. " Granted that it is a bad hurricane, what evidence have you got that it is going to hit this island? I believe you said that there is a ' strong possibility '; I would want more than that, Mr. Wyatt—I would want something more in the nature of a probability."

" I've produced some figures," said Wyatt, laying a sheaf of papers on the immaculate desk. " I believe that Commander Schelling is relying on standard theory when he states that

Mabel will not come here. He is, quite properly, taking into account the forces that we know act on tropical revolving storms. My contention is that we don't know enough to take chances."

He spread the papers on the desk. " I have taken an abstract of information from my records of all the hurricanes of which I have had personal knowledge during the four years I have been here—that would be about three-quarters of those occurring in the Caribbean in that time. I have checked the number of times a hurricane has departed from the path which strict theory dictates and I find that forty-five per cent. of the hurricanes have done so, in major and minor ways. To be quite honest about it I prepared another sheet presenting the same information, but confining the study to hurricanes conforming to the characteristics of Mabel. That is, of the same age, emanating from the same area, and so on. I find there is a thirty per cent. chance of Mabel diverging from the theoretical path enough to hit San Fernandez."

He slid the papers across the desk but Brooks pushed them back. " I believe you, Mr. Wyatt," he said quietly. " Commander, what do you say to this?"

Schelling said, " I think statistics presented in this way can be misused—misinterpreted. I am quite prepared to believe Mr. Wyatt's figures, but not his reasoning. He says there is a thirty per cent. chance of Mabel diverging from her path, and I accept it, but that is not to say that if she diverges she will hit San Fernandez. After all, she *could* go the other way."

" Mr. Wyatt?"

Wyatt nodded. " That's right, of course; but I don't like it."

Brooks put his hands together. " What it boils down to is this: the risk of Mabel hitting us is somewhere between vanishing point and thirty per cent., but even assuming that the worst happens, it's still only a thirty per cent. risk. Would that be putting it fairly, Mr. Wyatt?"

Wyatt swallowed. " Yes, sir. But I would like to point out one or two things that I think are pertinent. There was a hurricane that hit Galveston in 1900 and another that hit here in 1910; the high death-roll in each case was due to the same phenomena—floods."

" From the high rainfall?"

"No, sir; from the construction of a hurricane and from geographical peculiarities."

He stopped for a moment and Brooks said, "Go on, Mr. Wyatt. I'm sure the Commander will correct you if you happen to err in your facts."

Wyatt said, "The air pressure in the centre of a hurricane drops a lot; this release of pressure on the surface of the sea induces the water to lift in a hump, perhaps ten feet in a normal hurricane. Mabel is not a normal hurricane; her internal air pressure is very low and I would expect the sea level at her centre to rise to twenty feet above normal—perhaps as much as twenty-five feet."

He turned and pointed through the window. "If Mabel hits us she'll be coming from due south right into the bay. It's a shallow bay and we know what happens when a tidal wave hits shallow water—it builds up. You can expect flood waters to a height of over fifty feet in Santego Bay. The highest point on Cap Sarrat is, I believe, forty-five feet. You'd get a solid wall of water right over this Base. They had to rebuild the Base in 1910—luckily there wasn't much to rebuild because the Base hadn't really got going then."

He looked at Brooks, who said softly, "Go on, Mr. Wyatt. I can see you haven't finished yet."

"I haven't, sir. There's St. Pierre. In 1910 half the population was wiped out—if that happened now you could count on thirty thousand deaths. Most of the town is no higher than Cap Sarrat, and they're no more prepared for a hurricane and floods than they were in 1910."

Brooks twitched his eyes towards Schelling. "Well, Commander, can you find fault with anything Mr. Wyatt has said?"

Schelling said unwillingly, "He's quite correct—theoretically. But all this depends on the accuracy of the readings brought back from Mabel by Mr. Wyatt and Lieutenant-Commander Hansen."

Brooks nodded. "Yes, I think we ought to have another look at Mabel. Commander, will you see to it? I want a plane sent off right away with the best pilot you've got."

Wyatt said immediately, "Not Hansen—he's had enough of Mabel."

"I agree," said Schelling just as quickly. "I want a different flight crew and a different technical staff."

Wyatt stiffened. "That remark is a reflection on my professional integrity," he said coldly.

Brooks slammed the palm of his hand on the desk with the noise of a pistol shot. "It is nothing of the kind," he rasped. "There's a difference of opinion between the doctors and I want a third opinion. Is that quite clear?"

"Yes, sir," said Wyatt.

"Commander, what are you waiting around for? Get that flight organized." Brooks watched Schelling leave, and as Wyatt visibly hesitated he said, "Stay here, Mr. Wyatt, I want to talk to you." He tented his fingers and regarded Wyatt closely. "What would you have me do, Mr. Wyatt? What would you do in my position?"

"I'd get my ships out to sea," said Wyatt promptly, "loaded with all the Base personnel. I'd fly all aircraft to Puerto Rico. I'd do my damnedest to convince President Serrurier of the gravity of the situation. You should also evacute all American nationals, and as many foreign nationals as you can."

"You make it sound easy," observed Brooks.

"You have two days."

Brooks sighed. "It would be easy if that's all there were to it. But a military emergency has arisen. I believe a civil war is going to break out between insurgents from the mountains and the government. That's why this Base is now in an official state of emergency and all American personnel confined to Base. In fact, I have just signed a directive asking all American nationals to come to Cap Sarrat for safety."

"Favel is coming down from the mountains," said Wyatt involuntarily.

"What's that?"

"It's what I heard. Favel is coming down from the mountains."

Brooks nodded. "That may well be. He may not be dead. President Serrurier has accused the American Government of supplying the rebels with arms. He's a pretty hard man to talk to right now, and I doubt if he'd listen to me chit-chatting about the weather."

"Did the American Government supply the rebels with arms?" asked Wyatt deliberately.

Brooks bristled and jerked. "Definitely not! It has been our declared policy, explicitly and implicitly, not to interfere with local affairs on San Fernandez. I have strict instructions from my superiors on that matter." He looked down at the backs of his hands and growled, "When they sent in the Marines in that affair of the Dominican Republic it set back our South American diplomatic efforts ten years—we don't want that to happen again."

He suddenly seemed to be aware that he was being indiscreet and tapped his fingers on the desk. "With regard to the evacuation of this Base: I have decided to stay. The chance of a hurricane striking this island is, on your own evidence, only thirty per cent. at the worst. That sort of a risk I can live with, and I feel I cannot abandon this Base when there is a threat of war on this island." He smiled gently. "I don't usually expound this way to my subordinates—still less to foreign nationals—but I wish to do the right thing for all concerned, and I also wish to use you. I wish you to deliver a letter to Mr. Rawsthorne, the British Consul in St. Pierre, in which I am advising him of the position I am taking and inviting any British nationals on San Fernandez to take advantage of the security of this Base. It will be ready in fifteen minutes."

"I'll take the letter," said Wyatt.

Brooks nodded. "About this hurricane—Serrurier may listen to the British. Perhaps you can do something through Rawsthorne."

"I'll try," said Wyatt.

"Another thing," said Brooks. "In any large organization methods become rigid and channels narrow. There arises a tendency on the part of individuals to hesitate in pressing unpleasant issues. Awkward corners spoil the set of the common coat we wear. I am indebted to you for bringing this matter to my attention."

"Thank you, sir."

Brooks's voice was tinged with irony. "Commander Schelling is a *reliable* officer—I know precisely what to expect of him. I trust you will not feel any difficulty in working with him in the future."

"I don't think I will."

"Thank you, Mr. Wyatt; that will be all. I'll have the letter for Mr. Rawsthorne delivered to your office."

As Wyatt went back to his own office he felt deep admiration for Brooks. The man was on the horns of a dilemma and had elected to take a calculated risk. To abandon the Base

and leave it to the anti-American Serrurier would certainly
incur the wrath of his superiors—once Serrurier was in it
would be difficult, if not impossible, to get him out. On the
other hand, the hurricane was a very real danger and Boards
of Inquiry have never been noted for mercy towards naval
officers who have pleaded natural disasters as a mitigation.
The Base could be lost either way, and Brooks had to make a
coldblooded and necessary decision.

Unhappily, Wyatt felt that Brooks had made the wrong
decision.

I V

Under an hour later he was driving through the streets of St.
Pierre heading towards the dock area where Rawsthorne had
his home and his office. The streets were unusually quiet in
the fading light and the market, usually a brawl of activity,
was closed. There were no soldiers about, but many police
moved about in compact squads of four. Not that they had
much to do, because the entire town seemed to have gone into
hiding behind locked doors and bolted shutters.

Rawsthorne's place was also locked up solid and was only
distinguishable from the others by the limp Union Jack which
someone had hung from an upper window. Wyatt hammered
on the door and it was a long time before a tentative voice
said, "Who's that?"

"My name's Wyatt—I'm English. Let me in."

Bolts slid aside and the door opened a crack, then swung
wider. "Come in, come in, man! This is no time to be on the
streets."

Wyatt had met Rawsthorne once when he visited the Base.
He was a short, stout man who could have been typecast as
Pickwick, and was one of the two English merchants on San
Fernandez. His official duties as British Consul gave him the
minimum of trouble since there was only a scattering of
British on the island, and his principal consular efforts were
directed to bailing the occasional drunken seaman out of gaol
and half-hearted attempts to distribute the literature on
Cotswold villages and Morris dancing which was sent to him
by the British Council in an effort to promote the British Way
of Life.

He now put his head on one side and peered at Wyatt in the gloom of the narrow entrance. " Don't I know you?"

"We met at Cap Sarrat," said Wyatt. " I work there."

"Of course ; you're the weatherman on loan from the Meteorological Office—I remember."

" I've got a letter from Commodore Brooks." Wyatt produced the envelope.

" Come into my office," said Rawsthorne, and led him into a musty, Dickensian room dark with nineteenth-century furniture. A portrait of the Queen gazed across at the Duke of Edinburgh hung on the opposite wall. Rawsthorne slit open the envelope and said, " I wonder why Commodore Brooks didn't telephone as he usually does."

Wyatt smiled crookedly. " He trusts the security of the Base but not that of the outside telephone lines."

"Very wise," said Rawsthorne, and peered at the letter. After a while he said, " That's most handsome of the Commodore to offer us the hospitality of the Base—not that there are many of us." He tapped the letter. " He tells me that you have qualms about a hurricane. My dear sir, we haven't had a hurricane here since 1910."

" So everyone insists on telling me," said Wyatt bitterly. " Mr. Rawsthorne, have you ever broken your arm?"

Rawsthorne was taken aback. He spluttered a little, then said, " As a matter of fact, I have—when I was a boy."

"That was a long time ago."

"Nearly fifty years—but I don't see . . ."

Wyatt said, " Does the fact that it is nearly fifty years since you broke your arm mean that you couldn't break it again to-morrow?"

Rawsthorne was silent for a moment. " You have made your point, young man. I take it you are serious about this hurricane?"

" I am," said Wyatt with all the conviction he could muster.

"Commodore Brooks is a very honest man," said Rawsthorne. " He tells me here that, if you are right, the Base will not be the safest place on San Fernandez. He advises me to take that into account in any decision I might make." He looked at Wyatt keenly. " I think you had better tell me all about your hurricane."

So Wyatt went through it again, with Rawsthorne showing

a niggling appreciation of detail and asking some unexpectedly penetrating questions. When Wyatt ran dry he said, "So what we have is this—there is a thirty per cent chance at worst of this hurricane—so grotesquely named Mabel—coming here. That is on your *figures*. Then there is your overpowering conviction that it *will* come, and I do not think we should neglect that. No, indeed! I have a very great regard for intuition. So what do we do now, Mr. Wyatt?"

"Commodore Brooks suggested that we might see Serrurier. He thought he might accept it from a British source when he wouldn't take it from an American."

Rawsthorne nodded. "That might very well be the case." But he shook his head. "It will be difficult seeing him, you know. He is not the easiest man to see at the best of times, and in the present circumstances . . ."

"We can try," said Wyatt stubbornly.

"Indeed we can," Rawsthorne said briskly. "And we must." He looked at Wyatt with brightly intelligent eyes. "You are a very convincing young man, Mr. Wyatt. Let us go immediately. What decisions I make regarding the safety of British nationals must inevitably depend on what Serrurier will do."

The Presidential Palace was ringed with troops. Fully two battalions were camped in the grounds and the darkness was a-twinkle with their campfires. Twice the car was stopped and each time Rawsthorne talked their way through. At last they came to the final hurdle—the guard-room at the main entrance.

"I wish to see M. Hippolyte, the Chief of Protocol," Rawsthorne announced to the young officer who barred their way.

"But does M. Hippolyte want to see you?" asked the officer insolently, teeth flashing in his black face.

"I am the British Consul," said Rawsthorne firmly. "And if I do not see M. Hippolyte immediately he will be very displeased." He paused, then added as though in afterthought, "So will President Serrurier."

The grin disappeared from the officer's face at the mention of Serrurier and he hesitated uncertainly. "Wait here," he said harshly and went inside the palace.

Wyatt eyed the heavily armed troops who surrounded them, and said to Rawsthorne, "Why Hippolyte?"

"He's our best bet of getting to see Serrurier. He's big enough to have Serrurier's ear and small enough for me to frighten—just as I frightened that insolent young pup."

The "insolent young pup" came back. "All right; you can see M. Hippolyte." He made a curt gesture to the soldiers. "Search them."

Wyatt found himself pawed by ungentle black hands. He submitted to the indignity and was then roughly pushed forward through the doorway with Rawsthorne clattering at his heels. "I'll make Hippolyte suffer for this," said Rawsthorne through his teeth. "I'll give him protocol." He glanced up at Wyatt. "He speaks English so I can really get my insults home."

"Forget it," said Wyatt tightly. "Our object is to see Serrurier."

Hippolyte's office was large with a lofty ceiling and elaborate mouldings. Hippolyte himself rose to greet them from behind a beautiful eighteenth-century desk and came forward with outstretched hands. "Ah, Mr. Rawsthorne; what brings you here at a time like this—and at such a late hour?" His voice was pure Oxford.

Rawsthorne swallowed the insults he was itching to deliver and said stiffly, "I wish to see President Serrurier."

Hippolyte's face fell. "I am afraid that is impossible. You must know, Mr. Rawsthorne, that you come at a most inopportune time."

Rawsthorne drew himself up to the most of his insignificant height and Wyatt could almost see him clothing himself in the full awe of British majesty. "I am here to deliver an official message from Her Britannic Majesty's Government," he said pompously. "The message is to be delivered to President Serrurier in person. I rather think he will be somewhat annoyed if he does not get it."

Hippolyte's expression became less pleasant. "President Serrurier is . . . in conference. He cannot be disturbed."

"Am I to report back to my Government that President Serrurier does not wish to receive their message?"

Hippolyte sweated slightly. "I would not go so far as to say that, Mr. Rawsthorne."

"Neither would I," said Rawsthorne with a pleasant smile. "But I would say that the President should be allowed to make up his own mind on this issue. I shouldn't think he would like other people acting in his name—not at all. Why don't you ask him if he's willing to see me?"

"Perhaps that would be best," agreed Hippolyte unwillingly. "Could you tell me at least the ... er ... subject-matter of your communication?"

"I could not," said Rawsthorne severely. "It's a Matter of State."

"All right," said Hippolyte. "I will ask the President. If you would wait here ..." His voice tailed off and he backed out of the room.

Wyatt glanced at Rawsthorne. "Laying it on a bit thick, aren't you?"

Rawsthorne mopped his brow. "If this gets back to White-hall I'll be out of a job—but it's the only way to handle Hippolyte. The man's in a muck sweat—you saw that. He's afraid to break in on Serrurier and he's even more afraid of what might happen if he doesn't. That's the trouble with the tyranny of one-man rule; the dictator surrounds himself with bags of jelly like Hippolyte."

"Do you think he'll see us?"

"I should think so," said Rawsthorne. "I think I've roused his curiosity."

Hippolyte came back fifteen minutes later. "The President will see you. Please come this way."

They followed him along an ornate corridor for what seemed a full half mile before he stopped outside a door. "The President is naturally ... disturbed about the present critical situation," he said. "Please do not take it amiss if he is a little ... er ... short-tempered, let us say."

Rawsthorne guessed that Hippolyte had recently felt the edge of Serrurier's temper and decided to twist the knife. "He'll be even more short-tempered when I tell him how we were treated on our arrival here," he said shortly. "Never have I heard of the official representative of a foreign power being searched like a common criminal."

Hippolyte's sweat-shiny face paled to a dirty grey and he began to say something, but Rawsthorne ignored him, pushed open the door and walked into the room with Wyatt close behind. It was a huge room, sparsely furnished, but in the same over-ornate style as the rest of the palace. A trestle-table had been set up at the far end round which a number of uniformed men were grouped. An argument seemed to be in progress, for a small man with his back to them pounded on the table and shouted, "You will find them, General; find them and smash them."

Rawsthorne said out of the corner of his mouth, "That's Serrurier—with the Army Staff—Deruelles, Lescuyer, Rocambeau."

One of the soldiers muttered something to Serrurier and he swung round. "Ah, Rawsthorne, you wanted to tell me something?"

"Come on," said Rawsthorne, and strode up the length of the room.

Serrurier leaned on the edge of the table which was covered with maps. He was a small, almost insignificant man with hunched shoulders and hollow chest. He had brown chimpanzee eyes which seemed to plead for understanding, as though he could not comprehend why anyone should hate or even dislike him. But his voice was harsh with the timbre of a man who understood power and how to command it.

He rubbed his chin and said, "You come at a strange time. Who is the *ti blanc*?"

"A British scientist, Your Excellency."

Serrurier shrugged and visibly wiped Wyatt from the list of people he would care to know. "And what does the British Government want with me—or from me?"

"I have been instructed to bring you something," said Rawsthorne.

Serrurier grunted. "What?"

"Valuable information, Your Excellency. Mr. Wyatt is a weather expert—he brings news of an approaching hurricane —a dangerous one."

Serrurier's jaw dropped. "You come here at this time to talk about the weather?" he asked incredulously. "At a time when war is imminent you wish to waste my time with weather forecasting?" He picked up a map from the table and crumpled it in a black fist, shaking it under Rawsthorne's nose. "I thought you were bringing news of Favel. Favel! Favel—do you understand? He is all that I am interested in."

"Your Excellency——" began Rawsthorne.

Serrurier said in a grating voice, "We do not have hurricanes in San Fernandez—everyone knows that."

"You hade one in 1910," said Wyatt.

"We do not have hurricanes in San Fernandez," repeated Serrurier, staring at Wyatt. He suddenly lost his temper. "Hippolyte! Hippolyte, where the devil are you? Show these fools out."

"But Your Excellency——" began Rawsthorne again.

"We do not have hurricanes in San Fernandez," screamed Serrurier. "Are you deaf, Rawsthorne? Hippolyte, get them out of my sight." He leaned against the table, breathing heavily. "And, Hippolyte, I'll deal with you later," he added menacingly.

Wyatt found Hippolyte plucking pleadingly at his coat, and glanced at Rawsthorne. "Come on," said Rawsthorne bleakly. "We've delivered our message as well as we're able."

He walked with steady dignity down the long room, and after a moment's hesitation Wyatt followed, hearing Serrurier's hysterical scream as he left. "Do you understand, Mr. British Scientist? *We do not have hurricanes in San Fernandez!*"

Outside, Hippolyte became vindictive. He considered Rawsthorne had made a fool of him and he feared the retribution of Serrurier. He called a squad of soldiers and Wyatt and Rawsthorne found themselves brutally hustled from the palace to be literally thrown out of the front door.

Rawsthorne examined a tear in his coat. "I thought it might be like that," he said. "But we had to try."

"He's mad," said Wyatt blankly. "He's stark, staring, raving mad."

"Of course," said Rawsthorne calmly. "Didn't you know? Lord Acton once said that absolute power corrupts absolutely. Serrurier is thoroughly corrupted in the worst possible way— that's why everyone is so afraid of him. I was beginning to wonder if we'd get out of there."

Wyatt shook his head as though to clear cobwebs out of his brain. "He said, 'We do not have hurricanes in San Fernandez,' as though he has forbidden them by presidential decree." There was a baffled look on his face.

"Let's get away from here," said Rawsthorne with an eye on the surrounding soldiers. "Where's the car?"

"Over there," said Wyatt. "I'll take you back to your place —then I must call at the Imperiale."

There was a low rumble in the distance coming from the mountains. Rawsthorne cocked his head on one side. "Thunder," he said. "Is your hurricane upon us already?"

Wyatt looked up at the moon floating in the cloudless sky. "That's not thunder," he said. "I wonder if Serrurier has found Favel—or vice versa." He looked at Rawsthorne. "That's gun-fire."

Three

It was quite late in the evening when Wyatt pulled up his car outside the Imperiale. He had had a rough time; the street lighting had failed or been deliberately extinguished (he thought that perhaps the power-station staff had decamped) and three times he had been halted by the suspicious police, his being one of the few cars on the move in the quiet city. There was a sporadic crackle of rifle fire, sometimes isolated shots and sometimes minor fusillades, echoing through the streets. The police and the soldiers were nervous and likely to shoot at anything that moved. And behind everything was the steady rumble of artillery fire from the mountains, now sounding very distinctly on the heavy night air.

His thoughts were confused as he got out of the car. He did not know whether he would be glad or sorry to find Julie at the Imperiale. If she had gone to Cap Sarrat Base then all decision was taken out of his hands, but if she was still in the hotel then he would have to make the awkward choice. Cap Sarrat, in his opinion, was not safe, but neither was getting mixed up in a civil war between shooting armies. Could he, on an unsupported hunch, honestly advise anyone—and especially Julie—not to go to Cap Sarrat?

He looked up at the darkened hotel and shrugged mentally —he would soon find out what he had to do. He was about to lock the car when he paused in thought, then he opened up the engine and removed the rotor-arm of the distributor. At least the car would be there when he needed it.

The foyer of the Imperiale was in darkness, but he saw a faint glow from the American Bar. He walked across and halted as a chair clattered behind him. He whirled, and said,

C

"Who's that?" There was a faint scrape of sound and a shadow flitted across a window; then a door banged and there was silence.

He waited a few seconds, then went on. A voice called from the American Bar, "Who's that out there?"

"Wyatt."

Julie rushed into his arms as he stepped into the bar. "Oh, Dave, I'm glad you're here. Have you brought transport from the Base?"

"I've got transport," he said. "But I've not come directly from the Base. Someone was supposed to pick you up, I know that."

"They came," she said. "I wasn't here—none of us were."

He became aware he was in the centre of a small group. Dawson was there, and Papegaikos of the Maraca Club and a middle-aged woman whom he did not know. Behind, at the bar, the bar-tender clanged the cash register open.

"I was here," said the woman. "I was asleep in my room and nobody came to wake me." She spoke aggressively in an affronted tone.

"I don't think you know Mrs. Warmington," Julie said.

Wyatt nodded an acknowledgment, and said, "So you're left stranded."

"Not exactly," said Julie. "When Mr. Dawson and I came back and found everyone gone we sat around a bit wondering what to do, then the phone rang in the manager's office. It was someone at the Base checking up; he said he'd send a truck for us—then the phone cut off in the middle of a sentence."

"Serrurier's men probably cut the lines to the Base," said Wyatt. "It's a bit dicey out there—they're as nervous as cats. When was this?"

"Nearly two hours ago."

Wyatt did not like the sound of that but he made no comment—there was no point in scaring anybody. He smiled at Papegaikos. "Hello, Eumenides, I didn't know you favoured the Imperiale."

The sallow Greek smiled glumly. "I was tol' to come 'ere if I wan' to go to the Base."

Dawson said bluffly, "That truck should be here any time now and we'll be out of here." He waved a glass at Wyatt. "I guess you could do with a drink."

" It would come in handy," said Wyatt. " I've had a hard day."

Dawson turned. " Hey, you! where d'you think you're going?" He bounded forward and seized the small man who was sidling out of the bar. The bar-tender wriggled frantically, but Dawson held him with one huge paw and pulled him back behind the bar. He looked over at Wyatt and grinned. " Whaddya know, he's cleaned out the cash drawer, too."

" Let him go," said Wyatt tiredly. " It's no business of ours. All the staff will leave—there was one sneaking out when I came in."

Dawson shrugged and opened his fist and the bar-tender scuttled out. " What the hell! I like self-service bars better."

Mrs. Warmington said briskly, " Well, now that you're here with a car we can leave for the Base."

Wyatt sighed. " I don't know if that's wise. We may not get through. Serrurier's crowd is trigger-happy; they're likely to shoot first and ask questions afterwards—and even if they do ask questions we're liable to get shot."

Dawson thrust a drink into his hand. " Hell, we're Americans; we've got no quarrel with Serrurier."

" We know that, and Commodore Brooks knows it—but Serrurier doesn't. He's convinced that the Americans have supplied the rebels with guns—the guns you can hear now— and he probably thinks that Brooks is just biding his time before he comes out of the Base to stab him in the back."

He took a gulp of the drink and choked; Dawson had a heavy hand with the whisky. He swallowed hard, and said, " My guess is that Serrurier has a pretty strong detachment of the army surrounding the Base right now—that's why your transport hasn't turned up."

Everyone looked at him in silence. At last Mrs. Warmington said, " Why, I *know* Commodore Brooks wouldn't leave us here, not even if he had to order the Marines to come and get us."

" Commodore Brooks has more to think of than the plight of a few Americans in St. Pierre," said Wyatt coldly. " The safety of the Base comes first."

Dawson said intently, " What makes you think the Base isn't safe, anyway?"

" There's trouble coming," said Wyatt. " Not the war, but——"

"Anyone home?" someone shouted from the foyer, and Julie said, "That's Mr. Causton."

Causton came into the bar. He was limping slightly, there was a large tear in his jacket and his face was very dirty with a cut and a smear of blood on the right cheek. "Damn' silly of me," he said. "I ran out of recording tapes, so I came back to get some more." He surveyed the small group. "I thought you'd all be at the Base by now."

"Communications have been cut," said Wyatt, and explained what had happened.

"You've lost your chance," said Causton grimly. "The Government has quarantined the Base—there's a cordon round it." He knew them all except Mrs. Warmington, and regarded Dawson with a sardonic gleam in his eye. "Ah, yes, Mr. Dawson; this should be just up your street. Plenty of material here for a book, eh?"

Dawson said, "Sure, it'll make a good book." He did not sound very enthusiastic.

"I could do with a hefty drink," said Causton. He looked at Wyatt. "That your car outside? A copper was looking at it when I came in."

"It's quite safe," said Wyatt. "What have you been up to?"

"Doing my job," said Causton matter-of-factly. "All hell's breaking loose out there. Ah, thank you," he said gratefully, as Papegaikos handed him a drink. He sank half of it in a gulp, then said to Wyatt, "You know this island. Supposing you were a rebel in the mountains and you had a large consignment of arms coming in a ship—quite a big ship. You'd want a nice quiet place to land it, wouldn't you? With easy transport to the mountains, too. Where would such a spot be?"

Wyatt pondered. "Somewhere on the north coast, certainly; it's pretty wild country over there. I'd go for the Campo de las Perlas—somewhere round there."

"Give the man a coconut," said Causton. "At least one shipload of arms was landed there within the last month—maybe more. Serrurier's intelligence slipped up on that one—or maybe they were too late. Oh, and Favel *is* alive, after all." He patted his pockets helplessly. "Anyone got a cigarette?"

Julie offered her packet. "How did you get that blood on your face?"

Causton put his hand to his cheek, then looked with surprise at the blood on his fingertips. "I was trying to get in to see Serrurier," he said. "The guards were a bit rough— one of them didn't take his ring off, or maybe it was a knuckle-duster."

"I saw Serrurier," said Wyatt quietly.

"Did you, by God!" exclaimed Causton. "I wish I'd known; I could have come with you. There are a few questions I'd like to ask him."

Wyatt laughed mirthlessly. "Serrurier isn't the kind of man you question. He's a raving maniac. I think this little lot has finally driven him round the bend."

"What did you want with him?"

"I wanted to tell him that a hurricane is going to hit this island in two days' time. He threw us out and banished the hurricane by decree."

"Christ!" said Causton. "As though we don't have enough to put up with. Are you serious about this?"

"I am."

Mrs. Warmington gave a shrill squeak. "We should get to the Base," she said angrily. "We'll be safe on the Base."

Wyatt looked at her for a moment, then said to Causton in a low voice, "I'd like to talk to you for a minute."

Causton took one look at Wyatt's serious face, then finished his drink. "I have to go up to my room for the tapes; you'd better come with me."

He got up from the chair stiffly, and Wyatt said to Julie, "I'll be back in a minute," then followed him into the foyer. Causton produced a flashlight and they climbed the stairs to the first floor. Wyatt said, "I'm pretty worried about things."

"This hurricane?"

"That's right," said Wyatt, and told Causton about it in a few swift sentences, not detailing his qualms, but treating the hurricane as a foregone conclusion. He said, "Somehow I feel a responsibility for the people downstairs. I think Julie won't crack, but I'm not too sure about the other woman. She's older and she's nervous."

"She'll run you ragged if you let her," said Causton. "She looks the bossy kind to me."

" And then there's Eumenides—he's an unknown quantity but I don't know that I'd like to depend on him. Dawson is different, of course."

Causton's flashlight flickered about his room. " Is he? Put not your faith in brother Dawson—that's a word to the wise."

" Oh," said Wyatt. " Anyway, I'm in a hell of a jam. I'll have to shepherd this lot to safety somehow, and that means leaving town."

A cane chair creaked as Causton sat down. " Now let me get this straight. You say we're going to be hit by a hurricane. When?"

" Two days," said Wyatt. " Say half a day either way."

" And when it comes, the Base is going to be destroyed."

" For all practical purposes—yes."

" And so is St. Pierre."

" That's right."

" So you want to take off for the hills, herding along these people downstairs. That's heading smack into trouble, you know."

" It needn't be," said Wyatt. " We need to get about a hundred feet above sea-level and on the northern side of a ridge—a place like that shouldn't be too difficult to find just outside St. Pierre. Perhaps up the Negrito on the way to St. Michel."

" I wouldn't do that," said Causton definitely. " Favel will be coming down the Negrito. From the sound of those guns he's already in the upper reaches of the valley."

" How do we know those are Favel's guns?" said Wyatt suddenly. " Serrurier has plenty of artillery of his own."

Causton sounded pained. " I've done my homework. Serrurier was caught flat-footed. The main part of his artillery was causing a devil of a traffic jam just north of the town not two hours ago. If Favel hurries up he'll capture the lot. Listen to it—he's certainly pouring it on."

" That shipment of arms you were talking about must have been a big one."

" Maybe—but my guess is that he's staking everything on one stroke. If he doesn't come right through and capture St. Pierre he's lost his chips."

" If he does, he'll lose his army," said Wyatt forcibly.

" God, I hadn't thought of that." Causton looked thoughtful. "This is going to be damned interesting. Do you suppose he knows about this hurricane?"

"I shouldn't think so," said Wyatt. "Look, Causton, we're wasting time. I've got to get these people to safety. Will you help? You seem to know more of what's going on out there than anybody."

"Of course I will, old boy. But, remember, I've got my own job to do. I'll back you up in anything you say, and I'll come with you and see them settled out of harm's way. But after that I'll have to push off and go about my master's business—my editor would never forgive me if I wasn't in the right place at the right time." He chuckled. "I dare say I'll get a good story out of Big Jim Dawson, so it will be worth it."

They went back to the bar and Causton called out, "Wyatt's got something very important to tell you all, so gather round. Where's Dawson?"

"He was here not long ago," said Julie. "He must have gone out."

"Never mind," said Causton. "I'll tell him myself—I'll look forward to doing that. All right, Mr. Wyatt; get cracking." He sat down and began to thread a spool of tape into the miniature recorder he took from his pocket.

Wyatt was getting very tired of repeating his story. He no longer attempted to justify his reasons but gave it to them straight, and when he had finished there was a dead silence. The Greek showed no alteration of expression—perhaps he had not understood; Julie was pale, but her chin came up; Mrs. Warmington was white with two red spots burning in her cheeks. She was suddenly voluble. "This is ridiculous," she exploded. "No American Navy Base can be destroyed. I demand that you take me to Cap Sarrat immediately."

"You can demand until you're blue in the face," said Wyatt baldly. "I'm going nowhere near Cap Sarrat." He turned to Julie. "We've got to get out of St. Pierre and on to high ground, and that may be difficult. But I've got the car and we can all cram into it. And we've got to take supplies—food, water, medical kit and so on. We should find plenty of food in the kitchens here, and we can take soda- and mineral-water from the bar."

Mrs. Warmington choked in fury. "How far is it to the Base?" she demanded, breathing hard.

"Fifteen miles," said Causton. "Right round the bay. And there's an army between here and the Base." He shook his head regretfully. "I wouldn't try it, Mrs. Warmington; I really wouldn't."

"I don't know what's the matter with you all," she snapped. "These natives wouldn't touch *us*—the Government knows better than to interfere with Americans. I say we should get to the Base before those rebels come down from the hills."

Papegaikos, standing behind her, gripped her shoulder. "I t'ink it better you keep your mout' shut," he said. His voice was soft but his grip was hard, and Mrs. Warmington winced. "I t'ink you are fool woman." He looked across at Wyatt. "Go on."

"I was saying we should load up the car with food and water and get out of here," said Wyatt wearily.

"How long must we reckon on?" asked Julie practically.

"At least four days—better make it a week. This place will be a shambles after Mabel has passed."

"We'll eat before we go," she said. "I think we're all hungry. I'll see what there is in the kitchen—will sandwiches do?"

"If there are enough of them," said Wyatt with a smile.

Mrs. Warmington sat up straight. "Well, I think you're all crazy, but I'm not going to stay here by myself so I guess I'll have to come along. Come, child, let's make those sandwiches." She took a candle and swept Julie into the inner recesses of the hotel.

Wyatt looked across at Causton who was putting away his tape-recorder. "What about guns?" he said. "We might need them."

"My dear boy," said Causton, "there are more than enough guns out there already. If we're stopped and searched by Serrurier's men and they find a gun we'll be shot on the spot. I've been in some tough places in my time and I've never carried a gun—I owe my life to that fact."

"That makes sense," said Wyatt slowly. He looked at the Greek standing by the bar. "Are you carrying a gun, Eumenides?"

Papegaikos touched his breast and nodded. He said, "I keep it."

"Then you're not coming with us," said Wyatt deliberately. "You can make your own way—on foot."

The Greek put his hand inside his jacket and produced the gun, a stubby revolver. "You t'ink you are boss?" he asked with a smile, balancing the gun in his hand.

"Yes, I am," said Wyatt firmly. "You don't know a damn' thing about what a hurricane can do. You don't know the best place to shelter nor how to go about finding it. I do—I'm the expert—and that makes me boss."

Papegaikos came to a fast decision. He put the gun down gently on the bar counter and walked away from it, and Wyatt blew out his cheeks with a sigh of relief. Causton chuckled. "You'll do, Wyatt," he said. "You're really the boss now—if you don't let that Warmington woman get on top of you. I hope you don't regret taking on the job."

Presently Julie came from the kitchen with a plate of sandwiches. "This will do for a start. There's more coming." She jerked her head. "We're going to have trouble with that one," she said darkly.

Wyatt suppressed a groan. "What's the matter now?"

"She's an organizer—you know, the type who gives the orders. She's been running me ragged in there, and she hasn't done a damned thing herself."

"Just ignore her," advised Causton. "She'll give up if no one takes notice of her."

"I'll do that," said Julie. She vanished from the bar again.

"Let's organize the water," said Wyatt.

He walked towards the bar but stopped when Causton said, "Wait! Listen!" He strained his ears and heard a whirring sound. "Someone's trying to start your car," said Causton.

"I'll check on that," said Wyatt and strode into the foyer. He went through the revolving door and saw a dim figure in the driving seat of his car and heard the whine of the starter. When he peered through the window he saw it was Dawson. He jerked the door open and said, "What the devil are you doing?"

Dawson started and turned his head with a jerk. "Oh, it's you," he said in relief. "I thought it was that other guy."

"Who was that?"

"One of those cops. He was trying to start the car, but gave up and went away. I thought I'd check it, so I came out. It still won't start."

"You'd better get out and come back into the hotel," said Wyatt. "I thought that might happen so I put the rotor-arm in my pocket."

He stood aside and let Dawson step out. Dawson said, "Pretty smart, aren't you, Wyatt?"

"No sense in losing the car," said Wyatt. He looked past Dawson and stiffened. "Take it easy," he said in a low voice. "That copper is coming back—with reinforcements."

"We'd better get into the hotel pretty damn' fast," said Dawson.

"Stay where you are and keep your mouth shut," said Wyatt quickly. "They might think we're on the run and follow us in—we don't want to involve the others in anything."

Dawson tensed and then relaxed, and Wyatt watched the four policemen coming towards them. They did not seem in too much of a hurry and momentarily he wondered about that. They drew abreast and one of them turned. "*Blanc,* what are you doing?"

"I thought a thief was stealing my car."

The policeman gestured. "This man?"

Wyatt shook his head. "No, another man. This is my friend."

"Where do you live?"

Wyatt nodded towards the hotel. "The Imperiale."

"A rich man," the policeman commented. "And your friend?"

"Also in the hotel."

Dawson tugged at Wyatt's sleeve. "What the hell's going on?"

"What does your friend say?" asked the policeman.

"He does not understand this language," said Wyatt. "He was asking me what you were saying."

The policeman laughed. "We ask the same things, then." He stared at them. "It is not a good time to be on the streets, *blanc.* You would do well to stay in your rich hotel."

He turned away and Wyatt breathed softly in relief, but one of the other men muttered something and he turned back. "What is your country?" he asked.

"You would call me English," said Wyatt. "But I come from Grenada. My friend is American."

"An American!" The policeman spat on the ground. "But

you are English—do you know an Englishman called Manning?"

Wyatt shook his head. "No." The name rang a faint bell but he could not connect it.

"Or Fuller?"

Something clicked. Wyatt said, "I think I've heard of them. Don't they live on the North Coast?"

"Have you ever met them?"

"I've never seen them in my life," said Wyatt truthfully.

One of the other policemen stepped forward and pointed at Wyatt. "This man works for the Americans at Cap Sarrat."

"Ah, Englishman; you told me you lived in the hotel. Why did you lie?"

"I didn't lie," said Wyatt. "I moved in there to-night; it's impossible to get to Cap Sarrat—you know that."

The man seemed unconvinced. "And you still say you do not know the men, Fuller and Manning?"

"I don't know them," said Wyatt patiently.

The policeman said abruptly, "I'm sorry, *blanc*, but I must search you." He gestured to his colleagues who stepped forward quickly.

"Hey!" said Dawson in alarm. "What are these idiots doing?"

"Just keep still," said Wyatt through his teeth. "They want to search us. Let them do it—the sooner it's over the better."

For the second time that day he suffered the indignity of a rough search, but this time it was more thorough. The palace guards had been looking for weapons but these men were interested in more than that. All Wyatt's pockets were stripped and the contents handed to the senior policeman.

He looked with interest through Wyatt's wallet, checking very thoroughly. "It is true you work at Cap Sarrat," he said. "You have an American pass. What military work do you do there?"

"None," said Wyatt. "I'm a civilian scientist sent by the British Government. My work is with the weather."

The policeman smiled. "Or perhaps you are an American spy?"

"Nonsense!"

"Your friend is American. We must search him, too."

Hands were laid on Dawson and he struggled. "Take your filthy hands off me, you goddam black bastard," he shouted. The words meant nothing to the man searching him, but the tone of voice certainly did. A revolver jumped into his hand as though by magic and Dawson found himself staring into the muzzle.

"You damn' fool," said Wyatt. "Keep still and let them search you. They'll turn us loose when they don't find anything."

He almost regretted saying that when the policeman searching Dawson gave a cry of triumph and pulled an automatic from a holster concealed beneath Dawson's jacket. His senior said, "Ah, we have armed Americans wandering the streets of St. Pierre at a time like this. You will come with me—both of you."

"Now, look here——" began Wyatt, and stopped as he felt the muzzle of a gun poke into the small of his back. He bit his lip as the senior policeman waved them forward. "You bloody fool!" he raged at Dawson. "Why the hell were you carrying a gun? Now we're going to land in one of Serrurier's gaols."

II

Causton came out of the deep shadows very slowly and stared up the street to where the little group was hurrying away, then he turned and hurried back into the hotel and across the foyer. Mrs. Warmington and Julie had just come in from the kitchen bearing more sandwiches and a pot of coffee, and Papegaikos was busy stacking bottles of soda-water on top of the bar counter.

"Wyatt and Dawson have been nabbed by the police," he announced. "Dawson was carrying a gun and the coppers didn't like it." He looked across at the Greek, who dropped his eyes.

Julie put down the coffee-pot with a clatter. "Where have they been taken?"

"I don't know," said Causton. "Probably to the local lock-up—wherever that is. Do you know, Eumenides?"

"La Place de la Libération Noire," said the Greek. He shook his head. "You won't get them out of there."

"We'll see about that," said Causton. "We'll bloody well have to get them out—Wyatt had the rotor-arm of the car engine in his pocket, and now the cops have got it. The car's useless without it."

Mrs. Warmington said in a hard voice, "There are other cars."

"That's an idea," said Causton. "Do you have a car, Eumenides?"

"I 'ad," said Eumenides. "But the Army took all cars."

"It isn't a matter of a car," said Julie abruptly. "It's a matter of getting Dave and Dawson out of the hands of the police."

"We'll do that, too; but a car's a useful thing to have right now." Causton rubbed his cheek. "It's a long way to the docks from here—a bloody long walk."

Eumenides shrugged. "We wan' a car, not a sheep."

"Not a what?" demanded Causton. "Oh—a ship! No, I want the British Consul—he lives down there. Maybe the power of the state allied to the power of the press will be enough to get Wyatt out of the jug—I doubt if I could do it on my own." He looked regretfully at the sandwiches. "I suppose the sooner I go, the sooner we can spring Wyatt and Dawson."

"You've got time for a quick coffee," said Julie. "And you can take a pocketful of sandwiches."

"Thanks," said Causton, accepting the cup. "Does this place have cellars?"

"No—no cellars," said Eumenides.

"A pity," said Causton. He looked about the bar. "I think you'd better get out of here. This kind of party always leads to a lot of social disorganization and the first thing looters go for is the booze. This is one of the first places they'll hit. I suggest you move up to the top floor for the time being; and a barricade on the stairs might be useful."

He measured the Greek with a cold eye. "I trust you'll look after the ladies while I'm gone."

Eumenides smiled. "I see to ever't'ing."

That was no satisfactory answer but Causton had to put up with it. He finished off the hot coffee, stuffed some sandwiches into his pocket and said, "I'll be back as soon as I can—with Wyatt, I hope."

"Don't forget Mr. Dawson," said Mrs. Warmington.

"I'll try not to," said Causton drily. "Don't leave the hotel; the party's split up enough as it is."

Eumenides said suddenly, "Rawst'orne 'as a car—I seen it. It got them—them special signs." He clicked his fingers in annoyance at his lack of English.

"Diplomatic plates?" suggested Causton helpfully.

"Tha's ri'."

"That should come in handy. Okay, I hope to be back in two hours. Cheerio!"

He left the bar and paused before he emerged into the street, carefully looking through the glass panels. Satisfied that there was no danger, he pushed through the revolving doors and set off towards the dock area, keeping well in to the side of the pavement. He checked on his watch and was surprised to find that it was not yet ten o'clock—he had thought it much later. With a bit of luck he would be back at the Imperiale by midnight.

At first he made good time, flitting through the deserted streets like a ghost. There was not a soul in sight. As he got nearer the docks he soon became aware that he was entering what could only be a military staging area. There were many army trucks moving through the dark streets, headlights blazing, and from the distance came the tramp of marching men.

He stopped and ducked into a convenient doorway and took a folded map from his pocket, inspecting it by the carefully shaded light of his torch. It would be the devil of a job getting to Rawsthorne. Close by was the old fortress of San Juan which Serrurier had chosen to use as his arsenal—no wonder there were so many troops in the area. It was from here that his units in the Negrito were being supplied with ammunition and that accounted for the stream of trucks.

Causton looked closer at the map and tried to figure out a new route. It would add nearly an hour to his journey, but there was no help for it. As he stood there the faraway thunder of the guns tailed off and there was dead silence. He looked up and down the street and then crossed it, the leather soles of his shoes making more noise than he cared for.

He got to the other side and turned a corner, striking away from San Juan fortress and, as he hurried, he wondered what the silence of the guns presaged. He had covered many bush-

fire campaigns in his career—the Congo, Vietnam, Malaysia
—and he had a considerable fund of experience to draw upon
in making deductions.

To begin with, the guns were indubitably Favel's—he had
seen the Government artillery in a seemingly inextricable
mess just outside St. Pierre. Favel's guns had been firing at
something, and that something was obviously the main infantry force which Serrurier had rushed up the Negrito at the
first sign of trouble. Now the guns had stopped and that
meant that Favel was on the move again, pushing his own infantry forward in an assault on Serrurier's army. That army
must have been fairly battered by the barrage, while Favel's
men must be fresh and comparatively untouched. It was
possible that Favel would push right through, but proof would
come when next the artillery barrage began—if it was nearer
it would mean Favel was winning.

He had chosen to attack at night, something he had special-
ized in ever since he had retreated to the mountains. His men
were trained for it, and probably one of Favel's men was
equal to any two of Serrurier's so long as he was careful to
dictate the conditions of battle. But once get boxed in open
country with Serrurier's artillery and air force unleashed and
he'd be hammered to pieces. He was taking a considerable
risk in coming down the Negrito into the plain around Santego
Bay, but he was minimizing it by clever strategy and the
unbelievable luck that Serrurier had a thick-headed artillery
general with no concept of logistics.

Causton was so occupied with these thoughts that he nearly
ran into a police patrol head on. He stopped short and shrank
into the shadows and was relieved when the squad passed
him by unseen. He wanted to waste no time in futile arguments. By the time he got to Rawsthorne's house he had
evaded three more police patrols, but it took time and it was
very late when he knocked on Rawsthorne's door.

III

James Fowler Dawson was a successful writer. Not only was
he accepted by the critics as a man to be watched as a future
Nobel Prizewinner, but his books sold in enormous numbers
to the public and he had made a lot of money and was looking
forward to making a lot more. Because he liked making

money he was very careful of the image he presented to his public, an image superbly tailored to his personality and presented to the world by his press agents.

His first novel, *Tarpon*, was published in the year that Hemingway died. At the time he was a freelance writer concocting articles for the American sporting magazines on the glory of rainbow trout and what it feels like to have a grizzly in your sights. He had but average success at this and so was a hungry writer. When *Tarpon* hit the top of the bestseller lists no one was more surprised than Dawson. But knowing the fickleness of public taste he sought for ways to consolidate his success and decided that good writing was not enough—he must also be a public personality.

So he assumed the mantle that had fallen from Hemingway —he would be a man's man. He shot elephant and lion in Africa; he game-fished in the Caribbean and off the Seychelles; he climbed a mountain in Alaska; he flew his own plane and, like Hemingway, was involved in a spectacular smash; and it was curious that there were always photographers on hand to record these events.

But he was no Hemingway. The lions he killed were poor terrified beasts imprisoned in a closing ring of beaters, and he had never killed one with a single shot. In his assault on the Alaskan mountain he was practically carried up by skilled and well-paid mountaineers, and he heartily disliked flying his plane because he was frightened of it and only flew when necessary to mend his image. But game-fishing he had actually come to like and he was not at all bad at it. And, despite everything else, he remained a good writer, although he was always afraid of losing steam and failing with his next book.

While his image was shiny, while his name made headlines in the world press, while the money poured into his bank, he was reasonably happy. It was good to be well-known in the world's capitals, to be met at airports by pressmen and photographers, to be asked his opinion of world events. He had never yet been in a situation where the mere mention of his name had not got him out of trouble, and thus he was unperturbed at being put into a cell with Wyatt. He had been in gaol before—the world had chuckled many times at the escapades of Big Jim Dawson—but never for more than a few hours. A nominal fine, a donation to the Police Orphans' Fund, a gracious apology and the name of Jim Dawson soon set him free. He had no reason to think it was going to be different this time.

"I could do with a drink," he said grumpily. "Those bastards took my flask."

Wyatt examined the cell. It was in an old building and there was none of the modernity of serried steel bars; but the walls were of thick and solid stone and the window was small and set high in the wall. By pulling up a stool and standing on it he could barely see outside, and he was a fairly tall man. He looked at the dim shapes of the buildings across the square and judged that the cell was on the second floor of the building in which the Poste de Police was housed.

He stepped down from the stool and said, "Why the hell were you carrying a gun?"

"I always carry a gun," said Dawson. "A man in my position meets trouble, you know. There are always cranks who don't like what I write, and the boys who want to prove they're tougher than I am. I've got a licence for it, too. I got a batch of threatening letters a couple of years ago and there were some funny things happening round my place so I got the gun."

"I don't know that that was a good idea, even in the States," said Wyatt. "But it certainly got us into trouble here. Your gun licence won't cut any ice."

"Getting out will be easy," said Dawson angrily. "All I have to do is to wait until I can see someone bigger than one of those junior grade cops, tell him who I am, and we'll both be sprung."

Wyatt stared at him. "Are you serious?"

"Sure I'm serious. Hell, man; everyone knows me. The Government of this tin-pot banana republic isn't going to get in bad with Uncle Sam by keeping me in gaol. The fact that I've been picked up will make world headlines, and this Serrurier character isn't going to let bad change to worse."

Wyatt took a deep breath. "You don't know Serrurier," he said. "He doesn't like Americans in the first place and he won't give a damn who you are—if he's heard of you, that is, which I doubt."

Dawson seemed troubled by the heresy Wyatt had uttered. "Not heard of me? Of course he'll have heard of me."

"You heard those guns," said Wyatt. "Serrurier is fighting for his life—do you understand that? If Favel wins, Serrurier is going to be very dead. Right now he doesn't give a damn about keeping in with Uncle Sam or anyone else—he just doesn't have the time. And, like a doctor, he buries his mistakes, so if he's informed about us there'll probably be a shooting party in the basement with us as guests; that's why I hope to God no one tells him. And I hope his boys don't have any initiative."

"But there'll have to be a trial," said Dawson. "I'll have my lawyer."

"For God's sake!" exploded Wyatt. "Where have you been living—on the moon? Serrurier has had twenty thousand people executed in the last seven years without trial. They just disappeared. Start praying that we don't join them."

"Now that's nonsense," said Dawson firmly. "I've been coming to San Fernandez for the last five years—it makes a swell fishing base—and I've heard nothing of this. And I've met a lot of government officials and a nicer bunch of boys you couldn't wish to meet. Of course they're black, but I think none the less of them for that."

"Very broad-minded of you," said Wyatt sarcastically. "Can you name any of these 'nice boys'? That information might come in useful."

"Sure; the best of the lot was the Minister for Island Affairs—a guy called Descaix. He's a——"

"Oh, no!" groaned Wyatt, sitting on the stool and putting his head in his hands.

"What's the matter?"

Wyatt looked up. "Now, listen, Dawson; I'll try to get this over in words of one syllable. Your nice boy, Descaix, was the boss of Serrurier's secret police. Serrurier said, 'Do it,' and Descaix did it, and in the end it added up to a nice pile of murders. But Descaix slipped—one of his murders didn't pan out and the man came back to life, the man responsible for all those guns popping off up in the hills. Favel."

He tapped Dawson on the knee. "Serrurier didn't like that, so what do you think happened to Descaix?"

Dawson was looking unhappy. "I wouldn't know."

"Neither would anyone else," said Wyatt. "Descaix's gone, vanished as though he never existed—expunged. My own idea is that he's occupying a hole in the ground up in the Tour Rambeau."

"But he was such a nice, friendly guy," said Dawson. He shook his head in bewilderment. "I don't see how I could have missed it. I'm a writer—I'm supposed to know something about people. I even went fishing with Descaix—surely you get to know a man you fish with?"

"Why should you?" asked Wyatt. "People like Descaix have neatly compartmented minds. If you or I killed a man it would stay with us the rest of our lives—it would leave a mark. But Descaix has a man killed and he's forgotten about it as soon as he's given the order. It doesn't worry his conscience one little bit, so it doesn't show—there's no mark."

"Jesus!" said Dawson with awe. "I've been fishing with a mass murderer."

"You won't fish with him ever again," said Wyatt brutally. "You might not fish with anyone ever again if we don't get out of here."

Dawson gave way to petulant rage. "What the hell is the American Government doing? We have a base here—why wasn't this island cleaned up long ago?"

"You make me sick," said Wyatt. "You don't know what's going on right in front of your nose, and when your nose gets bitten you scream to your Government for help. The American Government policy on this island is 'hands off', and rightly so. If they interfere here in the same way they did in the Dominican Republic they'd totally wreck their diplomatic relations with the rest of the hemisphere and the Russians would laugh fit to burst. Anyway, it's best this way. You can't hand freedom to people on a plate—they've got to take it. Favel knows that—he's busy taking his freedom right now."

He looked at Dawson who was sitting huddled on the bed, strangely shrunken. "You were trying to take the car, weren't you? There was no policeman trying to drive it away at all. But you were."

Dawson nodded. "I went upstairs and heard you and Causton talking about the hurricane. I got scared and figured I'd better get out."

"And you were going to leave the rest of us?"

Dawson nodded miserably.

Wyatt stretched out his legs. "I don't understand it," he said. "I just don't understand it. You're Dawson—'Big Jim' Dawson—the man who's supposed to be able to outshoot, out-fight, out-fly any other man on earth. What's happened to you?"

Dawson lay on the bed and turned to the wall. "Go to hell!" he said in a muffled voice.

IV

The police came for them at four o'clock in the morning, hustling them out of the cell and along a corridor. The office into which they were shown was bare and bleak, the archetype of all such offices anywhere in the world. The policeman at the desk was also archetypal; his cold, impersonal eyes and level stare could be duplicated in any police office in New York, London or Tokyo, and the fact that his complexion was dark coffee did not make any difference.

He regarded them expressionlessly, then said, "Fool, I wanted them one at a time. Take that one back." He pointed his pen at Wyatt, who was immediately pushed back into the corridor and escorted to the cell again.

He leaned against the wall as the key clicked in the lock and wondered what would eventually happen to him—perhaps he would join Descaix, an unlikely bedfellow. He had not heard the guns for some time and he hoped that Favel had not been beaten, because Favel was his only chance of getting clear. If Favel did not take St. Pierre then he would either be shot or drowned in the cell when the waters of Santego Bay arose to engulf the town.

He sat on the stool and pondered. The policeman who had arrested them had shown a keen interest in Manning and Fuller, the two Englishmen from the North Coast, and he wondered why so much trouble should be taken over them in the middle of a civil war. Then he recalled Causton's questioning earlier about shipments of arms and wondered if Manning and Fuller lived in the Campo de las Perlas, the area in which Causton had said the arms had been landed. If they were involved in that, no wonder Serrurier's police were taking an interest in their doings—and in the doings of all other English people on San Fernandez.

Then, because he was very tired and had sat on the stool all night, he stretched out on the bed and fell asleep.

When he was aroused the first light of dawn was peering through the high window. Again he was taken down the corridor to the bleak room at the end and pushed through the doorway roughly. There was no sign of Dawson, and the policeman behind the desk was smiling. "Come in, Mr. Wyatt. Sit down."

It was not an invitation but an order. Wyatt sat in the hard chair and crossed his legs. The policeman said, in English, "I am Sous-Inspecteur Roseau, Mr. Wyatt. Do you not think my English is good? I learned it in Jamaica."

"It's very good," acknowledged Wyatt.

"I'm glad," said Roseau. "Then there will be no mis-understandings. When did you last see Manning?"

"I've never seen Manning."

"When did you last see Fuller?"

"I've never seen him, either."

"But you knew where they lived; you admitted it."

"I didn't 'admit' a damned thing," said Wyatt evenly. "I told your underling that I'd *heard* they lived on the North Coast. I also told him that I'd never seen either of them in my life."

Roseau consulted a sheet of paper before him. Without looking up he asked, "When were you recruited into American Intelligence?"

"Well, I'll be damned!" said Wyatt. "This is all a lot of nonsense."

Roseau's head came up with a jerk. "Then you are in British Intelligence? You are a *British* spy?"

"You're out of your mind," said Wyatt disgustedly. "I'm a scientist—a meteorologist. And I don't mind telling you something right now—if you don't get the people out of this town within two days there's going to be the most godawful smash-up you've ever seen. There's a hurricane coming."

Roseau smiled patiently. "Yes, Mr. Wyatt, we know that is your cover. We also know that you British and the Americans are working hand in hand with Favel in an attempt to overthrow the lawful government of this country."

"That'll do," said Wyatt. "I've had enough." He slapped the desk with the flat of his hand. "I want to see the British consul."

"So you want to see Rawsthorne?" inquired Roseau with a malicious smile. "He wanted to see you—he was here trying to get you out, together with another Englishman. It is un-fortunate that, because of his official position, we cannot

arrest Rawsthorne—we know he is your leader—but my
government is sending a strong protest to London about his
conduct. He is *non persona grata*." Roseau's smile widened.
" You see I have Latin, too, Mr. Wyatt. Not bad for an ignorant nigger."

" Ignorant is exactly the right word," said Wyatt tightly.

Roseau sighed, as a teacher sighs when faced with the
obtuseness of a particularly stubborn pupil. " This is not the
time to insult me, Wyatt. You see, your companion—your
accomplice—the American agent, Dawson, has confessed.
These Americans are not really so tough, you know."

" What the devil could he confess?" asked Wyatt. " He's as
innocent of anything as I am." He moved his hand and felt
a slight wetness on the palm. Turning his hand over he saw a
smear of blood, and there were a few more drops spattered
along the edge of the desk. He lifted his eyes and looked at
Roseau with loathing.

" Yes, Wyatt ; he confessed," said Roseau. He drew a blank
piece of paper from a drawer and placed it neatly before him.
" Now," he said with pen poised. " We will begin again.
When did you last see Manning?"

" I've never seen Manning."

" When did you last see Fuller?"

" I've never seen Fuller," said Wyatt monotonously.

Roseau carefully put down his pen. He said softly, " Shall
we see if you are more stubborn than Dawson? Or perhaps
you will be less stubborn—it is more convenient for you as
well as for me."

Wyatt was very conscious of the two policemen standing
behind him near the door. They had not moved or made a
sound but he knew they were there. He had known it ever
since Dawson's blood had stained his hand. He decided to
take a leaf out of Rawsthorne's book. " Roseau, Serrurier is
going to have your hide for this."

Roseau blinked but said nothing.

" Does he know I'm here? He's a bad man when he's
crossed—but who should know that better than you? When
I saw him yesterday he was giving Hippolyte a going over—
had Hippolyte shaking in his shoes."

" You saw our President yesterday?" Roseau's voice was
perhaps not as firm as it had been.

Wyatt tried to act as though he was always in the habit of

meeting Serrurier for afternoon drinks. "Of course." He leaned over the desk. "Don't you know who Dawson is— the man you've just beaten up? He's the famous writer. You must have heard of Big Jim Dawson—everyone has."

Roseau twitched. "He tried to make me believe he was ——" He stopped suddenly.

Wyatt laughed. "You've put Serrurier right in the middle," he said. "He has his hands full with Favel but that's all right —he can handle it. He told me so himself. But he was worried about the Americans at Cap Sarrat; he doesn't know whether they're going to come out against him or not. Of course you know what will happen if they do. The Americans and Favel will crack Serrurier between them like a nut."

"What has this got to do with me?" asked Roseau uncertainly.

Wyatt leaned back in his chair and looked at Roseau with well-simulated horror. "Why, you fool, you've given the Americans the chance they've been waiting for. Dawson is an international figure, and he's American. Commodore Brooks will be asking Serrurier where Dawson is in not too many hours from now, and if Serrurier can't produce him, alive and unhurt, then Brooks is going to take violent action because he knows he'll have world opinion behind him. Dawson is just the lever the Americans have been waiting for; they can't take up arms just because a few Americans got mixed up in your civil war—that's not done any more—but a potential Nobel Prizewinner, a man of Dawson's stature, is something else again."

Roseau was silent and twitchy. Wyatt let him stew for a few long seconds, then said, "You know as well as I do that Dawson told you nothing about Manning and Fuller. I know that because he knows nothing, but you used him to try to throw a scare into me. Now let me tell you something, Sous-Inspector Roseau. When Commodore Brooks asks Serrurier for Dawson, Serrurier is going to turn St. Pierre upside down looking for him because he knows that if he doesn't find him, then the Americans will break in the back door and stab him in the back just when he's at grips with Favel. And if Serrurier finds that Sous-Inspecteur Roseau has stupidly exceeded his duty by beating Dawson half to death I wouldn't give two pins for your chances of remaining alive for five more minutes. My advice to you is to get a doctor to Dawson as fast as you

can, and then to implore him to keep his mouth shut. How
you do that is your business."

He almost laughed at the expression on Roseau's face as he
contemplated the enormity of his guilt. Roseau finally shut
his mouth with a snap and took a deep breath. " Take this
man to his cell," he ordered, and Wyatt felt a firm grip on
his shoulder, a grip more welcome now than it would have
been five minutes earlier. After being thrust into the cell it
was a long time before he stopped shaking. Then he sat
down to contemplate the sheer, copper-bottomed brilliance of
the idea he had sold Roseau.

He thought that he and Dawson were safe from Roseau.
But there was still the problem of getting out before the
hurricane struck and that would not be easy—not unless he
could manage to work on Roseau's fears some more. He had
an idea that he would be seeing Roseau before long; the
Sous-Inspecteur would remember that Wyatt had claimed
acquaintance with Serrurier and he would want to know more
about that.

He looked at his watch. It was seven o'clock and the sun-
light was streaming through the small window. He hoped that
Causton would have sense enough to get the others out of St.
Pierre—even by walking they could get a long way.

The noise outside suddenly came to his attention. It had
been going on ever since he had been pushed into the cell
but he had been so immersed in his thoughts that it had not
penetrated. Now he was aware of the racket in the square
outside—the revving of heavy engines, the clatter of feet and
the murmur of many men interspersed by raucous shouts—
sergeants have the same brazen-voiced scream in any army ;
it sounded as though an army was massing in the square.

He kicked the stool across to the window and climbed up,
but the angle was wrong and he could not see the ground at
all, merely the façade of the buildings on the opposite side of
the square. He stood there for a long time trying to make
sense of the confused sounds from below but finally gave up.
He was just about to step off the stool when he heard the
sudden bellow of guns from so close that the hot air seemed
to quiver.

He stood on tiptoe, desperately trying to see what was
happening, and caught a glimpse of a deep red flash on the

roof of the building immediately opposite. There was a *slam* and the front of the building caved in before his startled eyes, seeming to collapse in slow motion in a billowing cloud of dust.

Then the blast of the explosion caught him and he was hurled in a shower of broken glass right across the cell to thud against the door. The last thing he heard before he collapsed into unconsciousness was the thump of his head against the solid wood.

Four

The drumfire of the guns jerked Causton from a deep sleep. He started violently and opened his eyes, wondering for a moment where he was and relieved to find the familiarity of his own room at the Imperiale. Eumenides, to whom he had offered a bed, was standing at the window looking out.

Causton sat up in bed. " God's teeth! " he said, " those guns are near. Favel must have broken through." He scrambled out of bed and was momentarily disconcerted to find he was still wearing his trousers.

Eumenides drew back from the window and looked at Causton moodily. " They will fight in town," he said. " Will be ver' bad."

" It usually is," said Causton, rubbing the stubble on his cheeks. " What's happening down there?"

" Many peoples—soldiers," said Eumenides. " Many 'urt."

" Walking wounded? Serrurier must be in full retreat. But he'll do his damnedest to hold the town. This is where the frightful part comes in—the street fighting." He wound up a clockwork dry shaver with quick efficient movements. " Serrurier's police have been holding the population down; that was wise of him—he didn't want streams of refugees impeding his army. But whether they'll be able to do it in the middle of a battle is another thing. I have the feeling this is going to be a nasty day."

The Greek lit another cigarette and said nothing.

Causton finished his shave in silence. His mind was busy

with the implications of the nearness of the guns. Favel must
have smashed Serrurier's army in the Negrito and pushed on
with all speed to the outskirts of St. Pierre. Moving so fast, he
must have neglected mopping-up operations and there were
probably bits of Serrurier's army scattered in pockets all down
the Negrito; they would be disorganized now after groping
about in the night, but with the daylight they might be a
danger—a danger Favel might be content to ignore.

For a greater danger confronted him. He had burst on to
the plain and was hammering at the door of St. Pierre in
broad daylight, and Causton doubted if he was well enough
equipped for a slugging match in those conditions. So far, he
had depended on surprise and the sudden hammer blow of
unexpected artillery against troops unused to the violence of
high explosives—but Serrurier had artillery and armour and
an air force. True, the armour consisted of three antiquated
tanks and a dozen assorted armoured cars, the air force was
patched up from converted civilian planes and Favel had
been able to laugh at this display of futile modernity when
still secure in the mountains. But on the plain it would be a
different matter altogether. Even an old tank would be master
of the battlefield, and the planes could see what they were
bombing.

Causton examined his reflection in the glass and wondered
if Favel had moved fast enough to capture Serrurier's artillery
before it had got into action. If he had, he would be the
luckiest commander in history because it had been sheer
inefficiency on the part of the Government artillery general
that had bogged it down. But luck—good and bad—was an
inescapable element on the field of battle.

He plunged his head into cold water, came up spluttering
and reached for a towel. He had just finished drying himself
when there was a knock on the door. He held up a warning
hand to Eumenides. "Who's that?"

"It's me," called Julie.

He relaxed. "Come in, Miss Marlowe."

Julie looked a little careworn; there were dark circles under
her eyes as though she had had very little sleep and she was
dishevelled. She pushed her hair back, and said, "That
woman will drive me nuts."

"What's La Warmington doing now?"

"Right now she's dozing, thank God. That woman's got a

nerve—she was treating me like a lady's maid last night and got annoyed because I wouldn't take orders. Then in the middle of the night she got weepy and nearly drove me out of my mind. I had to fill her full of luminol in the end."

"Is she asleep now?"

"She's just woken up, but she's so dopey she doesn't know what's going on."

"Perhaps it's just as well," said Causton, cocking his head as he listened to the guns. "It might be just as well to keep her doped until we get out of here. I hope to God Rawsthorne can make it in time." He looked at Julie. "You don't look too good yourself."

"I'm beat," she confessed. "I didn't sleep so well myself. I was awake half the night with Mrs. Warmington. I got her off to sleep and then found I couldn't sleep myself—I was thinking about Dave and Mr. Dawson. When I finally got to sleep I was woken up almost immediately by those damned guns." She folded her arms about herself and winced at a particularly loud explosion. "I'm scared—I don't mind admitting it."

"I'm not feeling too good myself," said Causton drily. "How about you, Eumenides?"

The Greek shrugged eloquently, gave a ferocious grin and passed his fingers across his throat. Causton laughed. "That about describes it."

Julie said, "Do you think it's any good trying to get Dave out of that gaol again?"

Causton resisted an impulse to swear. As a man who earned his living by the writing of the English language, he had always maintained that swearing and the use of foul language was the prop of an ignorant mind unable to utilize the full and noble resources of English invective. But the previous night he had been forced to use the dirtiest language he knew when he came up against the impenetrably closed mind of Sous-Inspecteur Roseau. He had quite shocked Rawsthorne, if not Roseau.

He said, "There's not much hope, I'm afraid. The walls of the local prison may be thick, but the coppers' heads are thicker. Maybe Favel may be able to get him out if he hurries up."

He put his foot up on the bed to lace his shoe. "I had a talk with Rawsthorne last night; he was telling me something about Wyatt's hurricane. According to Rawsthorne, it's not at all certain there'll be a hurricane here at all. What do you know about that?"

"I know that Dave was very disturbed about it," she said. "Especially after he saw the old man."

"What old man?"

So Julie told of the old man who had been tying his roof down and Causton scratched his head. He said mildly, "For a meteorologist, Wyatt has very unscientific ways of going about his job."

"Don't you believe him?" asked Julie.

"That's the devil of it—I do," said Causton. "I'll tell you something, Julie: I *always* depend on my intuition and it rarely lets me down. That's why I'm here on this island right now. My editor told me I was talking nonsense—I had no real evidence things were going to blow up here—so that's why I'm here unofficially. Yes, I believe in Wyatt's wind, and we'll have to do something about it bloody quickly."

"What can we do about a hurricane?"

"I mean we must look after ourselves," said Causton. "Look, Julie; Wyatt's immediate boss didn't believe him; Commodore Brooks didn't believe him, and Serrurier didn't believe him. He did all he can and I don't think we can do any better. And if you think I'm going to walk about in the middle of a civil war bearing a placard inscribed 'Prepare To Meet Thy Doom' you're mistaken."

Julie shook her head. "I know," she said. "But there are sixty thousand defenceless people in St. Pierre—it's terrible."

"So is civil war," said Causton gravely. "But there's still nothing we can do apart from saving ourselves—and that's going to be dicey." He took his map from the pocket of his jacket and spread it on the bed. "I wish Rawsthorne had been ready to leave last night, but he said he had to go back to the consulate. I suppose even a lowly consul has to burn the codebooks or whatever it is they do when you see smoke coming from the Embassy chimney on the eve of crisis. What time is it?"

"Nearly 'alf pas' seven," said Eumenides.

"He said he'd be here by eight, but he'll probably be late. Neither of us expected Favel to be so quick—I don't suppose Serrurier expected it, either. Rawsthorne might be held up, even in a car with diplomatic plates. Damn that bloody fool Dawson," he said feelingly. " If he hadn't messed things up we'd have been away in Wyatt's car hours ago."

He looked at the map. " Wyatt said we should find a place above the hundred-foot mark and facing north. This damned map has no contour lines. Eumenides, can you help me here?"

The Greek looked over Causton's shoulder. " There," he said, and laid his finger on the map.

" I dare say it is a nice place," agreed Causton. " But we'd have to go through two armies to get there. No, we'll have to go along the coast in one direction or another and then strike inland to get height." His finger moved along the coast road. " I don't think there's any point in going west towards Cap Sarrat. There are units of the Government army strung along there, and anyway, it's pretty flat as I remember it. The civil airfield is there and Favel will probably strike for it, so altogether it'll be a pretty unhealthy place. So it'll have to be the other way. What's it like this road, Eumenides? The one that leads east?"

" The road goes up," said Eumenides. " There is . . . there is . . ." He snapped his fingers in annoyance. " It fall from road to sea."

" There are cliffs on the seaward side—this side?" asked Causton, and the Greek nodded. " Just what we're looking for," said Causton with satisfaction. " What's the country like inland—say, here?"

Eumenides waved his hand up and down expressively. " 'Ills."

" Then that's it," said Causton. " But you'd better discuss it further with Rawsthorne when he comes."

" What about you?" asked Julie. " Where are you going?"

" Someone has to do a reconnaissance," said Causton. " We have to find if it's a practicable proposition to go that way. I'm going to scout around the east end of town. It's safe enough for one man."

He rose from his knees and went to the window. " There are plenty of civilians out and about now ; the police haven't been able to bottle them all up in their houses. I should be able to get away with it."

" With a white skin?"

" Um," said Causton. " That's a thought." He went over to his bag and unzipped it. " A very little of this ought to do the trick." He looked with distaste at the tin of brown boot-polish in his hand. " Will you apply it, Julie? Just the veriest touch—there are plenty of light-coloured Negroes here and I don't want to look like a nigger minstrel."

Julie smeared a little of the boot-polish on his face. He said, " Don't forget the back of the neck—that's vital. It isn't so much a disguise as a deception ; it only needs enough to darken the skin so that people won't take a second look and say ' Look at that *blanc*.' "

He rubbed some of the polish on his hands and wrists, then said, " Now I want a prop."

Julie stared at him. " A what?"

" A stage property. I've wandered all through the corridors of power in Whitehall and got away with it because I was carrying a sheaf of papers and looked as though I was going somewhere. I got a scoop from a hospital by walking about in a white coat with a stethoscope dangling from my pocket. The idea is to look a natural part of the scenery—a stethoscope gives one a *right* to be in a hospital. Now, what gives me a right to be in a civil war?"

Eumenides grinned maliciously, and said, " A gun."

" I'm afraid so," said Causton regretfully. " Well, there ought to be plenty of those outside. I ought to be able to pick up a rifle and maybe a scrap of uniform to make it look convincing. Meanwhile, where's that pop-gun of yours, Eumenides?"

" In the bar where I lef' it."

" Right—well, I'll be off," said Causton. There was a heavy explosion not far away and the windows shivered in their frames. " It's warming up. A pity this place has no cellars. Eumenides, I think you'd all better move downstairs—actually under the stairs is the best place. And if that Warmington woman gets hysterical, pop her one."

Eumenides nodded.

Causton paused by the door. " I don't think I'll be long, but if I'm not back by eleven I won't be coming back at all, and you'd better push off. With the townspeople coming out now the road might be difficult, so don't wait for me."

He left without waiting for a reply and ran down the stairs and into the bar. There were soda-water bottles stacked on the counter but no sign of the gun. He looked about for a couple of minutes then gave up, vaguely wondering what had happened to it. But he had no time to waste so he crossed the foyer and, with a precautionary glance outside, stepped boldly into the street.

II

Mrs. Warmington was still drugged with sleep, for which Julie was thankful. She opened one drowsy eye and said, "Wha' time is it?"

"It's quite early," said Julie. "But we must go downstairs."

"I wanna sleep," said Mrs. Warmington indistinctly. "Send the maid with my tea in an hour."

"But we must go now," said Julie firmly. "We are going away soon." She began to assemble the things she needed.

"What's all that *noise*?" complained Mrs. Warmington crossly. "I declare this is the noisiest hotel I've ever slept in." This declaration seemed to exhaust her and she closed her eyes and a faint whistling sound emanated from the bed—too ladylike to be called a snore.

"Come on, Mrs. Warmington." Julie shook her by the shoulder.

Mrs. Warmington roused herself and propped up on one elbow. "Oh, my head! Did we have a party?" Slowly, intelligence returned to her eyes and her head jerked up as she recognized the din of the guns for what it was. "Oh, my God!" she wailed. "What's happening?"

"The rebels have started to bombard the town," Julie said.

Mrs. Warmington jumped out of bed, all traces of sleep gone. "We must leave," she said rapidly. "We must go now."

"We have no car yet," said Julie. "Mr. Rawsthorne hasn't come." She turned to find Mrs. Warmington pushing her overfed figure into a tight girdle. "Good grief!" she said, "don't wear that—we might have to move fast. Have you any slacks?"

"I don't believe in women of . . . of my type wearing pants."

Julie surveyed her and gave a crooked smile. "Maybe you're right at that," she agreed. "Well, wear something sensible; wear a suit if it hasn't got a tight skirt."

She stripped the beds of their blankets and folded them into a bundle. Mrs. Warmington said, "I *knew* we ought to have gone to the Base last night." She squeezed her feet into tight shoes.

"You know it was impossible," said Julie briefly.

"I can't imagine what Commodore Brooks is thinking of—leaving us here at the mercy of these savages. Come on, let's get out of here." She opened the door and went out, leaving Julie to bring the large bundle of blankets.

Eumenides was at the head of the stairs. He looked at the blankets and said, "Ver' good t'ing," and took them from her.

There was a faint noise from downstairs as though someone had knocked over a chair. They all stood listening for a moment, then Mrs. Warmington dug her finger into the Greek's ribs. "Don't just stand there," she hissed. "Find out who it is."

Eumenides dropped the blankets and tiptoed down the stairs and out of sight. Mrs. Warmington clutched her bag to her breast, then turned abruptly and walked back to the bedroom. Julie heard the click as the bolt was shot home.

Presently Eumenides reappeared and beckoned. "It's Rawst'orne."

Julie got Mrs. Warmington out of the bedroom again and they all went downstairs to find Rawsthorne very perturbed. "They've started shelling the town," he said. "The Government troops are making a stand. It would be better if we moved out quickly before the roads become choked."

"I agree," said Mrs. Warmington.

Rawsthorne looked around. "Where's Causton?"

"He's gone to find the best way out," said Julie. "He said he wouldn't be long. What time is it now?"

Rawsthorne consulted a pocket watch. "Quarter to nine—sorry I'm late. Did he say when he'd be back?"

She shook her head. "He didn't think he'd be long, but he said that if he wasn't back by eleven then he wouldn't be coming at all."

There was a violent explosion not far away and flakes of plaster drifted down from the ceiling. Mrs. Warmington jumped. "Lead the way to your car, Mr. Rawsthorne. We must leave now."

Rawsthorne ignored her. "A little over two hours at the

most," he said. "But he should be back long before that.
Meanwhile . . ." He looked up meaningly at the ceiling.

"Causton said the best place for us was under the stairs,"
said Julie.

"You mean we're staying here?" demanded Mrs. Warmington. "With all this going on? You'll get us all killed."

"We can't leave Mr. Causton," said Julie.

"I fix," said Eumenides. "Come."

The space under the main staircase had been used as a
store-room. The door had been locked but Eumenides had
broken it open with a convenient fire axe, tossed out all the
buckets and brooms and had packed in all the provisions they
were taking. Mrs. Warmington objected most strongly to
sitting on the floor but went very quietly when Julie said
pointedly, "You're welcome to leave at any time." It was
cramped, but there was room for the four of them to sit, and
if the door was kept ajar Rawsthorne found he had a view of
the main entrance so that he could see Causton as soon as he
came back.

He said worriedly, "Causton should never have gone out—
I've never seen St. Pierre like this, the town is starting to boil
over."

"He'll be all right," said Julie. "He's experienced at this
kind of thing—it's his job."

"Thank God it's not mine," said Rawsthorne fervently.
"The Government army must have been beaten terribly in
the Negrito. The town is full of deserters on the run, and
there are many wounded men." He shook his head. "Favel's
attack must have come with shocking suddenness for that to
have happened. He must be outnumbered at least three to one
by the Government forces."

"You said Serrurier is making a stand," said Julie. "That
means the fighting is going to go on."

"It might go on for a long time," said Rawsthorne soberly.
"Serrurier has units that weren't committed to battle yesterday—Favel didn't give him time. But those fresh units are
digging in to the north of the town, so that means another
battle." He clicked deprecatingly with his tongue. "I fear
Favel may have overestimated his own strength."

He fell silent and they listened to the noise of the battle.
Always there was the clamour of the guns from the outskirts
of the town, punctuated frequently by the closer and louder

explosion of a falling shell. The air in the hotel quivered and gradually became full of a sifting dust so that the sunlight slanting into the foyer shone like the beams of searchlights.

Julie stirred and began to search among the boxes which Eumenides had packed at the back. "Have you had breakfast, Mr. Rawsthorne?"

"I didn't have time, my dear."

"We might as well eat now," said Julie practically. "I think I can cut some bread if we rearrange ourselves a little. We might as well eat it before it becomes really stale."

They breakfasted off bread and canned pressed meat, washing it down with soda-water. When they had finished Rawsthorne said, "What time is it? I can't seem to get at my watch."

"Ten-fifteen," said Julie.

"We can give Causton another three-quarters of an hour," said Rawsthorne. "But then we *must* go—I'm sorry, but there it is."

"That's all right," said Julie quietly. "He did tell us to go at eleven."

Occasionally they heard distant shouts and excited cries and sometimes the clatter of running boots. Eumenides said suddenly, "Your car . . . is in street?"

"No," said Rawsthorne. "I left it at the back of the hotel." He paused. "Poor Wyatt's car is in a mess; all the windows are broken and someone has taken the wheels; for the tyres, I suppose."

They relapsed into cramped silence. Mrs. Warmington hugged her bag and conducted an intermittent monologue which Julie ignored. She listened to the shells exploding and wondered what would happen if the hotel got a direct hit. She had no idea of the damage a shell could do apart from what she had seen at the movies and on TV and she had a shrewd idea that the movie version would be but a pale imitation of the real thing. Her mouth became dry and she knew she was very frightened.

The minutes dragged drearily by. Mrs. Warmington squeaked sharply as a shell exploded near by—the closest yet —and the windows of the foyer blew in and smashed. She started to get up, but Julie pulled her back. "Stay where you are," she cried. "It's safer here."

Mrs. Warmington flopped back and somehow Julie felt better after that. She looked at Eumenides, his face pale in the dim light, and wondered what he was thinking. It was bad for him because, his English being what it was, he could not communicate easily. As she looked at him he pulled up his wrist to his eyes. "Quar' to 'leven," he announced. "I t'ink we better load car."

Rawsthorne stirred. "Yes, that might be a good idea," he agreed. He began to push open the door. "Wait a minute—here's Causton now."

Julie sighed. "Thank God!"

Rawsthorne pushed the door wider and then stopped short. "No, it's not," he whispered. "It's a soldier—and there's another behind him." Gently he drew the door closed again, leaving it open only a crack and watching with one eye.

The soldier was carrying a rifle slung over one shoulder but the man behind, also a soldier, had no weapon. They came into the foyer, carelessly kicking aside the cane chairs, and stood for a moment looking at the dusty opulence around them. One of them said something and pointed, and the other laughed, and they both moved out of sight.

"They've gone into the bar," whispered Rawsthorne.

Faintly, he could hear the clinking of bottles and loud laughter, and once, a smash of glass. Then there was silence. He said softly, "We can't come out while they're there; they'd see us. We'll have to wait."

It was a long wait and Rawsthorne began to feel cramp in his leg. He could not hear anything at all and began to wonder if the soldiers had not departed from the rear of the hotel. At last he whispered, "What time is it?"

"Twenty past eleven."

"This is nonsense," said Mrs. Warmington loudly. "I can't hear anything. They must have gone."

"Keep quiet!" said Rawsthorne. There was a ragged edge to his voice. He paused for a long time, then said softly, "They *might* have gone. I'm going to have a look round."

"Be careful," whispered Julie.

He was about to push the door open again when he halted the movement and swore softly under his breath. One of the soldiers had come out of the bar and was strolling through the foyer, drinking from a bottle. He went to the door of the hotel and stood for a while staring into the street through the broken panes in the revolving door, then he suddenly shouted to someone outside and waved the bottle in the air.

Two more men came in from outside and there was a brief conference; the first soldier waved his arm towards the bar with largesse as though to say "be my guests". One of the two shouted to someone else outside, and presently there were a dozen soldiers tramping through the foyer on their way to the bar. There was a babel of sound in hard, masculine voices.

"Damn them!" said Rawsthorne. "They're starting a party."

"What can we do?" asked Julie.

"Nothing," said Rawsthorne briefly. He paused, then said, "I think these are deserters—I wouldn't want them to see us, especially . . ." His voice trailed away.

"Especially the women," said Julie flatly, and felt Mrs. Warmington begin to quiver.

They lay there in silence listening to the racket from the bar, the raucous shouts, the breaking glasses and the voices raised in song. "All law in the city must be breaking down," said Rawsthorne at last.

"I want to get out of here," said Mrs. Warmington suddenly and loudly.

"Keep that woman quiet," Rawsthorne hissed.

"I'm not staying here," she cried, and struggled to get up.

"Hold it," whispered Julie furiously, pulling her down.

"You can't keep me here," screamed Mrs. Warmington.

Julie did not know what Eumenides did, but suddenly Mrs. Warmington collapsed on top of her, a warm, dead weight, flaccid and heavy. She heaved violently and pushed the woman off her. "Thanks, Eumenides," she whispered.

"For God's sake!" breathed Rawsthorne, straining his ears to hear if there was any sudden and sinister change in the volume of noise coming from the bar. Nothing happened; the noise became even louder—the men were getting drunk. After a while Rawsthorne said softly, "What's the matter with that woman? Is she mad?"

"No," said Julie. "Just spoiled silly. She's had her own way all her life and she can't conceive of a situation in which getting her own way could cause her death. She can't adapt." Her voice was pensive. "I guess I feel sorry for her more than anything else."

"Sorry or not, you'd better keep her quiet," said Rawsthorne. He peered through the crack. "God knows how long this lot is going to stay here—and they're getting drunker."

They lay there listening to the rowdy noise which was sometimes overlaid by the reverberation of the battle. Julie kept looking at her watch, wondering how long this was going to go on. Every five minutes she said to herself, they'll leave in another five minutes—but they never did. Presently she heard a muffled sound from Rawsthorne. "What is it?" she whispered.

He turned his head. "More of them coming in." He turned back to watch. There were seven of them this time, six troopers and what seemed to be an officer, and there was discipline in the way they moved into the foyer and looked about. The officer stared across into the bar and shouted something, but his voice was lost in the uproar, so he drew his revolver and fired a shot in the air. There came sudden silence in the hotel.

Mrs. Warmington stirred weakly and a bubbling groan came from her lips. Julie clamped her hand across the woman's mouth and squeezed tight. She heard an exasperated sigh from Rawsthorne and saw him move his head slightly as though he had taken one quick look back.

The officer shouted in a hectoring voice and one by one the deserters drifted out of the bar and into the foyer and stood muttering among themselves, eyeing the officer insolently and in defiance. The last to appear was the soldier with the rifle—he was very drunk.

The officer whiplashed them with his tongue, his voice cracking in rage. Then he made a curt gesture and gave a quick command, indicating that they should line up. The drunken soldier with the rifle shouted something and unslung the weapon from his shoulder, cocking it as he did so, and the officer snapped an order to the trooper standing at his back. The trooper lifted his sub-machine-gun and squeezed the trigger. The stuttering hammer of the gun filled the foyer with sound and a spray of bullets took the rifleman across the chest and flung him backwards across a table, which collapsed with a crash.

A stray bullet slammed into the door near Rawsthorne's head and he flinched, but he kept his eye on the foyer and saw the officer wave his arm tiredly. Obediently the deserters lined up and marched out of the hotel, escorted by the armed troopers. The officer put his revolver back into its holster and looked down at the man who had been killed. Viciously he kicked the body, then turned on his heel and walked out.

Rawsthorne waited a full five minutes before he said cautiously, " I think we can go out now."

As he pushed open the door and light flooded into the store-room Julie released her grip of Mrs. Warmington, who sagged sideways on to Eumenides. Rawsthorne stumbled out and Julie followed, then they turned to drag out the older woman. "How is she?" asked Julie. "I thought I would suffocate her, but I had to keep her quiet."

Rawsthorne bent over her. " She'll be all right."

It was twenty minutes before they were in the car and ready to go. Mrs. Warmington was conscious but in a daze, hardly aware of what was happening. Eumenides was white and shaken. As he settled himself in the car seat he discovered a long tear in his jacket just under the left sleeve, and realized with belated terror that he had nearly been shot through the heart by the stray bullet that had frightened Rawsthorne.

Rawsthorne checked the instruments. " She's full up with petrol," he said. " And there are a couple of spare cans in the back. We should be all right."

He started off and the car rolled down the narrow alley at the back of the hotel heading towards the main street. The Union Jack mounted on the wing of the car fluttered a little in the breeze of their passage.

It was a quarter to two.

III

When Causton stepped out into the street he had felt very conspicuous as though accusing eyes were upon him from every direction, but after a while he began to feel easier as he realized that the people round him were intent only on their own troubles. Looking up the crowded street towards the Place de la Libération Noire he saw a coil of black smoke indicating a fire, and even as he watched he saw a shell burst in what must have been the very centre of the square.

He turned and began to hurry the other way, going with

the general drift. The noise was pandemonium—the thunder of the guns, the wail of shells screaming through the air and the ear-splitting blasts as they exploded were bad enough, but the noise of the crowd was worse. Everyone seemed to find it necessary to shout, and the fact that they were shouting in what, to him, was an unknown language did not help.

Once a man grasped him by the arm and bawled a string of gibberish into his face and Causton said, " Sorry, old boy, but I can't tell a word you're saying," and threw the arm off. It was only when he turned away that he realized that he himself had shouted at the top of his voice.

The crowd was mainly civilian although there were a lot of soldiers, some armed but mostly not. The majority of the soldiers seemed to be unwounded and quite fit apart from their weariness and the glazed terror in their eyes, and Causton judged that these were men who had faced an artillery barrage for the first time in their lives and had broken under it. But there were wounded men, trudging along holding broken arms, limping with leg wounds, and one most horrible sight, a young soldier staggering along with his hands to his stomach, the red wetness of his viscera escaping through his slippery fingers.

The civilians seemed even more demoralized than the soldiery. They ran about hither and thither, apparently at random. One man whom Causton observed changed the direction of his running six times in as many minutes, passing and repassing Causton until he was lost in the crowd. He came upon a young girl in a red dress standing in the middle of the street, her hands clapped to her ears and her prettiness distorted as she screamed endlessly. He heard her screams for quite a long time as he fought his way through that agony of terror.

He finally decided he had better get into a side street away from the press, so he made his way to the pavement and turned the first corner he came to. It was not so crowded and he could make better time, a point he noted for when the time came to drive out the car. Presently he came upon a young soldier sitting on an orange box, his rifle beside him and one sleeve of his tunic flapping loose. Causton stopped and said, " Have you got a broken arm?"

The young man looked up uncomprehendingly, his face

grey with fatigue. Causton tapped his own arm. "*Le bras*," he said, then made a swift motion as though breaking a stick across his knee. "Broken?"

The soldier nodded dully.

"I'll fix it," said Causton and squatted down to help the soldier take off his tunic. He kicked the orange box to pieces to make splints and then bound up the arm. "You'll be okay now," he said, and departed. But he left bearing the man's tunic and rifle—he now had his props.

The tunic was a tight fit so he wore it unbuttoned; the trousers did not match and he had no cap, but he did not think that mattered—all that mattered was that he looked approximately like a soldier and so had a proprietary interest in the war. He lifted the rifle and worked the action to find the magazine empty and smiled thoughtfully. That did not matter, either; he had never shot anyone in his life and did not intend starting now.

Gradually, by a circuitous route which he carefully marked on the map, he made his way to the eastern edge of the city by the coast road. He was relieved to see that here the crowds were less and the people seemed to be somewhat calmer. Along the road he saw a thin trickle of people moving out, a trickle that later in the day would turn to a flood. The sooner he could get Rawsthorne started in the car, the better it would be for everyone concerned, so he turned back, looking at his watch. It was later than he thought—nearly ten o'clock.

Now he found he was moving against the stream and progress was more difficult and would become even more so as he approached the disturbed city centre. He looked ahead and saw the blazon of smoke in the sky spreading over the central area—the city was beginning to burn. But not for long, he thought grimly. Not if Wyatt is right.

He pressed on into the bedlam that was St. Pierre, pushing against the bodies that pressed against him and ruthlessly using the butt of his rifle to clear his way. Once he met a soldier fighting his way clear and they came face to face; Causton reversed his rifle and manipulated the bolt with a sharp click, thinking, what do I do if he doesn't take the hint? The soldier nervously eyed the rifle muzzle pointing at his belly, half-heartedly made an attempt to lift his own gun but thought better of it, and retreated, slipping away into the crowd. Causton grinned mirthlessly and went on his way.

He was not far from the Imperiale when the press of the crowd became so much that he could not move. Christ! he thought; we're sitting ducks for a shell-burst. He tried to make his way back, but found that as difficult as going forward —something was evidently holding up the crowd, something immovable.

He found out what it was when he struggled far enough back, almost to the corner of the street. A military unit had debouched from the side street and formed a line across the main thoroughfare, guns pointing at the crowd. Men were being hauled out of the crowd and lined up in a clear space, and Causton took one good look and tried to duck back. But he was too late. An arm shot out and grabbed him, pulling him bodily out of the crowd and thrusting him to join the others. Serrurier was busy rounding up his dissolving army.

He looked at the group of men which he had joined. They were all soldiers and all unwounded, looking at the ground with hangdog expressions. Causton hunched his shoulders, drooped his head and mingled unobtrusively with them, getting as far away from the front as possible. After a while an officer came and made a speech at them. Causton couldn't understand a word of it, but he got the general drift of the argument. They were deserters, quitters under fire, who deserved to be shot, if not at dawn, then a damn' sight sooner. Their only hope of staying alive was to go and face the guns of Favel for the greater glory of San Fernandez and President Serrurier.

To make his point the officer walked along the front row of men and arbitrarily selected six. They were marched across to the front of a house—poor, bewildered, uncomprehending sheep—and suddenly a machine-gun opened up and the little group staggered and fell apart under the hail of bullets. The officer calmly walked across and put a bullet into the brain of one screaming wretch, then turned and gave a sharp order.

The deserters were galvanized into action. Under the screams of bellowing non-coms they formed into rough order and marched away down the side street, Causton among them. He looked at the firing squad in the truck as he passed, then across at the six dead bodies. *Pour encourager les autres*, he thought.

Causton had been conscripted into Serrurier's army.

I V

Dawson was astonished at himself.

He had lived his entire life as a civilized member of the North American community and, as a result, he had never come to terms with himself on what he would do if he got into real trouble. Like most modern civilized men, he had never met trouble of this sort ; he was cosseted and protected by the community and paid his taxes like a man, so that this protection should endure and others stand between him and primitive realities such as death by bullet or torture.

Although his image was that of a free-wheeling, all-American he-man and although he was in danger of believing his own press-clippings, he was aware in the dim recesses of his being that this image was fraudulent, and from time to time he had wondered vaguely what kind of a man he really was. He had banished these thoughts as soon as they were consciously formulated because he had an uneasy feeling that he was really a weak man after all, and the thought disturbed him deeply. The public image he had formed was the man he wanted to be and he could not bear the thought that perhaps he was nothing like that. And he had no way of proving it one way or the other—he had never been put to the test.

Wyatt's hardly concealed contempt had stung and he felt something approaching shame at his attempt to steal the car —that was not the way a *man* should behave. So that when his testing-time came something deep inside him made him square his shoulders and briskly tell Sous-Inspecteur Roseau to go to hell and make it damn' fast, buddy.

So it was that now, lying in bed with all hell breaking loose around him, he felt astonished at himself. He had stood up to such physical pain as he had never believed possible and he felt proud that his last conscious act in Roseau's office had been to look across at the implacable face before him and mumble, " I still say it—go to hell, you son of a bitch!"

He had recovered consciousness in a clean bed with his hands bandaged and his wounds tended. Why that should be he did not know, nor did he know why he could not raise his body from the bed. He tried several times and then gave up the effort and turned his attention to his new and wondrous self. In one brief hour he had discovered that he would never

need a public image again, that he would never shrink from
self-analysis.

"I'll never be afraid again," he whispered aloud through
bruised lips. "By God, I stood it—I need never be afraid
again."

But he *was* afraid again when the artillery barrage opened
up. He could not control the primitive reaction of his body;
his glands worked normally and fear entered him as the hail
of steel fell upon the Place de la Libération Noire. He shrank
back on to the bed and looked up at the ceiling and wondered
helplessly if the next shell would plunge down to take away
his newfound manhood.

v

Not far away, Wyatt sat in the corner of his cell with his hands
over his ears because the din was indescribably deafening. His
face was cut about where broken glass had driven at him, but
luckily his eyes were untouched. He had spent some time
delicately digging out small slivers of glass from his skin—a
very painful process—and the concentration needed had
driven everything else out of his mind. But now he was
sharply aware of what was going on.

Every gun Favel had appeared to be firing on the Place de
la Libération Noire. Explosion followed explosion without
ceasing and an acrid chemical stink drifted through the small
window into the cell. The Poste de Police had not yet been
hit, or at least Wyatt did not think so. And he was sure he
would know. As he crouched in the corner with his legs up,
grasshopper fashion, and his face dropped between his knees,
he was busy making plans as to what he would do when the
Poste was hit—if he still remained alive to do anything at all.

Suddenly there was an almighty *clang* that shivered the air
in the cell. Wyatt felt like a mouse that had crawled into a
big drum—he was completely deafened for a time and heard
the tumult outside as though through a hundred layers of
cloth. He staggered to his feet, shaking his head dizzily, and
leaned against the wall. After a while he felt better and began
to look more closely at the small room in which he was imprisoned. The Poste had been hit—that was certain—and
surely to God something must have given way.

He looked at the opposite wall. Surely it had not had that

bulge in it before? He went closer to examine it and saw a long crack zig-zagging up the wall. He put his hand out and pushed tentatively, and then applied his shoulder and pushed harder. Nothing gave.

He stepped back and looked around the cell for something with which to attack the wall. He looked at the stool and rejected it—it was lightly built of wood, a good enough weapon against a man but not against the wall. There remained the bed. It was made of iron of the type where the main frame lifts out of sockets in the head and foot. The bed head, of tubular metal, was bolted together, but the bolts had rusted and it was quite a task to withdraw them. However, at the end of half an hour he had a goodly selection of tools with which to work—two primitive crowbars, several scrapers devised from the bed springs and an object which was quite unnameable but for which, no doubt, he could find a use.

Feeling rather like Edmond Dantes, he knelt before the wall and began to use one of the scrapers to detach loose mortar from the crack. The mortar, centuries old, was hard and ungiving, but the explosion had not done the wall any good and gradually he excavated a small hole, wide enough and deep enough to insert the end of his crowbar. Then he heaved until his muscles cracked and was rewarded with the minutest movement of the stone block which he was attacking.

He stood back to inspect the problem and became conscious that the intense shell-fire directed at the square had ceased. The shell which had cracked the wall must have been one of the last fired in that direction, and all that could be heard now was a generalized battle noise away to the north of the town.

He dismissed the war from his mind and looked thoughtfully at his improvised crowbar. A crowbar is a lever, or rather, part of a lever—the other part is a fulcrum, and he had no fulcrum. He took the foot of the bed and placed it against the wall; it could be used as a fulcrum but not in the place he had made the hole. He would have to begin again and make another hole.

Again it took a long time. Patiently he scraped away at the iron-hard mortar, chipping and picking it to pieces, and when he had finished his knuckles were bruised and bleeding and his fingertips felt as though someone had sand-papered them raw. He was also beginning to suffer from thirst; he had drunk the small carafe of water that had been in the cell, and no one had come near since that last colossal explosion—a good sign.

He inserted the tip of his crowbar into the new hole and heaved again. Again he felt the infinitesimal shift in the wall. He took the bed foot and placed it within six inches of the wall and then plunged his crowbar into the hole. It rested nicely just on top of the metal frame of the bed. Then he took a deep breath and swung his whole weight on to the crowbar. Something had to give—the crowbar, the bed, the wall—or —maybe—Wyatt. He hoped it would be the wall.

He felt the metal tube of the crowbar bending under his weight but still bore down heavily, lifting his feet from the floor. There came a sudden grating noise and a sharp shift in pressure and he found himself abruptly deposited on the floor. He turned over and coughed and waved his hand to disperse the dust which eddied and swirled through the cell illuminated by a bright beam of sunlight which shone through the gaping hole he had made.

He rested for a few minutes, then went to look at the damage. By his calculations, he should merely have broken through to the next cell and it had been a calculated risk whether he would find the door to that cell locked. But to his surprise, when he looked through the hole he could see, though not very clearly, a part of the square partly obscured by a ragged exterior wall.

The shell that had hit the Poste had totally destroyed the next cell and it was only by the mercy of the excellent and he had forgotten the builders of his prison that he had not been blown to Kingdom Come.

He had dislodged only two of the heavy ashlar blocks that made up the wall and the hole would be a tight fit, but luckily he was slim and he managed to wriggle through with nothing more than a few additional scrapes. It was tricky finding a footing on the other side because half the floor had been blown away, leaving the ground-floor office starkly exposed to the sky. A man looked up at him from down there with shocked brown eyes—but he was quite dead, lying on his back with his chest crushed by a block of masonry.

Wyatt teetered on the foot-wide ledge that was his only perch and supported himself with his hands while he looked across the square. It was desolate and uninhabited save for the hundreds of corpses that lay strewn about, corpses dressed in the light blue of the Government army uniform. The only movement was from the smoke arising from the dozen or so fiercely burning army trucks grouped round what had been the centrepiece—the heroic statue of Serrurier. But the statue was gone, blown from its plinth by the storm of steel.

He looked down. It would be quite easy to descend to the ground and to walk away as free as the air. But then he looked across and saw the door of the ruined cell hanging loose with one hinge broken, and although he hesitated, he knew what he must do. He must find Dawson.

He picked his way carefully along the narrow ledge until he came to a wider and safer part near the door. From then on it was easy and inside thirty seconds he was in the corridor of the cell block. It was strange; apart from the heavy layer of dust which overlay everything, there was not a sign that the building had been hit.

Walking up the corridor, he called, "Dawson!" and was astonished to hear his voice emerge as a croak. He cleared his throat and called again in a stronger voice, "Dawson! Dawson!"

A confused shouting came from the cells around him, but he could not distinguish Dawson's voice. Angrily, he shouted, "*Taisez-vous!*" and the voices died away save for a faint cry from the end of the corridor. He hastened along and called again. "Dawson! Are you there?"

"Here!" a faint voice said, and he traced it to a room next to Roseau's office. He looked at the door—this was no cell, it would be easy. He took a heavy fire-extinguisher, and, using it as a battering ram, soon shattered the lock and burst into the room.

Dawson was lying in bed, his head and hands bandaged. Both his eyes were blackened and he seemed to have lost some teeth. Wyatt looked at him. "My God! What did they do to you?"

Dawson looked at him for some seconds without speaking, then he summoned up a grin. "Seen yourself lately?" he asked, speaking painfully through swollen lips.

"Come on," said Wyatt. "Let's get out of here."

"I can't," said Dawson with suppressed rage. "The bastards strapped me down."

Wyatt took a step forward and saw that it was true. Two broad straps ran across Dawson's body, the buckles well under the bed far beyond the reach of prying hands. He ducked under the bed and began to unfasten them. "What happened after you were beaten up?" he asked.

"That's the damnedest thing," said Dawson with perplexity. "I woke up in here and I'd been fixed up with these bandages. Why in hell would they do that?"

"I threw a scare into Roseau," said Wyatt. "I'm glad it worked."

"They still didn't want to lose me, I guess," said Dawson. "That's why they strapped me down. I've been going through hell, waiting for a shell to bust through the ceiling. I thought it had happened twice."

"Twice? I thought there was only one hit."

Dawson got out of bed. "I reckon there were two." He nodded to a chair. "Help me with my pants; I don't think I can do it myself—not with these hands. Oh, how I'd like to meet up with that son of a bitch, Roseau."

"How are your legs?" asked Wyatt, helping to dress him.

"They're okay."

"We've got a bit of climbing to do; not much—just enough to get down to street level. I think you'll be able to do it. Come on."

They went out into the corridor. "There's a cell a bit further along that's been well ventilated," said Wyatt. "We go out that way."

A shot echoed in the corridor shockingly noisily and a bullet sprayed Wyatt with chips of stone as it ricocheted off the wall by his head. He ducked violently and turned to find Roseau staggering down the corridor after them. He was in terrible shape. His uniform was hanging about him in rags and his right arm was hanging limp as though broken. He held a revolver in his left hand and it was perhaps that which saved Wyatt from the next shot, which went wide.

He yelled, "That cell there," and pushed Dawson violently. Dawson ran the few yards to the door and dashed through to halt, staggering, in an attempt to save himself falling over the unexpected drop.

Wyatt retreated more slowly, keeping a wary eye on Roseau who lurched haltingly down the passage. Roseau said nothing at all; he brushed the blood away from his fanatical eyes

with the back of the hand that held the gun, and his jaw
worked as he aimed waveringly for another shot. Wyatt
ducked through the cell door as the gun went off and heard a
distinct thud as the bullet buried itself in the door-jamb.

"Over here!" yelled Dawson, and Wyatt hastily trod over
the rubble and on to the narrow ledge. "If that crazy bastard
comes out we'll have to jump for it."

"It's as good a way to break a leg as any," Wyatt said. He
felt his fingers touch something loose and they curled round a
fist-sized piece of rock.

"Here he comes," said Dawson.

Roseau shuffled through the door, seemingly oblivious of
the drop at his feet. He staggered forward, keeping his eyes on
Wyatt, until the tips of his boots were overhanging space, and
he lifted the gun in a trembling hand.

Wyatt threw the rock and it hit Roseau on the side of the
head. The gun fired and he spun, losing his footing, to crash
face down in the ruins below. His arm lay across the shoulder
of the dead man as though he had found a lost comrade, and
the newly disturbed dust settled again on the dead man's
open and puzzled eyes.

Dawson took a deep breath. "Jesus! Now there was a
persistent son of a bitch. Thanks, Wyatt."

Wyatt was shaking. He stood on the ledge with his back to
the wall and waited for the quivers to go away. Dawson
looked down at Roseau and said, "He wanted to implicate
you—I didn't, Wyatt. I didn't tell him anything."

"I didn't think you had," said Wyatt quietly. "Let's get
down from here. There's nothing happening here now, but
that could change damn' quickly."

Slowly they made their way down to the street. It was
difficult for Dawson because his hands hurt, but Wyatt helped
him. When they stood on the pavement Dawson asked,
"What do we do now?"

"I'm going back to the Imperiale," said Wyatt. "I must
find Julie. I must find if she's still in St. Pierre."

"Which way is it?"

"Across the square," said Wyatt, pointing.

They set off across the Place de la Libération Noire and
Dawson stared at the carnage in horror. There were bodies
everywhere, cut down in hundreds. They could not walk in a
straight line for more than five yards without having to

deviate and they gave up trying and stepped over the corpses. Suddenly Dawson turned and retched; he had not drunk or eaten for a long time, and his heavings were dry and laboured.

Wyatt kicked something which rang with a hollow clang. He looked down to see the decapitated head of a man; the eyes stared blankly and there was a ghastly hole in the left temple.

It was the bronze head of the statue of Serrurier.

Five

Causton marched to the sound of the guns.

He sweated in the hot sun as he stepped out briskly in response to the lashing voice of the sergeant and wondered how he was going to get out of this pickle. If he could get out of the ranks for a few minutes, all he had to do was to rip off the tunic, drop the rifle and he would be a civilian again; but there did not seem much chance of that. The erstwhile deserters were watched carefully by troopers armed with sub-machine-guns and the officer, driven in a jeep, passed continually from one end of the column to the other.

He stumbled a little, then picked up the step again, and the man next to him turned and addressed him in the island *patois*, obviously asking a question. Causton played dumb—quite literally; he made some complicated gestures with his fingers, hoping to God that the soldier would not know he was faking. The man let out a shrill cackle of laughter and poked the soldier in front in the small of the back. He evidently thought it a good joke that they should have a dumb soldier in their midst and curious eyes were turned on Causton. He hoped the sweat was not making the boot-polish run.

Not far ahead he could hear the sound of small-arms firing —the tac-a-tac of machine-guns and the more unco-ordinated and sporadic rattle of rifles—much closer than he had expected. Favel had pushed the firing line far into the suburbs of St. Pierre and, from the sound of it, was expending ammunition at a fantastic rate. Causton winced as a shell burst a hundred yards to the right, ruining a shack, and there came a perceptible and hesitant slowing down of the column of men.

The sergeant screamed, the officer cursed, the column speeded up again. Presently they turned off into a side street and the column halted. Causton looked with interest at the army trucks which were parked nose to tail along the street, noting that most of them were empty. He also saw that men were siphoning petrol from the tanks of some of the trucks and refilling the tanks of others.

The officer stepped forward and harangued them again. At what was apparently a question several of the men in the ranks lifted rifles and waved them, so Causton did the same. At a curt command from the officer, those men broke ranks and lined up on the other side of the street, Causton with them. The officer was evidently sorting out the armed men from those who had thrown away their rifles.

A sergeant passed along the thin line of armed men. To every man he put a question and doled out ammunition from a box carried by two men who followed along behind. When he came to Causton and snapped out his question Causton merely snapped open the breech of his rifle to show that the magazine was empty. The sergeant thrust two clips of ammunition into his hands and passed on.

Causton looked across at the trucks. Rifles were being unloaded from one of them and issued to the unarmed men. There were not nearly enough to go round. He tossed the two clips of ammunition in his hand thoughtfully and looked at one lorry as it pulled away, replenished with petrol at the sacrifice of the others. Serrurier was running short of petrol, guns and ammunition, or, more probably, he had plenty but in the wrong place at the wrong time. It was very likely that his supply corps was in a hell of a mess, disrupted by Favel's unexpectedly successful thrust.

He loaded the rifle and put the other clip in his pocket. Serrurier's logistic difficulties were likely to be the death of a good foreign correspondent; this was definitely not a good place to be. Despite his aversion to guns, he thought it would be as well to be prepared. He looked about and weighed his chances of getting away and decided dismally that they were nil. But who knew what a change in the fortunes of war would bring?

More orders were barked and the men tramped off again, this time at right angles to their original march from the centre of the town, and Causton judged that they were moving parallel to the firing line. They entered one of the poorest areas of St. Pierre, a shanty town of huts built from kerosene cans beaten flat and corrugated iron. There were no civilians visible ; either they were cowering in the ramshackle dwellings or they had hurriedly departed.

The line of march changed again towards the noise of battle and they emerged on to an open place, an incursive tongue of the countryside licking into the suburbs. Here they were halted and spread out into a long line, and Causton judged that this was where they would make their stand. The men started to dig in, using no tools but their bayonets, and Causton, with alacrity, followed suit.

He found that a malodorous spot had been picked for him to die in. This open ground, so near to the shanty town, was a rubbish dump in which the unhygienic citizens deposited anything for which they had no further use. Incautiously he stabbed a borrowed bayonet into the bloated corpse of a dead dog which lay half-buried under a pile of ashes—the gases burst from it with a soft sigh and a terrible stench and Causton gagged. He moved away slightly and attacked the ground again, this time with better results, and found that digging in a rubbish dump did have advantages—it was very easy to excavate a man-sized hole.

Having got dug-in, he looked around, first to the rear in search of an avenue of escape. Directly behind him was the sergeant, tough-looking and implacable, the muzzle of whose rifle poked forward, perhaps intentionally, right at Causton. Behind the sergeant and just in front of the first line of shacks were the captain's bully-boys spread in a thin line, their sub-machine-guns ready to cut down any man who attempted to run ; and behind the troopers was the captain himself, leading from the rear and sheltering in the lee of a shack. Beside the shack the jeep stood with idling engine and Causton judged that the captain was ready to take off if the line broke. No joy there.

He turned his attention to the front. The strip of open ground stretched as far as he could see on either side, and was about a quarter of a mile across—maybe four hundred yards. On the other side were the better constructed houses of the more prosperous citizens of St. Pierre whose exclusiveness was accentuated and protected from the shanties by this strip of no-man's-land. A battle seemed to be going on across there ;

shells and mortar bombs were exploding with frightful regularity, tossing pieces of desirable residence about with abandon ; the fusillade of small-arms fire was continuous, and once a badly aimed projectile landed only fifty yards to Causton's front and he drew in his head and felt the patter of earth fragments all about him.

He judged that this was the front line and that the Government forces were losing. Why else would the army have whipped together a hasty second line of ill-equipped deserters? Still, the position was not badly chosen ; if the front line broke then Favel's men would have to advance across four hundred yards of open ground. But then he thought of the meagre two clips of ammunition with which he had been issued—perhaps Favel's men would not find it too difficult, after all. It depended on whether the Government troops over there could retreat in good order.

Nothing happened for a long time and Causton, lying there in the hot sun, actually began to feel sleepy. He had been informed by soldiers that war is a period during which long stretches of boredom are punctuated by brief moments of fright, and he was quite prepared to believe this, although he had not encountered it in his own experience. But then, his own job had mainly consisted of flitting from one hot spot to another, the intervals being filled in by a judicious sampling of the flesh-pots of a dozen assorted countries. He definitely found this small sample of soldiering very dreary.

Occasionally he turned to see if his chance of escape had improved, but there was never any change. The sergeant stared at him, stony-faced, and the rearguard troopers were always in position. The captain alternated between smoking cigarettes with quick puffs and gazing across at the front line through field glasses. Once, in order to ingratiate himself with the sergeant and in hope of future favours, Causton tossed him a cigarette. The sergeant stretched out an arm, looked at the cigarette in puzzlement, then smiled and lit it. Causton smiled back, then turned again to his front, hoping that a small bond of friendship had been joined.

Presently the uproar in the front line rose to a crescendo and Causton caught the first sight of human movement—a few distant figures flitting furtively on the nearside of the distant houses. He strained his eyes and wished he had the captain's binoculars. From behind him he heard the captain's voice issuing sharp orders and the nearer brazen scream of the sergeant, but he took no notice because he had just identified the distant figures as Government troops and they were running as hard as they could—the front line had broken.

The man nearest to him pushed his rifle forward and cocked it, and Causton heard a series of metallic clicks run down the line, but he did not take his eyes from the scene before him. The nearest blue-clad figure was half-way across—about two hundred yards away—when he suddenly threw up his hands and pitched helplessly forward as though he had stumbled over something. He collapsed into a crumpled heap, heaved convulsively and then lay still.

The field was now filled with running men, retreating in no form of order. Some ran with experience born of battle in short, scuttling zig-zags, constantly changing direction in order to throw the marksmen behind off their aim; these were the more intelligent. The stupid ones, or those crazed with fear, ran straight across, and it was these who were picked off by the rattling machine-guns and the cracking rifles.

Causton was abruptly astonished to find himself under fire. There was a constant twittering in the air about him which, at first, he could not identify. But when the dog in the periphery of his vision suddenly jerked its hind leg as though chasing rabbits in its sleep and the dry ground ten yards ahead of him fountained into a row of spurts of dust, he drew himself into his fox-hole like a tortoise drawing into its shell. However, his journalist's curiosity got the better of him, and he raised his head once more to see what was going on.

Mortar shells were beginning to drop into the field, raising huge dust plumes which drifted slowly with the wind. The first of the retreating men was quite near and Causton could see his wide-open mouth and staring eyes and could hear the hard thud of his boots on the dry earth. He was not ten yards away when he fell, a flailing tangle of arms and legs, and as he lurched into stillness Causton saw the gaping hole in the back of his head.

The soldier behind him swerved and came on, legs working like pistons. He jumped clear over Causton and disappeared behind in a panic of terror. Then there was another—and another—and still more—all bolting in panic through the second line of defence. The sergeant's voice rose in a scream

as the men in the foxholes nervously twitched as though to
run, and there was a near-by shot. We get killed if we run
and killed if we don't—later on, thought Causton. Better not
to run—yet.

For over half an hour the demoralized survivors of the
front line passed through and soon Causton heard scattered
shots coming from the rear. The survivors were being whipped
back into shape. He stared across the field, expecting to see
the assault of Favel's army, but nothing happened except that
the mortar fire lifted briefly and then plunged down again,
this time directly on their position. In that small moment of
time, when the smoke of battle was drifting away, Causton
saw dozens of bodies scattered over the field and heard a few
distant cries and wails.

Then he had no time even to think of anything else as the
shells began to rain down in an iron hail. He crouched in his
foxhole and dug his fingers into the nauseous detritus as the
ground shook and heaved underneath him. It seemed to go on
for an eternity although, on later recollection, he supposed it
to have lasted for not more than fifteen minutes. But at the
time he thought it would never end. Jesus, God! he prayed ;
let me get out of here.

The barrage lifted as suddenly as it had started. Causton
was stunned and lay for a while in the foxhole before he was
able to raise his head. When he did so, he expected to see the
first wave of Favel's assault upon them and strained to peer
through the slowly dispersing dust and smoke. But there was
still nothing—merely the field empty but for the crumpled
bodies.

Slowly he turned his head. The tin shacks immediately
behind the position had been destroyed, some of them totally,
and the ground was pitted with craters. The captain's jeep,
its rear wheels blown off, was burning furiously, and of the
captain himself there was no sign. Near-by lay the torso of a
man—no head, arms or legs—and Causton wondered drearily
if it was the sergeant. He stretched his legs painfully and
thought that if he was going to run for it, then this was the
time to do it.

From the next foxhole a man emerged, his face grey with
dust and fear. His eyes were glazed and blank as he levered

himself up and began to stagger away. The sergeant appeared from beneath the level of the ground and shouted at him, but the man took no notice, so the sergeant lifted his rifle and fired and the man collapsed grotesquely.

Causton sank back as a tirade of mashed French broke from the sergeant's foxhole. He had to admire the man—this was a tough, professional soldier who would brook no nonsense about desertion in the face of the enemy—but he was confoundedly inconvenient.

He looked about at the heads which were lifted, did a rough count and was surprised at the number of men who had survived the bombardment. He had read that troops well dug in could survive an enormous amount of punishment in the way of shelling—it had been the thing that had kept the First World War going—but experiencing the fact personally was quite a different thing. He looked across the field but could detect no movement that would presage an assault. Even the small-arms fire had ceased.

He turned to see the sergeant clamber out of his hole and walk boldly along the line to check on the men. Still not a shot came from across the field and Causton began to wonder what had happened. He looked uneasily at the steely blue sky as though expecting another storm of metal, and scratched his cheek reflectively as he watched the sergeant.

Suddenly the small-arms fire started up again. A machine-gun opened up shockingly closely and from an unexpected direction. A hail of bullets swept across the position and the sergeant spun like a top, punched by bullets, to fall sprawling and disappear into a foxhole. Causton ducked his head and listened to the heavy fire coming from the *left* and to the rear.

The position had been outflanked.

He heard the yells and the running steps as the rest of the men broke and ran, but he stayed put. He had a hunch they were running into trouble, and anyway he was fed up with being a part of Serrurier's army; the further that unit and he were separated, the better he would feel. So he lay in the foxhole and played dead.

The machine-gun fire stopped abruptly, but he lay there for fifteen minutes more before even poking his nose above the level of the ground. When he did so, the first thing he saw was a long line of men emerging from the houses on the other side of the field—Favel's men were coming over to mop up. Hastily he wormed his way out of the foxhole and crawled on his belly back towards the shacks, expecting to feel the thud of bullets at any moment. But there was plenty of cover since the ground had been churned up by the mortar fire and he found he could crawl from shell-hole to shell-hole with the minimum of exposure.

Finally he got to the cover of the shacks and looked back. Favel's men were nearly across the field and he had the notion they would shoot anything that moved and he had better find somewhere safer. He listened to the racket coming from the left flank—someone was putting up a fight there, but that would collapse as soon as these oncoming troops hit them. He began to move to the right, dodging from the cover of one shack to another, and always trying to move back.

As he went he ripped off the tunic he was wearing and rubbed at his face. Perhaps the sight of a white skin would cause hesitation of the trigger-finger—at least it was worth trying. He saw no sign of the Government army and all the indications were that Favel was on the verge of punching a hole right through the middle—there did not seem much to stop him.

Presently he had an idea and tried the door of one of the shacks. It had occurred to him that there was no point in running away; after all, he did not *want* to catch up with Serrurier's forces, did he? It would be much better to hide and then emerge in the middle of Favel's army.

The door was not barred, so he pushed it open with a creak and went inside. The shack was deserted; it consisted merely of two rooms and needed a minimum of inspection to show there was no one there. He looked about and saw a wash-basin on a rickety stand below a fly-blown and peeling mirror, which was flanked on one side by a highly coloured oleograph of the Madonna and on the other by the standard official portrait of Serrurier.

Hastily he pulled down the idealized photograph of Serrurier and kicked it under the bed. If anyone interrupted him, he did not want them getting any wrong ideas. Then he poured tepid water into the basin and began to wash his face, keeping a sharp ear cocked for anything going on outside. At the end of five minutes he realized in despair that he was still a light-complexioned Negro; the boot-polish was waterproof and would not come off, no matter how hard he rubbed. Many of the inhabitants of San Fernandez were even lighter complexioned and also had European features.

He was struck by an idea and unbuttoned the front of his shirt to look at his chest. Two days earlier he had been somewhat embarrassed at his pallidity, but now he thanked God that he had not felt the urge to sunbathe. As he stripped off his shirt he prepared for a long wait.

What brought him out was the sound of an engine. He thought that anyone driving a vehicle around there would be civilized enough not to shoot him on sight, so he came out of the cupboard and into the front room and looked through the window. The Land-Rover that was passing was driven by a white man.

"Hey—you!" he shouted, and dashed to the door. "You there—*arrêtez*!"

The man driving the Land-Rover looked back and the vehicle bumped to a halt. Causton ran up and the man looked at him curiously. "Who the devil are you?" he asked.

"Thank God!" said Causton. "You speak English—you *are* English. My name's Causton—I suppose you could call me a war correspondent."

The man looked at him unbelievingly. "You got off the mark pretty quickly, didn't you? The war only started yesterday afternoon. You don't look much like a war correspondent —you look more like a nigger minstrel who got on the wrong side of his audience."

"I'm genuine enough," assured Causton.

The man hefted a sub-machine-gun which was on the seat next to him. "I think Favel had better have a look at you," he said. "Get in."

"Just the man I want to see," said Causton, climbing into the Land-Rover and keeping a careful eye on the sub-machine-gun. "You a friend of his?"

"I suppose you could say so," said the man. "My name is Manning."

II

"It's too hot," said Mrs. Warmington querulously.

Julie agreed but did not say so aloud—Mrs. Warmington was the last person she felt like agreeing with about anything. She wriggled slightly, trying to unstick her blouse from the small of her back, and looked ahead through the windscreen. She saw exactly what she had seen for the last half-hour—a small handcart piled perilously high with trumpery household goods being pushed by an old man and a small boy who obstinately stuck to the crown of the road and refused to draw to the side.

Rawsthorne irritably changed down again from second gear to first. "The engine will boil if we carry on like this in this heat," he said.

"We mustn't stop," said Julie in alarm.

"Stopping might prove more difficult than moving," said Rawsthorne. "Have you looked behind lately?"

Julie twisted in her seat and looked through the back window of the car, which was now cresting a small rise. Behind, as far as she could see, stretched the long line of refugees fleeing from St. Pierre. She had seen this kind of thing on old newsreels but had never expected to see it in actuality. This was a people on the move, trudging wearily from the coming desolation of war, carrying as much of the material minutiæ of their lives as they could on an incredible variety of vehicles. There were perambulators loaded not with babies but with clocks, clothing, pictures, ornaments; there were carts pushed by hand or drawn by donkeys; there were beat-up cars of incredible vintage, buses, trucks and the better cars of the more prosperous.

But primarily there were people: men and women, old and young, rich and poor, the hale and the sick. These were people who did not laugh or speak, who moved along quietly like driven cattle with grey faces and downcast eyes, whose only visible sign of emotion was the quick, nervous twitch of the head to look back along the road.

Julie turned as Rawsthorne blasted on the horn at the obstinate old man ahead. "The damned fellow won't move aside," he grumbled. "If he'd move just a little to the side I could get through."

Eumenides said, "The road—it drop on side." He pointed to the cart. "'E fright 'e fall."

"Yes," said Rawsthorne. "That cart is grossly overloaded and there *is* a steep camber."

Julie said, "How much farther do we have to go?"

"About two miles." Rawsthorne nodded ahead. "You see where the road turns round that headland over there? We have to get to the other side."

"How long do you think it will take?"

Rawsthorne drew to a halt to avoid ramming the old man. "At this rate it will be another two hours."

The car crept on by jerks and starts. The refugees on foot were actually moving faster than those in vehicles and Rawsthorne contemplated abandoning the car. But he rejected the idea almost as soon as he thought of it; there was the food and water to be carried, and the blankets, too—those would be much too valuable in the coming week to leave behind with the car. He said, "At least this war is having one good result—it's getting the people out of St. Pierre."

"They won't all get out," said Julie. "And what about the armies?"

"It's damn' bad luck on Favel," said Rawsthorne. "Imagine taking a town and then being smashed by a hurricane. I've read a lot of military history but I've never heard of a parallel to it."

"It will smash Serrurier, too," said Julie."

"Yes, it will," said Rawsthorne thoughtfully. "I wonder who'll pick up the pieces." He stared ahead. "I like Wyatt, but I hope he's wrong about this hurricane. There's a chance he might be, you know; he's relying a lot on his intuition. I'd like Favel to have a fighting chance."

"I hope he's wrong, too," said Julie sombrely. "He's trapped back there."

Rawsthorne glanced at her drawn face, then bit his lip and lapsed into silence. The time dragged on as slowly as the car. Presently he pointed out a group of young men who were passing. They were fit and able-bodied, if poorly dressed; one had a fistful of bank-notes which he was counting, and another was twirling a gleaming necklace on his forefinger. He said meditatively, "I wish Causton hadn't taken your gun, Eumenides; it might have come in handy. Those boys have been looting. They've taken money and jewellery but soon they'll get hungry and try to take food from whoever has it."

Eumenides shrugged. "Too late; 'e took gun—I look."

At last they rounded the headland and Rawsthorne said, "Another few hundred yards and we'll pull off. Look for a convenient place to run the car off the road—what we really need is a side turning."

They ground on, still in bottom gear, and after a while Eumenides said, "Turn 'ere."

Rawsthorne craned his neck. "Yes, this looks all right. I wonder where it leads."

"Let's try," said Julie. "There's no one going up there."

Rawsthorne turned the car on to the unmetalled side road and was immediately able to change up to second gear. They bumped along for a few hundred yards and then came into the wide space of a quarry. "Damn!" he said. "It's a dead end."

Julie wriggled in her seat. "At least we can get out and stretch our legs before going back. And I think we ought to eat again while we have the chance, too," she said.

The bread was stale, the butter melted and going rancid, the water tepid and, on top of that, the heat had not improved their appetites, but they ate a little while sitting in the shade of the quarry huts and discussed their next move. Mrs. Warmington said, "I don't see why we can't stay here—it's a quiet place."

"I'm afraid not," said Rawsthorne. "We can still see the sea from here—to the south. According to Wyatt, the hurricane will come from the south."

Mrs. Warmington made an impatient noise. "I think that young man is a scaremonger; I don't think there is going to be a hurricane. I looked back when we could still see the Base and there are still ships there at anchor. Commodore Brooks doesn't think there'll be a hurricane, so why should we?"

"We can't take the chance that he'll be wrong," said Julie quietly. She turned to Rawsthorne. "We'll have to go back to the road and try again."

"I don't think so," said Rawsthorne. "I don't really think we can. This track left the road at an acute angle—I don't see how we could turn the car into the traffic stream. Nobody would stop to let us through." He looked up at the quarry face. "We've got to get on the other side of that."

Mrs. Warmington snorted. "I'm not even going to try to climb that. I'm staying here."

Rawsthorne laughed. "We don't have to climb it—we go round it. There's a convenient place to climb a little farther back down the track." He chewed the stale bread distastefully. "Wyatt said we must get on the north side of a ridge, didn't he? Well, that's what we're going to do."

Eumenides asked abruptly, "We leave car?"

"We'll have to. We'll take all we need from it, then park it behind these huts. With a bit of luck no one will find it."

They finished their brief meal and began to pack up. Julie looked at the wilting Mrs. Warmington and forced some humour into her voice. "Well, there's no dish-washing to be done." But Mrs. Warmington was past caring; she just sat in the shade and gasped, and Julie thought cattily, this is better than a diet for reducing her surplus poundage.

Rawsthorne ran the car down the track and they unpacked all the supplies. He said, "It's better we do this here; it's a nice out-of-the-way spot with none of those young thugs snooping at us." He looked up the hill. "It's not far to the top—I suppose this ridge isn't much more than two hundred feet high."

He took the car back to the quarry. Mrs. Warmington said pettishly, "I suppose we must, although I think this is nonsense." She turned to Eumenides. "Don't just stand there; pick up something."

Julie looked at Mrs. Warmington with a glint in her eye. "You'll have to do your share of carrying."

Mrs. Warmington looked doubtfully at the scrub-covered hill. "Oh, but I can't—my heart, you know."

Julie thought that Mrs. Warmington's heart was as sound as a bell and just as hard. "The blankets aren't heavy," she said. "Take some of those." She thrust a bundle of blankets into Mrs. Warmington's unready arms and she dropped her bag. It fell with a dull thud into the dust and they both stooped for it.

Julie picked it up and found it curiously heavy. "Whatever have you got in here?"

Mrs. Warmington snatched the bag from her, dropping the blankets. "My jewels, darling. You don't suppose I'd leave *those* behind."

Julie indicated the blankets. "Those might keep you alive—

your jewels won't." She stared hard at Mrs Warmington. "I suggest you concentrate more on doing work and less on giving orders; you haven't been right about a damn' thing so far, and you're just a dead weight."

"All right," said Mrs. Warmington, perhaps alarmed at the expression on Julie's face. "Don't drive so. You're too mannish, my dear; it's no wonder you haven't caught yourself a husband."

Julie ignored her and lifted a cardboard box full of bottled water. As she climbed the hill, she smiled to herself. A few days ago that gibe might have rankled, but not now. At one time she had thought that perhaps she was too self-reliant to appeal to a man; perhaps men *did* like the clinging ultra-feminine type, which she herself had always regarded as parasitic and not giving value for value received. Well, to hell with it! She was not going to disguise her natural intelligence for any man, and a man who was fooled by that sort of thing wasn't worth marrying, anyway. She would rather be herself than be a foolish, ineffectual, overstuffed creature like the Warmington woman.

But her heart turned over at the thought that she might not see Wyatt ever again.

It took them a long time to transport their supplies to the top of the ridge. Rawsthorne, although willing, was not a young man and had neither the strength nor the stamina for the sustained effort. Mrs. Warmington was totally unfit for any kind of work and after she had toiled to the top with her small load of blankets, she sat back and watched the others work. Julie was fit enough, but she was not used to the intense heat and the strong sun made her head swim. So it was Eumenides who carried the bulk of the supplies, willingly and without complaint. All he allowed himself was a contemptuous glance at Mrs. Warmington each time he deposited a load at the top.

At last all the stores had been moved and they rested for a while on the ridge-top. On the seaward side they could see the main coast road, still aswarm with refugees heading east away from St. Pierre. The city itself was out of sight behind the headland, but they could hear the distant thud of guns and could see a growing smudge of smoke in the western sky.

On the other side of the ridge the ground sloped down into a small green valley, heavily planted with bananas in long rows. Over a mile away was a long, low building with a few smaller huts scattered about it. Rawsthorne looked at the banana plantation with satisfaction. "At least we'll have plenty of shade. And the ground is cultivated and easy to dig. And a banana plant blowing down on one wouldn't hurt."

"I've always liked bananas," said Mrs. Warmington.

"I wouldn't eat any you find down there; they're unripe and they'll give you the collywobbles." Rawsthorne meditated for a moment. "I'm no expert on hurricanes like Wyatt, but I do know something about them. If the hurricane is coming from the south, then the wind will blow from the east to begin with—so we must have protection from that side. Later, the wind will come from the west, and that makes things complicated."

Eumenides pointed. "Over there—lil 'ollow."

"So there is," said Rawsthorne. He arose and picked up a spade. "I thought these might come in useful when I put them in the car. Shall we go? We can leave all this stuff here until we're sure we know where we're going to take it."

They descended into the plantation, which was quite deserted. "We'll keep away from that building," said Rawsthorne. "That's the barracks for the convict labour. I imagine Serrurier has given orders that the men be kept locked up, but there's no point in taking chances." He poked at the ground beneath a banana plant and snorted in disgust. "Very bad cultivation here; these plants need pruning—if they're not careful they're going to get Panama disease. But it's the same all over the island since Serrurier took over—the whole place is running down."

They reached the hollow and Rawsthorne adjudged it a good place. "It's nicely protected," he said, and thrust his spade into the earth. "Now we dig."

"How dig?" asked Eumenides.

"Foxholes—as in the army." Rawsthorne began to measure out on the ground. "Five of them—one for each of us and one for the supplies."

They took it in turns digging—Rawsthorne, Eumenides and Julie—while Mrs. Warmington panted in the shade. It was not very hard work because the ground was soft as Rawsthorne had predicted, but the sun was hot and they sweated copiously. Near the end of their labours Julie paused for a drink of water and looked at the five . . .*graves*? She thought sombrely of the unofficial motto of the Seabees—" First we dig 'em, then we die in 'em." In spite of the hot sun, she shivered.

When they had finally completed the foxholes and had brought down the supplies it was near to sunset, although it seemed hotter than ever. Rawsthorne cut some of the huge leaves from some near-by plants and strewed them over the raw earth. " In the middle of a civil war camouflage does no harm. Anyway, these plants need cutting."

Julie lifted her head. " Talking of the war—don't the guns sound louder . . . closer?"

Rawsthorne listened intently. " They do, don't they?" He frowned. " I wonder if . . ." He clicked his tongue and shook his head.

" If what?"

" I thought the battle might come this way," he said. " But I don't think so. Even if Favel takes St. Pierre he must attack Serrurier's forces between St. Pierre and Cap Sarrat—and that's on the other side."

" But the guns *do* sound nearer," said Julie

" A trick of the wind," said Rawsthorne. He said it with dubiety. There was no wind.

As the sun dipped down they prepared for the night and arranged watches. Mrs. Warmington, by common consent, was left to sleep all night as being too unreliable. They talked desultorily for a while and then turned in, leaving Julie to stand first watch.

She sat in the sudden darkness and listened to the sound of the guns. To her untutored ear they sounded as though they were just down the valley and round the corner, but she consoled herself with Rawsthorne's reasoning. But there was a fitful red glare in the west from the direction of St. Pierre— there were fires in the town.

She searched her pockets and found a crumpled cigarette, which she lit, inhaling the smoke greedily. It had been a bad day ; she was tense and the cigarette relaxed her. She sat with her back against a banana tree—or plant, or whatever it was—and thought about Wyatt, wondering what had happened to him. Perhaps he was already dead, caught up in the turmoil of war. Or maybe raging in a cell, waiting for the deadly wind he alone knew was going to strike. She wished with all her heart they had not been separated—whatever was going to happen, she wanted to be with him.

And Causton—what had happened to Causton? If he found his way back to the hotel he would find the note they had pinned on the door of the store-room under the stairs and know they had fled to safety. But he would not know enough to be able to join them. She hoped he would be safe—but her thoughts dwelt longer on Wyatt.

The moon had just risen when she awoke Eumenides as planned. "Everything quiet," she said in a low voice. "Nothing is happening."

He nodded and said, "The guns ver' close—more close than before."

"You think so?"

He nodded again but said nothing more, so she went to her own foxhole and settled down for the night. It is like a grave, she thought as she stretched on the blanket which lay on the bottom. She thought of Wyatt again, very hazily and drowsily, and then fell asleep before she had completed the thought.

She was awakened by something touching her face and she started up, only to be held down. "Ssssh," hissed a voice. "Keep ver' still."

"What's wrong, Eumenides?" she whispered.

"I don' know," he said in a low voice. "Man' peoples 'ere—lis'en!"

She strained her ears and caught an indefinable sound which seemed to emanate from nowhere in particular and everywhere at once. "It's the wind in the banana leaves," she murmured.

"No win'," said Eumenides definitely.

She listened again and caught what seemed to be a faraway voice. "I don't know if you're right or wrong," she said. "But I think we ought to wake the others."

He went to shake Rawsthorne, while Julie woke Mrs. Warmington, who squealed in surprise. "Damn you, be quiet," snapped Julie, and clapped her hand over Mrs.

E

Warmington's mouth as it opened again. "We might be in trouble. Just stay there and be prepared to move in a hurry. And don't make a sound."

She went over to where Rawsthorne and Eumenides were conferring in low tones. "There's something going on," said Rawsthorne. "The guns have stopped, too. Eumenides, you go up to the top and see what's happened on the seaward side of the ridge; I'll scout down the valley. The moon's bright enough to see for quite a distance." His voice held a note of perplexity. "But these damn' noises are coming from all round."

He stood up. "Will you be all right, Julie?"

"I'll be fine," she said. "And I'll keep that damned woman quiet if I have to slug her."

The two men went off and she lost sight of them as they disappeared in the plantation. Rawsthorne flitted among the rows, edging nearer and nearer to the convict barracks. Soon he came to a service road driven through the plantation and paused before he crossed—which was just as well for he heard a voice from quite close.

He froze and waited while a group of men went up the road. They were Government soldiers and from the sound of their voices they were weary and dispirited. From a word and a half-heard phrase he gathered that they had been defeated in a battle and had not liked it at all. He waited until they had gone by, then crossed the road and penetrated the plantation on the other side.

Here he literally fell over a wounded man lying just off the road. The man cried aloud in anguish and Rawsthorne ran away, afraid the noise would attract attention. He blundered about in the plantation, suddenly aware that there were men all about him in the leaf-shadowed moonlight. They were drifting through the rows of plants from the direction of St. Pierre in no form of order and with no discipline.

Suddenly he saw a spurt of flame and then the growing glow of a newly lit fire. He shrank back and went another way, only to be confronted by the sight of another fire being kindled. All around the fires sprang into being like glow-worms, and as he cautiously approached one of them he saw a dozen men sitting and lying before the flames, toasting unripe bananas on twigs to make them palatable enough to eat.

It was then that he knew he was in the middle of Serrurier's defeated army, and when he heard the roar of trucks on the service road he had just crossed and the sharp voice of command from close behind him, he knew also that this army was beginning to regroup for to-morrow's battle, which would probably be on the very ground on which he was standing.

I I I

Dawson felt better once he had left the Place de la Libération Noire and the sights that had sickened him. There was nothing wrong with his legs and he had no trouble keeping up with Wyatt who was in a great hurry. Although the town centre was not being shelled any more the noise of battle to the north had greatly intensified, and Wyatt felt he had to get to the Imperiale before the battle moved in. He had to make certain that Julie was safe.

As they moved from the square and the area of government administrative buildings they began to encounter people, at first in ones and twos, and then in greater numbers. By the time they got near to the Imperiale, which fortunately was not far, the press of people in the streets was great, and Wyatt realized he was witnessing the panic of a civilian population caught in war.

Already the criminal elements had begun to take advantage of the situation and most of the expensive shops near the Imperiale had been sacked and looted. Bodies lying on the pavement testified that the police had taken strong measures, but Wyatt's lips tightened as he noted two dead policemen sprawled outside a jewellery shop—the streets of St. Pierre were fast ceasing to be safe.

He pushed through the screaming, excited crowds, ran up the steps of the hotel and through the revolving doors into the foyer. "Julie!" he called. "Causton!"

There was no answer.

He ran across the foyer and stumbled over the body of a soldier which lay near an overturned table just outside the bar. He shouted again, then turned to Dawson. "I'm going upstairs—you see what you can find down there."

Dawson walked into the bar, crunching broken glass underfoot, and looked about. Someone had a hell of a party, he thought. He nudged at a half-empty bottle of Scotch with one bandaged hand and shook his head sadly. He would have liked a drink, but this was not the time for it.

He turned away, feeling a surge of triumph within him. Not long before he would have taken a drink at any time, but since he had survived the attentions of Sous-Inspecteur Roseau he felt a growing strength and a breaking of bonds. As he defied Roseau, stubbornly keeping his mouth shut, so he now defied what he recognized to be the worst in himself and, in that, found a new freedom, the freedom to be himself. "Big Jim" Dawson was dead and young Jimmy Dawson reborn—maybe a little older in appearance and a bit shrivelled about the edges, but still as new and shining and uncorrupted as that young man had been so many years ago. The only added quality was wisdom, and perhaps a deep sense of shame for what he had done to himself in the name of success.

He searched the ground floor of the hotel—discovered nothing, and returned to the foyer, where he found Wyatt. "Nothing down there," he said.

Wyatt's face was gaunt. "They've gone." He was looking at the dead soldier sprawled with bloody chest near the upturned table. There was a buzzing of flies about him.

Dawson said tentatively, "You think—maybe—the soldiers took them?"

"I don't know," said Wyatt heavily.

"I'm sorry it happened," said Dawson. "I'm sorry it happened because of me."

Wyatt turned his head. "We don't know it was because of you. It might have happened anyway." He felt suddenly dizzy and sat down.

Dawson looked at him with concern. "You know what?" he said. "I think we could both do with some food. When did we eat last?" He held out his bandaged hands and said apologetically, "I'd get it myself but I don't think I can open a can."

"What did they do to you?"

Dawson shrugged and put his hands behind his back. "Beat me up—roughed me around a bit. Nothing I couldn't take."

"You're right, of course," said Wyatt. "We must eat. I'll see what I can find."

Ten minutes later they were wolfing cold meat stew right

out of the cans. Dawson found he could just hold a spoon in
his left hand and by holding the can in the crook of his right
arm he could feed himself tolerably well. It was painful
because his left hand hurt like hell when he gripped the
spoon, but the last thing he wanted was for Wyatt to feed him
like a baby—he could not have borne that.

He said, "What do we do now?"

Wyatt listened to the guns. "I don't know," he said slowly.
"I wish Causton or Julie had left a message."

"Maybe they did."

"There was nothing in their rooms."

Dawson thought about that. "Maybe they weren't in their
rooms; maybe they were in the cellar. The guns were firing
at the square, and that's not very far away—maybe they
sheltered in the cellar."

"There is no cellar."

"Okay—but they might have sheltered somewhere else.
Where would you go in a bombardment?" He shifted in his
chair and the cane creaked. "I know a guy who was in the
London blitz; he said that under the stairs was the best place.
Maybe those stairs there."

Awkwardly he put down the spoon and walked over to the
staircase. "Hey!" he called. "There's something pinned on
this door."

Wyatt dropped his can with a clatter and ran after Dawson.
He ripped the note from the door. "Causton's vanished," he
said. "But the others got away in Rawsthorne's car. They've
gone east—out of the bay area." He drew a deep breath.
"Thank God for that."

"I'm glad they got away," said Dawson. "What do we do
—follow them?"

"You'd better do that," said Wyatt. "I'll give you all the
necessary directions."

Dawson looked at him in surprise. "Me? What are you
going to do?"

"I've been listening to the guns," said Wyatt. "I think
Favel is making a breakthrough. I want to see him."

"Are you out of your cotton-picking mind? You hang
round in the middle of a goddam war and you'll get shot.
You'd better come east with me."

"I'm staying," said Wyatt stubbornly. "Someone's got to
tell Favel about the hurricane."

"What makes you think Favel will listen to you?" demanded Dawson. "What makes you think you'll even get to see him? There'll be bloody murder going on in this city when Favel comes in—you won't have a chance."

"I don't think Favel is like that. I think he's a reasonable man, not a psychopath like Serrurier. If I can get to him I think he'll listen."

Dawson groaned, but one look at Wyatt's inflexible face showed the uselessness of argument. He said, "You're a goddam, pigheaded, one-track man, Wyatt; a stupid dope with not enough sense to come in out of the rain. But if you feel like that about it, I guess I'll stick around long enough to see you get your come-uppance."

Wyatt looked at him in surprise. "You don't have to do that," he said gently.

"I know I don't," complained Dawson. "But I'm staying, anyway. Maybe Causton had the right idea—maybe there's the makings of a good book in all this." He slanted a glance at Wyatt, half-humorous, half-frowning. "You'd make a good hero."

"Keep me out of anything you write," warned Wyatt.

"It's all right," said Dawson. "A dead hero can't sue me."

"And a dead writer can't write books. I think you'd better get out."

"I'm staying," said Dawson. He felt he owed a debt to Wyatt, something he had to repay; perhaps he would get the chance if he stayed around with him.

"As you wish," said Wyatt indifferently, and moved towards the door.

"Wait a minute," said Dawson.; "Let's not get shot right away. Let's figure out what's going on. What makes you think Favel is making a breakthrough?"

"There was a heavy barrage going on not long ago—now it's stopped."

"Stopped? Sounds just the same to me."

"Listen closely," said Wyatt. "Those guns you hear are on the east and west—there's nothing from the centre."

Dawson cocked his head on one side. "You're right. You think Favel has bust through the middle?"

"Perhaps."

Dawson sat down. "Then all we've got to do is to wait here and Favel will come to us. Take it easy, Wyatt."

Wyatt looked through a glassless window. "You could be right; the street is deserted now—not a soul in sight."

"Those people have brains," said Dawson. "No one wants to tangle with a driving army—not even Favel's. He may be as reasonable as you say, but reasonableness doesn't show from behind a gun. It's wiser to wait here and see what happens next."

Wyatt commenced to pace up and down the foyer and Dawson watched him, seeing the irritability boiling up. He said abruptly, "Got a cigarette—the cops took mine."

"They took mine, too." Wyatt stopped his restless pacing. "There should be some in the bar."

He went into the bar, found a pack of cigarettes, stuck one in Dawson's mouth and lit it. Dawson drew on it deeply, then said, "When are you expecting this hurricane of yours?"

"It could be to-morrow; it could be the day after. I'm cut off from information."

"Then take it easy, for Christ's sake! Favel's on his way, and your girl-friend is tucked away safely." Dawson's eyes crinkled as he saw Wyatt's head swing round. "Well, she *is* your girl-friend, isn't she?"

Wyatt did not say anything, so Dawson changed the subject. "What do you expect Favel to do about the hurricane? The guy's got a war on his hands."

"He won't have," promised Wyatt. "Not in two days from now. And if he stays in St. Pierre he won't have an army, either. He's *got* to listen to me."

"I surely hope he does," said Dawson philosophically. "Because he's the only chance we have of getting out of here." He lifted his left hand clumsily to take the cigarette from his mouth and knocked it against the edge of the table. He winced and a suppressed sound escaped his lips.

Wyatt said, "We'd better have a look at those hands."

"They're all right."

"You don't want them turning bad on you. Let's have a look at them."

"They're all right, I tell you," Dawson protested.

Wyatt looked at Dawson's drawn face. "I want to look at them," he said. "Things that are all right anywhere else go sour in the tropics." He began to unfasten one of the bandages and his breath hissed as he saw what it covered. "Good Christ! What did they do to you?"

The hand was mashed to a pulp. As he slowly drew the bandage away he saw, to his horror, two finger-nails come away with it, and the fingers were blue with one huge bruise where they weren't red-raw as beefsteak.

Dawson lay back in the chair. "They held me down and beat my hands with a rubber hose. I don't think they broke any bones, but I'll not be able to handle a typewriter for quite a while."

Wyatt had once caught his finger in a door—a trivial thing but the most painful happening of his life. The finger-nail had turned blue but his doctor saved it, and he had been careful of his hands ever since. Now, looking down at Dawson's raw hand, he felt sick inside; he could imagine how painful the battered nerve-endings would be. He said glumly, "Now I can stop being sorry I killed Roseau."

Dawson grinned faintly. "I never was sorry."

Wyatt was puzzled. There was more to Dawson than he had thought; this was not the same man who had tried to steal a car because he was scared—something must have happened to him. "You'll need some embrocation on that," he said abruptly. "And a shot of penicillin wouldn't do any harm, either. There's a place across the street—I'll see what I can find."

"Take it easy," said Dawson in alarm. "That street is not the safest place in the world right now."

"I'll watch it," said Wyatt, and went to the door. Opposite was an American-style drugstore; it had been broken into already but he hoped the drug supplies had not been touched. Before going out, he carefully inspected the street and, finding no movement, he stepped out and ran across.

The drugstore was in a mess but he ignored the chaos and went straight to the dispensary at the back, where he rummaged through the neat drawers looking for what he needed. He found bandages and codeine tablets and embrocation but no antibiotics, and he wasted little time on a further search. At the door of the drugstore he paused again to check the street and froze as he saw a man scuttle across to hide in a doorway.

The man peered out behind the muzzle of a gun, then waved, and three more men ran up the street, hugging the walls and darting from door to door. They were not in uniform and Wyatt thought they must be the forward skirmishers of Favel's army. Gently he opened the door and stepped out, holding his hands above his head and clutching his medical supplies.

Strangely, he was not immediately seen, and had got half-way across the street before he was challenged. He turned to face the oncoming soldier, who looked at him with suspicion. "There are none of Serrurier's men here," said Wyatt. "Where is Favel?"

The man jerked his rifle threateningly. "What is that?"

"Bandages," said Wyatt. "For my friend who is hurt. He is in the hotel over there. Where is Favel?"

He felt the muzzle of a gun press into his back but did not turn. The man in front of him moved his rifle fractionally sideways. "To the hotel," he ordered. Wyatt shrugged and stepped out, surrounded by the small group. One of them pushed through the revolving door, his rifle at the ready, and Wyatt called out in English, "Stay where you are, Dawson—we've got visitors."

The man in front of him whirled and pressed his gun into Wyatt's stomach. "*Pren' gar',*" he said threateningly.

"I was just telling my friend not to be afraid," said Wyatt evenly.

He went into the hotel, to find Dawson sitting tensely in his chair looking at a soldier who was covering him with a rifle. He said, "I've got some bandages and some codeine—that should kill the pain a bit."

Favel's men fanned out and scattered through the ground floor, moving like professionals. Finding nothing, they reassembled in the foyer and gathered round their leader, whom Wyatt took to be a sergeant although he wore no insignia. The sergeant prodded the dead soldier with his foot. "Who killed this one?"

Wyatt, bending over Dawson, looked up and shrugged. "I don't know," he said, and turned back to his work.

The sergeant stepped over and looked at Dawson's hands. "Who did that?"

"Serrurier's police," said Wyatt, keeping his eyes down.

The sergeant grunted. "Then you do not like Serrurier. Good!"

"I must find Favel," said Wyatt. "I have important news for him."

"What is this important news, *blanc*?"

"It is for Favel only. If he wants you to know he will tell you."

Dawson stirred. "What's going on?"

"I'm trying to get this man to take me to Favel. I can't tell *him* there's going to be a hurricane—he might not believe it and then I'd never get to see Favel."

The sergeant said, "You talk big, *ti blanc*; your so-important news had better be good or Favel will tear out your liver." He paused, then said with a grim smile, "And mine."

He turned to issue a string of rapid instructions, and Wyatt sighed deeply. "Thank God!" he said. "Now we're getting somewhere."

Six

The highest point of Cap Sarrat was a hillock, the top of which was forty-five feet above sea-level. On the top of the hillock was a 400-foot lattice radio mast which supported an array of radar antennae. From the antenna right at the top of the tower accurately machined wave-guides conducted electronic signals to a low building at the base; these signals, amplified many millions of times, were then projected on to a cathode-ray screen to form a green glow, which cast a bilious light on the face of Petty Officer (3rd Class) Joseph W. Harmon.

Petty Officer Harmon was both bored and tired. The Brass had been giving him the run-around all day. He had been standing-to at his battle station for most of the day and then he had been told off to do his usual job in the radar room that night, so he had had the minimum of sleep. At first he had been excited by the sound of gun-fire reverberating across Santego Bay from the direction of St. Pierre, and even more excited when a column of smoke arose from the town and he was told that Serrurier's two-bit army was surrounding the Base and they could expect an attack any moment.

But a man cannot keep up that pitch of excitement and now, at five in the morning with the sun just about due to rise, he felt bored and sleepy. His eyes were sore, and when he closed them momentarily it felt as though there were many grains of sand on his eyeballs. He blinked them open again and stared at the radar screen, following the sweep of the trace as it swept hypnotically round and round.

He jerked as his attention was caught by a minute green swirl that faded rapidly into nothingness and he had to wait until the trace went round again to recapture it. There it was again, just the merest haze etched electronically against the glass, fading as rapidly as it had arisen. He checked the direction and made it 174 degrees true.

Nothing dangerous there, he thought. That was nearly due south and at the very edge of the screen; the danger—if it came—would be from the landward side, from Serrurier's joke of an air force. There had been a fair amount of air activity earlier, but it had died away and now the San Fernandan air force seemed to be totally inactive. That fact had caused a minor stir among the officers but it meant nothing to Harmon, who thought sourly that anything that interested the officers was sure to be something to keep him out of his sack.

He looked at the screen and again caught the slight disturbance to the south. As an experienced radar operator he knew very well what it was—there was bad weather out there below the curve of the horizon and the straight-line radar beam was catching the top of it. He hesitated for a moment before he stretched out his arm for the telephone, but he picked it up decisively. His instructions were to call the Duty Officer if anything—repeat, *anything*—unusual came up. As he said, " Get me Lieutenant Moore," he felt some small satisfaction at being able to roust the Lieutenant from whatever corner he was sleeping in.

So it was that when Commander Schelling checked into his office at eight that morning there was a neatly typed report lying squared-up on his blotting-pad. He picked it up, his mind on other things, and got a jolt as the information suddenly sank into him like a harpoon. He grabbed the telephone and said hoarsely, " Get me Radar Surveillance—the Duty Officer."

While he waited for the connection he scanned the report again. It became visibly worse as he read it. The microphone clicked in his ear. " Lieutenant Moore . . . off duty? . . . who is that, then? . . . All right, Ensign Jennings, what's all this about bad weather to the south?"

He tapped impatiently on the desk as he heard what Jennings had to say, slammed down the telephone and felt the sweat break out on his brow. Wyatt had been right—Mabel had swerved to pay a visit to San Fernandez. His body acted efficiently enough as he selected all the information he had on Mabel and packed the sheets neatly into a folder, but a voice was yammering at the back of his mind: It's goddam unfair; why should Wyatt be right on an unscientific hunch? Why the hell didn't Mabel stick to what she should have done? How in God's name am I going to explain this to Brooks?

He entered the radar section at a dead run and one look at the screen was enough. He swung back on Jennings and snapped, "Why wasn't I told about this earlier?"

"There was a report sent to your office by Lieutenant Moore, sir."

"That was nearly three hours ago." He pointed at the thickening green streaks on the bottom edge of the radar screen. "Do you know what that is?"

"Yes, sir," said Jennings. "There's a bit of bad weather blowing up."

"A bit of bad weather?" said Schelling thickly. "Get out of my way, you fool." He pushed past Jennings and blundered out into the sunlit corridor. He stood there indecisively for a moment, then moistened his lips. The Commodore must be told, of course. He left the radar section like a man heading for his own execution with Ensign Jennings staring after him with puzzlement in his eyes.

The officer in Brooks's outer office was dubious about letting Schelling in to bother the Commodore. Schelling leaned over his desk and said deliberately, "If I don't get to see the Commodore within two minutes from now, you'll find yourself pounding the anchor cable for the next twenty years." A small flame of satisfaction leaped within him as he saw that he had intimidated this officer, a weak flame that drowned in the apprehension of what Brooks would have to say.

Brooks's desk was as neat as ever, and Brooks himself sat in the same position as though he had never moved during the last two days. He said, "Well, Commander? I understand you want to speak to me urgently."

Schelling swallowed. "Er . . . yes, sir. It's about Mabel."

Brooks did not move a muscle, nor was there any change in

his voice, but an air of tension suddenly enveloped him as he asked evenly, " What about Mabel?"

Schelling said baldly, " She seems to have swung off her predicted course."

" *Seems?* Has she or hasn't she?"

" Yes, sir ; she has."

" Well?"

Schelling looked into Brooks's hard grey eyes and gulped. " She's heading right for us." He became alarmed at the Commodore's immobility and his tongue loosened. " She shouldn't have done it, sir. It's against all theory. She should have passed to the west of Cuba. *I* don't know why she turned and I don't know any other meteorologist who could tell you either. There are so many things we don't . . ."

Brooks stirred for the first time. " Stop prattling, Schelling. How long have we got?"

Schelling put the folder down on the desk and opened it " She's a little over a hundred seventy miles away now, and she's moving along at eleven miles an hour. That gives us fifteen, maybe sixteen, hours."

Brooks said, " I'm not interested in your reasoning—I just wanted a time." He swung round in his chair and picked up a telephone. " Give me the Executive Officer . . . Commander Leary, I want you to put Plan K into action right now." He glanced at his watch. " As of 08:31 hours. That's right . . . immediate evacuation."

He put down the telephone and turned back to Schelling. " I wouldn't feel too bad about this, Commander. It was my decision to stay, not yours. And Wyatt didn't have any real facts—merely vague intuitions."

But Schelling said, " Maybe I was too rigid about it, sir."

Brooks waved that away. " I took that into my calculations, too. I know the capabilities of my officers." He turned and looked out of the window. " My one regret is that we can't do anything about the people of St. Pierre. But that, of course, is impossible. We'll come back as soon as we can and help clear up the mess, but the ships will take a beating and it won't be easy."

He looked at Schelling. " You know your station under Plan K?"

" Yes, sir."

"You'd better get to it."

He watched Schelling leave the office with something like
pity in his eyes, then called for his personal assistant. Things
had to be done—all the many necessary things. As soon as he
was alone again he walked over to a wall safe and began to
pack documents into a lead-weighted briefcase, and it was
only when he had completed his last official duties on Cap
Sarrat Base that he packed the few personal effects he wanted
to take, including a photograph of his wife and two sons
which he took from a drawer in his desk.

II

Eumenides Papegaikos was a very frightened man. He was
not the stuff of which heroes are made and he did not like the
position in which he found himself. True, running a night
club had its difficulties, but they were of the nature which
could be solved by money—both Serrurier's corrupt police
and the local protection racketeeers could be bought off,
which partly accounted for the high prices he charged. But
he could not buy his way out of a civil war, nor could a
hurricane be deflected by the offer of all the gold in the world.

He had hoped to be taken to Cap Sarrat with the American
women, but Wyatt and the war had put a stop to that. In a
way he was thankful he was among foreigners—he was
tongue-tied in English but that served to camouflage his fears
and uncertainties. He volunteered for nothing but did as he
was told with a simulated willingness which concealed his
internal quakings—which was why he was now stealthily
creeping through the banana plantation and heading towards
the top of the ridge overlooking the sea.

There were noises all about him—the singing cicadas and a
fainter, more ominous, series of noises that seemed to come
from all around. There was the clink of metal from time to
time, and the faraway murmur of voices and the occasional
rustle of banana leaves which should have been still in the
sultry, windless night.

He reached the top of the ridge, sweating profusely, and
looked down towards the coastal road. There was much
activity down there; the sound of heavy trucks, the flash of
lights and the movement of many men under the bright light
of the moon. The quarry, where they had left the car, was

now full of vehicles and there was a constant coming and going along the narrow track.

After a while Eumenides withdrew and turned to go back to the others. All over the plantation lights were springing up, the flickering fires of a camping army, and sometimes he could distinguish the movements of individual men as they walked between him and the flames. He walked down the hill, hoping that, if seen, he would only be another soldier stumbling about in the darkness, and made his way with caution towards the hollow where they had dug the foxholes. He made it with no trouble but at the expense of time, and when he joined Julie and Mrs. Warmington nearly an hour had elapsed.

From the bottom of her camouflaged foxhole Julie whispered cautiously, "Eumenides?"

"Yes. Where's Rawst'orne?"

"He hasn't come back yet. What's happening?"

Eumenides struggled valiantly with the English language. "Lot peoples. Soldiers. Army."

"Government soldiers? Serrurier's men?"

"Yes." He waved his arm largely. "All aroun'."

Mrs. Warmington whimpered softly. Julie said slowly, "Serrurier must have been beaten back—kicked out of St. Pierre. What do we do?"

Eumenides was silent. He did not see what they could do. If they tried to get away capture would be almost certain, but if they stayed, then daylight would give them away. Julie said, "Are any of the soldiers near?"

Eumenides pointed. "Maybe two 'undred feet. You speak loud—they 'ear."

"Thank goodness we found this hollow," said Julie. "You'd better get into your hole, Eumenides. Cover yourself with banana leaves. We'll wait for Mr. Rawsthorne."

"I'm frightened," said Mrs. Warmington in a small voice from out of the darkness.

"You think I'm not?" whispered Julie. "Now keep quiet."

"But they'll kill us," wailed Mrs. Warmington in a louder voice. "They'll rape us, then kill us."

"For God's sake, keep quiet," said Julie as fiercely as she could in a whisper. "They'll hear you."

Mrs. Warmington gave a low moan and lapsed into silence. Julie lay in the bottom of her foxhole and waited for Rawsthorne, wondering how long he would be, and what they could possibly do when he came back.

Rawsthorne was in difficulties. Having crossed the service road, he was finding it hard to recross it; there was a constant stream of traffic in both directions, the trucks roaring along one after the other with blazing headlights so that he could not cross without being seen. And it had taken him a long time to find the road at all. In his astonishment at finding himself in the middle of an army he had lost his way, stumbling about in the leaf-dappled darkness between the rows of plants and fleeing in terror from one group of soldiers, only to find another barring his way.

By the time he had calmed down he was a long way from the road and it took him nearly an hour and a half to get back to it, harried as he was by the dread of discovery. He had no illusions of what would happen to him if discovered. Serrurier's propaganda had been good; he had deceived these men and twisted their minds, and then trained and drilled them into an army. To them all *blancs* were Americans and Americans were bogeymen in the mythology Serrurier had built up—there would be a weird equation in which white man equals Americans equals spy, and he would be shot on the spot.

So he trod cautiously as he threaded his way among the banana plants. Once he had to remain motionless for a full half hour while a group of soldiers conversed idly on the other side of the plant under which he was hiding. He pressed himself against the broad leaves and prayed that one of them would not think to walk round the tree, and he was lucky.

When he was able to go on his way again he thought of what the men had been saying. The troops were tired and dispirited; they complained of the inefficiency of their officers and spoke in awe of the power of Favel's artillery. One recurring theme had been: where are *our* guns? No one had been able to answer. But the news was that the army was regrouping under General Rocambeau and they were going in to attack St. Pierre when the night was over. Although a lot of their military supplies had been captured by Favel, Rocambeau's withdrawing force had managed to empty San Juan arsenal and there was enough ammunition to make the attack. The men's voices lifted when they spoke of Rocambeau and they seemed to have renewed hope.

At last he found the road and waited in the shadows for a gap in the stream of traffic, but none came. He looked desperately at his watch—dawn was not far away and he would have to cross the road before then. At last, seeing no hope in a diminution of the traffic, he moved along the edge of the road until he found a curve. Here he might have a chance of crossing undetected by headlights. He waited until a truck went by, then ran across and hurled himself down on the other side. The lights of the next truck coming round the bend swept over him as he lay there winded.

There was light in the eastern sky when at last he located the approximate direction of the hollow in which the others were concealed. He moved along warily, thinking that this sort of thing might be all right for younger men like Wyatt and Causton, but might prove the death of an elderly man like himself.

Julie roused herself from her foxhole as the light grew in the sky. She sat up cautiously, lifting the huge green leaves, and looked about, wondering where Rawsthorne was. No one had come near the hollow and it seemed as though they might yet evade capture if they kept hidden and silent. But first she had to look about to see from which direction danger was most likely to threaten.

She whispered to Eumenides, " I'm going to the edge of the hollow."

There was a stir in the banana leaves. " All ri'."

" Don't leave me," Mrs. Warmington pleaded, sitting up. " Please don't go away—I'm frightened."

" Ssssh. I'm not going far—just a few yards. Stay here and be quiet."

She crawled away among the plants and found a place from which she could survey the plantation. In the dim morning light she could see the movement of men and heard a low hum of voices. The nearest group was a mere fifty yards away but the men were all asleep, huddled shapes lying round the dying embers of a fire.

She had come away to check on their camouflage in the light of day and before it was too late, so she looked back down into the hollow to see that the newly turned earth looked dreadfully raw, but it was nothing that could not be disguised by a few more leaves. The holes themselves were quite invisible or would be if that damned woman would keep still.

Mrs. Warmington was sitting up and looking about nervously, still clutching her purse to her breast. "Get down, you fool," breathed Julie, but to her astonishment Mrs Warmington opened her purse, produced a comb and began to comb her hair. She'll never learn, thought Julie in despair; she's quite unadaptable and habit-ridden. To attend to one's coiffure in the morning was, no doubt, quite laudable in suburbia, but it might mean death on this green hillside.

She was about to slip back and thrust the woman back into her foxhole, by force if necessary, when she was arrested by a movement on the other side of the hollow. A soldier was coming down, stretching his arms as he walked as though he had just risen from sleep, and adjusting the sling of his rifle to his shoulder. Julie stayed very still and her eyes switched to Mrs. Warmington, who was regarding herself in a small mirror. She distinctly heard the deprecating and very feminine sound which Mrs. Warmington made as she discovered how bedraggled she was.

The soldier heard it too and unslung his rifle and came down into the hollow very cautiously. Mrs. Warmington heard the metallic click as he slammed back the bolt, and she screamed as she saw him coming towards her, scrabbling at her purse. The soldier stopped in astonishment and then a broad grin spread over his face and he came closer, putting up his rifle.

Then there were three flat reports that echoed on the hot morning air. The soldier shouted and spun round to flop at Mrs. Warmington's feet, writhing like a newly landed fish. Blood stained his uniform red at the shoulder.

Eumenides popped up from his hole like a jack-in-a-box as Julie started to run. When she got down to the bottom of the hollow he was bending over the fallen soldier, who was moaning incoherently. He regarded his bloody hand blankly. "He was shot!"

"He was coming at me," screamed Mrs. Warmington. "He was going to rape me—kill me." She waved a pistol in her hand.

Julie let her have it, putting all her strength into the muscular open-handed slap. She was desperate—at all costs she must silence this hysterical woman. Mrs. Warmington was suddenly silent and the gun dropped from her nerveless fingers to be caught by Eumenides. His eyes opened wide as he looked at it. " This is mine," he said in astonishment.

Julie whirled as she heard a shout from behind and saw three soldiers running down the slope. The first one saw the prone figure on the ground and the pistol in Eumenides's hand and wasted no time in argument. He brought up his gun and shot the Greek in the stomach.

Eumenides groaned and doubled up, his hands at his belly. He dropped to his knees and bent forward and the soldier lifted his rifle and bayoneted him in the back. Eumenides collapsed completely and the soldier put his boot on him and pulled out the bayonet, to stab and stab again until the body lay in a welter of blood.

Rawsthorne, watching from the edge of the hollow, was sickened to his stomach but was unable to tear his eyes away. He listened to the shouting and watched the women being pushed about. One of the soldiers was ruthlessly pricking them with a bayonet and he saw the red blood running down Julie's arm. He thought they were going to be shot out of hand but then an officer came along and the two women were hustled out of the hollow, leaving behind the lifeless body of Eumenides Papegaikos.

Rawsthorne lingered for some minutes, held in a state of shock before his brain began to work again. At last he moved away, crawling on his belly. But he did not really know where he was going nor what he was going to do next.

III

Wyatt discovered that Favel was a hard man to find. With Dawson, he had been handed over to a junior officer who was too preoccupied with the immediate tactical situation to pay much attention to him. In order to rid himself of an incubus, the officer had passed them up the line, escorted by a single private soldier who was depressed at being taken out of the battle. Dawson looked at him, and said, " There's nothing wrong with the morale of these boys."

" They're winning," said Wyatt shortly. He was obsessed by the urgency of getting to see Favel, but he could see it was not going to be easy. The war had split into two separate battles to the west and east of St. Pierre. Favel's hammer blow in the centre had split Serrurier's army into two unequal halves, the larger part withdrawing to the east in a fighting retreat, and a smaller fragment fleeing in disorder to the west to join the as yet unblooded troops keeping a watch on Cap Sarrat.

A more senior officer laughed in their faces when Wyatt demanded to see Favel. "*You* want to see Favel," he said incredulously. "*Blanc, I* want to see him—everyone wants to see him. He is on the move all the time; he is a busy man."

"Will he be coming here?" asked Wyatt.

The officer grunted. "Not if I can help it. He comes only when there is trouble, and I don't want to be the cause of his coming. But he might come," he prophesied. "We are moving against Rocambeau."

"Can we stay here?"

"You're welcome as long as you keep out of the way."

So they stayed in battalion headquarters and Wyatt relayed to Dawson the substance of what he had learned. Dawson said, "I don't think you have a hope in hell of seeing him. Would you be bothered by a nutty scientist at a time like this?"

"I don't suppose I would," said Wyatt despondently.

He listened carefully to all that was going on about him and began to piece together the military situation as it stood. The name of Serrurier was hardly mentioned, but the name of Rocambeau was on everyone's lips.

"Who the hell is this Rocambeau?" demanded Dawson.

"He was one of the junior Government generals," said Wyatt. "He took over when old Deruelles was killed and proved to be trickier than Favel thought. Favel was relying on finishing the war in one bash but Rocambeau got the Government army out of the net in a successful disengaging action. He's withdrawn to the east and is regrouping for another attack, and the devil of it is that he managed to scrape together enough transport to empty San Juan arsenal. He's got enough ammunition and spare weapons to finish the war in a way Favel doesn't like."

"Can't Favel move in and finish him before he's ready? Sort of catch him off-balance?"

Wyatt shook his head. "Favel has just about shot his bolt. He's been fighting continuously against heavy odds. He's fought his way down from the mountains and his men are dropping on their feet with weariness. He also has to stop for resting and regrouping."

" So what happens now?"

Wyatt grimaced. "Favel stops in St. Pierre—he hasn't the strength to push further. So he'll fight his defensive battle in St. Pierre, and along will come Mabel and wipe out the lot of them. Neither army will have a chance on this low ground round Santego Bay. No one is going to win this war."

Dawson looked at Wyatt out of the corner of his eye. "Maybe we'd better get out," he suggested. "We could go up the Negrito."

" After I've seen Favel," said Wyatt steadily.

" Okay," said Dawson with a sigh. "We'll stick around and see Favel—maybe." He paused. "Where exactly is Rocambeau regrouping?"

" Just off the coast road to the east—about five miles out of town."

"Holy smoke!" exclaimed Dawson. "Isn't that where Rawsthorne and the others went?"

" I've been trying not to think of that," said Wyatt tightly.

Dawson felt depressed. "I'm sorry," he said abjectly. "About pulling that stupid trick with the car. If I hadn't done that we wouldn't have got separated."

Wyatt looked at him curiously. Something had happened to Dawson ; this was not the man he had met in the Maraca Club—the big, important writer—nor was it the grouchy man in the cell who had told him to go to hell. He said carefully, "I asked you about that before and you bit my ear off."

Dawson looked up. "You want to know why I tried to take your car? I'll tell you. I ran scared—Big Jim Dawson ran scared."

" That's what I was wondering about," said Wyatt thoughtfully. "It doesn't fit with what I've heard about you."

Dawson laughed sourly and there was not a trace of humour about him. "What you've heard about me is a lot of balls," he said bluntly. "I scare easy."

Wyatt looked at Dawson's hands. "I wouldn't say that."

" It's a funny thing," said Dawson. "When I came slap-bang against Roseau and knew I couldn't talk my way out of it, I ought to have got scared then, but I got mad instead.

That's never happened to me before. As for my reputation, that's a fake, a put-up job—and it was so easy, too. You go to Africa and shoot a poor goddam lion, everyone thinks you're a hero; you pull a fish out of the sea a bit bigger than the usual fish, you're a hero again. I used those things like a bludgeon and I built up Big Jim Dawson—what the Chinese call a paper tiger. And it's wonderful what an unscrupulous press agent can do, too."

"But why?" asked Wyatt helplessly. "You're a good writer —all the critics say so; you don't need artificial buttresses."

"What the critics think and what I think are two different things." Dawson looked at the point of his dusty shoe. "Whenever I sit at a typewriter looking at that blank sheet of paper I get a sinking feeling in my guts; and when I've filled up a whole lot of sheets and made a book the sinking feeling gets worse. I've never written anything yet that I've liked—I've never been able to put on paper what I really wanted to. So every time a book came out I was scared it would be a flop and I had to have some support so it would sell, and that's why Big Jim Dawson was invented."

"You've been trying to do an impossible thing—achieve perfection."

Dawson grinned. "I'll still try," he said cheerfully. "But it won't matter any more. I think I've got over being scared."

Many hours later Wyatt was shaken into wakefulness. He had not been aware of falling asleep, and as he struggled into consciousness he was aware of cramped limbs and aching joints. He opened his eyes, to be blinded by a flashlight and he blinked painfully. A voice said, "Are you Wyatt, or is it the other chap?"

"I'm Wyatt," he said. "Who are you?" He threw off the blanket which someone had thoughtfully laid over him and stared at the big bearded man who was looking down at him.

"I'm Fuller. I've been looking all over St. Pierre for you. Favel wants to see you."

"Favel wants to see me! How does he even know I exist?"

"That's another story; come on."

Wyatt creaked to his feet and looked through the doorway. The first faint light of dawn was breaking through and he saw the outline of a jeep in the street and heard the idling engine. He turned and said, "Fuller? You're the Englishman—one of them—who lives on the North Coast, in the Campo de las Perlas."

"That's right."

"You and Manning."

"You've got it," said Fuller impatiently. "Come on. We've got no time for chit-chat."

"Wait a minute," said Wyatt. "I'll wake Dawson."

"We've got no time for that," said Fuller. "He can stay here."

Wyatt turned and stared at him. "Look, this man was beaten up by Serrurier's bully-boys because of you—you and Manning. We were both within an ace of being shot for the same reason. He's coming with me."

Fuller had the grace to be abashed. "Oh! Well, make it snappy."

Wyatt woke Dawson and explained the situation rapidly, and Dawson scrambled to his feet. "But how the hell does he know about you?" was his first question.

"Fuller will no doubt explain that on the way," said Wyatt. The tone of his voice indicated that Fuller had better do some explaining.

They climbed into the jeep and set off. Fuller said, "Favel has established headquarters at the Imperiale—it's nice and central."

"Well, I'm damned," said Dawson. "We needn't have moved an inch. We were there this . . . last . . . afternoon."

"The government buildings took a battering during the bombardment," said Fuller. "They won't be ready for occupation for quite a while."

Dawson said feelingly, "You don't have to tell us anything about that—we were there."

"So I'm told," said Fuller. "Sorry about that."

Wyatt had been looking at the sky and sniffing the air. It was curiously hot considering it was so early in the morning, and the day promised to be a scorcher. He frowned and said, "Why has Favel sent for me?"

"An English newspaperman came in with a very curious story—something about a hurricane. A lot of nonsense really. Still, Favel was impressed enough to send search-parties out looking for you as soon as we settled in the city. You *are* the weather boffin, aren't you?"

"I am," said Wyatt with no expression in his voice.

"So Causton came through all right," said Dawson. "That's good."

Fuller chuckled. "He served a term in the Government army first. He told us that you'd landed in the jug—the one on Liberation Place. *That* wasn't encouraging because we plastered the Place pretty thoroughly, but there weren't any white bodies in the police station so there was a chance you'd got away. I've been looking for you all night—Favel insisted, and when he insists, things get done."

Wyatt said, "When does the war start again?"

"As soon as Rocambeau decides to make his push," said Fuller. "We're fighting a defensive action—we're not strong enough to do anything else right now."

"What about the Government troops to the west?"

"They're still grouped around Cap Sarrat. Serrurier is still afraid the Yanks will come out and stab him in the back."

"Will they?"

Fuller snorted. "Not a chance. This is a local fight and the Yanks want none of it. I think they'd prefer Favel to Serrurier —who wouldn't?—but they won't interfere. Thank God Serrurier has a different opinion."

Wyatt wondered where Fuller came into all this. He spoke as one who was high in the rebel hierarchy and he was definitely close to Favel. But he did not ask any questions about it—he had more important things on his mind. The best thing was that Favel wanted to see him and he began to marshal his arguments once again.

Fuller pulled up the jeep outside the Imperiale and they all climbed out. There was a great coming and going and Wyatt noticed that the revolving door had been taken away to facilitate passage in and out of the hotel. He chalked up another mark to Favel for efficiency and attention to minor detail. He followed Fuller inside to find that the hotel had been transformed; the foyer had been cleared and the American Bar had a new role as a map room. Fuller said, "Wait here; I'll tell the boss you've arrived."

He went off and Dawson said, "This is how I like to view a war—from the blunt end."

"You might change your mind when Rocambeau attacks."

"That's very likely," said Dawson. "But I refuse to be depressed."

There was a cry from the stairs and they saw Causton

hurrying down. "Welcome back," he said. "Glad you got out of the cooler."

Wyatt smiled wryly. "We were blown out."

"Don't believe it," said Dawson. "Wyatt did a great job—he got us both out." He peered at Causton. "What's that on your face—boot-polish?"

"That's right," said Causton. "Can't get rid of the damn' stuff. I suppose you'd like to clean up and put on some fresh clothing."

"Where's Julie—and Rawsthorne?" asked Wyatt.

Causton looked grave. "We got separated quite early. The plan was to head east."

"They went east," said Wyatt. "Now they're mixed up with Rocambeau's army."

There was nothing anyone could say further about that and, after a pause, Causton said, "You'd better both take the chance of cleaning up. Favel won't see you yet—he's in the middle of a planning conference, trying to get a quart out of a pint pot."

He took them up to his room and provided welcome hot water and soap. One glance at Dawson's hands produced a doctor, who hustled Dawson away, and then Causton found a clean shirt for Wyatt and said, "You can use my dry shaver."

Wyatt sat on the bed and shaved, already beginning to feel much better. He said, "How did you get separated from the others?"

Causton told him, then said, "I got to Favel in the end and managed to convince him you were important." He scratched his head. "Either he didn't need much convincing, or my powers of persuasion are a lot better than I thought—but he got the point very quickly. He's quite a boy."

"Hurricanes excepted—do you think he's got a chance of coming on top in this war?"

Causton smiled wryly. "That's an unanswerable question. The Government army is far stronger, and so far he's won by surprise and sheer intelligence. He plans for every contingency and the ground-work for this attack was laid months ago." He chuckled. "You know that the main force of the Government artillery never came into action at all. The guns got tangled in a hell of a mess not far up the Negrito and Favel came down and captured the lot. I thought it was luck, but I know now that Favel never depends on luck. The whole damn' thing was planned—Favel had suborned Lescuyer, the Government artillery commander ; Lescuyer issued conflicting orders and had two columns of artillery meeting head-on on the same road, then he ducked for cover. By the time Deruelles had sorted that lot out it was all over, and Deruelles himself was dead."

"That must have been when Rocambeau took over," said Wyatt.

Causton nodded. "That was a pity. Rocambeau is a bloody efficient commander—far better than Deruelles could ever be. He got the Government army out of the trap. God knows what will happen now."

"Didn't the Government armour cause Favel any trouble when he came out on the plain?"

Causton grinned. "Not much. He sorted out the captured artillery in quick time, ruthlessly junking the stuff that was in the way. Then he formed it into six mobile columns and went gunning for Serrurier's armour. The minute a tank or an armoured car showed its nose, up would come a dozen guns and blast hell out of it. He had the whole thing taped right from the start—the Government generals were dancing to *his* tune until Rocambeau took over. Like when he blasted the 3rd Regiment in the Place de la Libération Noire—he had artillery observers already in the city equipped with walkie-talkies, and they caught the 3rd Regiment just when they were forming up."

"I know." said Wyatt soberly. "I saw the result of that."

Causton's grin widened. "He disposed of Serrurier's comic opera air force in the same tricky efficient fashion. The planes started flying and bombing all right, but when each plane had flown three attacks they found they'd come to the end of the ready use petrol, so they broke open the reserve tanks on the airfield. The lot was doctored with sugar—there's plenty of *that* on San Fernandez—and now all the planes are grounded with sticky engines."

"He certainly gets full marks for effort," said Wyatt. "Where do Manning and Fuller come into all this?"

"I haven't got to the bottom of that yet. I think they had something to do with getting his war supplies. Favel certainly knew what he wanted—rifles, machine-guns and mobile artillery, consisting of a hell of a lot of mountain guns and mortars, together with bags of ammunition. It must have cost somebody a packet and I haven't been able to find out who financed all this."

"Manning and Fuller were in the right place," said Wyatt slowly. "And the police seemed to think they had a lot to do with Favel. They beat Dawson half to death trying to find out more."

"I saw his hands," said Causton. "What did he tell them?"

"What could he tell them? He just stuck it out."

"I'm surprised," said Causton. "He has the reputation among us press boys of being a phoney. We know that the air crash he had in Alaska a couple of years ago was a put-up job to boost the sales of his latest book. It was planned by Don Wiseman and executed by a stunt pilot."

"Who is Don Wiseman?"

"Dawson's press agent. I always thought that every view we've had of Dawson was through Wiseman's magnifying glass."

Wyatt said gently, "I think you can regard Wiseman as being Dawson's former press agent."

Causton lifted his eyebrows. "It's like that, is it?"

"There's nothing wrong with Dawson," said Wyatt, stroking his clean-shaven cheek. He put down the dry-shaver. "When do I get to see Favel?"

Causton shrugged. "When he's ready. He's planning a war, you know, and right now he may be on the losing end. I think he's running out of tricks; his preliminary planning was good but it only stretches so far. Now he faces a slugging match with Rocambeau and he's not in trim for it. He's got five thousand men against the Government's fifteen thousand, and if he tries a war of attrition he's done for. He may have to retreat back to the mountains."

Wyatt buttoned his shirt. "He'll have to make up his mind quickly," he said grimly. "Mabel won't wait for him."

Causton sat in silence for a moment, then he said, almost pleadingly, "Have you anything concrete to offer him, apart from this hunch of yours?"

Wyatt stepped to the window and looked up at the hot blue sky. "Not much," he said. "If I were back at the Base with my instruments I might have been able to come to some logical conclusions, but without instruments . . ." He shrugged.

Causton looked despondent, and Wyatt said, "This is hurricane weather, you know. This calm sultriness isn't natural—something has stopped the normal flow of the southeast wind, and my guess is that it's Mabel." He nodded towards the sea. "She's somewhere over there beyond the horizon. I can't prove for certain that she's coming this way, but I certainly think so."

Causton said, "There's a barometer downstairs; would that be any good?" He sounded half-heartedly hopeful.

"I'll have a look at it," said Wyatt. "But I don't think it will be."

They went downstairs into the hurly-burly of the army headquarters and Causton showed him the barometer on the wall of the manager's office. Wyatt looked at it in astonishment. "Good God, a Torricelli barometer—what a relic!" He tapped it gently. "It must be a hundred years old." Looking closely at the dial, he said, "No, not quite; 'Adameus Copenhans—Amsterdam—1872.'"

"Is it any good?" asked Causton.

Wyatt was briefly amused. "This is like handing a pickaxe to a nuclear physicist and telling him to split some atoms." He tapped the dial again and the needle quivered. "This thing tells us what is happening now, and that's not very important. What I'd like to know is what happened over the last twenty-four hours. I'd give a lot to have an aneroid barograph with a recording over the last three days."

"Then this is useless?"

"I'm afraid so. It will probably give a wrong reading anyway. I can't see anyone having taken the trouble to correct this for temperature, latitude and so on."

Causton waxed sarcastic. "The trouble with you boffins is that you've developed your instruments to such a pitch that now you can't do without them. What did you weathermen do before you had your satellites and all your electronic gadgets?"

Wyatt said softly, "Relied on experience and instinct—which is what I'm doing now. When you've studied a lot of hurricanes—as many as I have—you begin to develop a sixth sense which tells you what they're likely to do next. Nothing shows on your instruments and it isn't anything that can be analysed. I prefer to call it the voice of experience."

"I still believe you," said Causton plaintively. "But the point is: can we convince Favel?"

"That isn't worrying me," said Wyatt. "What is worrying me is what Favel will do when he *is* convinced. He's in a cleft stick."

"Let's see if he's finished his conference," said Causton. "As a journalist, I'm interested to see what he *does* do." He mopped his brow. "You know, you're right; this weather is unnatural."

Favel was still not free and they waited in the foyer watching the comings and goings of messengers from the hotel dining-room where the conference was being held. At last Fuller came out and beckoned. "You're next," he said. "Make it as snappy as you can." He looked at Wyatt with honest blue eyes. "Personally, I think this is a waste of time. We don't have hurricanes here."

"Serrurier told me the same thing in almost the same words," said Wyatt. "He isn't a meteorologist, either."

Fuller snorted. "Well, come on; let's get it over with."

He escorted them into the dining-room. The tables had been put together and were covered with maps and a group of men were conversing in low voices at the far end of the room. It reminded Wyatt irresistibly of the large ornate room in which Serrurier had been holding his pre-battle conference, but there was a subtle difference. There was no gold braid and there was no hysteria.

Causton touched his elbow. "That's Manning," he said, nodding to a tall white man. "And that's Favel next to him."

Favel was a lean, wiry man of less than average height. He was lighter in complexion than the average San Fernandan and his eyes were, strikingly and incongruously, a piercing blue—something very unusual in a man of Negro stock. He was simply dressed in clean khaki denims with an open-necked shirt, out of which rose the strong corded column of his neck. As he turned to greet Wyatt the crowsfeet round his eyes crinkled and the corners of his mobile mouth quirked in a smile. "Ah, Mr. Wyatt," he said. "I've been looking for you.

I want to hear what you have to say but—from what Mr. Causton tells me—I fear I won't like it." His English was smooth and unaccented.

"There's going to be a hurricane," said Wyatt baldly.

Favel's expression did not change. He looked on Wyatt with a half-humorous curve to his lips, and said, "Indeed!"

The tall white man—Manning—said, "That's a pretty stiff statement, Wyatt. There hasn't been a hurricane here since 1910."

"And I'm getting pretty tired of hearing the fact," said Wyatt wearily. "Is there some magic about the year 1910? Do hurricanes come at hundred-year intervals, and can we expect the next in 2010?"

Favel said softly, "If not in 2010, when may we expect this hurricane?"

"Within twenty-four hours," said Wyatt bluntly. "I wouldn't put it at longer than that."

Manning made a noise with his lips expressive of disgust, but Favel held up his hand. "Charles, I know you don't want anything to interfere with our war, but I think we ought to hear what Mr. Wyatt has to say. It might have a considerable bearing on our future course of action." He leaned comfortably against the table and pointed a brown finger directly at Wyatt. "Now, then; give me your evidence."

Wyatt drew in a deep breath. He *had* to convince this slim brown man whose eyes had suddenly turned flinty. "The hurricane was spotted five days ago by one of the weather satellites. Four days ago I went to inspect it on one of the usual reconnaissance missions and found it was a bad one, one of the worst I've ever encountered. I kept a check on its course, and up to the time I left the Base it was going according to prediction. Since then I haven't had the opportunity for further tracking."

"The predicted course," said Favel. "Does that bring the hurricane to San Fernandez?"

"No," admitted Wyatt. "But it wouldn't take much of a swing off course to hit us, and hurricanes do swerve for quite unpredictable reasons."

"Did you inform Commodore Brooks of this?" asked Manning harshly.

"I did."

"Well, he hasn't put much stock in your story. He's still

sitting there across the bay at Cap Sarrat and he doesn't look like moving."

Wyatt said carefully, looking at Favel, "Commodore Brooks is not his own master. He has other things to take into account, especially this war you're fighting. He's taking a calculated risk."

Favel nodded. "Just so. I appreciate Commodore Brooks's position—he would not want to abandon Cap Sarrat Base at a time like this." He smiled mischievously. "I would not want him to abandon the Base, either. He is keeping President Serrurier occupied by his masterly inactivity."

"That's beside the point," said Manning abruptly. "If he was as certain about this hurricane as Wyatt apparently is, he would surely evacuate the Base."

Favel leaned forward. "*Are* you certain about this hurricane, Mr. Wyatt?"

"Yes."

"Even though you have been kept from your instruments and so do not have full knowledge?"

"Yes," said Wyatt. He looked Favel in the eye. "There was a man up near St. Michel—two days ago, just before the battles started. He was tying down the roof of his hut."

Favel nodded. "I, too, saw a man doing that. I wondered . . ."

"For God's sake!" exploded Manning. "This isn't a meeting of a folklore society. The decisions we have to make are too big to be based on anything but facts."

"Hush, Charles," said Favel. "I am a West Indian, and so is Mr. Wyatt. Like is calling to like." He saw the expression on Wyatt's face and burst out laughing. "Oh yes, I know all about you; I have a dossier on every foreigner on the island." He became serious. "Did you talk to him—this man who was tying down the roof of his hut?"

"Yes."

"What did he say?"

"He said the big wind was coming. He said he was going to finish securing the roof of his house and then he was going to join his family in a cave in the hills. He said the big wind would come in two days."

"How did that coincide with your own knowledge of the hurricane?"

"It coincided exactly," said Wyatt.

Favel turned to Manning. " That man has gone to his cave where he will pray to an old half-forgotten god—older, even, than those my people brought from West Africa. Hunraken, the Carib storm god."

Manning looked at him blankly and Favel murmured, " No matter." He turned back to Wyatt and said, " I have a great belief in the instincts of my people for survival. Perhaps—" he wagged a lean, brown finger—" and only perhaps, there will be a hurricane, after all. Let us *assume* there will be a hurricane—what will be the probable result if it hits us, here in St. Pierre?"

" Mabel is a particularly bad . . ." began Wyatt.

" Mabel?" Favel laughed shortly. " You scientists have lost the instinct for drama. Hunraken is the better name." He waved his hand. " But go on."

Wyatt started again. " She'll hit from the south and come into Santego Bay; the bay is shallow and the sea will build up. You'll have what is popularly known as a tidal wave."

Favel snapped his fingers. " A map. Let us see what it looks like on a map."

A large-scale map was spread on one of the tables and they gathered round. Causton had watched with interest the interplay between Favel and Wyatt and he drew closer. Manning, in spite of his disbelief, was fascinated by the broad outline of tragedy which Wyatt had just sketched, and watched with as much interest as anyone. The less intellectual Fuller stood by with a half smile; to him this was just a lot of boffin's bumff—everyone knew they didn't have hurricanes in San Fernandez.

Favel laid his hand on the map, squarely in the middle of Santego Bay. " This tidal wave—how high will be the water?"

" I'm no hydrographer—that's not my line," said Wyatt. " But I can give you an informed guess. The low central pressure in the hurricane will pull the sea up to, say, twenty to twenty-five feet above normal level. When that hits the mouth of the bay and shallow ground it will build up. The level will also rise because of the constriction—you'll have more and more water confined in less and less space as the wave moves into the bay." He hesitated, then said firmly, " You can reckon on a main wave fifty feet high."

Someone's breath hissed out in a gasp. Favel handed a black

crayon to Wyatt. "Disregarding the high winds, will you outline the areas likely to be affected by flooding."

Wyatt stood over the map, the crayon poised in his hand. "The wind will be driving the sea, too," he said. "You'll get serious flooding anywhere below the seventy-foot contour line all around the bay. To be safe, I'd put it at the eighty-foot line." He dropped his hand and drew a bold sinuous line across the map. "Everything on the seaward side of this line you can say will be subject to serious flooding."

He paused and then tapped the map at the head of Santego Bay. "The Rio Negrito will back up because of the force of the waters coming into the mouth. All that water will have to go somewhere, and you can expect serious flooding up the Negrito Valley for, say, ten miles. The hurricane will also precipitate a lot of water in the form of rain."

Favel studied the map and nodded. "Just like before," he said. "Have you studied the 1910 hurricane, Mr. Wyatt?"

"Briefly. There's a shortage of statistics on it, though; not too much reliable information."

Favel said mildly, "Six thousand dead; I consider that a very interesting statistic." He turned to Manning. "Look at that line, Charles! it encloses the whole of Cap Sarrat, all the flats where the airfield is and right up to the foot of Mont Rambeau, the whole of the city of St. Pierre and the plain up to the beginning of the Negrito. All that will be drowned."

"*If* Wyatt is right," emphasized Manning.

Favel inclined his head. "Granted." His eyes became abstracted and he stood a while in deep thought. Presently he turned to Wyatt. "The man near St. Michel—did he say anything else?"

Wyatt racked his brains. "Not much. Oh, he did say there would be another wind, perhaps worse than the hurricane. He said that Favel was coming down from the mountains."

Favel smiled sadly. "Do my people think of me as a destructive force? I hardly think I am worse than a hurricane." He swung on Manning. "I am going to proceed as though this hurricane were an established fact. I can do nothing else. We will plan accordingly."

"Julio, we're fighting a war!" said Manning in an agonized voice. "You can't take the chance."

"I must," said Favel. "These are my people, Charles.

F

There are sixty thousand of them in this city, and this city may be destroyed."

"Jesus!" said Manning, and glared at Wyatt. "Julio, we can't fight Rocambeau, Serrurier and a hurricane, too. I don't think there is going to be a hurricane and I won't believe it until Brooks moves out. How the hell can we lay out a disposition of troops under these conditions?"

Favel put a hand on his arm. "Have you ever known me make an error of judgment, Charles?"

Manning gave an exasperated sigh, and it was as though he had yelled out loud in his fury. "Not yet," he said tightly. "But there's a first time for everything. And I've always had a feeling about you, Julio—when you do make a mistake, it'll be a bloody big one."

"In that case we'll all be dead and it won't matter," said Favel drily. He turned to Wyatt. "Is there anything you can do to provide any proof?"

"I'd like to have a look at the sea," said Wyatt.

Favel blinked, taken by surprise for the first time. "That is a small matter and easily provided for. Charles, I want you to see that Mr. Wyatt has everything he needs ; I want you to look after him personally." He looked at the writhing black line scored on the map. "I have a great deal of thinking to do about this. I would like to be alone."

"All right," said Manning resignedly. He jerked his head at Wyatt and strode towards the door. Wyatt and Causton followed him into the foyer, where Manning turned on Wyatt violently. He grasped him by the shirt, bunching it up in his big hand, and said furiously, "You bloody egghead! You've balled things up properly, haven't you?"

"Take your damned hands off me," said Wyatt coldly.

Manning was perhaps warned by the glint of fire in Wyatt's eye. He released him and said, "All right ; but I'll give you a warning." He stuck a finger under Wyatt's nose. "If there is no hurricane after all you've said, Favel will let the matter drop—but I won't. And I promise you that you'll be a very dead meteorologist before another twenty-four hours have passed."

He drew back and gave Wyatt a look of cold contempt. "Favel says I've got to nurse you ; there's my car outside—I'll drive you anywhere you want to go." He turned on his heel and walked away.

Causton looked after him. " You'd better be right, Wyatt," he murmured. " You'd better be very right. If Mabel doesn't turn up on time I wouldn't like to be in your shoes."

Wyatt was pale. He said, " Are you coming?"

" I wouldn't miss any of this for the world."

Manning was silent as he drove them down to the docks past the looted arsenal of San Juan and on to the long jetty. " Will this do?"

" I'd like to go to the end," said Wyatt. " If it's safe for the car."

Manning drove forward slowly and stopped the car within a few yards of the end of the jetty. Wyatt got out and stood looking at the oily swells as they surged in from the mouth of the bay and the open sea. Causton mopped his brow and said to Manning, " God, it's hot. Is it usually as hot as this so early in the morning?"

Manning did not answer his question. Instead, he jerked his head towards Wyatt. " How reliable is he?"

" I wouldn't know," said Causton. " I've only known him four days. But I'll tell you one thing—he's the stubbornest cuss I've ever struck."

Manning blew out his breath, but said nothing more.

Wyatt came back after a few minutes and climbed into the car. " Well?" asked Manning.

Wyatt bit his lip. " There's a strong disturbance out there big enough to kick up heavy swells. That's all I can tell you."

" For the love of God!" exclaimed Manning. " Nothing more?"

" Don't worry," said Wyatt with a crooked smile. " You'll get your wind." He looked up at the sky. " Wherever I am, I want to be told of the first sign of cloud or haze."

" All right," said Manning, and put the car into reverse. He was just about to let out the clutch when a heavy explosion reverberated across the water and he jerked his head. " What the devil was that?"

There came another *boom* even as the first echoed from the hills at the back of St. Pierre and Causton said excitedly, " Something's happening at the Base. Look!' '

They had a clear view across the four miles of water of Santego Bay which separated them from the Base. A column of black smoke was coiling lazily into the air and Wyatt knew that it must be tremendous to be seen at that distance. He had a sudden intuition and said, " Brooks is evacuating. He's getting rid of his surplus ammunition so that Serrurier can't grab it."

Manning looked at him, startled, and then a big grin broke out on his face as, one after the other, more explosions came in measured sequence. " By God! " he roared. " There *is* going to be a hurricane."

Seven

Favel said tolerantly, " Because Charles seems pleased does not mean that he does not realize the gravity of the situation. It is merely that he likes to face reality—he is no shadow boxer."

The dining-room of the Imperiale was stiflingly hot and Causton wished that the fans would work. Favel had promised to get the city electricity plant working as soon as possible, but there was no point in it now. He unstuck his shirt from the small of his back and looked across at Wyatt. Manning isn't the only happy man round here, he thought; Wyatt has made his point at last.

But if Wyatt was more relaxed he was not too happy; there was much to do and the time was slipping away, minute by minute, while Favel airily tossed off inconsequential comments. He shrugged irritably and then looked up as Favel addressed him directly, " What is your advice, Mr. Wyatt?"

" Evacuation," said Wyatt promptly. " Total evacuation of St. Pierre."

Manning snorted. " We're fighting a war, dammit. We can't do two things at once."

" I'm not too sure," said Favel in a low voice. " Charles, come over here—I want to show you something." He took Manning by the arm and led him to a table, where they bent over a map and conversed in a murmur.

Wyatt looked across at Causton and thought of what he had said just before this conference began. He had been a shade cynical about Favel and his concern for " my people " " Naturally he's concerned," Causton said. " St. Pierre is the biggest town on the island. It's the source of power—that's why he's here now. But the power comes from the people in the city, not from the buildings, and, as a politician, he knows that very well."

Wyatt had said that Favel seemed to be an idealist, and Causton laughed. "Nonsense! He's a thoroughly practical politician, and there's precious little idealism in politics. Serrurier's not the only killer—Favel has done his share."

Wyatt thought of the carnage in the Place de la Libération Noire and was forced to agree. But he could not agree that Favel was worse than Serrurier after he had seen them both in action.

Favel and Manning came back, and Favel said, "We are in trouble, Mr. Wyatt. The American evacuation of Cap Sarrat has made my task ten times more difficult—it has released a whole new army of Government troops to assault my right flank." He smiled. "Fortunately, we believe that Serrurier has taken command himself and I know of old that he is a bad general. Rocambeau on my left flank is another matter altogether, even though his men are tired and defeated. I tell you—if the positions of Serrurier and Rocambeau were reversed then this war would be over in twelve hours and I would be a dead man."

He shook his head sadly. "And in these conditions you want me to evacuate the entire population of our capital city."

"It must be done," said Wyatt stolidly.

"Indeed I agree," said Favel. "But how?"

"You'll have to make an armistice. You'll have . . ."

Manning threw back his head and laughed. "An armistice," he scoffed. "Do you think Serrurier will agree to an armistice now he knows he can crack us like a nut?"

"He will if he knows there's a hurricane coming."

Favel leaned forward and said intensely, "Serrurier is mad; he does not care about hurricanes. He *knows* this island does not have hurricanes. So you told me yourself in your account of your interview with him."

"He must believe it now," exclaimed Wyatt. "How else can he account for the evacuation of Cap Sarrat Base?"

Favel waved his hand. "He will find that easy to rationalize. The Americans withdrew because they feared an assault from the mighty army of Serrurier, the Black Star of the Antilles. The Americans ran away because they were afraid."

Wyatt looked at him in astonishment and then knew that Favel was right. Any man who could banish a hurricane

would automatically reason in that grandiloquent and para-
noiac manner. He said unwillingly, " Perhaps you're right."

" I *am* right," said Favel decisively. " So what must we do
now? Come, I will show you." He led Wyatt to the map
table. " Here we have St. Pierre—and here we have your line
which marks the limit of flooding. The population of St.
Pierre will be evacuated up the Negrito Valley, but keeping
away from the river. While this is being done the army must
contain the assaults of Serrurier and Rocambeau."

" And that's not going to be too bloody easy, "said Manning.

" I am going to make it less easy," said Favel. " I want two
thousand troops to supervise the evacuation. That leaves one
thousand to withstand Serrurier on the right, and two thousand to contain Rocambeau on the left. They'll have all the
artillery, of course."

" Julio, have a heart," yelled Manning. " It can't be done
that way. We haven't the men to spare. If you don't have
enough infantry to protect the guns they'll be overrun. You
can't do it."

" It must be done," said Favel. " There is not much time.
To move a whole population, we will need the men to get the
people from their homes, by force if necessary." He looked at
his watch. " It is now nine-thirty. In ten hours from now I
do not want a single living being left in the city apart from
the army. You will be in charge of the evacuation, Charles.
Be ruthless. If they won't move, prod them with bayonets ; if
that fails, then shoot a few to encourage the others. But get
them out."

Wyatt listened to Favel's flat voice and, for the first time,
knew the truth of what Causton had implied. This was a man
who used power like a weapon, who had the politician's view
of people as a mass and not as individuals. Perhaps it was
impossible for him to be otherwise: he had the ruthlessness
of a surgeon wielding a knife in an emergency operation—to
cure the whole he would destroy the part.

" So we get them out," said Manning. " Then what?"

Favel gestured at the map, and said softly, " Then we let
Serrurier and Rocambeau have St. Pierre. For the first time
in history men will use a hurricane as a weapon of war."

Wyatt drew in his breath, shocked to the core of his being.

He stepped forward and said in a cracked voice, "You can't do that."

"Can't I?" Favel swung on him. "I've been trying to kill those men with steel, and if I had my way I would kill every one of them. And they want to kill me and my men. Why shouldn't I let the hurricane have them? God knows how many of my men will be lost saving the inhabitants of St. Pierre; they'll be outnumbered five to one and a lot of them will die—so why shouldn't the hurricane exact my revenge?"

Wyatt momentarily quailed before those blazing blue eyes and fell back. Then he said, "I gave you the warning to save lives, not to take them. This is uncivilized."

"And the hydrogen bomb is civilized?" snapped Favel. "Use your brains—what else *can* I do? This afternoon, when the evacuation is complete, my men will be in sole possession of St. Pierre. I am certainly not going to leave them there. When they withdraw the Government forces will move in, thinking we are in retreat. What else would they think? I am not *asking* them to be drowned in St. Pierre—they enter the city at their own risk."

"How far will you withdraw?" asked Wyatt.

"You drew the line yourself," said Favel remorselessly. "We will hold, as far as we can, on the eighty-foot contour line."

"You could withdraw further," said Wyatt heatedly. "They'd follow you on to higher ground."

Favel's hand came down on the table with the sound of a pistol shot. "I have no wish to fight further battles. There has been enough of killing men. Let the hurricane do its work."

"This is murder."

"What else is war but murder?" asked Favel, and turned his back on Wyatt. "Enough, we have work to do. Charles, let us see which men I can spare you."

He walked to the end of the room, leaving Wyatt shattered. Causton came over and put his hand on his shoulder. "Don't worry your head about the policies of princes," he advised. "It's dangerous."

"This is against all I've ever worked for," said Wyatt in a low voice. "I never intended this."

"Otto Frisch and Lise Meitner didn't mean trouble when

they split the uranium atom back in 1939." Causton nodded up the room towards Favel. " If you find a way of controlling hurricanes, it's men like that who'll decide what they'll be used for."

" He could save everyone," said Wyatt in a stronger voice. " He could, you know. If he retreated up into the hills the Government forces would follow him."

" I know," said Causton.

" But he's not going to do that. He's going to pen them in St. Pierre."

Causton scratched his head. " That may not be as easy as it sounds. He's got to stand off Rocambeau and Serrurier until the evacuation is completed, then he has to conduct a controlled retreat without being smashed while he's doing it. Next, he has to establish his perimeter on the eighty-foot line and that's a hell of a long line to hold with five thousand men—less what he'll have lost while all this has been going on. And on top of all that he'll have to dig in against the wind." He shook his head doubtfully. " A tricky operation altogether."

Wyatt looked at Favel. " I think he's as power-mad as Serrurier."

" Look, laddie," said Causton. " Start thinking straight. He's doing what he has to do in the circumstances. He's begun something he's got to go through with and in the dicey position he's in now, he'll use any weapon at hand—even a hurricane." He paused thoughtfully. " Maybe he's not as bad as I thought. When he said he didn't want any more battles, I think he meant it."

" He might well," said Wyatt. " As long as he comes out on top."

Causton grinned. " You're getting an education in the political facts of life. Damn it, some of you scientists are bloody naïve."

Wyatt said, with something of despair in his voice, " I'd have liked to have gone into atomic physics—my tutor wanted me to—but I didn't like the end results of what they were doing. Now it's happening to me anyway."

" You can't live in an ivory tower all your life," said Causton roughly. " You can't escape the world outside."

" Perhaps not," said Wyatt, frowning. " But there's something I've got to do. What about Julie and Rawsthorne and the others? We must do something about them."

Causton made a strangled noise. "What were you thinking of doing?" he asked with caution.

"We've got to do *something*," said Wyatt angrily. "I want transport—a car or something—and an escort for part of the way."

Causton struggled for a while to sort out his emotions. At last he said, "You weren't intending—by any chance—going into the middle of Rocambeau's army, were you?"

"It seems to be the only way," said Wyatt. "I can't think of anything else."

"Well, I wouldn't worry Favel about it now," advised Causton. "He's busy." He regarded Wyatt thoughtfully, trying to decide if he could be entirely sane. "Besides, Favel won't want to lose you."

"What do you mean by that?" demanded Wyatt.

"He'll expect you to consult the skies and give him a time-table for his operations."

"I'm not lending myself to that sort of thing," said Wyatt through his teeth.

"Now, look here," said Causton in a hard voice. "Favel has over sixty thousand people to think of. You have only four—and you're really only thinking of one. He *is* getting the people out of St. Pierre, you know—and that is not essential to his military plans. In fact, the effort might damn' well cripple him. I'll leave it to you to see where your duty lies." He turned on his heel and walked away.

Wyatt looked after him with a sinking feeling in his stomach. Causton was right, of course; too damnably right. He was caught up in this thing whether he liked it or not—in saving the population of St. Pierre he would help to destroy the Government army. Perhaps it would be better to think of it the other way round—in helping to destroy the army he would save the people. He thought about that, but it did not make him feel much better.

II

At eleven o'clock the city of St. Pierre boiled over. Manning's plan was brutally simple. Starting simultaneously in the

eastern and western suburbs, just behind the troops drawn up
ready for battle, his evacuating force pitched the inhabitants
into the streets, going systematically from house to house. The
people could take the clothes they stood up in and as much
food as they could carry—nothing else. The result was as
though someone had thrust a stick into an ants' nest and given
it a vicious twist.

Manning issued maps of the city to his officers, scored with
red and blue lines. The red lines indicated the lines of communication of the army; no civilians were allowed on those
streets at all on pain of death—at all costs the army must be
protected and serviced and nothing must stand in the way of
that. The blue lines led to the main road leading up through
the Negrito Valley, the road along which Wyatt had driven
with Julie what seemed a hundred years before.

There were incidents. The blue lines indicated one-way
traffic only, a traffic regulation enforced with violence. Those
attempting to go against the stream were brusquely ordered
to turn round, and if this failed, then the point of a bayonet
was a convincing argument. But sometimes, against a frantic
father looking for his family, even the bayonet was not convincing enough and the rifle beyond the bayonet spoke a
louder word. The body would be dragged to the side of the
road so as not to impede the steady shuffle of feet.

It was brutal. It was necessary. It was done.

Causton, wearing the brassard of a rebel officer, roamed the
city. In all the hot spots of a troubled world he had covered
in the course of his work he had never seen anything like this.
He was simultaneously appalled and exultant—appalled at
the vast scale of the tragedy he was witnessing, and exultant
that he was the only newspaperman on the spot. The batteries
of his tape recorder having run down, he wrote the quick,
efficient shorthand he had learned as a cub reporter in note-
books looted from a stationery shop, and recorded the scene
for a news-hungry world.

The people were apathetic. For years Serrurier had systematically culled the leaders from among them and all that
were left were the sheep. They resisted vocally on being told
to get out of their homes but the sight of the guns silenced
them, and, once in the street, they fell into the long line
obediently and shuffled forward with Favel's men at their

heels chivvying them to greater speed. Inevitably there were
confusions and bottlenecks as the greater mass of the populace
came on to the streets; at one corner where two broad streets
debouched into a third at a narrow angle there was chaos—
a tangled inextricable mass of bodies crushed against one
another which took Favel's bawling non-coms two hours to
straighten out, and when at last this traffic jam was eased
it left a couple of dozen crushed and suffocated corpses as
evidence of anarchy.

Causton, in his borrowed car, toured the city and finally
turned to the Negrito, checking on his map to find the quickest
way on a red-lined route. He arrived by means of a side road
at the main road leading into the Negrito valley quite close
to where Serrurier's artillery had been captured, and saw the
long line of refugees streaming away in the distance. Here
there was a sizeable force of rebel soldiers, about two hundred
strong. They were weeding out able-bodied men from the
passing stream, forming them into squads and marching
them away. Curious, Causton followed one of these squads to
see where they were going and saw them set to digging under
the rifles of Favel's men.

Favel was establishing his final defence line on the eighty-
foot contour.

When Causton returned to his car he saw a little pile of bodies
tossed carelessly into a heap by the roadside behind the rebel
troops—the conscientious objectors, the men who would not
dig for victory.

Sickened by death, he contemplated driving up the Negrito
to safety. Instead, he turned the car and went back into the
city because he still had his job to do and because his job was
his life. He drove back to general headquarters at the
Imperiale and asked for Wyatt, finding him eventually on the
roof, looking at the sky.

He looked up too, and saw a few feathery clouds barely
veiling the furnace of the sun. "Anything doing yet?" he
asked.

Wyatt turned. "Those clouds," he said. "Mabel's on her
way."

Causton said, "They don't seem much. We get clouds like
that in England."

"You'll see the difference pretty soon."

Causton cocked an eye at him. "Got over your bloody-mindedness?"

"I suppose so," said Wyatt gloomily.

"I have a thought that might console you," Causton said. "The people who are going to get it in the neck are Serrurier's soldiers, and soldiers are paid to get killed. That's more than you can say for the women and children of St. Pierre."

"What's it like out there?"

"Grim," said Causton. "There was a bit of looting, but Favel's men soon put a stop to that." He deliberately refrained from mentioning the methods being used to get the people on the move; instead, he said, "The devil of it is that there's only one practicable road out of town. Have you any idea how much road-space a city full of people takes up?"

"I've never had occasion to work it out," said Wyatt sourly.

"I did some quick mental arithmetic," said Causton. "And I came up with the figure of twelve miles. Since they're not moving at more than two miles an hour, it takes six hours for the column to pass any given spot."

"I spent an hour looking at maps," said Wyatt. "Favel wanted me to outline safe areas for the people. I did my best, looking at bloody contours, but—" he thumped a fist into the palm of his hand—"safe? I don't know. This town ought to have had a hurricane plan ready for lifting from a pigeon-hole and putting into action," he said savagely.

"That's not Favel's fault," pointed out Causton reasonably. "You can blame Serrurier for that." He looked at his watch. "One o'clock and Rocambeau hasn't made a move yet. He must have been mauled more seriously than we thought. Have you eaten yet?"

Wyatt shook his head, so Causton said, "Let's see what we can rustle up. It might be the last time we'll eat for quite a while."

They went downstairs and were buttonholed by Manning, who had just walked in. "When's that hurricane due?" he asked abruptly.

"I can't tell you yet," said Wyatt. "But give me another couple of hours and I'll tell you exactly."

Manning looked disgusted, but said nothing. Causton said, "Is there anything to eat around here? I'm getting peckish."

Manning grinned. "We did find a few stray chickens. You'd better come with me."

He took them into the manager's office, which had been converted into an officers' mess, and they found Favel just finishing a meal. He also questioned Wyatt, going into it much more thoroughly than Manning had, and then he went back to his map room, leaving them to eat in peace.

Causton gnawed on a chicken leg and then paused, pointing it at Manning. "Where do you come into all this?" he asked. "How did you get tangled up with Favel?"

"A matter of business," said Manning off-handedly.

"Such as professional advice on how to organize a war?"

Manning grinned. "Favel doesn't need any teaching about that."

Causton looked profound. "Ah," he said, as though enlightenment had suddenly come to him. "Your business is A.F.C. business."

Wyatt looked up. "What's that?"

"The Antilles Fruit Corporation—very big business in this part of the world. I was wondering where Favel got his finance."

Manning put down a bone. "I'm not likely to tell you, am I? I wouldn't shoot off my mouth to a reporter."

"Not in the normal way," agreed Causton. "But if the reporter had the smell of the right idea and he was good enough at his job to ferret out the rest of it, you'd want him to get the right story, wouldn't you? From your angle, I mean."

Manning laughed. "I like you, Causton; I really do. Well, I can give you some kind of story—but it's off the record and don't quote me on it. Let's say I'm having a quiet talk with Wyatt here, and you're eavesdropping with those long ears." He looked at Wyatt. "Let's say there was a big American corporation which had a lot of capital invested in San Fernandez at one time, and all its holdings were expropriated by Serrurier."

"A.F.C.," said Causton.

"Could be," said Manning. "But I'm not saying so out loud. The officers of this corporation were as mad as hornets, naturally—their losses were more than twenty-five million dollars—and the shareholders weren't pleased, either. That's one half of it. The other half is Favel—he's the chap who could do something about it—for reasons of his own. But he had no money to buy arms and train men, so what more natural than they get together?"

"But why pick you as a go-between?" asked Causton.

Manning shrugged. "I'm in the business—I'm for hire. And they didn't want an American; that might not have looked right. Anyway, I went shopping with the corporation's money—there's a chap in Switzerland, an American, who has enough guns to equip the British army, let alone our piddling little effort. Favel knew exactly what he wanted—rifles, machine-guns, mortars to pack a big wallop and yet be easily moved, recoilless rifles and a few mountain guns. He got his best men off the island and set up a training school—and I'd better not tell you where. He hired a few artillery instructors to train his men and then gradually started to recruit again on the island. When he had enough men we shipped in the arms."

Wyatt said incredulously, "Do you mean to tell me that all this has been done so that a fruit company can make a few dollars more profit?"

Manning looked at him sharply and his hand curled into a ball. "It has not," he said crisply. "Where do you get that idea?"

Causton said hastily, "Pray forgive my young friend. He's still wet behind the ears—he doesn't understand the facts of life, as I've had occasion to tell him."

Manning pointed his finger at Wyatt. "You say that to Favel and you'll get your head chopped off. Somebody had to get Serrurier out and Favel was the only one with guts enough. And it couldn't be done constitutionally because Serrurier abolished the constitution, so it had to be done with blood—a surgical operation. It's a pity, but there it is."

He relaxed and grinned at Causton. "Our hypothetical fruit corporation might have caught a tiger by the tail—Favel is no one's dummy. He's a bit of a reformer, you know, and he'll hold out for fair pay and good working conditions on the plantations." He shrugged. "I'm no company man; it's no skin off my nose if Favel bites the hand that's fed him."

Wyatt winced. It seemed that Causton was right again. Nothing in this topsy-turvy world of politics made sense to him. It was a world in which black and white merged into an indeterminate grey, where bad actions were done for good reasons and good actions were suspect. It was not his world and he wished he were out of it, in his own uncomplicated sphere of figures and formulae where all he had to worry about was whether a hurricane would behave itself.

He was about to apologize but he saw that Manning was still talking to Causton. ". . . will be better when San Fernandez can build up a fund of development capital instead of it being siphoned off into Serrurier's pocket. A bit of spare money round here would make all the difference—it could be a good place."

Causton said, "Can Favel be trusted?"

"I think so. He's liberally inclined, but he's not a milk-and-water liberal, and he's got no inclination to be taken over by the Russians like Castro. He'll stand up to the Americans, too." Manning grinned. "He'll make them pay a hell of a lot more for Cap Sarrat Base than they've been paying." He became serious. "He'll be a dictator because he can't be anything else right now. Serrurier beat the stuffing out of these people, killed their natural leaders and drained them of guts—they're not fit for government yet. But I don't think he'll be a bad dictator, certainly not as bad as Serrurier."

"Um," said Causton. "He'll have to take a lot of criticism from well-meaning fools who don't know what's been going on here."

"That won't worry him," said Manning. "He doesn't give a damn about what people say about him. And he can give as good as he gets."

The table shook and there came a roll of thunder rumbling from the east. Manning lifted his head. "The party's started—Rocambeau has begun his attack."

III

Julie looked through a crack in the door of the corrugated iron hut, paying no attention to the shrill voice of Mrs. Warmington who sat crouched on a box behind her. There still seemed to be a lot of trucks in the quarry, although she had heard many drive away. And there were still many soldiers about, some standing in groups, talking and smoking, and others moving about intent on their business. She was thankful that the officer had not considered it necessary to post a guard on the hut; he had merely tested the bolt on the outside of the door before pushing them inside.

She had had a hard time with Mrs. Warmington—the woman was impossible. When they were captured and brought down to the quarry Mrs. Warmington had tried to talk her way out of it, raising her voice in an attempt to get her point over—which was that she was an American and not to be treated like a criminal when she had merely been defending her life and honour. It had not worked because no one understood English, no matter how loudly shouted, and they had been thrust into the hut and, Julie hoped, forgotten.

She turned from the door, irritated with Mrs. Warmington's monologue. "For God's sake, will you be quiet?" she said wearily. "What do you want them to do—come in here and shut you up with a gun? They will, you know, once they get as tired of you as I am."

Mrs. Warmington's mouth shut with a snap—but not for long. "This is intolerable," she said with the air of a victim. "The State Department will know of this when I get home."

"*If* you get home," said Julie cruelly. "You shot a man, you know. You shot him with Eumenides's gun." She cocked her head at the door. "They're not going to like that."

"But they don't know," said Mrs. Warmington craftily. "They think it was that Greek."

Julie looked at her in disgust for a long moment. "They don't know," she agreed. "But they will if I tell them."

Mrs. Warmington gulped. "But you wouldn't do that . . . would . . . you?" Her voice tailed away as she saw the expression on Julie's face.

"I will if you don't keep your big trap shut," said Julie callously. "You killed Eumenides—you killed him as surely as if you'd shot him and pushed a bayonet into his back yourself. He was a nice guy; not very brave maybe—who is?— but a nice guy. He didn't deserve that. I'm not going to forget it, you know, so you'd better watch yourself. If I killed you here and now it wouldn't be murder, just decent execution."

She spoke levelly and without emphasis, but her words were chilling and Mrs. Warmington shrank into a corner with horror in her eyes. Julie said, "So walk carefully round me, you big bag of wind, or I might be tempted. I *could* kill you, it shouldn't be too difficult." Her voice was detached, but when she looked down at her hands she saw they were shaking violently.

She turned and looked again through the crack in the door, astonished at herself. Never before had she struck at another person with such deadly intent to hurt, never before had she trembled in such fury. For too long she had exercised the tact drilled into her as an air hostess and it felt good to let rip at this futile and dangerous woman. She felt a surge of strength and knew she had done the right thing.

She felt a warm trickle run down her thigh, and looked at her arm and saw the drying blood where she had been jabbed by a bayonet. There was much activity outside but no one seemed to be taking particular notice of the hut, so she stripped off her slacks and examined the wounds in her legs.

Incredibly, Mrs. Warmington had retained her purse when they were dragged down the hill, and now Julie picked it up and dumped the contents on to the floor. It contained no more than the usual rat's nest found in a woman's purse; lipstick, compact, comb, money in notes and coins—quite a lot of that, travellers' cheques, pen, notebook, a packet of tissues, a bottle of aspirin, a small flask of spirit which proved to be bourbon, an assortment of hairpins, several loose scraps of paper and a cloying scent of spilled face powder.

She stirred the heap with her finger and said sardonically, "You've lost your jewels." She took the tissues and began to stanch her wounds. They were not too bad; the worst was not a quarter of an inch deep, but they bled freely and she knew that when they stopped bleeding her legs would become very stiff and painful to move. She took two of the aspirin tablets and dumped half of the contents of the bottle into her shirt pocket. As she swallowed the aspirins she wished they had water, and wondered what could be done about that. Then she donned her slacks and tossed the remainder of the tissues to Mrs. Warmington. "Clean yourself up," she ordered abruptly, and went to the door again.

She stayed to observe the scene for a long time. The quarry apparently formed a convenient military park close to the main road but not in the way of traffic. There were many trucks moving in and out but she noted that the general trend was to lessen the number of vehicles standing idle. She hoped briefly, but with no great assurance, that everyone would go away, forgetting the white women imprisoned in the hut, and wondered how much chance there was of that happening.

After a while she tired of the changing scene that always remained the same and began to explore the hut. Mrs. Warmington sat mutely in her corner, looking at Julie with frightened eyes, and Julie ignored her. Most of the boxes were empty, but behind a large tea chest filled with bits and pieces of scrap iron she found a sledge-hammer and a pickaxe, both in reasonably good condition.

Julie hefted the hammer and then explored the walls of the hut. The wooden framework was rotten and the nails that held the rusty iron sheets were corroded, and she thought she would have no difficulty in battering her way out provided there was no one within earshot—an unlikely eventuality. She put the tools close to hand behind the door where they would not be easily seen and settled down again to her vigil.

The morning wore on and slowly the quarry emptied of vehicles. As the sun rose higher in the sky the hut warmed to an oven-like heat and the iron walls were too hot to touch. The two women sat there and sweated, listening to the noisy clash of gears and the roar of engines as trucks drove to and fro—and they became very thirsty.

She wondered what had happened to Rawsthorne and concluded that he must also have been taken prisoner, or perhaps killed. It had only been the fortunate arrival of the Negro officer that had saved them, and maybe Rawsthorne had not been so lucky. She coldly contemplated the grim fact that if she did not get out of this hut she would die. Rawsthorne had already rejected the quarry as being safe from the hurricane, and however the fortunes of the civil war turned she would die if she could not escape.

Her thoughts again turned to Wyatt. It was a great pity that now they had come together at last they should be parted and that both would probably die. At the moment she did not give much for her own chances, and while she was ignorant of what had happened to Wyatt, she was doubtful of his having survived the war that had washed over St. Pierre.

She was aroused from her reverie by Mrs. Warmington. " I'm thirsty."

" So am I," said Julie. " Shut up!"

Something was happening—or rather, not happening—and

she made a quick gesture with her hand, pressing Mrs. Warmington to silence. It had suddenly gone very quiet. True, there was the noise of traffic from the main coast road, but the closer rumble of trucks from the quarry had ceased. She looked through the crack in the door again and found the quarry empty except for one soldier, who squatted in the shade a dozen yards away and seemed to be dozing. There had been a guard, after all.

Julie turned and snatched the purse from Mrs. Warmington's grasping hand and took out the wad of notes. Mrs. Warmington flared up. "Don't take that—it's mine."

"You want water, don't you?" asked Julie. "We might be able to buy some." She looked at the thick bundle of money. "We might even be able to buy our way out of here—if you keep quiet." Mrs. Warmington closed her mouth abruptly, and Julie said, "I don't know my way around in this language, but I'll try; the money will speak loud enough, anyway."

She went to the door and looked through the crack. "Hey —you, there!"

The soldier turned round lazily and blinked at the door. He saw what appeared to be a bank-note of large denomination protruding through the door of the hut and moving gently up and down. He scrambled to his feet, seized his rifle, and approached the hut with circumspection diluted with avarice. The bank-note flashed from sight as he made a grab for it, and a feminine voice said, "*L'eau . . . agua.* Can you get us some?"

Julie watched the puzzlement on the man's face, and said urgently, "Bring us water. Water . . . *l'eau . . . agua.* You can have the money."

The soldier scratched his head, and then his face cleared. "Ah—*l'eau!*"

"That's right. You can have the money—the money, see— when you bring *l'eau.*"

He broke into a jabber of incomprehensible *patois*, finally ending with, "*L'argent . . . la monnaie . . . pour l'eau?*"

"That's right, buster; you've got it."

He nodded and went away and Julie breathed a sigh of relief. Her throat was parched and felt like sand-paper, and the thought of cool water made her feel dizzy for a moment. But there was something that had to be done before the soldier returned. It was not likely he would unlock the door—he probably had no key—and how would he get the water into the hut?

She seized the sledge-hammer and prodded tentatively at the bottom of the door where it seemed to be weakest. Then she swung the hammer like a golf club and crashed it once against the rotten wood. A piece gave way leaving a small opening, and she dared not do more. She did not know how far the soldier had gone and he could still be within earshot—one sharp noise he might dismiss, but not the constant repetition necessary to break down the door.

She saw him coming back bearing a bottle and a tin cup and he paused a moment and looked helplessly as she rattled the door. He said something and shrugged his shoulders and she knew he could not open the door, so she bent down and put her hand through the hole she had made. "Down here," she shouted, hoping he did not realize the opening was new.

He squatted before the door and put the bottle and cup just out of her reach. "L'argent," he said in a bass growl. "La monnaie."

She cursed him and pushed a bank-note through the hole. He grabbed it and pushed the tin cup within her reach. She drew it through the hole gently, careful not to spill it, and passed it to Mrs. Warmington. When she reached for the bottle it was still beyond her grasp. The soldier grinned and said cheerfully, "L'argent?" and she was forced to give him more money before he would let her have the bottle.

The water, tepid though it was, was a benison to her dry throat. She drank half the bottle in one swallow and then paused, looking at Mrs. Warmington who was licking the last drop from the rim of the dirty cup. She said, "Take it easy; this stuff is expensive—it's costing you over four dollars a cup." She put the bottle in the corner and looked at her watch. It was twelve-thirty.

The soldier had gone back to sitting in the shade, but he kept his eye on the hut, hoping for more easy money. Julie said, "I wish to hell he'd go away."

She heard a tapping sound from behind her and turned to look at Mrs. Warmington, who was gazing hopefully into the cup as though she expected it to fill up by magic. The tapping continued and came from the back of the hut, so Julie went to the back wall and listened closely. There was a familiar but incomplete rhythm which she recognized as the old shave-and-a-haircut of her childhood days, so she gave the two taps necessary to complete the phrase and said in a low voice, "Who's that?"

"Rawsthorne—don't make a noise."

Her heart leaped in her breast. "How did you get here?"

"I followed you when you were brought down here. I've been watching from the top of the quarry. I was only able to get down when that bloody guard went away just now."

"Where did he go?" asked Julie urgently.

"Up the track and out of sight," said Rawsthorne. "I think he went as far as the main road."

"Good!" said Julie. "I think I can make him do it again. If he goes that far we can get out of here. Can you wait there?"

"Yes," said Rawsthorne. He sounded very much his age and as though he was desperately tired. "I can wait."

Julie went back and found that Mrs. Warmington had finished the bottle of water. She looked up defiantly, and said, "Well, it was my money, wasn't it?"

Julie snatched the bottle from her hands. "It doesn't matter now; we're getting out of here. Get ready—and keep quiet."

She went to the door and called out, "L'eau . . . more l'eau, please," and fluttered another bank-note through the crack. This time she wasn't quick enough and the soldier snatched it from her before she could withdraw it. He grinned in satisfaction as he stuffed it into his pocket but made no objection to taking the bottle and cup.

She watched him walk out of sight and forced herself to wait two full minutes, then she swung at the door with the hammer and with her full strength. One of the planks split along its length; it was rotten with age and lack of paint and another blow shattered it. Rawsthorne called, "Wait!" and stuck his head through the opening she had made. "Hit it down there." he said, indicating the area of the lock.

She swung the hammer again and the hasp and staple burst out of the rotten wood and the door creaked open. "Come on," she said. "Make it fast." And ran outside, not really caring if Mrs. Warmington followed or not.

"Over here," called Rawsthorne, and she ran after him

round a corner of rock and out of sight of the hut. "We're still in a trap," Rawsthorne told her. "This quarry is a dead end, and if we go along the track we'll meet that guard coming back."

"How did you get down?"

Rawsthorne pointed upwards. "I came down there—and nearly broke my neck. But we can't get up that way—not before the guard comes back—he'd pick us off the cliff like ducks in a shooting gallery." He looked around. "The only thing we can do is to hide."

"But where?"

"There's a ledge up there," said Rawsthorne. "If we lie flat we should be out of sight of anyone down here. Come on, Mrs. Warmington."

It was an awkward climb. Julie and Rawsthorne gave the ungainly Mrs. Warmington a boost, and then Rawsthorne went up and turned to give Julie his hand. She rolled on to the narrow ledge with skinned knees and flattened herself out. Although she kept her head down she could still see the corner of the hut in the distance and expected to see the guard return with the water at any moment.

She whispered, "Supposing we do get on top of the quarry —what then?"

"All the troops have gone from the top," said Rawsthorne. "They moved out of the plantation back towards St. Pierre. I think General Rocambeau is going to attack very soon. I thought we could cut across country behind his army, moving over the hills until we reach the Negrito. We should be safe enough there." He paused. "But we might not have time; have you looked at the sky?"

Julie twisted her neck and looked up, wincing as the sun bit into her eyes. "I don't see much—just a few high clouds. Feathery ones."

"There's a halo round the sun," said Rawsthorne. "I think the hurricane will be here soon."

Julie saw a movement near the hut. "Hush, he's come back."

The soldier looked at the hut in astonishment and dropped the bottle and the cup, spilling the water carelessly on the dusty ground. He unslung his rifle and Julie heard quite clearly the snap of metal as he slipped off the safety-catch. He looked around the quarry and she froze—if she could see him, then he could see her if he looked carefully enough in the right direction.

Slowly the soldier walked around the hut; he walked with deliberation, his rifle held ready to shoot, and she heard the dry crunch of his boots on the ground. He came forward intent on searching the quarry, and cast in a wide circle, peering into all the nooks and crannies left by the blasting. As he came closer he vanished from sight and Julie held her breath and hoped the Warmington woman would keep quiet, because now the man was very close—she could even hear the rasp of his breath as he stood below the ledge.

And he stood there for a long time. There was no movement of his feet at all, and Julie pictured him looking up at the ledge and wondering if it was worth while climbing up to investigate. There was a clink and a scraping sound as of metal on rock, and she thought: he's put down his gun; he needs both hands for climbing. He's coming up!

She jerked at the sound of a shattering explosion, and then there was another—and another. She heard the thud of boots and, after a few seconds, saw the man running across the quarry away from them to stand looking up the track with his hand shielding his eyes from the glare of the sun. The explosions continued in rapid succession. It was a noise Julie was becoming familiar with—an artillery barrage. Rocambeau had attacked and Favel was laying down protective fire.

The soldier hesitated and looked about the quarry again, then slung his rifle on his shoulder and disappeared from her view at a rapid trot, heading towards the track. "I think he's gone," she said after a long moment.

Rawsthorne lifted himself up and looked about. "Then we must go too," he said. "We must strike for the high ground."

IV

Favel's force in the east resisted the first assault, shattering the wave of Government troops that tried to cross the open ground before the furthest suburbs with a deluge of shells and mortar bombs. Rocambeau had no artillery and was impotent in the face of this onslaught of fire, but he had the men— seven thousand to Favel's two thousand—and he used them ruthlessly.

He lost five hundred in that first attack, but when it was

beaten off he occupied a line within two hundred yards of
the nearest houses, his men burrowing into the shell-holes that
pitted the ground; and he filtered in reinforcements from the
rear, crawling on their bellies from crater to crater, until his
position was unassailable.

Not that Favel meant to counter-attack—or could attack.
Over half his force was serving the guns and he had only nine
hundred infantrymen to cover them—a dangerously small
force. But his infantry were exceptionally well equipped to
fight a decisive battle; they had all the automatic weapons
which had been withdrawn from the men now evacuating the
city and they had had time to site them well. Rocambeau was
going to lose a lot more men before he had a chance of getting
at those murderous guns which were hammering his force—
if he ever could get at them. For the guns were prepared to
retreat at a moment's notice; their limbers and transport lay
close at hand and they could retreat in echelon to already
prepared positions when the order was given, and Rocambeau
would be left to go through the whole futile, man-killing process again.

Favel did not even leave his headquarters. His officers knew
what was expected of them and he knew he could rely on
them to carry out the master plan, so he was left free to concentrate on the coming attack from the west. That morning
he had gone down to the docks and watched the American
evacuation of Cap Sarrat Base, powerful binoculars shortening
the distance across the water. One by one the ships went and
the aircraft roared towards the north-east in the direction of
Puerto Rico and safety. A hazy pall of black smoke covered
the Cap as the oil tanks went up in flames. Commodore
Brooks was not leaving anything behind that would do anyone
any good.

Favel thought of what Serrurier would do. Putting last
things first, he would immediately occupy the Base. The
American occupation of Cap Sarrat had always been a sore
point with him and several times he had sought to break the
agreement, only to be faced with the inflexible refusal of the
American Government to be thrown out. Now it was open
for him to take and take it he would—an empty victory with
the promise of defeat lurking in the background. He would
waste time on Cap Sarrat instead of organizing an attack on
St. Pierre with his reserve of fresh and unblooded troops now

freed from the irrational fear of a stab in the back by the Americans.

So when Favel heard the guns from the east bellow in response to Rocambeau's assault he smiled thinly. Rocambeau with his defeated and demoralized army had come into action first and Serrurier was still wallowing in his fool's paradise on Cap Sarrat. Good! Let him stay there. If he knew there were but a thousand men to oppose his eight thousand perhaps he might change his mind—but there was no one to tell him, and if anyone did he would not believe it. He was a suspicious man and, fearing a trap, he would not believe anything so ridiculous.

Favel called an orderly and instructed him to bring Manning and Wyatt as soon as they could be found. Then he sat back in his chair and placidly lit a long thin cigar.

Wyatt was again on the roof when the orderly found him, scanning the horizon with binoculars. The high cirrus clouds, feathery and fragile, now covered the sky and were giving place to cirrostratus from the south, extending in a great flat sheet. It was still intensely hot and the air was still and sultry without the trace of a breeze. The sun was haloed—an ominous sign to Wyatt as he checked the time again.

He went down to see Favel and found Manning giving a progress report. "We're moving along as fast as we can," he said. "But it takes time."

Wyatt said abuptly, "Time is something we haven't got. Mabel is moving faster than I thought."

"How long?" asked Manning.

"She'll hit about five o'clock."

"Christ!" said Manning. "It can't be done."

"It must be done," said Favel curtly. He turned to Wyatt. "What do you mean when you say it will hit at five o'clock?"

"You'll have winds of sixty miles an hour."

"And the flooding?"

Wyatt shrugged. "I don't know," he said honestly. "That's one aspect of hurricanes I haven't studied. I don't really know when you can expect the tidal wave—but I wouldn't put it much after six o'clock."

Favel said reflectively, "It is two o'clock now—that gives us four hours, or three at the worst. What is likely to happen between now and then?"

"Not much," said Wyatt. "The clouds will thicken very perceptibly in the next hour and a breeze will spring up. From then on it just gets worse."

"Charles, how is the evacuation going in the east? Can we withdraw to the second prepared line?"

Manning nodded unwillingly. "I've got all that area cleared—but you'll be pushing it a bit hard. If Rocambeau breaks through—and he could if we aren't careful on this retreat—he'll be right in the middle of us and we won't have a chance."

Favel pulled a telephone towards him. "We retreat," he said firmly. "Speed things up, Charles. I want every effort made."

"All right, Julio," said Manning wearily. "I'll do my best." He strode out. Wyatt hesitated, wondering if he should go too, but Favel held up his hand while speaking into the telephone, so he leaned on the edge of the table and waited.

Favel put down the handset gently, and said, "You mentioned rain, Mr. Wyatt. Is this going to be a serious factor?"

"You can expect a lot of rain—more than you've ever seen before; it will add to the flooding problem in the Negrito but I took it into account when you asked me to outline the safe areas. The worst rainfall will occur in the right front quadrant of the hurricane, but I think that will be to the west of here. Still, you can expect between five and ten inches spread over twenty-four hours."

"A lot of rain," observed Favel. "That is likely to preclude serious military operations."

Wyatt laughed grimly. "I hope you aren't thinking of doing *any* military operations during the next day or so. The wind will stop you if the rain doesn't."

Favel said, "I was thinking of afterwards. Thank you, Mr. Wyatt. Keep me informed of any serious developments."

So Wyatt went back on the roof and watched the dark line of nimbostratus gather on the horizon.

Rocambeau's second blow fell on thin air. True, the shelling was just as severe as before but there was no small-arms fire until his men had penetrated over half a mile into the city. They rushed into this sudden vacuum and became overextended, and when they came up against opposition they were thin on the ground. The stragglers were lucky, but the enthusiasts in the forefront suffered heavy casualties from strong machine-gun fire and retreated a little way to lick their wounds.

But they did not mind because they heard the sudden rumble of guns from the other side of the city and knew that Serrurier had begun his attack at last. Now Favel and his rebels would surely be crushed.

Serrurier was even more brutal and callous about losses than Rocambeau. His bull-headed rush against the pitiful thin line of defenders was overwhelming. Despite the artillery and the plentiful machine-guns he cracked Favel's line in three places, threatening to split the small force into fragments. Favel took over decisively and ordered an immediate retreat into the city. In the open he had no chance against eight-to-one odds, but street fighting was another matter.

The fighting became brisk on both fronts and Favel's men gave way slowly, suffering many losses but not nearly as many as the Government armies. There was a constant coming and going at the Imperiale as Favel demanded news and yet more news of the evacuation, carefully timing his withdrawals on both flanks to accommodate the slow ebbing of the human tide from St. Pierre, and grudgingly trading ground for enemy casualties. It was a risky business and it lost him more good men than he liked, but he stubbornly kept to his plan and somehow made it work.

The city was in flames to east and west as he withdrew. His men had orders to set all buildings on fire to put a barrier of flame before the advancing and victorious Government troops. The flames, fanned by the brisk breeze that had sprung up, roared to the sky and the smoke drifted north to lie over the Negrito.

At four o'clock he decided that he could not possibly save his artillery and gave orders for the guns to be spiked and abandoned as his commanders thought fit. The road to the Negrito was jammed with refugees and it was impossible to push the guns through at the same time, and he knew the guns would not be needed when the hurricane had passed. Already more than fifteen hundred of the troops Manning had used to evacuate the city were in position in the defence line on the eighty-foot contour, and Serrurier and Rocambeau were pushing in faster and pressing harder.

Five minutes later he gave the order to abandon headquarters, and an orderly passed the news to Wyatt, who cast one more glance at the dark horizon and hurried downstairs. Favel was waiting in the foyer, watching maps being loaded into a truck standing outside the hotel and seemingly more intent on the lighting of his cigar than on the din of battle.

"We will let Serrurier and Rocambeau join hands," he said. "I think they will waste time greeting each other, and perhaps they'll split a bottle of rum together. We will also form one line—but we are united." He smiled. "I do not think Rocambeau will take kindly to being superseded by Serrurier."

A soldier shouted from the truck and Favel, after making sure his cigar was lit, applied the still burning match to a twist of paper. "Excuse me," he said, and walked back into the bar. As he came back Wyatt saw the quick glow of fire behind him.

"Come, we must go," said Favel, and pushed Wyatt through the door and into the street. As the truck pulled off Wyatt looked back at the Imperiale and saw smoke pouring through the windows to be whipped away in the rising wind.

It was four-thirty in the afternoon.

Eight

Wyatt had advocated evacuation—now he saw the reality and was shocked.

The truck travelled through the deserted streets in the centre of the town, while all around the clamour of battle echoed from the blank faces of the buildings as the rebel army grimly retreated in their narrowing circle. The sky was darkening and a wind had risen which blew tattered papers along dirty pavements. The city smelled of fire and the smoke, instead of rising, was now driven down into the streets to catch in the throat.

Wyatt coughed and stared at a body lying on the pavement. A little way along the street he saw another, then another—all male, all civilian. He jerked his head round and said to Favel, "What the devil has been going on?"

Favel stared straight ahead. He asked tonelessly, "Have

you any conception of what is needed to evacuate a city in a few hours? If the people will not move, then they must be made to move."

The truck slowed to swerve round another corpse in the middle of the street—a woman in a startlingly patterned red floral dress and a yellow bandanna about her head. She was sprawled like a toy abandoned by a child, her limbs awry in the indecency of violent death. Favel said, "We share the guilt, Mr. Wyatt. You had the knowledge; I had the power. Without your knowledge this would never have happened, but you brought your knowledge to one who had the power to make it happen."

"Need there have been killing?" asked Wyatt in a low voice.

"There was no time to explain, no plans already made, no knowledge in the people themselves." Favel's face was stern. "Everyone knows we do not have hurricanes in San Fernandez," he said as though he were quoting. "The people did not *know*. That is another crime of President Serrurier— perhaps the worst of all. So the people had to be forced."

"How many dead?" asked Wyatt grimly.

"Who knows? But how many shall be saved? Ten thousand? Twenty—thirty thousand? One must make a balance in these things."

Wyatt was silent. He knew he would have to live with this thing and that it would hurt. But he could still try to sway Favel in his decision to contain and destroy the Government army. He said, "Need there be more killing? Must you still stand and fight around St. Pierre? How many will you kill in the city, Julio Favel? Five thousand? Ten—fifteen thousand?"

"It is too late," said Favel austerely. "I cannot do otherwise if I wished. The evacuation took a long time—it is not yet complete—and my men will be lucky if they can get to their prepared positions in time." His voice became sardonic. "I am not a Christian—it is a luxury few honest politicians can afford—but I have justification in the Bible. The Lord God parted the waters and let the Israelites through the flood dry-shod; but he stayed his hand and drowned the pursuing Egyptians—every soldier, every horse, every chariot was destroyed in the Red Sea."

The truck pulled up at a check-point, beyond which Wyatt could see a long line of refugees debouching from a side road. A rebel officer came up and conferred with Favel, and a white man waved and hurried over. It was Causton. "You took your time," he said. "How far has the Government army got into the city?"

"I don't know," said Wyatt He climbed out of the truck. "What's happening up here?"

Causton indicated the refugees. "The last of the many," he said. "They should be all through in another fifteen minutes." He stretched his arms wide. "This is where Favel makes his stand—this is the eighty-foot contour line." The rising wind plucked at his shirt-sleeves. "I've got a hole already picked out for us—unless you want to push on up the Negrito."

"You're staying here, then?"

"Of course," said Causton in surprise. "This is where the action will be. Dawson is here, too ; he said he was waiting for you."

Wyatt turned and looked back at the city. In the distance he could see the sea, no longer a beaten silver plate but the dirty colour of uncleaned pewter. The southern sky was filled with the low iron-grey mass of the coming nimbostratus, bringing with it torrential rain and howling wind. Already it was perceptibly darker because of the lowering clouds and the smoke from the city.

Above the faint keening of the wind he could hear the sound of battle, mostly small-arms fire and hardly any artillery. The noise fluctuated as the wind gusted, sometimes seeming far away and sometimes very close. The ground sloped away down to the city, and between the top of the low ridge on which he was standing and the nearer houses there was not a soul to be seen.

"I'll stay here," he said abruptly. "Though I'm damned if I know why." Of course he *did* know. His desire was a curious amalgam of professional interest in the action of a hurricane on the sea in shallow waters and a macabre fascination at the sight of a doomed city and a doomed army. He looked up the road. "Where exactly is Favel making his stand?"

"On this ridge. There are positions dug in on the reverse slope—the men can nip down there when the weather gets really bad."

"I hope those holes are well drained," said Wyatt grimly.

"It's going to rain harder than you've seen it rain before. Any hole dug without provision for drainage is going to get filled up fast."

"Favel thought of that one," said Causton. "He's pretty bright."

"He asked me about rainfall," said Wyatt. "I suppose that was why."

Favell called, "Mr. Wyatt, headquarters has been established about three hundred yards up the road."

"I'm staying with Causton," said Wyatt, moving nearer the truck.

"As you wish." Favel's lips quirked. "There is nothing more you or I can do now, except perhaps to send a prayer to Hunraken or any other appropriate god." He spoke to his driver and the truck pulled into the thinning line of refugees.

"Let's join Dawson," said Causton. "We've established our new home just over there."

He led the way off the road and down the reverse side of the ridge, where they found Dawson sitting cross-legged by the side of a large foxhole. He looked pleased when he saw Wyatt, and said, "Well, hello! I thought you'd been captured again."

Wyatt looked at the foxhole. It had a drainage trench at the rear which was obviously going to be inadequate. "That wants deepening—and there should be two. Are there any spades around?"

"Those are in short supply," said Dawson. "But I'll see what I can find."

Wyatt looked along the ridge and saw that it was alive with men, a long, thin line of them burrowing into the earth like moles. At the top of the ridge overlooking the city others were busy, siting machine-guns, excavating more foxholes for cover against enemy fire rather than the coming wind, and keeping careful watch on the city in case Serrurier's men broke through. Causton said, "I hope you're right about the flooding. If it doesn't happen all hell will break loose. Favel abandoned his guns—he couldn't bring these out and the refugees, too."

Wyatt said, "Mabel is going to hit us head-on. There'll be floods."

"There'd better be. From a military point of view Serrurier is right on top. I'll bet he's crowing."

"He won't if he looks behind him—out to sea."

Dawson came back carrying a thin piece of sheet metal under his arm. "No spades; but this might do it."

Causton and Wyatt deepened the drainage trench and scooped out another while Dawson watched them. Wyatt looked up. "How are your hands?"

"Okay," said Dawson. "A doctor fixed them up."

"What are you hanging round here for?" asked Wyatt. "You should get away up the Negrito while you have the chance."

Dawson shook his head. "Have you seen those people? I've never seen a more beaten, dispirited crowd. I'm scared that if I joined them I'd get to feeling like that. Anyway, maybe I can help out here, somehow."

"What do you think you can do?" asked Causton. "You can't use your hands, so you can't fire a gun or dig a hole. I don't see the point of it."

Dawson shrugged. "I'm not running any more," he said stubbornly. "I've been running like hell for a long time, a lot of years. Well, I'm stopping right here on top of this ridge."

Causton looked across at Wyatt and raised his eyebrows, then smiled faintly, but he merely said, "I think that's all we can do here. Let's go up and see what trouble is coming."

The last of the people of St. Pierre had passed by on their way up into the Negrito Valley, but the road in the far distance was speckled with trudging figures making their way to high ground. The verdant greenness of the sugar-cane fields looked like a raging sea as the strengthening wind blew waves across the springy canes. Only the soldiers were left, and very few of those in the thin line of trenches scored across the ridge, but there would soon be more as the embattled army in St. Pierre retreated on this position.

Wyatt strode to the top of the ridge and dropped flat near a rebel soldier, who turned and grinned at him. He said, "What is happening, soldier?"

The man's grin widened. "There," he said, and stabbed out a finger. "They come soon—maybe ten minutes." He checked the breech of his rifle and laid some clips of ammunition before him.

Wyatt looked down the bare slope of the ridge towards the city. The sound of firing was very close and an occasional stray bullet whistled overhead. Soon he saw movement at the bottom of the slope and a group of men began to trudge up the hill, unhurriedly but making good time. From behind him an officer called out an order and the three men grouped round a machine-gun a dozen yards away got busy and swivelled the gun in the direction of the officer's pointing finger.

The men climbing the ridge reached the top and passed over. They were carrying a mortar which they assembled quickly on the reverse slope. Causton watched them and said critically. " Not many mortar bombs left."

More men were climbing the ridge now, moving steadily in disciplined retreat and covered by their comrades still fighting the confused battle among the houses below. Causton guessed he was witnessing the last jump in the controlled and planned leap-frogging movement which had brought Favel's defending force across St. Pierre, and he was impressed by the steady bearing of the men. This was no rout in undisciplined panic like the débâcle he had been involved in earlier, but an orderly withdrawal in the face of the enemy, one of the most difficult of military operations.

Wyatt, after casting a brief glance at the retreating men, had lifted his eyes to the south. The horizon was dark, nearly black, lit only by the dim flickering of distant lightning embedded in thick cloud, and the nearer nimbostratus was a sickly yellow, seemingly illuminated from the inside. The wind was backing to the west and was now much stronger. He estimated it to be force seven verging on force eight— about forty miles an hour and gusting up to fifty miles an hour. It was nothing to worry anyone who did not know what was coming and was merely a gale such as San Fernandez had known many times. Probably Rocambeau, if he was still in command, would welcome it as bringing rain to extinguish the many fires in the city.

The retreating soldiers were now streaming over the ridge and were marshalled by their non-coms into the firing line and issued with more ammunition. They lay on the crest of the ridge in the shallow foxholes that had been dug for them and again set their faces towards the oncoming enemy.

Causton nudged Wyatt. " Those houses down there—how high are they above sea-level?"

Wyatt considered. The ridge was not very high and the slope to the city was long. He said, " If this ridge is on the eighty-foot contour, then they shouldn't be more than fifty feet up."

"Then the tidal wave should wash as high as that, then?"

"It will," said Wyatt. "It will probably wash half-way up the slope."

Causton pulled at his lower lip. "I think the idea here is to pin the Government troops against those houses. They're three hundred yards away and the troops will have to attack uphill and across open ground. Maybe Favel will be able to do it, after all. But it'll be tricky disengaging the last of his men."

Dawson said, "I hope you're right, Wyatt. I hope this tidal wave of yours doesn't come boiling over this ridge. It would drown the lot of us." He shook his head and grinned in wonder. "Christ, what a position to be in—I must be nuts."

"Perhaps we're all light-headed," said Causton. "We're seeing something that's never been tried before—the use of a hurricane to smash an army. What a hell of a story this will be when—and if—I get out of here."

"It has been done before," said Wyatt. "Favel quoted a precedent—when Moses crossed the Red Sea with the Egyptians after him."

"That's right," said Causton. "I hadn't thought of that one. It's a damned good——" He pointed suddenly. "Look, something's happening down there."

A long line of men had emerged on to the slope, flitting about and on the move all the time, stopping only briefly to fire back at the houses. The machine-gun near-by cleared its throat in a coughing burst, then settled down to a steady chatter, and all the men along the ridge began to shoot, giving covering fire to the last of the rebel army retreating towards them. They had the advantage of height, little though it was, and could fire over the heads of their own men.

There was a sharp crack from behind as the mortar went off, and seconds later the bomb burst just short of the nearest house. There were more explosions among the houses, and from the rear came a louder report and the whistle of a shell as one of the few remaining guns fired. Again Causton heard that unearthly twittering in the air about him and pulled down his head below the level of the ridge. "The bastards haven't any *politesse*," he said. "They're shooting back."

The last of Favel's men came pouring over the ridge, to

stumble and collapse in the shelter of the reverse slope. They
had left some of their number behind—Wyatt could see three
crumpled heaps half-way up the slope, and he thought of the
sacrifices these men must have made to hold back the Government army until the city had been evacuated. The men
rested and got back their breath and then, after a drink of
water and a quick snack which was waiting for them, they
rejoined the line.

Meanwhile there was a pause. Desultory and sporadic firing
came from the houses, which had little or no effect, and the
rebels did not fire at all under strict instructions from their
officers—there was little enough ammunition left to waste any
of it. It was obvious that the Government general was regrouping in the cover of the city for the assault on the ridge.

In spite of the rapidly cooling air Causton sweated gently.
He said, " I hope to God we can hold them. When the attack
comes it's going to be a big one. Where's that damned
hurricane of yours, Wyatt?"

Wyatt's eyes were on the horizon. "It's coming," he said
calmly. "The wind is rising all the time. There are the rain
clouds coming up—the nimbostratus and the fractonimbus.
The fighting will stop pretty soon. No one can fight a battle in
a hurricane."

The wind was now fifty miles an hour, gusting to sixty, and
the smoke clouds over St. Pierre had been broken down into
a diffused haze driving before the wind. This made it difficult
to see the sea, but he managed to see the flecks of white out
there which indicated even higher winds.

"Here they come," said Causton, and flattened himself out
as the shooting from the houses suddenly increased to a
crescendo. A wave of soldiers in light blue uniforms emerged
at the foot of the slope and began to advance, the individual
men zig-zagging and changing direction abruptly, sometimes
dropping on one knee to fire. They came on quickly and when
they had advanced a hundred yards another wave broke from
the houses to buttress the assault.

"Jesus!" said Dawson in a choked voice. "There must be a
couple of thousand of them down there. Why the hell don't
we shoot?"

Not a shot came from the top of the ridge as the flood of
blue-clad men surged up the slope. The wind was now strong

enough to hamper them and Wyatt could see the fluttering of their clothing, and twice the black dot of a uniform cap as it was blown away. Some of the men lost their footing and, taken off balance, were pushed by the gusting wind, but still they came on, scuttling at the crouch and continually climbing higher.

It was not until the first of them were half-way up that a Very light soared up from the top of the ridge, to burst in red stars over the slope. Immediately pandemonium broke loose as the rebels opened up a concentrated fire. The rifles cracked, the machine-guns hammered, and from behind came the deeper cough of the few guns and mortars.

The oncoming wave of men shivered abruptly and then stopped dead. Causton saw a swathe of them cut down like wheat before the scythe as a defending machine-gun swivelled and chopped them with a moving blade of bullets, and all over that open ground men were falling, either dead, wounded or desperately seeking cover where there was none. He noted that half of Favel's machine-guns were firing on fixed lines so that the attackers were caught in a net stitched in the air with bullets—they would die if they advanced and they would die if they ran because in either event they would run right into the line of fire of the angled machine-guns.

Mortar bombs and shells dropped among the trapped men— Favel was firing his last ammunition with extravagant prodigality, staking everything on the coming hurricane. The earth shook and fountained with darkly blossoming trees and the clouds of smoke and dust were snatched by the wind and blown away. A pitifully thin fire came from below, perhaps there were few to shoot or perhaps those alive were too shattered to care.

For five minutes that seemed an eternity the uproar went on and then, suddenly, as though on command, the line of attackers broke and ebbed away, leaving a wrack of bodies behind to mark the highest level of the assault, a bare hundred yards from the crest of the ridge. And as they ran back in panic, so they still died, hit by rifle bullets, cut in two by the murderous machine-guns and blown to pieces by the mortar bombs. When all was still again the ground was littered with the shattered wreckage of what had been men.

"Oh, my God!" breathed Dawson. His face was pale and

sickly and he let out his breath with a shuddering sigh. "They must have lost a quarter of their men."

Causton stirred. "Serrurier must have taken over," he said quietly. "Rocambeau would never have made a damn'-fool frontal attack like that—not at this stage of the game." He turned and looked back at the mortar team just behind. "These boys have shot their bolt—they have no ammunition left. I don't know if we can stand another attack."

"There'll be no more attacks," said Wyatt with calm certitude. "As far as the fighting goes this war is over." He looked down the slope at the tumbled heaps of corpses. "I wish I could have said that half an hour ago, but it doesn't really make any difference. They'll all die now." He withdrew from the ridge and walked away towards the foxhole.

Down in St. Pierre thousands of men would be killed in the next few hours because he had told Favel of the approaching hurricane, and the guilt weighed heavily upon him. But he could not see what else he could have done.

And there was something else. He could not even look after the safety of a single girl. He did not know where Julie was—whether she was dead or alive or captured by Rocambeau's men. He had not properly seen her in his preoccupation with the hurricane, but now he saw her whole, and he found the tears running down his cheeks—not tears of self-pity, or even tears for Julie, but tears of blind rage at his stupidity and impotent futility.

Wyatt was very young for his years.

Causton listened to the fire-fight still crackling away to the left. "I hope he's right. When Favel was faced with a similar problem he outflanked the position." He jerked his head towards the distant sound of battle. "If Serrurier breaks through along there he'll come along the ridge rolling up these rebels like a carpet."

"I think Wyatt's right, though," said Dawson. "Look out to sea."

The city was lost in a writhing grey mist through which the fires burned redly, and the horizon was black. Streamers of low cloud fled overhead like wraiths in the blustering wind which had sharply increased in violence and was already raising its voice in a devil's yell. Lightning flickered briefly over the sea and a single drop of rain fell on Causton's hand.

He looked up. "It does look a bit dirty. God help sailors on a night like this."

"God help Serrurier and his army," said Dawson, staring down at St. Pierre.

Causton looked back to where Wyatt was sitting at the edge of the foxhole. "He's taking it badly—he thinks he's failed. He hasn't yet realized that perfection doesn't exist, the damned young fool. But he'll learn that life is a matter of horse-trading—a bit of bad for a lot of good."

"I hope he never does learn," said Dawson in a low voice. "I learned that lesson and it never did me any good." He looked Causton in the eye and, after a moment, Causton looked away.

II

Rawsthorne was not a young man and two days of exertion and life in the open had told on him. He could not move fast over the hilly ground—his lungs had long since lost their elasticity and his legs their driving power. The breath in his throat rasped painfully as he tried to keep up a good pace and the muscles of his thighs ached abominably.

But he was in better shape than Mrs. Warmington, whom the years of cream cakes and lack of exercise had softened to a doughy flesh. She panted and floundered behind him, her too generous curves bouncing with the effort, and all the time she moaned her misery in a wailing undertone, an obbligato to the keening of the rising wind.

In spite of her wounds, Julie was the fittest of the three. Although her legs were stiff and sore because of the bayonet jabs, her muscles were hard and tough and her breath came evenly as she followed Mrs. Warmington. The brisk sets of hard-played tennis now paid off and she had no difficulty in this rough scramble over the hills.

It was Rawsthorne who had made the plan. "It's no use going further west to escape the army," he said. "The ground is low about St. Michel—and we certainly can't stay here because Rocambeau might be beaten back again. We'll have to cut across the back of his army and go north over the hills —perhaps as far as the Negrito."

"How far is that?" asked Mrs. Warmington uneasily.

"Not far," said Rawsthorne reassuringly. "We'll have to

walk about eight miles before we're looking into the Negrito Valley." He did not say that those eight miles were over rough country, nor that the country would probably be alive with deserters.

Because Rawsthorne had doubts about his ability to climb the quarry cliff—and private, unexpressed doubts about Mrs. Warmington's expertise as a climber—they went down the track towards the main road, moving stealthily and keeping an eye open for trouble. They did not want to meet the guard who had disappeared in that direction. They left the track at the point where they had originally climbed up to the banana plantation, and Julie got a lump in her throat when she saw the imprint of Eumenides's shoe still visible in the dust.

The plantation seemed deserted, but they went with caution all the same, slipping through the rows of plants as quietly as they could. Rawsthorne led them to the hollow where they had dug the foxholes in the hope of finding a remnant of food and, more important, water. But there was nothing at all, just four empty holes and a litter of cans and bottles.

Julie looked at the hole that had been filled in and felt a great sorrow as she thought of the Greek. First we dig 'em, then we die in 'em. Eumenides had fulfilled the prophecy.

Rawsthorne said, " If it wasn't for the war I would recommend that we stay here." He cocked his head on one side. " Do you think the fighting is going away or not?"

Julie listened to the guns and shook her head. " It's difficult to say."

"Yes, it is," said Rawsthorne. " If Rocambeau is defeated again he'll be thrown back through here and we'll be back where we started."

Mrs. Warmington surveyed the hollow and shuddered. " Let's get away from this horrible place," she said in a trembling voice. " It frightens me."

And well it might, thought Julie; you killed a man here.

"We'll go north," said Rawsthorne. " Into this little valley and over the next ridge. We must be very careful, though ; there may be desperate men about."

So they went through the plantation, across the service road and, carefully avoiding the convict barracks, pushed on up the ridge on the other side. At first Rawsthorne kept up a cracking pace, but he did not have the stamina for it and gradually his pace slowed so that even Mrs. Warmington could keep up with him. The going was not difficult while they were on cultivated ground and in spite of their slower pace they made good time.

At the top of the first ridge they left the banana plantations and entered pineapple fields, where all was well as long as they walked between the rows and avoided the sharp, spiky leaves. But then they came to sugar-cane and, finding the thicket too hard to push through, had to cast about to find a road leading in the right direction. It was a narrow dusty track between the high green canes, which rustled and crackled under the press of the breeze. In spite of the breeze and the high feathery clouds which veiled and haloed the sun it was still very hot, and Julie fell into a daze as she mechanically plodded behind Mrs. Warmington.

They saw no one and seemed to be travelling through an empty land. The track dipped and rose but climbed higher all the time, and Julie, when she looked back, saw huts in the distance, but no smoke arose from these small settlements nor was there any sign of life. Where the tracks came out of the cane-fields they came upon more huts, and as soon as he saw them Rawsthorne held up his hand. "We must be careful," he whispered. "Better safe than sorry. Wait here."

Mrs. Warmington sat down on the spot and clutched her feet. "These shoes are crippling me," she said.

"Hush!" said Julie, looking at the huts through the cane. "There may be soldiers here—deserters."

Mrs. Warmington said no more, and Julie thought in astonishment: she is capable of being taught, after all. Then Rawsthorne came back. "It's all right," he said. "There isn't a soul here."

They emerged from the cane and moved among the huts, looking about. Mrs. Warmington stared at the crude rammed earth walls and the straw roofs and sniffed. "Pig-sties, that's all these are," she announced. "They're not even fit to keep pigs in."

Rawsthorne said, "I wonder if there's any water here. I could do with some."

"Let's look," said Julie, and went into one of the huts. It was sparsely furnished and very primitive, but also very clean. She went into a small cubicle-like room which had obviously been a pantry, to find it like Mother Hubbard's cupboard— swept bare. Going into another hut, she found it the same and when she came out in the central clearing she found that Rawsthorne had had no luck either.

"These people have run away," he said. "They've either taken all their valuables with them or buried them." He held up a bottle. "I found some rum, but I wouldn't recommend it as a thirst-quencher. Still, it may come in useful."

"Do you think they've run away from the war?" asked Julie. "Or the hurricane—like that old man near St. Michel?"

Rawsthorne rubbed his cheek and it made a scratchy sound. "That would be difficult to say. Off-hand, I'd say because of the war—it doesn't really matter.'

"These people must have got their water from somewhere," said Julie. "What about from down there?" She indicated a path that ran away downhill along the edge of the cane-field. "Shall we see?"

Rawsthorne hesitated. "I don't think we should hang about here—it's too dangerous. I think we should push on."

From the moment they entered the scrub the going was harder. The ground was poor and stony and the tormented trees clung to the hillside in a frozen frenzy of exposed roots over which they stumbled and fell continually. The hillside was steeper here and what little soil there had been had long since been washed to the bottom lands where the fertile plantations were. Underfoot was rock and dust and a sparse sprinkling of tough grass clinging in stubborn clumps wherever the stunted trees did not cut off the sun.

They came to the top of a ridge to find themselves confronted by yet another which was even higher and steeper. Julie looked down into the little depression. "I wonder if there's a stream down there."

They found a watercourse in the valley but it was dry with not a drop of moisture in it, so they pushed on again. Mrs. Warmington was now becoming very exhausted; she had long since lost her ebullience and her propensity for giving instructions had degenerated into an aptitude for grumbling. Julie prodded her relentlessly and without mercy, never allowing herself to forget the things this woman had done, and Rawsthorne ignored her complaints—he had enough to do in dragging his own ageing body up this terrible dusty hill.

When they got to the top they found the ground levelling into a plateau and it became less difficult. There was a thin covering of dubious soil and the vegetation was a little lusher.

They found another small gathering of huts in a clearing cut out of the scrub—this was deserted too, and again they found no water. Rawsthorne looked about at the small patch of maize and cane, and said, " I suppose they rely on rainfall. Well, they're going to get a lot of it presently—look back there."

The southern sky was dark with cloud and the sun was veiled in a thicker grey. It was perceptibly cooler and the breeze had increased to a definite wind. In the distance, seemingly very far away, they could still hear the thudding of the guns, and to Julie it seemed very much less impressive, although whether this was the effect of distance or whether there was less firing she had no way of knowing.

Rawsthorne was perturbed by the oncoming weather. " We can't stop now. All we have to do is to get over that." He pointed to an even higher ridge straight ahead. " On the other side of that is the Negrito."

" Oh, God! " said Mrs. Warmington. " I can't do it—I just *can't* do it."

" You must," said Rawsthorne. " We have to get on a northern slope, and it's on the other side. Come on."

Julie prodded Mrs. Warmington to her feet and they left the huts. She looked at her watch—it was four-thirty in the afternoon.

By five-thirty they had crossed the plateau and were half-way up the ridge, and the wind had strengthened to a gale. It seemed to be darkening much earlier than usual—the clouds were now thick overhead but no rain had fallen as yet. The wind plucked at them as they scrambled up, buffeting them mercilessly, and more than once one or other of them lost his footing and slid down in a miniature landslide of dust and small stones. The wind whipped the branches of the stunted trees, transforming them into dangerous flails, and the dry leaves were swept away along the ridge on the wings of the gale.

It seemed an eternity before they got to the top, and even then they could not see down into the Negrito. " We must . . . get down . . . other side," shouted Rawsthorne against the wind. " We mustn't . . . stay . . ." He choked as the wind caught him in the mouth, and staggered forward in a crouch.

Julie followed, kicking Mrs. Warmington before her, and they stumbled across the top of the hill, exposed to the raging violence of the growing hurricane. There was a thick, clabbery yellow light about them which seemed almost tangible, and the dust swirled up from the barren earth in streaming clouds. Julie could taste it as she ran, and felt the grittiness between her teeth.

At last they began to descend and could see the floor of the Negrito Valley a thousand feet below dimly illuminated in that unwholesome light. As soon as they dropped below the crest of the hill there was some relief from the wind and Rawsthorne stopped, looking down in amazement. "What the devil's happening down there?"

At first Julie could not see what he meant, but then she saw that the lower slopes were alive with movement and that thin columns of people were moving up from the valley. "All those people," she said in wonder. "Where did they come from?"

Rawsthorne gave an abrupt laugh. "There's only one place they could have come from—St. Pierre. Someone must have got them out." He frowned. "But the battle is still going on —I think. Can you hear the guns?"

"No," said Julie. "But we wouldn't—not in this wind."

"I wonder . . ." mused Rawsthorne. "I wonder if . . ." He did not finish his sentence but Julie caught the implication and her heart lifted. All the people down there must have left St. Pierre long before there was any indication that there was going to be a hurricane, and as far as she knew, there was only one man who believed the hurricane was on its way— an undeviating, obstinate, stubborn, thick-headed man— David Wyatt. He's alive, she thought, and found an unaccountable lump in her throat. *Thank God, he's alive!*

"I don't think we'd better go right down," said Rawsthorne. "Isn't that a ravine over there?"

There was a cleft in the hillside, an erosion scored deep by weather and water which would give shelter from the wind on three sides. They crossed the hillside diagonally and clambered down the steep sides of the ravine. Here the blast of wind was even less although they could hear it howl above their heads on the open hill, and they found a little hollow carved beneath a large rock, almost a cave, in which they could sit.

It was here that Rawsthorne finally collapsed. He had only been held together by his will to get the women to safety, and now, having done what he had set out to do, his body rebelled

against the punishment it had been forced to take. Julie
looked at his grey face and slack lips in alarm. " Are you all
right, Mr. Rawsthorne?"

" I'll be all right, my child." He managed a pallid smile
and moved his hand weakly. " In my pocket . . . bottle . . .
rum. Think we all . . . deserve . . . drink."

She found the rum, uncocked the bottle and held it to his
lips. The raw spirit seemed to do him good for some colour
came back to his cheeks, or so she thought, for it was difficult
to see in the fading light. She turned to Mrs. Warmington,
who was equally prostrated, and forced some of the rum
through her clenched teeth.

She was about to have some herself when there was an ear-
splitting crash and a dazzle of vivid blue light, followed by
the steady rolling of thunder. She rubbed her eyes and then
heard the rain, the heavy drops smacking the dusty ground.
Wriggling out of the little shelter she let it pour on her face
and opened her mouth to let the drops fall in. Thirstily she
soaked up the rain, through her mouth and through her skin,
and felt her shirt sticking wetly to her body. The water did
her more good than the rum would ever do.

III

The wind roared across St. Pierre, fanning the flames of the
burning buildings so that the fires jumped broad streets and
it seemed as though the whole city would be engulfed in an
unquenchable furnace.

Then the rain came and quenched it in fifteen minutes.

It rained over two inches in the first hour, a bitter, painful
downpour, the heavy drops driven by the wind and bursting
like shrapnel where they hit. Causton had never been *hurt* by
rain before: he had never thought that a water drop could be
so big, nor that it could hit with such paralysing force. At
first he mistook it for hail, but then he saw the splashes
exploding on the ground before the foxhole, and each drop
seemed to be as much as would fill a cup. He blinked and
shook the hair from his eyes, and then a drop hit him on the
side of the face with frightening force and he ducked to the
bottom of the hole.

Dawson moaned in pain and turned over on his side, holding his bandaged hands under his body to shield them. No one heard his sudden cry, not even Causton who crouched next to him, because the noise of the wind had risen to a savage howl drowning all other sounds.

Wyatt listened to the wind with professional and knowledge-able interest. He estimated that the wind-speed had suddenly risen to force twelve, the highest level on the Beaufort Scale. Old Admiral Beaufort had designed the scale for the use of sailing-ship captains and had been sensible about it—his force twelve was the wind-speed at which, in his opinion, no reason-able seaman would be found at sea if he could help it. Force twelve is sixty-five knots or seventy-four miles an hour, and the Admiral was not concerned about wind-speeds greater than that because to a sailing captain caught *in extremis* it would not matter either. There are no degrees in sudden death.

But times have changed since Admiral Beaufort and Wyatt, who had helped to change them, knew it very well. His con-cern here was not for the action of the wind on a sailing ship but on an island, on the buildings of the towns. A force twelve wind exerts a pressure of seventeen pounds on each square foot, over three tons on the sides of an average house. A reasonably well-built house could withstand that pressure, but this hurricane was not going to be reasonable.

The highest estimated wind-speed in Mabel's gusts had been 170 miles an hour, producing pressures of well over a hundred pounds a square foot. Enough to pick a man off his feet and hurl him through the air as far as the wind cared to take him. Enough to lean on the side of a house and cave it in. Enough to uproot a strong tree, to rip the surface soil from a field, to destroy a plantation, to level a shanty town to the raw earth from which it had sprung.

Wyatt, therefore, listened to the raging of the wind with unusual interest.

Meanwhile, he held his head down and sat with Causton and Dawson in a hole full of water. The two drains spouted like fire hoses at full pressure, yet the hole never emptied. It was like sitting in the middle of a river. All around them streams of water gushed down the slope of the ridge, inches deep, carving courses in the soft earth. Wyatt knew that would not last long—as the wind-speed increased it would become strong enough to lift up that surface water and make it airborne again in a driving mist of fine spray. That was one thing—no one he had heard of had died of thirst in a hurricane.

This rain, falling in millions of tons, was the engine which drove the monster. On every square mile over which the hurricane passed it would drop, on average, half a million tons of water, thus releasing vast quantities of heat to power the circular winds. It was a great turbine—three hundred miles in diameter and with almost unimaginable power.

Causton's thoughts were very different. For the first time in his life he was really frightened. In his work he covered the activities of men, and man, the political animal, he thought he understood. His beat was the world and he found himself in trouble-spots where students rioted in the streets of big cities and where bush wars flared in the green jungles. Other men covered the earthquakes, the tidal waves, the avalanches—the natural disasters.

He had always known that if he got into trouble he could somehow talk his way out of it because he was dealing with men and men could be reasoned with. Now, for the first time in his life, he found himself in trouble where talking was futile. One could no more reason with a hurricane than with a Bengal tiger; in fact, it was worse—one could at least shoot the tiger.

He had listened with vague interest to Wyatt's lecture on hurricanes back at Cap Sarrat Base, but he had been more curious about Wyatt than about the subject under discussion. Now he wished he had listened more closely and taken a keener interest. He nudged Wyatt, and shouted, "How long will this go on ?"

The dark shape of Wyatt turned towards him and he felt warm breath in his ear. "What did you say?"

He put his mouth next to Wyatt's ear, and bellowed, "How long will this go on?"

Wyatt turned again. "About eight hours—then we'll have a short rest."

"Then what happens?"

"Another ten hours, but coming from the opposite direction."

Causton was shocked at the length of time he would have to undergo this ordeal. He had been thinking in terms of three or four hours only. He shouted, " Will it get worse?"

It was difficult to detect any emotion in Wyatt's answering shout, but he thought he heard a cold humour. " It hasn't really started yet."

Causton crouched deeper in the hole with the rain flailing his head and thought in despair, how *can* it get worse?

The sun had set and it was pitchy black, the impenetrable darkness broken only by the lightning flashes which were becoming more frequent. Any thunder there might have been was lost in the general uproar of the gale, which, to Wyatt's ear, was taking on a sharper edge—the wind-speed was still increasing, although it was impossible to tell without instruments any reasonably exact speed. One thing was certain, though—it was pushed well over the further edge of the Beaufort Scale.

Wyatt thought with grim amusement of Causton's question: will it get worse? The man had no conception of the forces of nature. One could explode an atomic bomb in the middle of this hurricane and the puny added energy would be lost—swallowed up in the greater cataclysm. And this was not too bad. True, Mabel was a bad bitch, but there had been worse—and there had been far greater wind-speeds recorded.

He closed his mind to the howling of the wind. Now what was it—oh, yes—two hundred and thirty-one miles an hour recorded at Mount Washington before the instrument smashed—that was the record reading. And then there were the theoretical speeds of the tornadoes. No chance of recording those, of course—the very fast winds in excess of six hundred miles an hour—but it took a fast wind to drive a straw through an inch-thick plank of wood.

And yet tornadoes were small. Comparing a tornado with a hurricane was like comparing a fighter plane with a bomber—the fighter is faster, but the bomber has more total power. And a hurricane has immeasurably more power than any tornado, more power than any other wind system on earth. He remembered the really bad one that crossed the Atlantic when he had been a student in England back in 1953. It had been the very devil in the west Atlantic, but then it had crossed

and passed to the north of England, choking up the waters
of the North Sea very much as Mabel was doing down there
in Santego Bay. The dykes of Holland had been overwhelmed
and the waters had surged over East Anglia, bringing the
worst weather disaster Europe had known for hundreds of
years. The hurricane was the devil among winds.

Dawson held his hands to his chest. He was soaked to the
skin and felt that he would never be dry again. Had he not
liked game fishing, he thought that he would have spent the
rest of his life in some nice desert which never knew a wind
like this—say, Death Valley. But he did like fishing and these
were the waters for it and he knew that if he survived this
experience he would come back. On the other hand—why go
away at all? Why not settle in San Fernandez? There was
nothing to keep him in New York now and he might as well
live where he liked.

He grinned tightly as he thought that even in this he would
be continuing the programme mapped out for him by his
press agent, Wiseman, who had plotted mightily to cut
Hemingway's mantle to fit Dawson's different figure. Hadn't
Hemingway lived in Cuba? To hell with that! It was what
he wanted to do and he would do it.

Curiously enough, he was not frightened. The unexpected
courage he had found in facing up to Roseau and his thugs
followed by the catharsis of his confession to Wyatt had
released something within him, some fount of manhood that
had been blocked and diverted to corrupt ends. He should
have been frightened because this was the most frightening
thing that had ever happened to him, but he was not and the
knowledge filled him with strength.

Smeared with viscous mud, he lay in a water-filled hole
with the wind and the rain lashing him cruelly and was very
content.

The hurricane achieved its greatest strength just after midnight. The very noise itself was a fearsome thing, a malignant
terrifying howl of raw power that seared the mind. The rain
had slackened and there were no large drops, just an atomized
mist driving level with the ground at over a hundred miles
an hour, and, as Wyatt had predicted, the flooding ground
water had been lifted in the wind's rage.

Lightning now flashed continuously, illuminating the ridge in a blue glare, and once, when Wyatt lifted his eyes, he saw the dim outlines of the mountains, the Massif des Saints. They would resist the terrible wind; standing there rooted deep in the bowels of the earth they were a match for the hurricane which would batter its life away against them. Perhaps this slight barrier would take the vicious edge off Mabel and she would go on her way across the Caribbean only to die of the mortal wound she had received. Perhaps. But that would not help the agony of San Fernandez.

Again in a lightning flash he saw something huge and flat skim overhead like a spinning playing card. It struck the ground not five yards away from the foxhole and then took off again in sharply upward flight. He did not know what it was.

They lay in their hole, hugging to the thick, viscous mud at the bottom, deafened by the maniacal shriek of the storm, sodden to the skin and becoming colder as the wind evaporated the moisture from their clothing, and with their minds shattered by the intensity of the forces playing about them. Once Causton inadvertently lifted his arm above ground level and the wind caught his elbow and threw his arm forward with such power that he thought it was broken, and if the arm had been thrown against the shoulder joint instead of with it, it very well might have been.

Even Wyatt, who had a greater understanding of what was happening than the others, was astonished at this violence. Hitherto, when he had flown into the depths of hurricanes, he had felt a certain internal pride, not at his own bravery but at the intrepidity and technical expertise of mankind who could devise means of riding the whirlwind. But to encounter a hurricane without even the thin Duralumin walls of an aircraft to enfold a shrinking and vulnerable body was something else again. This was the first hurricane he had experienced from the ground and he would be a better meteorologist for it—if he lived through it, which he doubted.

Gradually they fell into a stupor. The brain—the mind—can only take so much battering and then it automatically raises its defences. Over the hours the incredible noise became so much a part of their environment that they ceased to hear it, their tensed bodies relaxed when the adrenalin stopped being pumped into the bloodstream and, beaten into tiredness, they fell into an uneasy doze, their limbs flaccid and sprawled in the mud.

At three in the morning the wind began to ease slightly and Wyatt, his expert ear attuned to the noise even in his unquiet inertness, noticed the change immediately. The rain had stopped completely and there was only the cruel wind left to hurt them, and even the wind was pausing and hesitating, sometimes gusting a little harder as though regretting a slight check, yet always dying a little more.

At four o'clock he stirred and looked at his watch, rubbing away the slimy mud from the dial so that he could see the luminous fingers. It was still pitch dark and there was less lightning, but now he could hear the thunder rolling among the clouds, which meant the wind was not as intense. He stirred his limbs and tentatively thrust his hand above ground-level. The wind pushed hard at it but not so much that he could not resist and he concluded that the wind-strength was now just back on the Beaufort Scale—a nice, comfortable storm.

Once roused, his mind was active again. He had an intense curiosity about what was happening on the other side of the ridge, and the itch to know got the better of him. He tested the strength of the wind again and thought it was not too bad, so he turned over and eased himself out of the foxhole on his belly and began to crawl up the slope. The wind plucked at him as he inched his way through the mud and it was worse than he thought it would be. There was a great difference between sitting in a hole and being caught in the open, and he knew that but for the foxhole they would not have survived. However, driven by the need to know, he persevered and, although it took him fifteen minutes to traverse the twenty yards to the top of the ridge, he made it safely and tumbled into water two feet deep in a foxhole that had been dug to protect against a storm of steel rather than a storm of air.

He rested for a few minutes in this shelter, glad to be out of the worst of the wind, then lifted his head and peered into the darkness, his hands cupped blinkerwise about his eyes. At first he saw nothing, but in a momentary lull before a gust he heard something that sounded very much like the sea and the splash of waves. He blinked and stared again and, in the glare of a lightning flash, he saw a terrifying sight.

Not more than two hundred yards away was a storm-driven sea with short and ugly waves, the tops sheered off by the fierce wind to blow horizontally across the waste of water. An eddy of wind blew spray into his face and he licked his lips and tasted salt water.

St. Pierre had been totally engulfed.

Nine

As the first grey light of dawn touched the sky Julie eased her cramped legs. She had tucked them under her body in an attempt to keep them reasonably dry and she had failed, but at least they were not lying under a running torrent of water. The wind had dropped with the coming of day; no longer did it howl ferociously nor did it fling cascades of water at them, but still the water ran in a muddied flood down the ravine.

It had been a bad night. In their little cave under the great rock they were well protected from the wind; it had roared about them but they were untouched by it. The water was something else. It came from above, slowly at first, and then in an increasing rush, pouring over the rock that protected them in a dirty brown waterfall which splashed with increasing violence at their feet, and carried with it the tree-fallen detritus which littered the ravine above.

As the wind grew in strength the wall of water before their faces was torn and shredded, blowing away in a fine spray across the hillside, and when the wind backed and eddied they were deluged as though someone had thrown a bathful of water into the cave. This happened a dozen times an hour with monotonous regularity.

Their shelter was cramped, small—and safe. The walls of the ravine rose sheer on each side and the wind, tearing over the open hillside, sometimes actually sucked the air out of this cleft at the height of the storm and left them gasping for breath for the space of a couple of heart-beats. But this did them no harm and indeed helped, because the water also went with the air, giving them momentary respite.

They could either sit with their legs oustretched and have

the waterfall pouring over their feet and the danger of bruises or worse as the flood swept down tree branches and stones, or they could sit on them and get cramp. They alternated between these methods, extending their legs when the cramp became too bad. The water was not too cold, for which Julie was thankful, and she thought hysterically that she was being washed so clean that she would never need to take another shower ever again. The very thought of the hissing spray of water in her bathroom at home made her feel physically sick.

At first they could talk quite comfortably. Rawsthorne was feeling better for the rum. He said, "We might get a bit wet here, but I think we'll be safe with this rock behind us."

"It won't move?" said Mrs. Warmington nervously.

"I doubt it. It seems to be firmly embedded—in fact, I think it's an outcropping of the bedrock." He looked through the waterfall before him. "And there's a good run-off for the water down there. It won't back up and drown us. All we have to do is sit here until it's all over."

Julie listened to the rising shriek of the wind overhead. "It seems as though the whole island will blow away."

Rawsthorne chuckled weakly. "It didn't in 1910—I see no reason why it should now."

Julie pulled her legs in from under the waterfall and tucked them underneath herself. "We've got enough water now—more than enough." She paused. "I wonder how all those people got out of St. Pierre in the middle of a battle."

"My guess is that Favel had something to do with it," said Rawsthorne thoughtfully. "He must have had because they are in the Negrito—his line of communication with the mountains."

"You think Dave Wyatt told him about the hurricane?"

"I hope so. It will mean that that young man is alive. But perhaps Favel had other sources of information; perhaps there was a message from the Base, or something like that."

"Yes," she said slowly, and lapsed into silence.

The rainfall increased and the torrent coursing down the ravine became a flood swirling over the top of the big rock. The wind strengthened and now it was that the eddies hurled back water into the cave, to leave them gasping for breath and clutching at the stone around them for fear of being washed away. Mrs. Warmington was very frightened and wanted to leave to find a safer place, but Julie held her back.

Rawsthorne was not feeling well. The events of the last two days had been too much for him, and his heart, not too good in normal circumstances, was beginning to act up. He doubted if he could have gone on any longer on their flight from the coast and was thankful for this respite, unpleasant though it was. He thought of Julie; this was a good girl, strong and tough when the necessity arose and not frightened of taking a chance. He could tell that young Wyatt was on her mind, and hoped that both of them would be preserved during this terrible night so that they could meet again and pick up their normal lives. But neither of them would be the same again, not in their approach to the world and, especially, to each other. He hoped they would find each other again.

As for that damned Warmington woman with her eternal nagging moan, he did not care if she was washed out of the cave there and then. It would at least leave more room and they would be rid of a strength-sapping incubus. He gasped as he was soaked by a solid wall of water and all thought left him save for the one desire for survival.

So the night went on, a terror measured in hours, a lukewarm hell of raging wind and blowing water. But the wind died towards morning and the cave became drier, no longer inundated every few minutes. Julie eased her cramped legs and thought that, incredibly enough, they were going to survive. She roused Rawsthorne, who said, " Yes, the wind is dropping. I think we'll be all right."

" My God, I'll be glad to get out of here," said Julie. " But I don't know if I'll be able to stand. The way I feel now I'll have to learn to walk all over again."

" Can we go out?" asked Mrs. Warmington with the first animation she had shown for a long time.

" Not yet. We'll wait until it's lighter, and the wind will have dropped even more by then." Rawsthorne hunched his shoulders and peered forward. " I have the idea it would be easy to get drowned out there, especially stumbling around in the dark."

So they stayed in their cramped shelter until the dim light revealed the sides of the ravine and then they went out into the glorious daylight, first Julie, ducking cautiously through the rapidly flowing curtain of water, then Mrs. Warmington, and finally Rawsthorne, who moved slowly and painfully as though his joints were seized up. Julie's hair streamed in the wind that swooped boisterously down the ravine—it was blowing hard by any standards but it was no hurricane.

She waded knee deep through the rushing water and gained the bank, then turned to give a hand to Mrs. Warmington, who squeaked and slipped. " My shoe," she cried. " I've lost my shoe."

But it was gone, washed swiftly down into the valley in the fast water. " Never mind," said Julie. " It doesn't really matter. Maybe we won't have to do much walking from now on."

Rawsthorne joined them, and said, " I wonder what's happening down in the valley. I think it's important we should find out."

Julie glanced at him. " If we climb out of here on to the hillside we should be able to see. I think we can get up that way."

The earth had turned to mud, thick and slimy, and it was not easy to climb out of the ravine. They floundered and slid on the slippery surface, but eventually reached the top by tugging on convenient branches and tough tufts of grass. Everything they grasped to pull themselves up by held firm —only the strong was left, the weak had been destroyed by the wind.

Even the barren hillside had been wrecked. Most of the low, gnarled trees showed white wood where branches had been ripped off, and there were raw scars in the red earth to show where entire trees had been uprooted. Hardly a tree had a leaf left on it and the whole slope had been scraped free of everything that could be moved.

Rawsthorne looked down into the valley. " My God!" he exclaimed. " Look at the Gran Negrito—the river!"

The whole floor of the valley was covered with a leaden sheet of water. The Negrito Valley drained most of the southern slopes of the Massif des Saints and the vast run-off of water from the mountains had met the floods pressing in from the mouth of the river in Santego Bay. The river had burst its banks, flooding the rich plantations, destroying roads and bridges and drowning farms. Even from where they stood, so high above the valley, and despite the dying wind, they could hear the murmur of the flood waters.

Mrs. Warmington was white-faced. "Isn't there *anyone* alive down there?"

"The people we saw were climbing the slopes," said Rawsthorne. "There's no reason to suppose they were caught in the floods."

"Let's go down and find out," suggested Julie.

"No!" said Rawsthorne sharply, and Julie looked at him in surprise. "I don't think we've finished with the hurricane yet."

"That's nonsense," said Mrs. Warmington. "The wind's dropping all the time. Of course it's over."

"You don't understand," said Rawsthorne. "I think we're in the eye of the hurricane. We've got the other half to go through yet."

"You mean we've got to go through all that again?" asked Julie in alarm.

Rawsthorne smiled ruefully. "I'm afraid we might have to."

"But you don't really know," said Mrs. Warmington. "You don't really know, do you?"

"Not really, but I don't think we ought to take a chance on it just yet. It all depends on whether we encountered the hurricane dead centre or whether it just caught us a glancing blow. If it hit us dead centre, then we're in the eye and we've still got to go through the other half. I'm not a good enough weather expert to tell, though; Wyatt could tell us if he were here."

"But he's not," said Mrs. Warmington. "He landed himself in gaol." She hobbled along the hillside and looked down. "There are people down there—I can see them moving."

Rawsthtorne and Julie crossed over to where she was standing and saw the hillside crawling with people on the lower slopes. Rawsthorne scratched his chin. "It's a good thing the valley is flooded, in a way," he said. "They can't get down into the bottom again where they might be caught in the winds next time round."

"Well, I'm going down there," said Mrs. Warmington with unexpected decision. "I'm sick and tired of being pushed around by you two. Besides, I'm *hungry*."

"Don't be a fool," said Julie. "Mr. Rawsthorne knows more about it than you do. You're safer up here."

"I'm going," said Mrs. Warmington, stepping out of arm's

reach. "And you're not going to stop me." Her chin quivered with foolish obduracy. "I think it's nonsense to say that we'll have another storm like the one we've just gone through—things don't happen that way. And there'll be food down there and I'm starving."

She edged away as Julie stepped forward. "And you blame me for everything, I know you do. You're always bullying me and hitting me—you wouldn't do it if I were stronger than you. I think it's disgraceful the way you hit a woman older than yourself. So I'm going—I'm going down to those people down there."

She darted away as Julie made a grab for her and went stumbling down the hill in an awkward limping gait due to the loss of her shoe. Rawsthorne called Julie back. "Oh, let the damned woman go; she's been a bloody nuisance all along and I'm glad to see her back."

Julie halted in mid-step and slowly walked up the hill again. "Do you think she'll be all right?" she asked doubtfully.

"I don't give a damn," said Rawsthorne tiredly. "She's meant nothing but trouble all along and I don't see why we should get ourselves killed trying to save her neck. We've done our best for her and we can't do more." He sat down on a rock and put his head in his hands. "God, but I'm tired."

Julie bent over him. "Are you all right?"

He lifted his head and gave her a wan smile. "I'm all right, my dear. There's nothing wrong with me but too many years of living. Sitting about in wet clothing isn't too good at my age." He looked down the hill. "She's out of sight now. She went in the wrong direction, too."

"What?"

Rawsthorne smiled and waved his hand in the direction of St. Pierre. "The St. Michel road is over there; it leaves St. Pierre and sticks to the upper slopes of the Negrito Valley before it climbs over to join the coast road. If we were leaving I would suggest going that way—I don't think that road would be flooded."

"But you don't think we ought to leave," Julie said in a flat statement.

"I don't. I fear we're going to have more wind. We've found a safe place here and we might as well stick to it as long as we're not entirely sure. If the wind doesn't blow up in another three or four hours then it will be safe to move."

"All right—we'll stay," said Julie. She moved over and looked down into the ravine at the smooth sheet of water flowing over the big rock. The cave was completely hidden behind that watery curtain. She laughed and turned back to Rawsthorne. "There's one good thing—we'll have a lot more room now that fat bitch has left us."

II

Wyatt stood on the top of the ridge overlooking St. Pierre and looked down over the city. The waters had ebbed since his first startled vision in the flash of lightning, yet half the city was still flooded. The climacteric wave had left nasty evidence of destruction, the wrack of a broken city at the high-water mark half-way up the ridge. The houses at the bottom from which the battle assault had been made just a few hours before had disappeared completely, as had the wide stretches of shanties in the middle distance. Only the core of the city was left standing—the few modern towers of steel and concrete and the older stone buildings which had already withstood more than one hurricane.

Away in the distance the radar tower that marked Cap Sarrat Base had vanished, cut down by the wind as a sickle cuts a stalk of grass. The Base itself was too low-lying and too far away to see if much more damage had been done, although Wyatt saw the glint of water where no water should be.

And of the Government army there was no sign—no movement at all from the ruined city.

Causton and Dawson walked up the slope behind Wyatt and joined him. "What a mess!" said Causton, and blew out his cheeks expressively. "I'm glad we got the population out." He dug into his pocket and produced a cigarette-lighter and a soggy packet of disintegrating cigarettes. "I always pride myself on being prepared. Here I have a waterproof lighter guaranteed to work under any conditions." He flicked it and a steady flame sprang forth. "But look at my damned cigarettes."

Dawson looked at the flame which burned without a flicker in the still air. "Are we really in the middle of this hurricane?"

Wyatt nodded. "Right in the eye. Another hour or so and we'll be in the thick of it again. I don't think Mabel will drop much more rain, though, not unless the bitch decides to stand still. They do that sometimes."

"Don't pile on the agony," pleaded Causton. "It's enough to know that we have another packet of trouble coming."

Dawson rubbed his ear awkwardly with a bandaged hand. "I've got a hell of an ear-ache."

"That's funny," said Causton. "So have I."

"It's the low pressure," said Wyatt. "Hold your nose and blow to equalize the pressure in the sinuses." He nodded towards the flooded city. "It's the low pressure that's keeping all that water there."

As the others made disgusting snorting sounds he looked up at the sky. There was a layer of cloud but he had no means of knowing how thick it was. He had heard that sometimes one could see blue skies in the eye of a hurricane, but he had never seen it himself nor had he ever encountered any who had, and he was inclined to dismiss it as one of the tall tales so often found in weather lore. He felt the sleeve of his shirt and found it was nearly dry. "Low pressure," he said. "And low humidity. You'll dry off quickly. Look at that." He nodded to where the ground was beginning to steam gently.

Causton was watching a group of men march down the slope towards St. Pierre. "Are you sure Favel knows that more wind is due?" he asked. "Those boys are in for trouble if they don't get back here smartly."

"He knows it," said Wyatt. "We discussed it. Let's go and see him—where did he say headquarters were?"

"Just up the road—it's not far." Causton chuckled suddenly. "Are we dressed to go visiting?"

Wyatt looked at the others—they were caked with sticky mud from head to foot and he looked down at himself to find the same. "I doubt if Favel will be in better condition," he said. "Come on."

They walked back, skirting their foxhole, and suddenly Causton stopped dead. "Good grief!" he breathed. "Look at that."

In the next foxhole lay a body with an outflung arm. The back of the hand which would normally be a rich brown in

colour was dirty grey as though all the blood had been
drained from it. But what had made Causton pause was the
fact that the body had no head, nor was there a head anywhere
to be seen.

"I think I know what did that," said Wyatt grimly. "Something came over when the wind was really bad and I think it
was a sheet of corrugated iron. It hit the ground just about
there, then took off again."

"But where's the goddam head?" said Dawson wildly.

"That will have blown away, too. It was a strong wind."

Dawson looked sick and walked away. Causton said with a
catch in his breath, "That . . . that could have happened to
any of us."

"It could," agreed Wyatt. "But it didn't. Come on."

His emotions were frozen. The sight of violent death did
not affect him and he found himself unstirred by the sight. He
had seen too much killing, too many men shot dead and
blown to bits. He had killed a man himself. Admittedly
Roseau deserved killing if ever a man did, but Wyatt was a
product of his environment and killing did not come easily to
him. The sight of an accidental death in a hurricane meant
nothing to him and left him untouched because he compared
it to the death of a whole army of men—also killed in a
hurricane, but not accidentally.

Headquarters was a series of holes in the ground. Headquarters was a hurry of officers. Headquarters was a widening
circle of effects with Favel as the calm centre.

Wyatt could not get to see him right away. He did not mind
because he had weighed up Favel and knew that he was not
forgotten and that Favel would see him in time. There were
priorities and Wyatt was not among the first. With Dawson,
he hovered on the outskirts of the busy group and watched
the activity. Men were being sent up into the Negrito in ever
increasing numbers and Wyatt hoped that Favel knew what
he was doing.

Causton had vanished, presumably about his work, although
what greater disasters he could find for his eager readers Wyatt
could not imagine. Dawson was impatient. "I don't see the
point in waiting round here," he grumbled. "We might as
well just sit back there in our hole."

"I wouldn't want Favel to make a mistake now," said Wyatt. "I'll stick around. You can go back if you like, and I'll join you later."

Dawson shrugged. "It's the same here as anywhere else." He did not move away.

After a while a tall Negro walked over to Wyatt and he was astonished to see, on closer inspection, that it was Manning, his face smeared with the all-pervading mud. "Julio would like to see you," he said. His face cracked into a grim smile. "You certainly called the shot on that hurricane."

"It's not over yet," said Wyatt shortly.

Manning nodded. "We know that. Julio is doing a hell of a lot of forward planning to see what we can salvage out of this mess. That's what he wants to talk to you about. After you've seen him I think I can find you a bite to eat; you're not likely to get any more until we've got rid of bloody Mabel."

Favel received Wyatt with the same quirk of the lips curved in a half smile. Incredibly, he looked smart in a clean shirt and had found time to wash, although his denim pants were stiff with mud. He said, "You did not exaggerate your hurricane, Mr. Wyatt. It was every bit as bad as your prognosis."

"It still is," said Wyatt bluntly. "What about those troops you've sent up the Negrito? They'll get caught if they're not careful."

Favel waved his hand. "A calculated risk. I find I am always forced to make these decisions. Let us look at the map."

It was the same map on which Wyatt had sketched out the supposedly safe areas up the Negrito. It was damp and mud-smeared and the crayon lines had run and blotched. Favel said, "Messengers were selected to report back here during this break in the hurricane and they've been coming in during the last half hour—not as many as I would have liked, but enough to let me know the broad situation."

His hand hovered over the map. "You were right to tell me to get the people off the valley bottom—the whole valley is flooded from the mouth to about here." He sketched in the area quickly with a pencil. "That's about eight miles. The Gran Negrito has broken its banks and there is yet more water coming from the mountains down the Gran Negrito itself and down the P'tit Negrito. The bridges are down and the roads under water."

"It looks a mess," said Wyatt.

"It is," agreed Favel. "This road, the short cut to St. Michel up the Negrito, is pretty clear. At this moment it's the only usable road in or out of St. Pierre. Because it hangs on the side of the valley it missed the floods. There are a few blockages such as fallen trees, and the three bridges are not too safe. Men are clearing it now and looking at the bridges. Other men are digging in for protection against the second half of the hurricane. As soon as it is over they will come out and do whatever final repairs are necessary on those bridges."

Wyatt nodded. That sounded reasonable.

"Now, Mr. Wyatt, how long is St. Pierre going to be flooded?"

Wyatt looked at the map. "What's this line you've drawn here?"

"That's the extent of flooding that exists now—as far as we can tell."

"That's on the twenty-foot contour—we can extend that." He took the pencil and drew a quick, curved line. "It takes in half the city, a lot of Cap Sarrat, all the flat ground including your airfield, but there's not much east of here because of the higher ground by this headland. All that area is under water because of the present low pressure, but as soon as Mabel moves on things will return to normal very quickly."

"So we can go down into St. Pierre as soon as the hurricane passes."

"Yes, there'll be nothing to stop you."

"What about the flooding in the Negrito—how long will that take to subside?"

Wyatt hesitated. "That's a different matter. The river has backed up from the mouth and it's still blocked by the floods here, in Santego Bay. Then there's all the water coming down from the mountains to make things worse and it will all have to drain to the sea on the original river course. That's going to take a long time, but I couldn't tell you exactly how long."

"That is what I thought," said Favel. "My estimate is a week, at least." His finger traced a line on the map. "I've sent a regiment up the St. Michel road with instructions to spread out along the ridge over the Negrito and dig in. When the hurricane has gone they will go down and conduct the people over the hills to the St. Michel road, bringing them back that way to avoid the floods."

He looked up. "Others of that regiment will push on to St. Michel and down the coast. There are other towns on San Fernandez besides St. Pierre. Sending those men now is risky but it will save two hours, and a lot of lives can be saved in two hours, Mr. Wyatt." He shook his head. "We will need medical supplies, blankets, clothing; we will need everything it takes to keep men alive."

"The Americans will be coming back," said Wyatt. "Commodore Brooks will have radioed for assistance. I'll bet they're loading up rescue planes in Miami right now."

"I hope so," said Favel. "Do you think the airfields will be usable?"

"That's hard to say. I should think your own airfield will be written off, but the military airfield at the Base is built for heavy weather so it may be all right."

"I will have it checked as soon as the hurricane is past," said Favel. "Thank you, Mr. Wyatt—you have been of great service. How much longer have we got?"

Wyatt stared at the grey sky, then looked at his watch. He felt the faintest of zephyrs blowing on his cheek. "Less than an hour," he said. "Call it three-quarters of an hour, then the wind will come again. I don't think there'll be much rain this time."

Favel smiled gently. "A small blessing."

Wyatt withdrew a little way and Manning thrust an open can into his hand. "You'd better eat while you can."

"Thanks." Wyatt looked about. "I don't see your pal Fuller around."

A look of pain crossed Manning's face. "He was killed," he said in a low voice. "He was wounded in the last attack and died during the hurricane."

Wyatt did not know what to say. To say that he was sorry would be inadequate, so he said nothing.

Manning said, "He was a good chap—not too good with his brains but dependable in a tight corner. I suppose you. could say I killed him—I got him into this."

It came to Wyatt that others had their guilts as well as he.

It did not make him feel any better, but it gave him more understanding. He said, "How did it all happen?"

"We were in the Congo," said Manning. "Working for Tshombe—mercenaries, you know. That job was coming to an end when I got on to this job and I asked Fuller if he'd like to come along. The pay was so bloody good that he jumped at it, not that good pay will do him much good now." He shrugged. "But that's in the game."

"What will you do now?"

"There's not much left here," said Manning. "Julio asked me to stay on, but I don't think he really wants a white man to play any big part in what's going to come next. I hear that there are jobs open in the Yemen, working for the Royalists—maybe I'll go across there."

Wyatt looked at this big man who spoke of working when he meant fighting. He said, "For God's sake, surely you can find easier ways of making a living?"

Manning said gently, "I don't think you've got it, after all. Sure, I get paid for fighting—most soldiers do—but I pick the side I fight for. Do you think I'd have fought for Serrurier?"

Wyatt groped for an apology and was glad to be interrupted by Dawson, who came over and said excitedly, "Hey, Dave, I think there's something you ought to know. One of these guys has just come down from the Negrito—he says there's an American woman up there. At least, that's what I think he says; this is a bastard of a language."

Wyatt swung round. "Which man?"

"That guy there—the one who's just finished talking to Favel."

Wyatt strode over and grasped the man's arm. "Did you see an American woman in the Negrito?" he asked in the island *patois*.

The man turned an exhausted face towards him and shook his head. "I was told of her. I did not see her."

"Where was this?"

"Beyond the St. Michel road—down in the valley."

Wyatt tugged at him urgently. "Can you show me on the map?"

The soldier nodded tiredly and suffered himself to be led. He bent over the map and laid down a black finger. "About there."

Wyatt looked at the map blankly and his heart sank. Julie would not be there, so far down in the Negrito. The party had gone along the coast road. He said, "Was this an old woman?—A young woman?—What colour hair?—How tall?"

The soldier blinked at him stupidly, and Dawson cut in, "Wait a minute, Dave. This guy's beat, he can hardly stand up." He pushed a bottle into the man's hand. "Have a snort of that, buster; it'll wake you up."

As the man drank from the neck of the rum bottle Dawson looked at the map. "If this guy has come from where he says he has, he's come a hell of a long way in double-quick time."

"It can't be Julie," said Wyatt in a depressed voice. "That note she left in the Imperiale said they were going up the coast road."

"Maybe they didn't," said Dawson. "Maybe they couldn't. There was a war going on at the time, remember." He stared at the map. "And if they did go to where they said, they'd get mixed up with Rocambeau's army when it retreated. If Rawsthorne had any sense he'd move them out of there fast. Look, Dave; if they travelled in a straight line over the hills they could get into the Negrito. It would be one hell of a tough trip, but it could be done."

Wyatt turned again to the man and questioned him again but it was no use. He had not seen the woman himself, he did not know her age or her colouring or anything more about her other than that an American woman had been seen up the Negrito. And Wyatt knew that this meant nothing, not even that she was American; to these people all whites were American.

He said drearily, "It could be anybody, but I can't take a chance. I'm going up there."

"Hey!" said Dawson in alarm, and made a grab at him but could not get a grip because of his ruined hands. Wyatt threw him off and began to run for the road.

Manning came up behind and said, "What's the matter?"

Dawson choked. "All hell's going to break loose in half an hour and that obstinate guy is taking off for the Negrito—he thinks his girl's up there."

"The Marlowe girl?"

Dawson looked after Wyatt. "That's the one. I'll be seeing you—someone's got to look after that crazy idiot."

He began to run after Wyatt, and Manning began to run too. They caught up with him and Manning said, " I'm a fool, but I think I can get you up there faster. Follow me."

That brought Wyatt up short. He stared at Manning, then followed, as Manning led the way back to a place further along the ridge where there was a low stone structure. " This is where I've been hiding during the hurricane," said Manning. " I've got my Land-Rover inside ; you can take it."

Wyatt went inside and Dawson said, " What is this thing?"

" An old gun casemate—perhaps three hundred years old. It was part of the harbour fortifications in the old days. Favel wouldn't come in here—he said he wouldn't have better protection than his men. But I had Fuller to look after."

They heard the engine roar as Wyatt started up and the Land-Rover backed out. Dawson jumped in, and Wyatt said, " There's no need for you to come."

Dawson grinned. " I'm a goddam lunatic, too. I've got to look after you—see you safely back to the nuthouse."

Wyatt shrugged and rammed the gear-lever home. Manning shouted, " Try not to bend it ; it belongs to me, not the corporation." He waved as the Land-Rover lurched past him, its wheels slipping in the mud, and he looked after it with a thoughtful expression. Then he went back to headquarters because Favel would need him.

When they got on to the road the going was easier, and Dawson said, " Where exactly are we going?"

The Land-Rover bounced as Wyatt pressed on the accelerator. " We go as high up overlooking the Negrito as we can," he said. " To where the road turns off to go down to the coast and St. Michel." That was where he and Julie had admired the view and drunk weak Planter's Punch. " I hope the bridges are all right."

Dawson tried to wedge himself in as the Land-Rover swung recklessly round a corner. " How far is it?"

" We ought to get there in half an hour if we can keep moving fast. Favel said the road was blocked by fallen trees but he was having it cleared."

They began to climb and Dawson looked over to the left. " Look at that goddam river. It's like a sea—the whole valley is under water."

Wyatt concentrated on the road. " That'll be salt water, or

very brackish. It won't do the agriculture any good." He did
not even give it a glance; all his attention was on his driving.
He was going too fast for this road with all its bends and
climbing turns, and he tended to swing wide at the corners.
It was unlikely there would be anything coming the other way
but the chance was there. It was a chance he was prepared
to take for the sake of speed.

Dawson twisted and looked back anxiously at the sea. It
was too far away for him to see the waves but he caught a
glimpse of the distant horizon before the Land-Rover slid
round the next corner. It was boiling with clouds—great black
masses of them splintered with lightning. He looked sideways
at Wyatt's set face and then up at the wet road coiling and
climbing along the southern slopes of the Negrito Valley. This
was going to be a near thing.

The plantations on each side were ruined, the soft banana
plants hammered flat into a pulpy mass on the ground by the
blast. The few plants left standing waved shredded leaves like
forlorn battle flags, but it was doubtful if they would survive
the next few hours. The sugar-cane was tougher; the stiff
canes still stood upright, rattling together in the rising wind,
but the verdant green top leaves had been stripped away completely and the plants would die.

They turned another corner and came upon men marching
stolidly up the road. Wyatt swerved to avoid running them
down, lost speed and cursed as he had to change gear. The
soldiers waved as they passed and Dawson waved back. He
hoped they found shelter soon—this was no time to be on an
open road.

Then they came to the first bridge spanning a watercourse
which was normally dry but which now gushed water, a
spouting torrent that filled the narrow gash in the hillside and
streamed under the bridge to hurl itself in a waterfall down
the almost sheer drop on the other side of the road. There
were men standing by the bridge who looked up in amazement
as the Land-Rover came up and Wyatt made a gesture with
his arm to indicate he was going to cross. A sergeant shrugged
and waved him forward and Wyatt drove slowly on to the
bridge.

Dawson looked over the side and held his breath. He
thought he could feel a vibration as the fast-moving water

slapped at the underside of the bridge and he hoped fervently that it had not been weakened. There was a sheer drop down there of over a hundred feet and he had never had a head for heights. He closed his eyes and opened them a few seconds later when he heard Wyatt change gear to find that the bridge was behind and they were continuing the long climb.

Every minute or so Wyatt flicked his eyes to the sky. The clouds were thickening as the southern edge of the hurricane drew closer. The few remaining banana plants still standing streamed their tattered leaves and he knew the big winds were not far away. He said, " We'll probably get to the top just in time."

" Then what?"

" Then we take shelter below the crest of the ridge. We should have company—Favel pushed a regiment up there."

" That seems goddam stupid to me," commented Dawson. " What good can it do?"

" It's a matter of organization. The people down in the valley don't have it—they're undisciplined and fragmented, and they'll be worse after the hurricane. If Favel can get a disciplined group among them as soon as the wind dies he can save a lot of lives. Ever heard of disaster shock?"

" I can't say I have."

" When a disaster hits a community the survivors come out in a state of shock. They're absolutely helpless. It's not merely a question of not wanting to help themselves—they're not capable of it. They just sit around, absolutely numb, while hundreds of them die for lack of minimal attention—things as elementary as putting a blanket over an injured man just don't get done even if the blanket's there. It's a sort of mass catalepsy."

" That sounds bad."

" It is bad. It happens in war, too, in cases of heavy bombing or shelling. The rescue organizations like the Red Cross or the special alpine teams they have in Switzerland know that the only thing to do is to get people in from the outside as fast as possible."

" But Favel's men aren't coming in from the outside," objected Dawson. " They'll have taken as big a battering as anyone else—apart from having just fought a war."

" Disaster shock doesn't have as great an effect on disciplined groups which have the backbone of an existing organization, but it hits civilian populations seriously. Favel's men can do a hell of a lot to help."

They crossed the second bridge. This was an old stone structure which stood as firm as the rock of which it was built.

Then, a few miles further on, they ran into water on the road, just a skim at first, but deepening to over six inches, which made the steering groggy. Wyatt cursed. "Favel told me this bloody road wasn't flooded."

The water was surging down the open hillside and flowing across the road, and the wind flickered across the surface of the water blowing away a fine mist. Wyatt drove slowly and came to the last bridge with the usual army squad about it. "What's happened?" he asked.

A sergeant turned and pointed upwards. "*Blanc*, there has been a landslide in the ravine."

"How's the bridge?"

The soldier shook his head. "Not good. You must not cross."

"Be damned to that," said Wyatt, and put the Land-Rover into gear. "I'm going over."

"Hey!" said Dawson, looking forward. "It doesn't look too good to me." This was a wooden trestle bridge and it seemed decidedly rickety. "That thing has moved—it's been slung sideways."

Wyatt drove forward and stopped just short of the bridge. The whole structure was leaning and the road bed was tilted at a definite angle. He put his head out of the side window and stared down at the supports in the gorge below and saw the raw wood where baulks had broken. The wind blew his hair into his eyes and he drew back and glanced at Dawson. "Shall we chance it?"

"Why not leave the truck here?" asked Dawson. "You said it wasn't far to the top."

"We might need the truck on the other side. I'll take it across—you get out and walk."

"Oh, nuts!" said Dawson. "Get on with it."

The Land-Rover crept forward on to the bridge and leaned the way the bridge was tilting. There was an ominous and long-drawn creak from somewhere beneath and then a sudden loud crack, and the whole bridge shuddered. Wyatt kept moving at the same slow pace even though the tilt was perceptibly worse. He eased out his breath as the front wheels touched solid ground and permitted his foot to press a little harder on the accelerator. The Land-Rover jolted and there came a rending crash from behind, and Wyatt frantically fed fuel to the engine. He felt the rear wheels spin under the sudden surge of power and then they were bowling along the road too fast for safety.

Dawson looked back and saw the gap where the bridge had been and he heard the tearing and rending sounds coming from the gorge. There were beads of sweat on his forehead as he said, " Favel isn't going to like that—you busted a bridge."

" It would have gone anyway," said Wyatt. His face was pale. " We haven't far to go."

III

When the wind strengthened again after that incredible calm Julie said dully, " You were right—it's coming again."

" I'm afraid so," said Rawsthorne. " A pity."

She grimaced. " Just when I'd got dry. Now we have to sit under that damn' waterfall again."

" It's better in the ravine," said Rawsthorne tiredly. " At least we have more protection than the people down there."

It had been so quiet during the lull that they had been able to hear the murmur of voices from the multitude below quite clearly. Sometimes it had been more than a murmur ; when the wind dropped they heard a woman screaming at the top of her voice, in long, sobbing wails. She had screamed for a long time, and then had stopped, her voice suddenly cut short. Julie looked at Rawsthorne, but neither of them made any comment.

She had expected the people to move, to come up the hill since the floods had made the valley impassable, but nothing like that happened. " They are West Indians," said Rawsthorne. " They know hurricanes—they know it is not over yet."

" I wonder what's happened to the war," said Julie.

" The war!" Rawsthorne gave a short laugh. " There will be no more war. Did Wyatt tell you what would happen to St. Pierre in the event of a hurricane?"

" He said there'd be flooding."

"We English have a fatal gift for understatement. If the armies were fighting in St. Pierre when the hurricane struck then there are no more armies. No Government army—no rebel army; a complete solution of conflict. There might be a few remnants left, of course; scattered and useless and in no condition to fight, but the war is over."

Julie looked up at the grey sky through leafless branches. She hoped Wyatt had got out of the city. Perhaps he was somewhere down there—on the lower slopes of the Negrito. She said, "What about the Base?"

Rawsthorne shook his head. "The same," he said. "Young Wyatt estimated that the big wave would completely cover the Base." He tried to cheer her up. "Commodore Brooks might have reconsidered and evacuated, you know. He's no fool."

"Dave tried to tell him, but he wouldn't listen. He couldn't get past that fool Schelling. I don't think he would evacuate; he's too stiff-necked—a real Navy man with his 'Damn the torpedoes!' and 'Damn the hurricanes!'"

"I didn't get that impression of Brooks," said Rawsthorne quietly. "And I knew him very well. He had a very difficult decision to make, and I'm sure he made the right one for all concerned."

Julie looked up at the tall tree on the edge of the ravine and saw the topmost branches straining in the wind. It would soon be time to take shelter again. She knew it was futile to worry about Wyatt—there was nothing she could do—and there was someone closer at hand to trouble her.

Rawsthorne looked very ill. His breathing was bad and, when he spoke, it seemed to strain him. His face had lost its floridity and turned the colour of dirty parchment and his eyes were shrunk into dark smudges in his head. He also had trouble in moving; his actions were slow and uncertain and there was a trembling palsy in his hands. To be soaked to the skin for the next few hours would be the worst thing that could happen to him.

She said again, "Wouldn't it be wiser to go down the hill?"

"There is no better shelter there than we have here. The ravine provides complete shelter from the wind."

"But the water . . ."

He smiled gently. "My dear, one would get just as wet anywhere else." He closed his eyes. "You're worried about me, aren't you?"

"I am," said Julie. "You don't look too good."

"I don't feel too well," he confessed. "It's an old complaint which I thought I'd got rid of. True, my doctor said I mustn't exert myself, but he didn't take account of wars and hurricanes."

"It's your heart, isn't it?"

He nodded. "Running over these hills is all very well for younger men. Don't worry, my dear; there is nothing you can do. I certainly don't intend to do any more running. I shall sit placidly under that waterfall and wait for the wind to stop." He opened his eyes and looked at her. "You have a great capacity for love, child. Wyatt is a very lucky man."

She coloured, then said softly, "I don't know if I'll ever see him again."

"Wyatt is a very stubborn man," said Rawsthorne. "If he has something to work towards he will not permit himself to be killed—it would interfere with his plans. He was very concerned about you, you know, the night the battle began. I don't know which was on his mind more, the hurricane or your safety." He patted her hand and she felt the tremble of his fingers. "He will be looking for you still."

The wind gusted among the leafless trees, drying the sudden tears that ran down her cheeks. She gulped and said, "I think it's time to go back into our hole; the wind's getting stronger."

Rawsthorne looked up. "I suppose we must go. It won't be pleasant out here when the wind really starts." He got to his feet, creaking almost audibly, and his steps were uncertain. He paused for a moment, and said, "A few minutes longer won't hurt. I don't relish that waterfall at all."

They walked over to the edge of the ravine and looked down. The water still coursed over the big rock, although perhaps not as strongly. Rawsthorne sighed. "It's not a comfortable bed for old bones like mine." The wind blew his sparse hair.

"I think we ought to go down," said Julie.

"In a moment, my dear." Rawsthorne turned to look over the windy hillside. "I thought I heard voices quite close— from up there." He pointed towards the top of the ridge in the direction of St. Pierre.

"I didn't hear anything," said Julie.

The wind rose to a greater violence, singing crazily among

the branches of the trees. "Perhaps it was just the wind," said
Rawsthorne. He smiled tightly. "Did you hear what I said
then? Just the wind! Rather silly of me to say that about a
hurricane, don't you think? All right, my dear; we'll go
down now. The wind *is* very strong."

He walked over to the tall tree and used it to lean on while
he felt for his footing on the edge of the ravine. Julie came
forward. "I'll give you a hand."

"It's all right." He lowered himself over the edge and
started to climb down, and Julie prepared to follow. There
was a roar like an express train as a squall of wind passed
overhead and an ominous creaking came from the tree.

Julie whirled and looked up. "Watch out!" she screamed.

The tree was not securely rooted; water pouring from
above had undercut the roots and the sudden hard pressure of
the wind was too much for them. The tree began to topple,
the roots wrenched themselves from the side of the ravine and
the bole of the tree came forward like a battering ram straight
at Rawsthorne.

Julie dashed forward and cannoned into him and, caught
off balance, he lost his footing and fell down among the
rocks. As it dropped the tree twisted and turned and a branch
caught Julie a glancing blow on the head. She staggered back
and the tree fell on top of her, crushing her legs painfully.
The world was suddenly a twisting, turning chaos of red pain,
and there were many crackling and popping noises as twigs
and branches snapped off short on violent contact with the
ground. Then all the noise faded away, even the howling of
the wind, and the redness became grey and finally a total
black.

At first, Rawsthorne did not know what had happened. He
heard Julie's shout and then found himself thrust into space.
He was thoroughly winded by his fall into the ravine and lay
for a while struggling for breath. There was a tightness in
his chest, an old enemy which presaged no good, and he knew
he must not move very much or his heart would begin to go
back on him. But after a while, when he began to breathe
more easily, he sat up and looked at the tangle of branches on
the edge of the ravine.

"Julie!" he called. "Are you all right?"

His voice was painfully thin and lost in the suddenly risen
wind. He shouted again and again but heard no reply. He

looked up in despair at the wall of ravine, knowing that he must force himself to climb it, and wondered hazily if he would make it. Slowly he began to climb, nursing his ebbing strength and resting often when he found a firm footing.

He nearly made it to the top.

As he stretched out his hand to grasp a firm rock on the lip of the ravine he cried out in pain. It felt as though some vicious enemy had thrust a red-hot sword into his chest and his heart seemed to swell and break asunder. He cried out once more at the awful agony and fell back into the ravine, where he lay with the torrent of water lapping at his hair.

Ten

It seemed to Dawson that the second half of the hurricane was not as bad as the first half, but perhaps that was because there was little rain. Still, it was bad enough. When Wyatt left the road he had driven the Land-Rover into the rough bush on the hillside and had found an almost imperceptible dip in the ground. This was the best he could do to ensure the safety of their vehicle.

Dawson said, "Why not stay inside?"

Wyatt disillusioned him. "It wouldn't take much to push it over on to its side even though I've jammed it among the trees. We can't risk it."

So Dawson gave up hope of being out of the wind and rain and they began looking for personal shelter further along the hillside. The wind was already bad and steadily increased in strength and in the more violent gusts they were hard put to it to retain their footing. Presently they encountered the outlying flank of the regiment that Favel had sent to the ridge above the Negrito. The men were digging in and Wyatt was able to borrow an entrenching tool to do a bit of burrowing himself.

Digging in was harder than it had been outside St. Pierre; the ground was hard and stony with bedrock not far beneath the thin layer of poor soil and all he could manage was a shallow scrape. But he took as much advantage of inequalities of the ground as he could and chose a place where there was an outcropping of rock to windward which would give immovable protection.

When he had finished he said to Dawson, "You stay here. I'm going to see if I can find one of the officers of this crowd."

Dawson huddled behind the rock and looked apprehensively at the sky. "Take it easy—that's no spring zephyr you're walking in."

Wyatt crept away, keeping very close to the ground. The wind closed about him like a giant's hand and tried to pick him up and shake him, but he flattened out to elude its grip and crawled on his belly to the nearest foxhole, where he found a curled-up bundle of clothing which, when straightened out, would be a soldier.

"Where's your officer?" he yelled.

A thumb jerked, indicating that he should go further along the hillside.

"How far?"

Spread fingers said three hundred feet—or was it metres? A long way in either case. Puzzled brown eyes watched Wyatt as he crawled away and then were shrouded in a coat as the wind blew harder.

It took Wyatt a long time to find an officer, but when he did so he recognized him as one he had seen in Favel's headquarters. Better still, the officer recognized Wyatt and welcomed him with a white-toothed grin. "'Allo, ti blanc," he shouted. "Come down."

Wyatt dropped into the foxhole and jammed himself next to the officer. He regained his breath, then said, "Have you seen a white woman round here?"

"I have seen no one. There is no one this high up the hillside but the regiment." He grinned widely. "Just unfortunate soldiers."

Wyatt was disappointed even though he had not really expected good news. He said, "Where are the people—and how are they taking this?"

"Down there," said the officer. "Near the bottom of the valley. I don't know how they are—we didn't have time to find out. I sent some men down there but they didn't come back."

Wyatt nodded. The regiment had done a magnificent job—a forced march of nearly ten miles and then a frantic burrowing into the ground, all in two hours. It was too much to expect them to have done more.

The officer said, "But I expected to find some of them up here."

"It's more exposed at this height," said Wyatt. "They're safer down there. I don't suppose they'll get a wind much above eighty or ninety miles an hour. Up here it's different. How do you think your men will take it?"

"We will be all right," said the officer stiffly. "We are soldiers of Julio Favel. There have been worse things than wind."

"No doubt," said Wyatt. "But the wind is bad enough."

The officer nodded his agreement vigorously, then he said, "My name is André Delorme. I had a plantation higher up the Negrito—I will get it back now that Serrurier is gone. You must come and see me, *ti* Wyatt, when this is over. You will always be welcome—you will be welcome anywhere in San Fernandez."

"Thank you," said Wyatt. "But I don't know if I'll stay."

Delorme opened his eyes wide in surprise. "But why not? You saved the people of St. Pierre ; you showed us how to kill Serrurier. You will be a great man here—they will make you a statue better than the one of Serrurier in the Place de la Libération Noire. It is better to make a statue to one who saves lives."

"Saves lives?" echoed Wyatt sardonically. "But you say I showed you how to kill Serrurier—and his whole army."

"That is different." Delorme shrugged. "Julio Favel told me you saw Serrurier and he did not believe you when you said there would be a hurricane."

"That is so."

"Then it is his own fault he is dead. He was stupid."

"I must get back," said Wyatt. "I have a friend."

"Better you stay here," said Delorme, raising his head to listen to the wind.

"No, he is expecting me."

"All right, *ti* Wyatt ; but come and see me at La Carrière when this is over." He held out a muscular brown hand which Wyatt gripped. "You must not leave San Fernandez, *ti* Wyatt ; you must stay and show us what to do when the hurricane comes again." He grinned. "We are not always fighting in San Fernandez—only when it is necessary."

Wyatt climbed out of the foxhole and gasped as the wind buffeted him. He had been tempted to stay with Delorme but he knew he had to get back. If Dawson got into trouble he could not do much to help himself with his injured hands and Wyatt wanted to be with him. It took him over half an hour to find Dawson and he was exhausted as he climbed round the outcrop and tumbled into the shallow hole.

" I thought you'd been blown away," shouted Dawson as he rearranged his limbs. " What's going on?"

" Nothing much. There's been no sign of Julie or Mrs. Warmington. They're probably down on the lower slopes, and it's just as well."

" How far are we from the map position that guy gave us back in St. Pierre?"

" It's a little over a mile up the valley."

Dawson pulled his jacket about his chest and huddled against the rock. " We'll just have to sit this one out, then."

He had been doing a lot of thinking in Wyatt's absence, planning what to do when the hurricane was over. He would not stay in St. Pierre ; he would go right back to New York and rearrange his affairs. Then he would come back to San Fernandez, buy a house overlooking the sea, and buy a boat and do a lot of fishing. And write a book once in a while. His last three books had not been too good ; they had sold because of Wiseman's jazzy publicity, but in his heart he knew they were not good books even though the critics had let them by. He wondered why he had lost his steam and had been troubled about it, but now he knew he could write again as well, or better, than he had ever done.

He smiled slightly as he thought of his agent. Wiseman would have already written a lot of junk about Big Jim Dawson, the great hero, practically saving San Fernandez single-handed, but he wouldn't really give a damn whether Dawson was alive or dead—in fact, if Dawson had been killed it would be a red-hot story. Dawson would take great pleasure in reading all the press releases and then tearing them up and littering Wiseman's desk with the fragments. This was one episode in his life that wasn't going to be dirtied and twisted for profit by a conniving press agent. Or a conniving and bastardly writer, for that matter.

Maybe he would write the story of the last few days himself. He had always wanted to tackle a great non-fiction subject and this was it. He would tell the story of Commodore Brooks, of Serrurier and Favel, of Julie Marlowe and Eumenides Papegaikos, and of the thousands of people caught in the double disaster of war and wind. And, of course, it would be the story of Wyatt. There would be little, if anything, in it of himself. He had done nothing but get Wyatt in gaol and cause trouble all round. That would go in the book—but no false heroics, none of Wiseman's synthetic glorification. It would be a good book.

He twisted and lay closer to the ground in an effort to avoid the driving wind.

The day wore on and again San Fernandez was subject to the agony of the hurricane. Once more the big wind tormented the island, sweeping in from the sea like a destroying angel and battering furiously at the central core of mountains as though it would sweep even those back into the sea from where they had come. Perhaps the hurricane did contribute towards the time when this small piece of land would be finally obliterated —a landslide here, a new watercourse gouged in the earth there, and a fraction of a millimetre removed from the top of the highest mountain in the Massif des Saints. But the land would survive many more hurricanes before being finally defeated.

Life was more vulnerable than inanimate rock. The soft green plants were uprooted, torn from the soil to fly on the wind ; the trees broke, and even the tough grasses, stubbornly clumped with long spreading roots, felt the very earth dissolve beneath. The animals of the mountains died in hundreds ; the wild pig was flung from the precipice to spill its brains against the stone, the wild dog whimpered in its rocky shelter and scratched futilely against the earthfall that sealed the entrance, and the birds were blown from the trees to be whirled away in the blast and to drown in the far sea.

And the people?

On the slopes of the Negrito alone were almost 60,000 exposed men, women and children. Many died. The old and tired died of exposure, and the young and fit died of the violence of air. Some died of stupidity, not having the sense to find proper shelter, and some died in spite of their intelligence through mere ill-luck. Others died of illness—those with weak hearts, weak chests and other ailments. Some, even, died

of shock; perhaps one can say that these died of surprise at
the raw violence of the world in which they lived.

But not as many died as would have perished if they had
stayed in the ruined city of St. Pierre.

For ten hours the storm raged at the island—the hurricane—
the big wind. Ten hours, every minute of which was a stupe-
fying eternity of shattering noise and hammering air. There
was nothing left to do except to cower closer to the earth and
hope to survive. Wyatt and Dawson crouched in their shallow
trench behind the rock and, as Dawson had said, they " sat
this one out."

At first Wyatt thought in some astonishment of what
Delorme had said, and he smiled sardonically. So this was
how legends were created. He was to be cast as a saviour, a
hero of San Fernandez—the man who had saved a whole
population and won a war. He would be praised for the good
he had done and the bad he had been unable to prevent.
Obviously Delorme had been quite sincere. To him, Serrurier
and all who followed him had been devils incarnate and deserved no better than they had received. But to Wyatt, Serrurier had been sick with madness, and his followers, while
misguided, had been men like any others, and he had been the
one who had shown Favel the trap into which they might be
led. Others might forgive him, or even not realize there was
anything to forgive, but he would never forgive himself.

And then the hurricane drowned all thought and he lay
there supine, waiting patiently for the time when he would
be allowed to rouse himself to action and go down into the
valley in search of the one person in the world he wanted to
bring out in safety—Julie Marlowe.

The hurricane reached its height at eleven in the morning and
from that time the wind began to decrease in violence very
slowly. Wyatt knew there would not be any sudden drop in
wind-speed as when the eye of the hurricane came over the
island; the wind would quieten over a period of hours and
would remain blustery for quite a long time.

It was not until three in the afternoon that it became safe
enough for a man to stand in the open, and even then it was
risky but Wyatt was in no mood for waiting any longer. He
said to Dawson, " I'm going into the valley now."

" Think it's safe?"

"Safe enough."

"Okay," said Dawson, sitting up. "Which way do we go?"

"It will be best to go right down, and then across the lower slopes." Wyatt turned and looked across the hillside in the direction of Delorme's foxhole. "I'm going to have a word with that officer again."

They walked gingerly across the slope and Wyatt bent down and shouted to Delorme, "I'd wait another hour before you get your men out."

Delorme looked up. His face was tired and his voice was husky as he said, "Are you going down now?"

"Yes."

"Then so will we," said Delorme. He heaved himself up and groped in his pocket. "Those people down there might not be able to wait another hour." He blew shrilly on a whistle and slowly the hillside stirred as his men emerged from a multitude of holes and crevices. One of his sergeants came up and Delorme issued a rapid string of instructions.

Wyatt said, "I'd take it easy on the way down—it's not so difficult to break a leg. If you come across any white people I'd be glad to know."

Delorme smiled. "Favel said we were to watch for a Miss Marlowe. He said you were worried about her."

"Did he?" said Wyatt in surprise. "I wonder how he knew."

"Favel knows everything," said Delorme with pride. "He misses nothing. I think he talked with the other Englishman—Causton."

"I'll have to thank him."

Delorme shook his head. "We owe you a lot, *ti* Wyatt; what else could we do? If I find Miss Marlowe I will let you know."

"Thanks." Wyatt looked at Delorme and knew he had changed his mind. "And I'll certainly come to see you at your plantation. Where did you say it was?"

"Up the Negrito—at La Carrière." Delorme grinned. "But wait until I have cleaned it up and re-planted—it will not look good now."

"I'll wait," promised Wyatt, and turned away.

It was not easy going down the hill. The wind plucked at them viciously and the surface had been loosened at the height

of the storm so that small landslides were easy to start. There
were many fallen trees round which they had to make their
way, and the ripped-up trees left gaping holes. It was three-
quarters of an hour before they reached the first of the survivors, a huddle of bodies lying in a small depression. The
wind was still fierce and they had not yet stirred.

Dawson looked at them with an expression of horror.
" They're dead," he said. " The whole lot of them are dead."

Wyatt stepped down and shook the nearest shoulder. Slowly
the man lifted his head and looked at Wyatt with a vacant
expression, then he curled up again as Wyatt let go. " They'll
be all right," said Wyatt. " Let's push on. The army will
look after them."

Dawson looked up the hill. " They're coming down now."
He pointed through the bare trees to the long line of men
descending the slope.

They went further down the hill and saw more and more
people, a scattering of bodies among the trees looking like
bundles of old clothes that had been carelessly cast away.
None of them moved, and from time to time Wyatt investi-
gated more closely. He said to Dawson, " They're all alive, but
they need attention. They have no greater drive than to
survive, and they don't know if they *have* survived yet."

" Is this disaster shock?"

" This is it," said Wyatt. " I've never seen it before; I've
just read about it in accounts of hurricanes." He straightened
up from the woman he was examining. " A person has to
have a greater purpose than mere survival to resist it—a purpose like *they* have." He indicated the soldiers coming down
the hill. " Let's move on; there's nothing we can do here that
can't be done better by Favel's men. We'll go right down to
the water and then up the valley."

At the water's edge they found their first corpses, those
drowned and cast ashore at the rim of this strange new lake.
And they found the first survivors to have any constructive
life in them, a few men and women looking about anxiously,
probably for members of their families. They wandered about
like zombies and when Wyatt spoke to them they would not
—or could not—answer. He gave up, and said, " Let's go up
the valley to where that soldier reported the white woman."

It was a harrowing journey. After they had gone half a
mile Dawson looked about and said, " What a mess! What a

hopeless, goddam mess!" He pointed to a woman who was hugging a child in her arms ; the child was obviously dead—the head hung unnaturally on one side like that of a broken-jointed doll—but the woman seemed not to be aware of it. "What can you do about a thing like that?" he asked.

"We can't do anything," said Wyatt. "It's best to leave her to her own people."

Dawson looked back along the hill. "But there are thousands here—what can one regiment of men do? There are no medical supplies, no doctors, no hospitals left standing in St. Pierre. A lot of these people are going to die—even those who have survived so far."

"There are a lot of people on the other side of the valley, too," said Wyatt, pointing across the flood. "It's like this all along the Negrito—on both sides."

The hillside heaved with slow, torpid movement as the inhabitants of St. Pierre came to the tired realization that their agony was over. Favel's men were now among them, but there was little they could do beyond separating the living from the dead, and the men who had enough first-aid knowledge to be able to splint a broken limb were kept very busy.

Wyatt said hopelessly, "How can we find one person in this lot?"

"Julie's white," said Dawson. "She ought to stand out."

"A lot of these people are as white as we are," said Wyatt glumly. "Let's get on."

They took to the slopes again where an incursion of the flood crept inland, and Wyatt paused constantly to ask the more alert-seeming survivors if they had seen a white woman. Some did not answer, others replied with curses, and others were slow and incoherent in their replies—but none knew of a white woman. Once Wyatt yelled, "There she is!" and plunged back down the hill to grasp a woman by the arm. She turned and looked at him, revealing the creamy skin of an octoroon, and he let her arm fall limply.

At last they arrived at their goal and started a more systematic search, patrolling up and down the hill and looking very closely at each group of people. They searched for nearly an hour and did not find Julie or any other white person, male or female. Dawson was sickened by what he saw, and estimated that if what he saw was a fair sample there must have been a thousand killed on the one side of the Negrito alone—and the injured were beyond computation.

The people seemed unable to fight their way clear of the state of shock into which they had been plunged. The air was alive with the moaning and screaming of the injured, while the fit either just sat looking into space or moved aimlessly with the gait of tortoises. Only a minute few seemed to have recovered their initiative enough to leave the hillside or help in the rescue work.

Wyatt and Dawson met again and Dawson shook his head heavily in response to Wyatt's inquiring and wild-eyed look. "The man can't have made a mistake," said Wyatt frantically. "He *can't* have."

"All we can do is keep on looking," said Dawson. "There's nothing else we can do."

"We *could* go over to the coast road. That's where they went in the first place. That we *know*."

"We'd better finish checking here first," said Dawson stolidly. He looked over Wyatt's shoulder. "Hey, there's one of Favel's boys coming this way—it looks as though he wants us."

Wyatt spun on his heel as the soldier ran up. "You looking for a *blanc*?" asked the man.

"A woman?" asked Wyatt tersely.

"That's right; she's over there—just over the rise."

"Come on," shouted Wyatt and started to run, with Dawson close behind. They came to the top of the slight rise and looked down at the couple of hundred people, some of whom raised inquiring black faces and rolling eyes in their direction.

"There!" jerked out Dawson. "Over there." He stopped and said quietly, "It's the Warmington woman."

"She'll know where Julie is," said Wyatt exultantly, and ran down the slope. He pushed his way among the people and reached out to grasp Mrs. Warmington's arm. "You're safe," he said. "Where's Julie—Miss Marlowe?"

Mrs. Warmington looked up at him and burst into tears. "Oh, thank God—thank God for a white face. Am I glad to see you!"

"What happened to Julie—and the others?"

Her face crumpled. "They killed him," she said hysterically. "They shot him and stabbed a bayonet in his back . . . again . . . and again. My God . . . the blood . . ."

Wyatt went cold. "Who was killed? Rawsthorne or Papegaikos?" he demanded urgently.

Mrs. Warmington looked at the backs of her hands. "There was a lot of blood," she said with unnatural quietness. "It was very red on the grass."

Wyatt held himself in with an effort. "Who . . . was . . . killed?"

She looked up. "The Greek. They blamed me for it. It wasn't my fault ; it wasn't my fault at all. I had to do it. But they blamed me."

Dawson said, "Who blamed you?"

"That girl—that chit of a girl. She said I killed him, but I never did. He was killed by a soldier with a gun and a bayonet."

"Where is Julie now?" asked Wyatt tensely.

"I don't know," said Mrs. Warmington shrilly. "And I don't care. She kept on hitting me, so I ran away. I was frightened she'd kill me—she said she would."

Wyatt looked at Dawson in shocked surprise, then he said dangerously softly, "Where did you run from?"

"We came from the other side, near the sea," she said. "That's where we were locked up. Then I ran away. There was a river and a waterfall—we all got wet." She shivered. "I thought I'd get pneumonia."

"Is there a river between here and the coast?" asked Dawson.

Wyatt shook his head. "No." Mrs. Warmington was obviously in a state of shock and would have to be treated with kid gloves if they were going to get anything out of her. He said gently, "Where was the river?"

"On the top of a hill," said Mrs. Warmington incomprehensibly. Dawson sighed audibly and she looked up at him. "Why should I tell you where they are? They'll only tell you a lot of lies about me," she said spitefully. "I'm not going to tell you anything." She clenched her fists and the nails dug into her palms. "I hope she dies like she meant me to."

Dawson tapped Wyatt on the shoulder. "Come over here," he said. Wyatt was looking horrified at Mrs. Warmington, but he backed away under Dawson's pressure until they stood a few paces away from her. Dawson said, "I don't know what this is all about. I think that woman has gone crazy."

"She's raving mad," said Wyatt. He was trembling.

"Maybe—but she knows where Julie is all right. Something's thrown a hell of a scare into her, and it wasn't the hurricane, although that might have tipped her over the edge. Maybe she *did* kill Eumenides and Julie saw her do it—that means she's scared of a murder charge. She may be crazy, but I think she's crazy like a fox—faking it up, I mean."

"We've got to get it out of her," said Wyatt. "But how?"

"Leave it to me," said Dawson savagely. "You're an English gentleman—you wouldn't know how to handle her kind. Now, me—I'm an eighteen-carat diamond-studded American son-of-a-bitch—I'll get it out of her even if I have to beat her brains in."

He walked back to her and said in a deceptively conciliatory manner, "Now, Mrs. Warmington; you'll tell me where Julie Marlowe and Mr. Rawsthorne are, won't you?"

"I'll do no such thing. I don't like people tattling and telling lies about me."

Dawson's voice hardened. "Do you know who I am?"

"Sure. You're Big Jim Dawson. You'll get me out of here, won't you?" Her voice broke pathetically into a wail. "I want to go back to the States."

He said dangerously, "So you'll know my reputation. I'm supposed to be a bad bastard. You've got one chance to get back to the States quick. Tell me where Rawsthorne is or I'll have you held here pending the inquiry into the disappearance of the British consul. There's sure to be an inquiry—the British are conservative, they don't like losing officials, even minor ones."

"On top of the hill," she said sullenly. "There's a gully up there."

"Point it out." His eyes followed the direction of her wavering hand, then he looked back at her. "You've come out of this hurricane pretty well," he said grimly. "Someone must have been looking after you. You should be thankful, not spiteful."

He went back to Wyatt. "I've got it. There's a gully up there somewhere." He waved his hand. "Over in that direction."

Without a word Wyatt left at a run and started to climb the hill. Dawson grinned and moved after him at a slower, more economical pace. He heard a noise in the air and looked up to see a helicopter coming over the brow of the hill like a huge grasshopper "Hey!" he shouted. "Here comes the Navy—they've come back."

But Wyatt was far ahead, climbing the hill as though his life depended on it. Perhaps it did.

II

Causton stood on the concrete apron near the ruined control tower of the airfield on Cap Sarrat Base and watched the helicopters come in from the sea in a straggling and wavering line. Commodore Brooks had been quick off his mark—the aircraft carrier under his command must have been idling just on the outskirts of Mabel and he had sent off his helicopters immediately the weather was fit for flying. And this was only the first wave. Planes would soon pour into San Fernandez, bringing much-needed medical aid.

He looked across at the small group of officers surrounding Favel and grinned. The Yanks were due for a surprise—but perhaps not just yet.

Favel had been quite clear about it. " I am going to occupy Cap Sarrat Base," he said. " Even if only with a token force. This is essential."

So a platoon of men had made the dangerous trip across the flooded mouth of the Negrito and here they were, waiting for the Americans. It all hinged on the original treaty of 1906 in which Favel had found a loophole. " The position is simple, Mr. Causton," he said. " The treaty states that if the American forces voluntarily give up the Base and it is thereafter claimed by the government of San Fernandez, then the treaty is abrogated."

Causton raised his eyebrows. " It'll look a pretty shabby gesture," he said. " The Americans come in to bring you unstinting aid, and you reciprocate by taking the Base."

" The Americans will bring us nothing they do not owe already," said Favel drily. " They have rented eight square miles of valuable real estate for sixty years at a pittance, on a lease forced at a time when they occupied San Fernandez as though it were an enemy country." He shook his head seriously. " I do not want to take the Base away from them,

Mr. Causton. But I think I will be in a position to negotiate another, more equitable lease."

Causton took a notebook from his pocket and refreshed his memory. "One thousand, six hundred and ninety-three dollars a year. I think it's worth more than that, and I think you ought to get it."

Favel grinned cheerfully. "You forgot the twelve cents, Mr. Causton. I think the International Court at The Hague will give us just judgment. I would like you to be at the Base as an independent witness to the fact that the San Fernandan government has assumed control of Cap Sarrat."

So now he was watching the first helicopter touch down on the territory of the sovereign government of San Fernandez. He watched men climb out and saw the gleam of gold on a flat cap. "My God, I wonder if that's Brooks," he murmured, and began to walk across the apron. He saw Favel move forward and watched the two men meet.

"Welcome back to Cap Sarrat," said Favel, offering his hand. "I am Julio Favel."

"Brooks—Commodore in the United States Navy."

The two men shook hands and Causton wondered if Brooks knew about the flaw in the treaty. If he did, he showed no awareness of his changed position, nor did he evince any surprise as he flicked his eyes upwards at the sodden green and gold flag of San Fernandez which hung limply from an improvised mast on the control tower. He said, "What do you need most, Mr. Favel, and where do you need it? Anything we've got, you just have to ask for it."

Favel shook his head sadly. "We need everything—but first, doctors, medical supplies, food and blankets. After that we would like some kind of large-scale temporary housing— even tents would do."

Brooks indicated the helicopters landing on the runways. "These boys are going to check the airfield to see if it's safe for operation. We'll set up a temporary control tower over there. When that's done the big planes can start to move in— they're already waiting for a signal in Miami and Puerto Rico. In the meantime, we have five choppers full of medics. Where do you want them to go?"

"Up the Negrito. They will have plenty of work."

Brooks raised his eyebrows. "The Negrito? Then you got your people out of St. Pierre."

"With the help of your Mr. Wyatt. That is a very forceful and persuasive young man."

They began to move away. "Yes," said Brooks. "I wish I had . . ." His voice was lost to Causton as they walked up the runway.

III

Dawson caught up with Wyatt when he was nearly at the top of the hill. "Take it easy," he gasped. "You'll bust a gut."

Wyatt kept silent, reserving his breath to power his legs which were working like pistons. They reached the crest and he looked around, his chest heaving and the muscles of his legs sore with the effort he had made. "I don't . . . see . . . a gully."

Dawson looked over the other side towards the sea and saw a line of welcome blue sky on the horizon. He turned back. "Suppose they had come up from the coast—where would they go from here?"

Wyatt shook his head in irritation. "I don't know."

"My inclination would be to edge in towards St. Pierre," said Dawson. "So I wouldn't have so far to go home when it was all over." He pointed to the left. "That way. Let's have a look."

They walked a little way along the crest of the hill, and Wyatt said, "That's it—I suppose you'd call that a gully."

Dawson looked down at the cleft cut into the hillside. "It's our best bet so far," he said. "Let's go down."

They climbed down into the ravine and looked about. Pools of water lay trapped among the rocks, and Wyatt said, "There'd be quite a bit of water coming down here during the hurricane. That's what Mrs. Warmington meant when she talked of a river on the top of a hill." He filled his lungs with air. "Julie!" he shouted. "Julie! Rawsthorne!"

There was no answer. Everything was silent save for the distant roar of a helicopter landing at the bottom of the valley.

"We'll go a bit further," said Dawson. "Perhaps they're lower down. Perhaps they've left already—gone down to the valley."

"They wouldn't do that," objected Wyatt. "Rawsthorne knows that the St. Michel road is easier."

"Okay, perhaps they've gone that way."

"We'll look down here first," said Wyatt. He began to climb among the tumbled rocks at the bottom of the ravine, wading through pools, heedless of the water. Dawson followed him, and kept a careful watch all round. From time to time Wyatt shouted, and then they paused to listen but heard no answering cry.

After a while Dawson said, "That Warmington cow said something about a waterfall. You see anything that could have been a waterfall?"

"No," said Wyatt shortly.

They went further down the ravine and found themselves enclosed within its sheer walls. "This would be as good a place to sit out a hurricane as any," commented Dawson. "Better than the goddam holes we had."

"Then where the hell are they?" demanded Wyatt, losing his temper.

"Take it easy," said Dawson. "We'll find them if they're here. I'll tell you what; you carry on down the ravine, and I'll get up on the hillside. I can move faster up there and still see most of what there is to be seen down here."

He climbed up the ravine wall and regained the open hillside, and as he thought, he was immediately able to keep up a better speed. Even though he was hampered by fallen trees, they were easier to negotiate than the jumble of rocks in the ravine. He carried on down the hill, outstripping Wyatt, and returned to the lip of the ravine frequently to scan the bottom very carefully. It was quite a while before he found anything.

At first he thought it was some kind of animal moving very slowly, and then his breath hissed as he saw it was a man crawling painfully on his belly. He climbed down to the bottom and stumbled across the rocks to where the crawling figure had stopped. When he turned the man over he lifted his head and yelled, "Wyatt, come here—I've found Rawsthorne!"

Rawsthorne was in a bad way. His face was deathly pale, accentuating the blood streaks on the side of his head. His right side appeared to be completely paralysed and he made ineffectual pawing movements with his left arm as Dawson gently cradled him. His eyes flickered open and his lips moved but he made no sound.

"Take it easy," said Dawson. "You're safe now."

Rawsthorne's breath rasped and he whispered, "Heart . . . heart . . . attack."

"Don't worry," said Dawson. "Relax."

Small stones clattered as Wyatt came up, and Dawson turned his head. "The poor guy's had a heart attack. He's not too good."

Wyatt took Rawsthorne's wrist and felt the faint thread of pulse and then looked into the glazing eyes which seemed focused an infinity away. The grey lips moved again. "Water-fall . . . tree . . . tree . . ."

Rawsthorne suddenly sagged and lay in Dawson's arms, gazing vacantly at the sky, his jaw dropped open.

Dawson eased him down on to the rocks. "He's dead."

Wyatt stared down at the body and his face looked haggard. "Was he crawling?" he whispered.

Dawson nodded. "He was going down the ravine. I don't know how he expected to make it."

"Julie would never have left him," said Wyatt in an over controlled voice. "Not if he was sick. Something must have happened to her."

"He said something about a waterfall, too—just like Warmington."

"It must be higher up," said Wyatt. "And I think I know where it is." He rose to his feet and stumbled away, moving much too fast for the broken ground and reckless of twisted or broken ankles. Dawson followed him more cautiously and found him beneath an outcrop of rock too hard and stubborn to be worn away. He stooped and picked up something from the cleft in the base of the rock. It was a woman's purse.

"This was Warmington's," he said. "This is the waterfall." His head jerked upwards to the tangle of tree roots above his head on the edge of the ravine. "And that's the tree—he said 'tree', didn't he?"

He scrambled up the side of the ravine and then turned to give a hand to Dawson. "Let's have a closer look at this bloody tree."

They walked around the tree and saw nothing, and then Wyatt pushed in among the branches and suddenly gave a choked sound. "She's here," he said brokenly.

Dawson pushed his way through and looked over Wyatt's shoulder, then turned away. He said heavily, "Well—we found her."

She was lying with the trunk of the tree across her legs and hips and a branch across her right arm, pinning it to the ground. The fingertips of her left hand were scraped bloodily raw where she had scrabbled at the trunk in her efforts to move it. Her face, smudged with dirt, was otherwise marble-white and drained of blood, and the only thing about her that moved was a strand of her hair that waved gently in the wind.

Wyatt stepped back away from the tree and looked at it calculatingly. He said in a repressed voice, " Let's move this tree. Let's shift this damned tree."

" Dave," said Dawson quietly, " she's dead."

Wyatt turned in a flash, his face furious. " We don't know," he shouted. "*We don't know that!*"

Dawson fell back a step, intimidated by the controlled violence emanating from this man. He said, " All right, Dave. We'll move the tree."

" And we'll do it carefully, do you hear?" said Wyatt. " We'll do it very carefully."

Dawson looked at the tree dubiously. It was big and heavy and awkward. " How do we start?"

Wyatt attacked a broken branch and wrenched it free by sheer force. He stepped back panting. " We take the weight off her . . . her body, then one of us can draw her out."

That did not look so easy to Dawson, but he was willing to give it a try. He took the branch which Wyatt offered and walked round the tree looking for a convenient place to wedge it under the trunk. Wyatt collected some rocks and followed him. " There," he said abruptly. " That's the place." His face was very white. " We must be careful."

Dawson rammed the branch beneath the trunk and cautiously tested the leverage. He doubted if the trunk would move but said nothing. Wyatt pushed him out of the way and swung his weight on to the branch. There was a creak, but otherwise nothing. " Come on," he said. " You can push on this, too."

" Who is going to push the stones under?" asked Dawson reasonably. " Neither of us can do it if we're both heaving on that branch."

" I can do it with my foot," said Wyatt impatiently. " Come on."

Both of them leaned heavily on the branch and Dawson felt an agony of pain in his hands. The trunk of the tree moved fractionally and he set his teeth and held on. Slowly the trunk lifted, inch by inch, and Wyatt, both his feet off the ground, nudged one of the rocks with the tip of his shoe until it slid underneath. Then another, a larger one, went under, and he gasped, " That's enough—for now."

Slowly they released the branch and the trunk settled again, but it was slightly raised on the rocks. Dawson staggered back, his hands aflame with pain, and Wyatt looked up and saw his face. "What's the matter?" Then he caught on. " Oh, my God, I'm sorry. I didn't realize."

Dawson suppressed the sickness that welled up within him and grinned weakly. " It doesn't matter," he said, trying to keep his voice steady. " There's nothing to it. I'm all right."

" Are you sure?"

" I'm fine," he said nonchalantly.

Wyatt switched his attention back to the tree. " I'll see if I can pull her out now." He crawled under the branches and was silent for some minutes, then said in a muffled voice. " It needs one more swing." He came out. " If you can get under there and pull her out while I lift this damned tree, I think we'll do it."

He carefully chocked in the rocks he had already inserted under the trunk while Dawson got in position, and when Dawson shouted that he was ready he swung again on the lever. Nothing happened, so he swung harder, again and again, leaning his whole weight on the branch and pushing down until he thought his bones would crack. The thought entered his mind dizzily that he had gone through all this before in the prison cell. Well, he had done it before and he would do it again.

The tree-trunk did not move.

Dawson called a halt and came out from under the branches. He had been close to Julie's body and was now certain that she was dead, but whatever he privately thought of the uselessness of all this did not show on his face for one moment. He said, "What we need here is weight—not strength. I'm sixty pounds heavier than you are—it may not be all muscle, but that doesn't matter. You pull her out while I do the lifting."

" What about your hands?"

" They're my hands, aren't they? Get under there."

He waited until Wyatt was ready, then leaned on the branch

and thrust down with all his force and weight. He almost screamed at the cruel torment in his hands and sweat beaded his forehead. The trunk moved and Wyatt gave a shout. "Keep it up! For God's sake, keep it up!"

Dawson went through an eternity of purgatory and for a fraction of a second he wondered if he would ever be able to use his hands again—say, on a typewriter. Hell! he grunted to himself, I can always dictate—and pressed down harder. Out of the corner of his eye he saw Wyatt backing out, drawing something with him, and it was with exquisite relief that he heard a faint and faraway voice say, "Okay, you can let it go."

He released the branch and flopped to the ground, thankfully feeling the flaming hell centred in his hands dying to a welcome numbness. With lacklustre eyes he watched Wyatt bend over Julie, rip open her shirt and apply his ear to her chest. And it was with something approaching shock that he heard him shout exultantly, "She's alive! She's still alive! It's faint, but it's there."

It took a long time for them to signal a helicopter, but when they did action was swift. The chopper hovered over them and swirled the dust while Wyatt lay over Julie and protected her from the blast. A man was lowered by a winch and dropped to the ground, and Dawson lurched up to him. "We need a doctor."

The man gave a brief grin. "You've found one—what's the trouble?"

"This woman." He led the way to where Julie was lying and the doctor dropped to one knee beside her and produced a stethoscope. After a few seconds he fumbled in a cartouche at his waist and drew forth a hypodermic syringe and an ampoule. While Wyatt watched anxiously he gave Julie an injection. Then he waved back the helicopter and, speaking through a microphone at the bottom of the dangling hoist, he gave terse instructions.

The hoist was reeled in and presently another man came down, bearing a folded stretcher and a bundle of splints, and the helicopter retreated again to continue its circling. Julie was tenderly bound in a complex of splints and given another injection. Wyatt said, "How is . . . will she . . .?"

The doctor looked up. "We got to her in time. She'll be

all right if we can get her off this hillside real fast." He waved to the helicopter which came in again, and Julie was hoisted up on the stretcher.

The doctor surveyed them. "You coming?" He looked at Dawson. "What's the matter with your hands?"

"What hands?" asked Dawson with tremulous irony. He thrust bandaged claws forward. "Look, doc, no hands!" He began to laugh hysterically.

The doctor said, "You'd better come with us." He looked at Wyatt. "You, too; you look half beat to death."

They were hoisted up by the winch one at a time, and the doctor followed and tapped the pilot once on the shoulder. Wyatt sat next to the stretcher and looked at Julie's white face. He wondered if she would consider marrying a man who had failed her, who had let her go into the storm to die. He doubted it—but he knew he would ask her.

He stared down blindly at the receding hillside and at the broad waters of the flooded Negrito and felt a touch on his hand. He turned quickly and saw that Julie was awake and that her hand touched his. Two tears ran down her cheeks and her lips moved, but all sound was lost in the roar of the aircraft.

Quickly he bent down with his ear to her lips and caught the faint thread of sound. "Dave! Dave! You're alive!" Even in the thin whisper there were overtones of incredulity.

He smiled at her. "Yes, we're alive. You'll be back in the States to-day."

Her fingers tightened weakly on his hand and she spoke again. He missed something of what she said, but caught the gist of it. ". . . come back. I want house . . . overlooking sea . . . St. Pierre."

Then she closed her eyes but her fingers still held his hand and he felt half his burden taken from him. She was going to be all right and they were going to be together.

And so he went back to Cap Sarrat Base and into fame and history. He did not know that the headlines of the world's newspapers would blazon his name in a hundred languages as the man who saved a whole city's people—as the man who had destroyed an army. He did not know that honours awaited him, to be bestowed by lesser men. He did not know that one day, when he was a very old man, he would be the one who was to show the way to the taming of the big wind—the hurricane.

He knew nothing of all this. All he knew was that he was very tired and that he was a professional failure. He did not know how many soldiers had died in the trap of St. Pierre—many hundreds or many thousands—but even if only one had died it would serve to proclaim to the world his failure in his work and he felt miserable.

David Wyatt was a dedicated scientist, unversed in the ways of the world and very young for his years.

Desmond Bagley

'Mr Bagley is nowadays incomparable.' *Sunday Times*

THE ENEMY   £1.35
FLYAWAY   £1.65
THE FREEDOM TRAP   £1.50
THE GOLDEN KEEL   £1.35
HIGH CITADEL   £1.25
LANDSLIDE   £1.50
RUNNING BLIND   £1.50
THE SNOW TIGER   £1.50
THE SPOILERS   £1.50
THE TIGHTROPE MEN   £1.50
THE VIVERO LETTER   £1.50
WYATT'S HURRICANE   £1.50
BAHAMA CRISIS   £1.50

FONTANA PAPERBACKS

Fontana Paperbacks

Fontana is a leading paperback publisher of fiction and non-fiction, with authors ranging from Alistair MacLean, Agatha Christie and Desmond Bagley to Solzhenitsyn and Pasternak, from Gerald Durrell and Joy Adamson to the famous Modern Masters series.

In addition to a wide-ranging collection of internationally popular writers of fiction, Fontana also has an outstanding reputation for history, natural history, military history, psychology, psychiatry, politics, economics, religion and the social sciences.

All Fontana books are available at your bookshop or newsagent; or can be ordered direct. Just fill in the form and list the titles you want.

FONTANA BOOKS, Cash Sales Department, G.P.O. Box 29, Douglas, Isle of Man, British Isles. Please send purchase price, plus 8p per book. Customers outside the U.K. send purchase price, plus 10p per book. Cheque, postal or money order. No currency.

NAME (Block letters)

ADDRESS